# CRAIG RUSSELL

# THE QUIET DEATH OF THOMAS QUAID

Quercus

First published in Great Britain in 2016 by Quercus
This paperback edition published 2016 by

Quercus Editions Ltd
Carmelite House
50 Victoria Embankment
London EC4Y 0DZ

An Hachette UK company

A CIP catalogue record for this book is available
from the British Library

PB ISBN 978 178087 491 3
EBOOK ISBN 978 1 78429 239 3

10 9 8 7 6 5 4 3

Typeset by Jouve (UK), Milton Keynes

Printed and bound in Great Britain by Clays Ltd, St Ives plc

# THE QUIET DEATH OF THOMAS QUAID

'I have a story to tell you,' I said, after a while. 'I'm afraid it's not a pretty story and you won't thank me for the telling of it. It's also a story that a lot of people would kill – and have killed – to stop being told. Once I tell it to you, there are things that I will expect from each of you. But, I warn you, once you hear my story, you won't be able to unhear it.'

They said nothing.

So I told them it.

I told them Quiet Tommy Quaid's story.

# Part One

Part One

# 1

I liked Quiet Tommy Quaid.

Everyone liked him: every thief, thug, racketeer and ne'er-do-well in Glasgow liked Quiet Tommy Quaid; every street-corner kid, every shopkeeper and publican had a good word to say about him; women in particular had a fondness for Quaid's quiet but potent charms. Even the police liked him. In fact, I had heard it had been the police who had christened him 'Quiet Tommy' in the certain knowledge that whenever they caught him – not that they caught him often these days – Tommy would invariably put his hands up and 'come quiet'. And, of course, in all the many crimes he had committed over the years, Quiet Tommy Quaid had never once used violence.

In fact, violence seemed to be a language Quaid neither spoke nor understood, which was somewhat at odds with his wartime service as a commando – a highly decorated commando, I'd been told. I dare say that Adolf's *Kommandobefehl* notwithstanding, if they had captured him, the Germans would probably have liked Quiet Tommy Quaid too.

And everyone seemed to like him *totally*: without that hidden ire we tend secretly to reserve for the naturally amiable. Yep . . . Quiet Tommy Quaid was a thoroughly likeable cove. He had practically no vices – except for equally excessive womanizing and drinking, which in nineteen fifty-eight Glasgow were pretty much looked on as virtues, not vices. And in that respect I myself was to be considered virtuous to the point of sainthood. But unlike me, Thomas Quaid was the most equanimous person you could encounter: a calm, easy-going, friendly sort who accepted the occasional misfortune – especially the misfortune of arrest – with calm resignation.

The strange thing was Quiet Tommy Quaid also happened to be one of the wisest men I'd ever known, with a calm, deep-flowing intelligence that he shared seldom and only with those he chose to trust. I felt honoured to be amongst the few allowed the odd rare glimpse into the deep waters beneath the still surface.

But Quiet Tommy did have one flaw – a mental deficiency, I suppose you'd call it. Everybody has something they find diffi-cult to understand: I personally struggled to wrap my mind around the musings of Niels Bohr or Albert Einstein; the City of Glasgow Police failed to understand the lexical difference between the nouns 'Catholic' and 'suspect'; but for Quiet Tommy Quaid, the one concept that eluded comprehension was that of private ownership. That isn't to say he was one of Glasgow's many red-flag-waving, Lenin-quoting, class-warrior idealists – it was simply that Tommy couldn't seem to understand that if something belonged to someone else, he couldn't just up and take it.

I'm not saying that Tommy was some kind of common thief: Quaid was most definitely a thief, and every bit as definitely anything but common. He had intelligence, he had flair, he had style. He had inches on other Glaswegians. When it came to the population's height, Glasgow was the kind of place where Snow White would have felt right at home – generations of bad diet, hard labour and equally hard drinking, coupled with appalling living conditions, had stunted the city's population – but Tommy Quaid was unusually tall for Glasgow; he was always immaculately groomed, his expensively barbered, copper-coloured hair sleeked but not oily and combed back from a broad-browed, handsome and vaguely aristocratic face, a neat moustache lining his top lip. Speaking for myself as someone who was known for his appreciation of good tailoring, I can tell you that the perpetually well-turned-out Tommy Quaid's suits were always top-notch. I had once been tempted to ask him who his tailor was, but thought better of it, realizing that he probably gave new depth to the concept of *prêt à porter* – *prêt à porter* through the skylight window of a tailor's storeroom, usually.

But the thing I liked most about Quiet Tommy Quaid, and I guessed that everyone else liked most, was that you knew exactly where you were with him, exactly who it was you were dealing with. Here, everybody realized, was someone who was precisely, simply and totally who and what he seemed to be.

We had no idea how wrong we were.

## 2

I would have good cause to remember that day; most people would remember it, but for a different reason.

Friday the eleventh of July, nineteen fifty-eight was an auspicious day all right. An auspicious day for Glasgow – for all of Scotland, for that matter. The reason that day would live in so many memories was because a lever was pulled and an insignificant-looking, five-foot-four-inch monster – known in the press as 'The Beast of Birkenshaw' – took the shortest of journeys through a Barlinnie Prison trap door and into the afterlife. And as multiple murderer Peter Manuel breathed his last, the rest of the country breathed a sigh of relief.

Manuel had been on my mind a lot that day. I'd come across him once, in the Horsehead Bar: a short-arsed loudmouth with a cod American accent, he had been the object of ridicule. But what I remembered most were his eyes: Manuel had had the palest complexion under an oily mop of jet-black hair, the frame for small, dark eyes that glittered black like Airdrie anthracite and seemed to bore into you. Or maybe it was just hindsight that made me wax lyrical, having read about his monstrous crimes in the papers. As we had learned from Herr Hitler, monsters rarely look like monsters and guise themselves as insignificant, even comical-looking.

At the time I was not aware that Manuel's hanging would not be the event that would mark out the day for me. What would, in the fullness of time, make Friday the eleventh of July nineteen fifty-eight an auspicious day was something else completely.

It was the day I met Mr McNaught.

The post-war landscape of my life could generally have been described as less than easy-going, but the years fifty-seven and fifty-eight had been especially rocky – both personally and professionally. The women in my life had always had a tendency towards dramatic exits and for the second time a woman for whom I had had something like genuine above-the-waist feelings had died. After I had found out that cancer had taken Fiona White, I had become lost for a while.

A year before, I'd hired Archie McClelland, an ex-City of Glasgow policeman, to help in the business. After Fiona's death, I hadn't exactly left Archie to carry the business on his own, but he had shouldered more than his share while I had not so much gone off the rails as taken a branch line for a while. I had drunk too much even by my standards and had buried myself in the soft folds of female comfort a little more than Errol Flynn would have found seemly; but I had, by and large, managed to keep myself together. Or at least functioning.

Lugubrious, chain-smoking Archie, who had the tall, stooping posture of an undertaker and the doleful eyes of Alastair Sim, had done much to keep me on the straight and narrow, but I'd still managed to get into a few dodgy areas, both morally and legally – which, of course, weren't always the same thing.

Archie had never complained, never asked for anything as reward; but because of everything he'd done, the sign on the door now said *Lennox and McClelland Enquiry Agents*. At least I kidded myself that my partnership offer was simply about rewarding Archie. My gratitude really was a big part of it, of course, but the truth was also that having straight-as-a-die, ex-City of Glasgow Police beat-man Archie as a partner took off my shoulders a lot of the aspects of the work I couldn't be bothered with. Most importantly, it helped me legitimize the business that little bit more.

Before Archie had come along, most of the work I'd done had been for the Three Kings, the triumvirate of crook monarchs who ran much that was legal and everything that wasn't in Glasgow. Some of the waters I'd gotten into had been so murky that they made the Clyde look limpid. The war had messed me up – me and a million others – and more than once I'd found myself in a situation that had brought out the old demons. On a couple of occasions, the prison yard – even the hanging shed – had beckoned and I'd decided to straighten myself, my life and my business out. I'd hired ex-cop Archie and, between us, we had successfully steered the business away from providing services to the Three Kings.

But the Three Kings – Willie Sneddon, Hammer Murphy and Handsome Jonny Cohen – were not the kind of people who generally accepted no as an answer, so the price I had paid was still to do the odd job for the Kings 'off the books' – and very much out of Archie's sight. Generally, I liked to think I had much in common with Mae West: we both tried to remain as white as snow, but had a tendency to drift.

So on that auspicious Friday morning of the eleventh of July, nineteen fifty-eight – as I stood staring out of my office window, bereaved, mildly hungover, generally pissed with everything, and morally overdrawn if not completely bankrupt – the stage was set for Mr McNaught's entrance.

*

Archie had just left for a meeting with the Scottish and North-ern Bank, around the corner from our Gordon Street offices and for whom we had been providing transfer security for two years. It didn't occur to me at the time that McNaught's arrival coin-cided with Archie's departure, with just enough time for them not to pass each other in the stairwell. It wasn't something that would have occurred to anyone: that no one ever saw Mr McNaught except me.

Of course, there was the distraction of the goings-on over at the station.

Even I didn't see McNaught arrive, despite the fact that I had been looking out the third-floor window of my office when he must have come in through the street entrance below. I had been drawn to the window by the urgent trilling of bells from approaching police cars and an ambulance.

Our Gordon Street office was directly opposite Central Sta-tion, looking down on the ornate Victorian latticed ironwork of its entrance. Three police cars had arrived with the ambulance and had pulled up immediately outside the main entry. The cop-pers and the ambulance men, carrying a stretcher, had trotted off into the main concourse of the station. I was as subject to morbid curiosity as the next man – perhaps even more so – and I lit a cigarette and watched the comings and goings below.

Another police car arrived, this time with an inspector and driver, both of whom also disappeared into the railway station. It was another cigarette's length before the ambulance men reappeared, their stretcher empty, and drove off in the ambu-lance, only to be replaced a minute or so later by a Black Maria police van. Two more coppers answered the question as to why the ambulance had left by taking out what looked like a black coffin from the back of the Black Maria. I knew it was a 'body shell', as the boys in blue called it – the rigid but lightweight container the police used to remove dead bodies to the mortuary, and made out of fibreglass because the effluent residue of the leaving of life could be easily hosed from it.

Obviously someone had died in the station. It could have been anything from a heart attack – from which, it seemed to me, every Glaswegian over the age of sixteen was at danger – or an accident involving a rail worker. I reflected that if it had been a typical accident on the rails, then they probably wouldn't have needed the body shell: a couple of good-sized suitcases would have done the job.

Whatever the cause, someone's light, an entire universe of experiences and senses, had been extinguished somewhere inside the station. And I would completely forget the incident by the end of the day.

A third police Wolseley pulled up and three men, two in uniform, one in plainclothes, got out. The plainclothesman was older – almost too old to still be in police service – but clearly senior in more than age as all the other officers obviously deferred to him. They headed in through the ornate entrance and disappeared from my view and interest.

When I turned from the window, McNaught was there, framed in my office doorway, watching me in lopsided silence. History was something that tended to be written as much in the faces of men as in books: McNaught's face contained several volumes' worth. With appendices.

Mr McNaught – he never did give a first name and I guessed his surname was about as genuine as Hemingway's machismo – introduced himself as a 'businessman'. He didn't look the business type, although he didn't look the criminal type either. But there was something about him that told you he was no stranger to violence: he had a build that made the Forth Bridge look flimsy and a face that some event had stripped of symmetry.

A decade or so after the war there were a lot of lopsided faces about, some deficient to the tune of an eye, some twisted into unintentional sneers by inexpert battlefield surgery. McNaught's face wasn't that bad, but it was worse than mine. I'd been left with a faint web of white scars on one side of my face from a German grenade that had landed not too close to me but conveniently close to one of my men, who had unintentionally shielded me from the brunt of the blast. A plastic surgeon had done his stuff on me but, nearly a decade and a half on, the scars were still visible if you got close enough. Whatever the plastic surgeon had done had changed my appearance, making the skin taut and emphasizing my cheekbones. The Jack Palance look, I'd been told. The unintentional result was a subtle transformation that, while it hadn't robbed me of my looks, had given me a harder, crueller appearance. It was something that seemed to make me more attractive to women. And coppers.

McNaught, on the other hand, just looked a little fucked up. The odd thing was that neither half of his face would have looked wrong by itself or married to its mirror image, it was more that each cheek was at a different angle and location from its opposite number, like mismatched socks. A clue to the cause lay in the deep crease of a crescent-shaped scar that arced around the bottom of his right cheek. My guess was that McNaught had been that little bit closer to a shell, grenade or machine-gun burst but, unlike me, hadn't had one of his men to run interference for him; the result being he'd lost flesh and a little bone on the right side of his face.

'Sorry . . . I didn't see you come in.' I waved a thumb vaguely at the window as if he should know what had distracted me.

'I'd like to hire your services,' he said, after he had introduced himself, we had shaken hands and I'd invited him to take a seat. McNaught had a military bearing, all right; the kind who managed to stand at attention even when sitting down. 'It won't take up much of your time, but it will be financially very worthwhile for you.'

I smiled, which was something of a Pavlovian response with me to the stimulus of easy money. I took a second to weigh McNaught up: his accent was Scottish middle-class and his tailoring was very British: sharp, neat and completely and studiously devoid of style. He was one of those men you saw a lot after the war, wearing immaculately pressed tweed suits and immaculately polished burgundy brogues as if they were still in uniform. He also wore a lovat-green mac over his suit, despite it being a July afternoon. There again, in Glasgow, the concept of seasons could be at best abstract.

'What can I do for you, Mr McNaught?'

'I have a job for you. More correctly, my client has a job for you.'

'Your client?'

'I am an intermediary. A broker, if you like. I have been hired by a party who wishes to remain anonymous. They instruct and pay me, I instruct and pay you.'

'Pay me for what?'

'An idea. Or at least for you to secure that idea for them. It's your business to gather information for clients; there's a single, specific piece of information that is of great commercial value to my client. To *our* client.'

'What kind of information?'

'I'll give you the details if and when we come to an arrangement, but what we're talking about is basically a design for something. Something my client's competitors have developed and that gives them an unfair commercial advantage. My client would very much like to obtain the details of this advantage.'

Again I studied McNaught, taking a moment to work out exactly whose army he'd been in.

'It sounds to me like the *information* you're talking about is more like secrets,' I said. 'They hang people for stealing those, in this country.'

McNaught laughed lopsidedly, the damage to his face restricting the movement on the right. It turned his smile into something ugly and disturbing. 'You're right, Mr Lennox, I'm asking you to steal secrets and get involved in espionage. But not those kinds of secrets nor that kind of espionage. What we're talking about is purely *industrial* espionage. And, technically, industrial espionage isn't illegal in this country.'

'But what you're asking me to do is of dubious legality.'

'No it's not. There's absolutely no dubiety about it whatsoever – it's illegal. Stealing industrial secrets may be no crime, but those secrets are, of course, kept under lock and key. The means of gaining access to those premises – breaking and entering – is a crime, even if it's only intellectual property that ends up being stolen. I'm asking you to conspire to commit a crime, even if that crime is petty.' He paused, leaning the ramrod he had for a spine back in the chair and taking his turn to study me. 'From what I've been able to gather about you, Mr Lennox, bending the law shouldn't present much of a problem. And that's why you're being paid a premium. I'm authorized to offer you a deal that compensates for the risk.'

'How much compensation are we talking about?'

'Two hundred pounds now, a further five hundred when the files are delivered to me. But I have to point out that once the two hundred pounds is paid, you are committed to delivering the files. Failure to do so could have *unpleasant* results. My clients may be respectable and conventional, but my associates and I are not. We have a reputation for delivering what we promise to deliver . . . and we take that reputation very, very seriously. If you say yes, you're committed. If you cannot commit fully, then say no now and I'll leave. Are we clear?'

The darkness of his threat was lost in the cosy glow generated by the idea of seven hundred pounds, at least three hundred of which would warm my back pocket. I nodded. He dipped a hand into his briefcase. When it came out, the hand was holding a satisfyingly thick bundle of banknotes, tight-bound with elastic bands. Homely as the reigning monarch might have been, I always felt an almost erotic thrill when I saw her face on a Bank of England twenty-pound note. McNaught sat the bundle on the desk between us; Pavlov rattled my dish and I smiled again.

'So, for whom would I be working?'

'You're working for me. I thought I made that clear.'

'Okay then . . . for whom are *you* working?'

'I hope we're not going to have a difficulty, Mr Lennox. You do not need to know – you should not know nor try to find out – who my client is. Like you, I'm self-employed. Another link in the chain, as it were. Or a buffer between my client and you. Between my client and everyone else, for that matter. All you need to know is that I represent someone who will benefit from the information you obtain.'

I nodded. 'You realize that I won't be visiting the premises myself? I have to hire a specialist contractor for that.' Whenever entering somewhere without the convenience of a legally held key came to mind, so did Quiet Tommy Quaid. But I was going to be as tight-lipped about who I'd use as McNaught was about his client's identity.

'I assumed you would,' he said, 'and that you would have someone particular in mind. It has to be someone who's good with heights and whose discretion can be relied upon. You're being well paid for this, so I don't expect you to cut corners.'

'I won't. The person I'm thinking about has worked for me before and he's the best in the business. But it means I will have additional expenses. Shall we round it up to a thousand?'

McNaught's hand reached out for the two hundred on the desk and the cosy glow began to dim.

'Okay . . .' I surrendered faster than a Govan girl on a Saturday night. 'Seven hundred it is. How do I contact you?'

McNaught withdrew his hand and I again basked in the glow. 'You don't,' he said. 'I'll stay in touch with you. I take it I can trust you to keep this business strictly to yourself and your *contractor*? Absolutely no one else.'

'I won't even discuss it with my associate here,' I promised. 'Heights?'

McNaught frowned. 'Heights?'

'You said whomever I hired had to be good with heights.'

'Oh, I see. It's your business, of course, but the best way into the premises is through the roof. It's a large industrial complex and entry is through a skylight, six floors up and across pitched roofs. There is minimal security but a night watchman is based on the ground floor and does – or is supposed to do – an hourly walk around and checks the doors at ground level.'

'I think that my guy would rather make his own plan. He's a bit of a perfectionist.'

'That is of course entirely a matter for you and him, but we have taken the liberty of surveying the building and the security arrangements. Just to save you time.'

'Speaking of time, when do you need the stuff?'

'Before the end of the month. That gives you enough time to plan and execute the break-in. But I will need to know when you plan to carry it out. The exact date and time.'

'Sounds like someone needs an alibi.'

'Again, that's not your concern. All you need to focus on is getting your man in and out with the plans, ideally leaving little or no trace of his presence. I need to know which night you're planning to go through with it. Exact times.' Reaching again into his briefcase, he brought out a foolscap envelope, which he set next to the cash on the desktop. 'In there you will find the address of the company, photographs and plans of the building and details of what you're looking for and where to find it.'

I reached for the envelope but McNaught laid his hand on top of it.

'If you open this and see where the job is, you are committed to taking it. Understand?'

I nodded. I didn't pick up the envelope but I didn't withdraw my hand either.

McNaught sat back. 'If there's anything you want to ask before taking the job, now's the time to ask it.'

'Are these plans kept under lock and key? If there's a safe, then that could be tricky and, whatever you say, the cost would have to go up.'

McNaught shook his head. 'No safe. The blueprints we want are kept in a draughtsman's office on the third floor, stored in a plan chest. There's always a chance that the chest will be secure, so your contractor should be able to deal with locks, although it shouldn't be anything too challenging. I have to say that if the person you use is skilful enough, there is a good chance that not only will he get in and out without detection, but also it might be some time before the removal of the plans is discovered. Which would actually be preferable.'

'Why not just photograph them? The plans, I mean,' I added helpfully, and a little cleverly, I thought. McNaught's expression suggested he didn't share my opinion of my intelligence.

'You read too many spy novels, Mr Lennox. Admittedly it would be one way of making sure no one would know that the ideas had been stolen, but all it takes is for your man's skills as a photographer not to match his as a burglar and the photographs turn out blurry and unreadable – or for something to go wrong in the developing process. A chain is only as strong as its weakest link. I always think it's an idea to have as few links as possible. Anyway, like I say, it could be days, even weeks, before these original blueprints are noticed missing.' He paused. 'This really is a high-pay, low-risk opportunity, Mr Lennox. Seven hundred pounds for a single night's work. If you're not interested, then there are plenty of others I could ask.'

'So why haven't you?' I saw a contradiction in what McNaught was saying: as far as I could see, I was an unnecessary link in the chain; a little asking around and he could probably have found and hired Quiet Tommy Quaid himself. And more cheaply.

'Because most of them are criminals. This enterprise lies only partly on the wrong side of the law; criminals are completely on the wrong side of the law. Less reliable. And more chance of complications with the police.'

'And I fit your picture of someone with a foot planted on both sides of the law, is that it?'

'I'm asking you to do what your business card says you do. I just need you to bend the law a little to do it. So yes – I not only believe you have the skills needed to manage this perfectly, but that your door would not be the first port of call for the police, should they become involved. And I'm guessing you would only hire someone you can guarantee to keep their mouth shut should they be unlucky enough to be caught.'

'That's something I can absolutely guarantee.' My hand still rested on the envelope and I looked questioningly at McNaught. He nodded and I lifted and opened it.

'This looks like—'

'The Saracen Ironworks. Yes,' McNaught interrupted me.

'What are these plans you're stealing?' I asked, confused. I had expected the layout of some top-secret laboratory somewhere. 'The pattern for a 'phone box? I could sketch that out for you here and now.' The red 'phone box had become, for those like myself not born in the sceptred isle, an icon of Britishness. Most red 'phone boxes in the UK had been cast at the Saracen Foundry. The romance of this particular cultural icon had faded for me over my years in Glasgow, mainly because of the locals' custom of using them as public conveniences. I also reflected that only minutes before, as I had watched the police arrive at Central Station, I had been looking at the Saracen Foundry's work in the shape of the station entrance's elaborate cast iron canopy.

'I'm sure you're aware that the foundry produces more than fountains, bandstands and 'phone boxes,' said McNaught. 'The nature of the item we're interested in is none of your concern. The details in there tell you what your man is looking for and where to find it.'

'Okay.' I shrugged. McNaught was right: it would be a walk in the park for Quiet Tommy Quaid. Security was light and the works were out of town and there wouldn't be many coppers pounding the Possilpark beat. Possilpark was a part of Glasgow that had been created out of the green fields of some toff's estate and built over with tenements exclusively used as housing for the foundry's workers. Medieval serfdom had simply been replaced with a newer, post-Industrial Revolution version. At Possilpark's heart and surrounded by a high wall, the foundry buildings themselves covered acres of land. I still was confused as to why an ironworks would be the target of industrial espionage – but as McNaught had pointed out, that was his and his client's business, not mine.

Before he left, McNaught told me to be by my home 'phone on Sunday, 'between thirteen hundred and thirteen-thirty hours', when he or an associate would 'phone me to get the exact day and time the 'mission' would take place.

I nodded, but there was something about McNaught's military way of phrasing things that seemed heavy-handed: *carrying out your mission* instead of *pulling off the job*; *between thirteen hundred and thirteen-thirty hours* not *between one and one-thirty p.m.* It was almost as if he had been trying too hard to paint a military background.

Archie returned about twenty minutes after McNaught had left. He told me all about his bank meeting with his usual lugubrious wit. We were being entrusted with an extra delivery on the wages run, he explained, and were expected to go at least three-handed – usually the runs were handled by the unlikely duo of Archie and Twinkletoes McBride. Unlikely because Archie was an ex-copper and Twinkletoes McBride was, well, Twinkletoes. If you put 'ex' in front of just about any criminal activity that involved extreme violence, then you'd get a snapshot of McBride's curriculum vitae. But Twinkle had turned over a new leaf – mainly thanks to me, it had to be said – and his intimidating physical presence had proved a successful deterrent on the bank runs.

'Anything new while I was away?' Archie asked.

I told him about the excitement over at Central Station. Some kind of accident, I guessed.

'Nothing else?'

I shook my head. 'It's been as quiet as the grave, Archie.'

## 3

I had a date, of sorts, that night. Or at least the early part of the evening.

My venturesome time as an officer in occupied Hamburg at the end of the war had presented me with unexpected entrepreneurial opportunities – the result being that I'd managed to stash away my little *Nibelungengold* hoard. Generally speaking, people didn't have any kind of moral or legal problem with you making your fortune by playing the market – I could never grasp the difference between a stockbroker and a bookie – and that's all I could be accused of doing in Hamburg: playing the market.

However, the particular market I had played had been on the dark side of black, and the military police and the local German authorities seemed to have had a problem with it – especially when a German associate of mine took a face-down dip in the harbour. It all ended with my hasty – and almost-but-not-quite-dishonourable – exit from military life.

My time in Glasgow since had also provided other earning opportunities I hadn't wanted to be a nuisance to the taxman about. Altogether it had meant a very tidy sum had accrued in my under-a-loose-floorboard-beneath-the-bed bank account.

My plan had always been to use my Nibelungen Hoard to get back to Canada some day when I was less fucked up and my hands were that little bit cleaner. Before the war, I'd been someone else, somewhere else: the bright-eyed, idealistic Kennebecasis Kid growing up in Canada and careless privilege. After the war, a different Lennox was demobbed from the 1st Canadian Army, and Glasgow had been waiting for him, like an accomplice hanging about prison gates.

But, scathing as I was about the place, I'd grown fond of Glasgow. It was the kind of place and the kind of people that got under your skin, and it had remained my dark accomplice, our characters suiting each other. A match made somewhere other than in heaven.

Given that my Glaswegian sojourn had turned semi-permanent, I'd decided to place a chunk of my gains, ill-gotten and otherwise, into a stylish little place in a nineteen-thirties Art Deco apartment building – one of those redbrick and stucco deals – in Kelvin Court.

It was a bright and elegant flat with a largish lounge, two bedrooms, biggish bathroom and a separate kitchen. Most importantly, it had a dining room, which was the most significant social identifier in Glasgow: Glaswegians who unwrapped the newspaper from their fish suppers in a separate room considered themselves quite the cut above. French windows opened out from the dining room onto a narrow balcony and the whole place looked out over a tree-fringed square of car park and gardens to Great Western Road.

It was a nice place in a nice part of town and, sickeningly, my property ownership brought out more than a little petty bourgeois pride in me. But not bourgeois enough to stop me entertaining ladies there. I was discreet, but my social life had still attracted the disapproving attention of some of the other residents.

Which brings me to Irene.

After the war, after I had all of the bright-eyed, pre-war Kennebecasis Kid naivety kicked out of me, I generally saw things the way they were: all of the absurdity and crap we build into ways of living. It wasn't as if I spent all my time looking for the emotional and psychological wreckage all around me, it was just that I couldn't help tripping over it.

It was especially true in Glasgow when you saw life stories written before they'd been lived: seen the face of a passing teenage girl filled with the resignation of a sixty-year-old; or watching some tenement kid, happy and grimy from street-play, smile as his paper boat sailed on oil-sleeked gutter water towards a storm-drain, unaware of deep metaphorical irony. The fact was that the whole determinism or free-will hoopla just didn't fly here in Glasgow: it was the kind of place your future was handed to you the second you were born. And it usually was crap.

The truth was that most were complicit in their own doom. You could never have described nineteen-fifties Britain – especially Scotland – as the most progressive of societies. They were all still there: all the fossilized ideas and forms, codes and systems that had been impressed into the British social consciousness. It wasn't just a case of keeping people in their place, but getting them to keep themselves, and each other, in their place. It was how ships got built, how wars got fought, how the machinery of Empire was kept running. It was odd that no one seemed to have noticed that the Empire wasn't there any more.

And one of the codes that still adhered was that relating to pregnancy. In Presbyterian Scotland, there was a prescribed and immutable chronology to pregnancy: conception and pregnancy followed marriage. If conception preceded marriage, then marriage had better follow in short order and well before birth, or mother and baby would soon part company.

There was something of that sort written in the history of Irene Christie.

Irene was a good-looking woman, and she knew it. Her hair was dark, nearly as black as mine, kept short and in a permanent so it curled at the nape of her neck and over her delicate ears. Her eyes were large and blue-green beneath the black arches of her eyebrows, her nose smallish and her lips promisingly full and lipsticked crimson. She had the kind of curvy hourglass figure that hinted that gravity would eventually do its work on the hourglass's sand but at the moment it was a delight to behold.

Irene was very much the kind of woman I seemed to have leant towards of late. And I had done an awful, awful lot of leaning. She was undemanding – except to make the same kind of demands on me that I made on her – and she was wise enough to be beyond romantic foolery. The talk we made was almost exclusively small, but I had gotten the idea that Irene had started out an attractive girl who, not realizing she would mature into a beautiful woman, had seen her prettiness as a diminishing asset and had chosen to make the most of it while she still could.

Whatever the background, teenage behind-the-ballroom and back-row-picture-house fumbles had led to a fruitful exchange – but without a union to be blessed. So, pregnant and eighteen, Irene had married. Her husband, reading between the lines, or the sheets, had been the best of the bunch at the time, but was an unexceptional man of little ambition and less ability: a tradesman of some sort whom the socially ambitious Irene had mercilessly harried into better tailoring, a Bearsden bungalow and his own business.

Dragging her hapless and reluctant husband bumping up the steep steps of social advance had clearly fatigued Irene; she had chosen me to rub her aching muscles.

In a place and time – and of a class – where women were more often than not simply their husbands' shadows, Irene was an independent woman. She drove her own car and, at the beginning, we would meet for a drink somewhere out of town where we'd be unlikely to meet anyone who might know either of us; but once we'd pretty much exhausted the few conversation topics of vaguely mutual interest, we decided Irene should just park her car around the corner and come directly to my place where we could get on with the business at hand.

As agreed, she turned up at my apartment at eight that evening.

'I can only stay an hour,' she said as way of greeting when I let her into the flat. 'George thinks I'm at my sister's so I better show face there later.' She walked straight past me, along the hall and into the bedroom.

Irene was my kind of woman, all right.

I followed her in and was about to ask her how she was but the sudden presence of two tongues in my mouth at the same time made clear diction difficult. We fell onto the bed and did what we did best.

Sex with Irene was always explosive, almost violent. She navigated the male anatomy with an expertise probably matched only by the Flying Dutchman's knowledge of the world's seaways – and more than once she'd put her finger on a sequestered point on the map that I myself hadn't known existed. It was almost perfect sex. Almost. The only negative aspect of it was Irene's propensity for cheering me on. During the act of love, particularly approaching its climax, Irene had a tendency, well, to provide *instruction*. 'Come on, Lennox! Come oaaaan! No . . . no' like that . . . aye . . . like THAT!'

In my usual perverse way, it called to mind a football trainer on the sidelines yelling encouragement or criticism of the on-pitch performance of his players. It was mildly off-putting, but given the other compensations, more than tolerable. I was just relieved that she'd never brought a football rattle to bed or had, on the point of orgasm, yelled out, 'Ya *BEAUTY*!'

After we'd rattled the bedposts a couple of times, Irene and I lay smoking. It became clear she was in a stinker of a mood for some reason she couldn't be bothered explaining and in any case I didn't care about. But whatever was troubling her, it had been a bonus for me, because the pent-up heat of her frustration had combusted in my bed. I had struggled to match it and worried momentarily that I was about to be relegated to the substitutes' bench.

'Are you okay?' I asked to fill a silence. 'You seem tense.'

'I'm fine. Just a bit fed up.'

'Fed up with what?'

'Wi' George, mostly. He could do so much more with the business. With everything. And he's been acting funny. Moody.'

'Do you think he suspects?'

Irene shook her head. 'George? Christ no. He doesnae have enough imagination. I don't know what's wrong with him. Don't worry, he isnae on to us. He hasnae the imagination even for that.'

I watched her profile as she lay next to me: under her frown her big eyes were fixed on the ceiling as if concentrating on a sum she couldn't add up. Her crimson lipstick had smudged, leaving her lips lighter, and her skin was pale and freckled. Suddenly I saw the girl who had got herself knocked up and trapped in a device that, for all I knew, had been of her own making. I suddenly didn't feel very good about myself, which wasn't that unusual.

I put my arm around her to comfort her but the signal was misunderstood and before I knew it we were rattling the bed-head for the third time. Afterwards she got up, dressed quickly and left. We had hardly exchanged anything other than our brief intercoital chat.

After Irene was gone, I took a bath and dressed in a fresh set of clothes: I'd been down in London that spring and had picked up a couple of seersucker shirts I was particularly fond of – white with a navy chalk stripe – and I put one on with a knotted plum silk tie. I had been lucky, after a lot of searching, to have found a tailor in Glasgow capable of rising to the challenge of the new Continental style and he had made me a lightweight, mid-grey single-breasted Prince of Wales check suit.

I finished the outfit off with a pair of burgundy wingtips: a French chum had once told me that black shoes should only be worn to weddings and funerals and the custom had sort of stuck with me. Similarly I'd given up on wider-brimmed Borsalinos and the hat I chose from the coat-rack on the way out was a narrow-snap-brimmed trilby, which was becoming the fashion in the world outside and a decade ahead of Glasgow. Before I left the flat to meet with Quiet Tommy Quaid, I checked myself in the hall mirror by the door: I was looking good. Empty, but good.

I would maybe have chosen a different outfit if I'd known what lay ahead.

## 4

Quiet Tommy Quaid was dressed every bit as sharply as I was.

Like me, Quaid wasn't the type to give away much about himself, but from what I'd been able to find out he had spent a not inconsiderable chunk of his early adult life behind bars and his childhood had been in some shitty mining village in the distant back of beyond, or somewhere even worse, like Lanarkshire.

But, as I saw him sitting with his drink over in the corner of the lounge bar, I could easily have believed he was the scion of some noble lineage out slumming it for the night. It was the leisurely expectation with which he sat – a quiet patience that said the world was there for him, not the other way around – that gave him the composed, graceful ease of an aristocrat. Only the lingering Motherwell in his accent when he spoke gave away a less illustrious background. That, and the fact that the deep-blue suit he wore – Continental-cut with cuffless trousers – was far too elegant for the British aristocracy. The thought again crossed my mind that I should maybe give Tommy my measurements for the next time he went skylight shopping.

We were a couple of swells, all right, and whenever Tommy and I met we did so in the few bars in Glasgow where you didn't order a punch in the puss with your pint to save time and formality. So, for our business discussion, we had arranged to meet in a less-rough-than-the-usual bar in the West End, close to one of the dance halls. Drinking sessions with Tommy had usually ended up with us scoring a couple of women, but this was business and an element of discretion, sobriety and unaccustomed moral continence was called for.

As I came in, Tommy saw me through the blue-grey smoke haze, stood up and waved. When I reached him I saw he already had a Canadian Club sitting waiting for me on the table. We drank a couple or three before we got down to business.

'The Saracen Foundry?' Tommy's confused reaction when I'd filled him in on the details matched mine when McNaught had told me.

'I know.' I shrugged. 'Not what you imagine as the typical target for industrial espionage, but it's the client's money.'

'Speaking of which . . . ?'

'Four hundred for you – a hundred now and the rest paid on delivery. I get a finder's fee and you deal only with me. Not my decision, but it's the way the client wants it.'

'Four hundred . . . that's a lot for a job like this.'

'You think it'll be easy?'

'Piece of pish, as my dear old da used to say.' He frowned. 'Seems far too easy for that kind of cash.'

I shrugged. 'Whatever these plans are, they obviously have a lot more value than we would think. I guess whoever's behind my contact is paying a premium to get the job done as professionally as possible. No mistakes and no obvious trail for the coppers to follow. So much so, they want to know exactly when you'll do the job and they'd like it if you could do your best to cover your traces so the break-in isn't discovered for a while.'

'Not a problem.' Tommy paused, his expression thoughtful. 'But this is an odd one, Lennox. The only security worth a damn will be at the other end of the complex, where the wages office is, and even that doesn't keep cash overnight – they bring the wages in from the bank on payday.'

'There's a night watchman.'

Tommy shook his head. 'Some old codger doing his rounds at ground level isn't worth shite. The only other worry, and it's hardly that, is that the foundry's such a huge place there's bound to be a nightshift working somewhere. But, apart from that, it's a piece of cake. I mean, it's an ironworks for fuck's sake – there's nothing much worth stealing and anything that *is* worth stealing is too heavy to carry out unless you take it out on a flatbed. They won't be looking for thieves and that means bugger all chance of getting caught. Like I say, it's almost too good to be true.' He frowned again; this time I saw something else in his expression, something deeper and darker than doubt. It troubled me because Tommy Quaid's inner feelings never seemed to break through to the surface. 'You do think it's all kosher?' he asked.

I shrugged. 'The money certainly is. And these plans, whatever they're for, obviously have great value to my contact's client. A value we can't see – maybe only they can see.'

'That's the other thing. All the cloak-and-dagger stuff makes me jumpy. You say this guy looked like a tough nut?'

'Not in the usual way. More military. For all I know he's really the client himself but just wants to fudge things up a bit. Listen, Tommy, if you just don't like the feel of it, I understand. But you know you're the only guy I trust with these jobs.'

Tommy thought for a while. I'd noticed that my mention that McNaught had had a military look had caused his frown to deepen. Again I got the feeling there was something else in the mix I didn't know about; and again it troubled me.

'I'd like to scope the place out first,' he said eventually.

'They've done their own survey. Watchman rounds, ways in and out, that kind of thing. I can give it to you.'

'I'd still like to do my own scope.'

'I guessed you would.'

'And will you do the driving and lookout?'

I thought for a moment. I hadn't considered going along on the job and had imagined that while Tommy was slipping quietly into the foundry, I'd be doing pretty much the same with Irene, cosy at home. I nodded. 'If you need me, then yes. No problem. You in?'

Tommy thought it all through; then he said, very seriously, something I would have cause to recall later: 'I trust you, Lennox. You know that, don't you?' The gravity with which he said it took me aback.

'Sure, Tommy. I trust you too. Explicitly. That's why you're the only man for this job . . .'

Again Tommy paused thoughtfully, then grinned. Whatever it was that had caused the darkness in his expression, it was gone like the shadow of a cloud passing in front of the sun. 'That amount of money for a walk in the park? I'm in. When does it need to be done?'

I ran through everything that McNaught had told me, including that he wanted the file for the end of the month. I suggested we do the foundry the following Friday, but Tommy said he had another job on that night.

'This bugger's less of a walk in the park,' he said. I wondered if it had been this other job that had preoccupied him, but I knew better than to quiz Tommy on matters that weren't my concern.

I ran through the job and Tommy sat quietly, nodding. When

I was finished he asked questions in a systematic way, taking the job apart piece by piece and stretching me to remember all the details. Tommy was smart, very smart: his interrogation of the job reminded me, not for the first time, that there was a keen intelligence working behind the calm, quiet exterior. He read my mind.

'I'm thorough, eh? You're wondering how, if I'm so careful, I spent so much time in chokey?' he asked when we'd finished the business of the day.

'I was, as a matter of fact.'

'I'm a journeyman, a tradesman – maybe even a craftsman. Like every tradesman I served an apprenticeship.'

'And part of that apprenticeship was getting caught?'

Before he could answer, the door of the bar opened and two young women, a blonde and a brunette, walked into the lounge. Dressed-up factory girls, their mayfly youth and freedom squeezed between school and marriage, they were young, sleek and unexceptionally pretty and looked around the bar with the Friday-night-hungry eyes of willing prey. They saw us looking at them and leant heads together, exchanging a giggled something.

Tommy turned back to his drink and me and shrugged. 'Occupational hazard. I made stupid mistakes – it's all part of learning your trade. And even if you don't make stupid mistakes, this is a risky business. There's always the chance that there'll be a copper where he shouldn't be, or an alarm pad that you missed. It's been years since I've been caught and I intend to keep it that way. But when you've not been caught for so long it can make you sloppy. Even with a job as easy as this, all it takes is one bit of bad luck. One foot put wrong. That's why I plan everything out to the last detail.'

'I couldn't do it. The prison time, I mean,' I said and I meant it: there had been a couple of times, including in Hamburg, where prison had become a distinct possibility.

Tommy was distracted while he exchanged mating rituals with the blonde of the two women who now sat at the opposite side of the lounge, but deliberately in eyeline. Tommy had a naturally easy way with women. He seemed genuinely interested in them, in what they had to say. Me? Women seemed to expect me to be bad; being a polite Canadian, I didn't like to disappoint them.

'Prison's just a place, like any other,' he said eventually. 'People ask me how I put up with it, I ask them how they put up with *this* . . .' He waved a hand to indicate our surroundings. 'The truth is, Lennox, we're all born into a prison. Just some walls are easier to see than others.'

'And some prisons are easier to live in.'

He smiled and shook his head. 'You're wrong, Lennox, all prisons are the same. Remind me to tell you about my old da—' Tommy broke off as he looked past me, grinned and raised his glass. I turned in the direction of the two girls.

'Anyway, Lennox old chum,' he said, draining his glass, and rising from the table, 'business over. I think it's time we had our bells rung . . .'

## 5

I had done enough bedhead rattling for one day but stayed long enough as support act while Tommy worked his gentle magic on the blonde. The brunette seemed to be happy to be paired off with me and she was a cute enough girl, but I was tired and I wanted to get home to bed.

She got all swoony over my 'American' accent and I got the impression that, if I'd made the obligatory moves and for-appearances persuasions, she would have happily accompanied me, but once I'd made final arrangements to meet with Tommy to do the job, I made my excuses and left.

For form's sake I asked the brunette for her 'phone number. Explaining that she wasn't on the 'phone, she scribbled her name and address down on a handbag-scrabbled-for piece of paper and eagerly handed it to me. I was tired and tempted to point out that I'd be looking for a shag, not a pen-pal, but instead smiled gallantly and took her note.

I could have given David Niven tips on how to be a gentleman.

The weather outside was still sluggishly warmish but there was what Glaswegians, with their usual poetic turn of phrase, called a smirr: an all-pervading fine rain that hung like muslin gauze in the air. With a logic that only the Scots could under-stand, they believed that this kind of rain got you wetter than any other. On leaving the bar, my main concern was that I hadn't brought a coat and that the damp would play havoc with the fine worsted of my suit.

It was stupid that I let such a trivial concern force me into a half-run along the street to where I'd parked the Sunbeam Alpine. Glasgow at night was generally a place you had to keep your wits about you and I was about to pay dearly for my sartorial conceit.

I suddenly felt propelled forward, the flat of someone's boot slamming into the small of my back and adding to the momentum of my run. The impetus snapped my head back and I lost my hat and footing in the same instant. Arms flailing, I struggled and failed to keep upright and fell face down, skidding to a halt on the wet pavement. Instinct and experience told me to get to my feet as fast as possible, but kicks were already slamming into my ribs on both sides.

Two of them.

The one on my left aimed a kick at my head but I moved and his boot glanced painfully off my scalp. I should have rolled up into a ball and turtled it out, but the old dark fire that had gotten me into – and out of – so many scrapes kicked in. I rolled sideways, over and over as fast as I could, throwing myself into the legs of my right-side attacker. He staggered a little and I wrapped a bicep around his calf and yanked. He went down hard and his friend ran forward to kick me again. I didn't let the kick stop me getting up and as I did so I stamped my heel down hard on the mouth of the thug I'd downed.

When I turned to the second guy, I could see in his face that this was not the kind of playtime nor was I the kind of playmate he and his chum had expected. He was big, broad and prognathous and in the middle of my anger and pain I couldn't stop a *fuck-me-he's-the-spit-of-Victor-McLaglen* thought running through my head.

Despite his hard look, he didn't strike me as a street thug type; he confirmed my suspicion by taking a swing at me that told me he'd done most of his fighting in a boxing ring and not on the street – or in the mud and blood of Anzio, where I'd learned many of my best dance steps.

I moved forward inside the arc of his punch and slammed my forehead into his face. He staggered back, nose streaming with blood, his eyes dazed and startled at the same time. I startled him again, harder this time, and he dropped.

I took the time to check out what had happened. I saw that behind us was a doorway set in shadow by a heavy stone lintel – I realized my playmates had been hiding in there. Waiting for me. This was no ordinary street robbery: they had had a reason for picking me out and I was going to find out why.

The first guy I'd dropped and on whose dental records I'd made a permanent mark was coming round. My ribs hurt like hell and I knew I was going to wake up the next morning stiffer than a Bridgeton bridegroom, so I decided that my new chums would remember the encounter too. I kicked the inside of his thigh to part his legs and followed up by slamming the heel of my wingtip into his groin. He doubled up like a jack-knife and started gagging.

'Victor McLaglen' was now on his feet and stared disbelievingly at his chum, then me. I took a step towards him and, courageously loyal to his comrade to the end, he turned on his heel and ran for it.

'Lennox!' I turned and saw Tommy Quaid running towards me, leaving the two girls standing slack-mouthed at the door of the pub. I used the seconds it took Tommy to reach me to land some good, hard kicks on the fallen guy's back and head. I felt strong hands grab me by the upper arms and pull me back. I spun around, breaking the hold and turning to face Tommy. The fire must have still burned in my face because he held his hands up appeasingly.

'For fuck's sake, Lennox – take it easy.'

I made a move towards the moaning man on the ground and again Tommy grabbed my arm, this time even more firmly. 'Enough! For God's sake calm down or you're going to kill him.'

I let him pull me back.

'Are you all right?' he asked.

'I'm fine,' I said, although every breath was beginning to hurt. 'Help me get laughing boy here to his feet and I'll find out what this was all about.'

Tommy looked down at the guy on the ground who lay on his side moaning, his knees drawn up to his chest. His mouth was a bloody mess and one side of his face was badly split and bleeding, fleshy puffs already closing up the eye.

'Christ, Lennox,' said Tommy. 'Did you have to do that to him?'

'There were two of them – the bastards jumped me. I want to know why.'

Tommy looked back up towards the pub. I turned too and saw that a small knot of drinkers had spilled out and were looking in our direction. The ringing bells of an approaching police car sounded in the distance and I guessed we'd picked one of the few pubs in Glasgow who'd care enough to report a fight within fifty feet of their door.

'We've got to get out of here,' said Tommy. 'There may've been two of them but there's only one now, and from the look of him you've put him in hospital. You'll be hard pushed to talk your way out of this, Lennox. Where's your car?'

'Just around the corner.' I winced, a pain shooting through my right side. 'I think the bastards have busted a rib.'

The sound of the police bells drew closer. The girls had melted into the growing crowd at the pub door and out of involvement. No one to tell the police about my charming 'American' accent.

'Let's get the fuck out of here,' said Tommy, looping an arm around my shoulders and easing me along the street and around the corner to where the Alpine was parked.

'I want to know why they did it,' I protested when we reached the car, but I was too weak and hurting to push the point.

'Give me your keys, I'll drive.' The police bells were louder now and there was a hint of urgency in Tommy's tone. I handed him the keys and allowed him to slide me gently into the passenger seat.

Any successful professional thief needs to have a thorough memory for geography, knowing every street and alley in his patch making the difference between an escape route or one straight into the welcoming bosom of the police. Tommy Quaid knew his patch inside-out and, taking the first turning he could off the main road, followed a circuitous but efficient route that took us away from the scene quickly, but without the risk of running into an approaching car full of coppers. I sank back into the leather of the Alpine and closed my eyes. Out of danger and with the adrenalin in my system burned up, a dark, leaden pain and nausea started to wash over me in sluggish waves. My ribs hurt whenever I breathed and my head hurt whenever I moved it.

And the old self-loathing claimed me too: the sense of shame I always felt whenever I'd gotten so het up that I'd ended up in that same old dark-hot place that the war had taken me. I was also embarrassed that Tommy had seen that side of me; it was like being seen naked and exposed, all of your baser instincts – the type most people keep locked up tight – out there in the open for the world to see.

That had been the thing about war: there had always been some dark and shadowed place where you found yourself doing things that no one would ever find out about. Things only you saw. Things you didn't know were inside you. After the war, like so many others, I had done my best to lock the darkness back inside.

But there was always some bastard, like tonight, who would come along and bang on the door and ask it out to play.

We crossed the Clyde to the South Side.

Quaid must have had his own Nibelungen Hoard stashed somewhere because his place was a downstairs flat in a Victorian blond sandstone in Pollockshields. I'd been once before, but that had been after a hard night's drinking with Tommy and I'd been in a greater – and in that case self-inflicted – state of stupor than I was now. Quaid steered me into a tastefully decorated if a little Spartan lounge and I dropped down onto the red chesterfield. I could see that my handmade Prince of Wales had taken a battering: the worsted at one knee had split and frayed and I was beginning to understand why the Scots had a penchant for industrial-grade tweed.

Tommy handed me a Scotch, the taste of which made me wince more than my ribs did, but it warmed the right cockles and my nausea lessened a little.

I eased out of my jacket and opened my shirt. Taking another swallow of whisky, I ran my hands over my ribs; although the pressure on one side sent a jolt through me, I couldn't feel any deformity.

'What's the damage?' asked Tommy.

'As far as I can see there's nothing broken, but with ribs you can never tell. I think all I've got is a crack in a couple.'

'You should maybe go for an X-ray.' Tommy sipped his whisky. There was something vaguely off about his tone, as if he was talking to someone he didn't know as well as he thought he had.

I shook my head. 'I think I should avoid hospitals and the questions that come with them. I'll strap up tight when I get home.'

'I've got bandages here, I'll fix you up . . .' Tommy put down his glass and went through to the kitchen. While he was gone I looked around the room. Tommy lived here; but it was living without touching, without personal investment. The walls were bare of pictures, mirrors or any other adornment and there wasn't much in the way of furniture: the deep-red leather chesterfield I sat on, the club chair that matched it, a heavy teak coffee table in between, and a large bookcase against the wall. Everything looked expensive, but there was an incompleteness to the room – a sense of temporariness, as if Tommy had left his personality unpacked in a moving crate.

There was one thing that promised to give away something about the man who lived there: I gingerly eased myself up from the chesterfield and went across to the stacked-full bookcase. It perhaps didn't do me much credit that I was surprised by the erudite and eclectic choice of literature of a boy from a Lanarkshire pit village. I had always known Tommy was bright: he would often surprise with a literary allusion or the extent of his general knowledge. But the books in the bookcase were of a different order.

It was sophisticated stuff, all right: dictionaries, encyclopaedias, political biographies, and various technical manuals on all sorts of disciplines from locksmithing to architecture that I suspected had some bearing on Tommy's trade. But it was the other books that surprised me. There was some, but not much, of the usual stuff: paperbacks by Nevil Shute, Dennis Wheatley, Nicholas Monsarrat, that kind of thing. But the majority of Tommy's personal library was totally unexpected: hardbacks of Dostoevsky, Franz Kafka, *The Tartar Steppe* by Dino Buzzati, another three by Albert Camus, and the Roads to Freedom trilogy by Jean-Paul Sartre.

There was a host of other titles by writers I hadn't heard of – and I had read a lot and widely. I picked out a hardback copy of *The Outsider* by Camus and was about to flick through it when I was interrupted by Tommy coming back into the room, carrying a canvas musette bag marked with a faded red cross; I recognized it as a standard first-aid kit from the war. Once more I was a little put off by the expression on Tommy's face when he saw me looking at his books, almost as if I no longer had the status that afforded that kind of privilege. But again it was a cloud that passed.

'Did you do over a library?' I asked, indicating his book collection. It was a lame joke made lamer by Tommy's lack of reaction to it.

'I read a lot,' he said. 'I like Sartre and Camus. Have you ever read *The Outsider*?'

I shook my head.

'It's interesting that you should pick that one out. You know, with everything we were talking about earlier, you really should read it. It's a good book. A great book, probably.' He gave a strange, small, almost wistful laugh. 'It's a book that speaks to me.'

I was about to ask if I could borrow it when he took the Camus from my hand. He examined it for a moment, then examined me in the same way, as if I too had been something to be read.

'It's been a very special book for me, Lennox. I want you to remember that. I tell you what – if ever anything happens to me, I'll leave it to you in my will. Remember that too. I think you'd get an awful lot out of it – maybe, one day, this'll be a book that will speak to you too. And most important of all, always remember that you can never judge a book by its cover. This book particularly. Or people.' He put the book back in its place in the bookcase. 'Anyway, I've got the bandages. Sit down and I'll strap you up.'

I nodded and eased my way out of my shirt. My ribs, especially on the right, hurt like hell but there was no sense of bone grinding on bone. Tommy told me to take another swallow of whisky, then to raise my arms up, but not too high. I did what he said and he started wrapping the bandages around my torso, sending a loop over one shoulder for extra stability. He wrapped tight and it hurt, but at least I knew I wouldn't do more damage. It was an expert job.

'I'll fix you another drink,' he said when he was finished and I eased back into my shirt and jacket. 'The bathroom's at the end of the hall: you look like shite – why don't you go and clean up?'

I nodded my thanks and did what he said. The bathroom was fitted out with expensive porcelain furniture and tiling, and was even equipped with a shower, but again the only personal touches were a toothbrush and Tommy's shaving kit. Once more I had the impression that it was all ready to be scooped up and packed if Tommy had to move on in a hurry.

I checked my reflection in the mirror. My handmade Prince of Wales check looked pretty much beyond the magic of dry cleaner or tailor. The shoulder seam of my jacket had burst and there was an oily smear on one sleeve where I'd reclined unwillingly on Glasgow Corporation tarmac. My pride-and-joy shirt had lost buttons and was creased and grimy. But what I liked least was the face that looked back out at me: cold, hard, weary. Bad.

My black hair was mussed up and an ugly bruise was creeping out from below the hairline, from where the boot of one of my playmates had grazed the scalp. I felt another, stronger wave of nausea but fought it back hard: I knew if I vomited the spasms would jangle my ribs. I scooped up some cold water and rinsed my mouth, splashed my face and smoothed back my hair.

There was a tap on the door and when I opened it Tommy stood holding a suit on a hanger. It was very like the one I had ruined, except the grey check was perhaps a shade or two darker.

'You can borrow this,' he said. 'We're roughly the same size. And here's a change of shirt.'

'Thanks . . .'

After he left I changed into the clothes. The suit was a Continental too and very similar in cut to the one I'd ruined. The freshly laundered shirt wasn't of the same quality as mine, but at least it was clean so I changed into that too.

Tommy had made some bad coffee – the fake chicory crap that the Scots drank – and handed me a cup when I came back into the living room.

'You don't think much of the way I handled things tonight, do you?' I said.

'I don't like violence, Lennox. I've seen too much for one lifetime and don't have a taste for it any more.'

'Nor do I, Tommy . . .' I tried to put force behind it but it didn't even convince me. 'It's just that . . . I don't know. The war. It messed me up. When something like tonight happens and I get into it with someone, I just lose my head. It becomes more than a punch-up. There's just all this . . . all this *rage*.'

'I know all that. You're not the only one who was in the war. I had to do things I never want to talk about. Or think about. But I swore that I'd never do them again, or let anyone force me to do them again. I promised myself that I wouldn't let all of that shite claim me. I saw your face tonight, Lennox. You didn't just want to hurt that guy, you wanted to kill him.'

'I just lost the place—'

'There was more to it than that.' Tommy cut me off. 'I saw something in you I haven't seen for a long while. I saw it in the war – men who wouldn't have hurt a fly in civilian life suddenly finding a part of themselves they didn't know existed. The part that enjoys killing. You'd see it in their faces – like they were hungry for it. Like they were glad the war had come along and shown them who they really were. I knew someone like that, someone in my unit during the war who called himself my friend too. He had that look.' He took a sip of chicory coffee. 'It's been years since I saw that look but I saw it tonight. You had fucking murder in your eyes, Lennox.'

'That's not who I am. I know the type you're talking about, but that isn't me. It's just . . .' I struggled for the best way of putting it, then gave up.

'Forget about it,' said Tommy.

But I didn't want to forget it. For some reason it was important to me that Tommy understood. 'When I was a kid I used to go to Saturday matinees at the Capitol in Saint John. Westerns or Buck Rogers. Kids whistling and booing and chucking stuff at the screen whenever the bad guys rode into town. It was all so simple: black hats and white hats, heroes and villains, good and evil. I believed it. I believed I had to be one or the other. But life's not like that. Christ knows you know that, Tommy. Nothing's black and white: everything is shades of grey. You, me, everyone – we can be the good guy *and* the bad guy, depending on what life throws at us. I admit there were lots of things I did during the war that I'm not proud of – but I never, ever enjoyed killing. I hated it. In fact, that's where that crap comes from: all that anger and fear I had to go through.' I sipped the chicory coffee; regretting it instantly, I set the cup and saucer down on the table. 'Sometimes I wear the black hat instead of the white. Because it's been handed to me.'

'You're wrong,' said Tommy. 'You choose who you are, what you are. Whatever's happened to you, whatever you've been through, whatever shitty deal you've been handed – *you* decide what you make of it. Because if you don't, then there's always some other bastard who'll decide for you – officers, cops, judges, politicians. And you're wrong about there being shades of grey. There are some bad fucking bastards out there, believe me. And not our kind of bad bastards . . . not some pissed-up hard cunt with a razor, or gangster from the Gorbals. I'm talking about people who have everything, who've had everything handed to them and have no reason to do the shite they do. And the shite they do is beyond fucking belief. Real evil.'

And there it was again, hiding in the shadows behind Tommy's eyes. In that instant I saw Tommy, just like me, kept something locked up inside. Then it was gone. He smiled and shook his head as if annoyed at his own folly.

'If you think I was – that I am – one of those guys you talked about, then you're wrong,' I said. 'What you saw tonight is my own little demon that I've been fighting ever since the war. You wouldn't have seen it if those guys hadn't jumped me. What I really want to know is *why* they jumped me.'

'You have no idea?'

'None. Sometimes when I'm working on a divorce, an irate

husband might turn up handy; but I haven't got anything on remotely like that at the moment.'

'Maybe they were simply after your wallet.'

I shook my head. 'They weren't the type. I got the impression that their experience of rough-and-tumble has more to do with the rugby club or amateur boxing than real street stuff. They weren't pros and they got more than they bargained for. If they hadn't jumped me from behind and got me on the ground, they wouldn't have cut the mustard at all. The fact that they had me on the ground and that I managed to get to my feet and give them a hiding speaks for itself.'

'Amateurs or not, they've given you something to think about for the next week or so.' Tommy nodded to my chest. 'There's no way it could be connected to this ironworks job?'

'I can't see how. Maybe it was a case of mistaken identity.' I smiled, but then a thought occurred to me. I looked down at the suit trousers I now wore – the ones Tommy had lent me. He read my thoughts and laughed.

'Aye . . . I thought about that too – I do wear that suit a fair bit, and we're roughly the same height and build – but unlike you, Lennox, my disposition is famously sunny. No one has a grudge against me and everybody I do business with knows I'm fair and square. So no . . . they weren't after me.'

I shrugged and my ribs shouted at my shoulders to be still. 'Maybe we'll never know. Tell me about your father.'

'What?'

'In the pub you said to remind you to tell me about him.' I had sensed a thaw in Tommy and I wanted to steer the conversation away from the events of that night.

'Oh, that . . . Forget it. Sometimes I get too philosophical for my own good.'

'Tell me anyway. It'll take my mind off my ribs.'

Tommy shrugged. 'All right . . . you asked me about how I was able to do the prison time . . . how I was able to give up my freedom. Well my old da had freedom: he never spent a day of his life in a cell – born free, lived free, died free. Never *bent* a law in his life, never mind break one. But the laws and rules he lived his life by had fuck all to do with him, they were other people's rules. Any freedom he had was what someone else decided was freedom. My old man died free all right – at fifty-three years old, coughing and spitting up black phlegm and blood. And he lived free too . . . a free life spent three fathoms deep working a coal seam, one eye always on the water seeping through the gallery walls or on the gas alert. Even the food we ate wasn't up to us – the pit foreman would come knocking and looking for answers if you didn't buy your groceries from the mine company store. Aye, my da lived free – free with the constant threat of drowning or suffocating and ended up doing both on his deathbed. Fuck that, Lennox. If you call that freedom, give me a Barlinnie cell any day.' He took a drink.

'I never took you for a Marxist . . .'

Tommy laughed. 'They're as bad as the bosses. Just a different set of rules. Just a different set of bosses.'

'It doesn't mean you have to turn to crime and accept being chucked in chokey. There are easier ways—'

'Are there? Oh you mean education? Learning your way out of the pit? I must have missed the scouts from Oxford and Cambridge waiting for me when I left Dalziel Secondary at fourteen. The pit foremen were there though, looking for apprentices to bury in the mine.'

'You've got brains, Tommy—'

He cut me off with a laugh. 'Brains? Do you think they count for anything? My da had plenty to spare. Down the pit since he was twelve, practically no education – but he spent hours in the miners' library, then the Motherwell library. Then the Mitchell Library in Glasgow. He used to learn stories and poems by heart so he could repeat them in his head when he was down in the dark.'

Tommy took another sip of his drink.

'My da had brains all right, and you're right to say he passed them on – to both me and my sister – but they never got him out of the pit. I could never understand why he lived his life by some-one else's rules. You know . . . why he worked so hard for fuck-all except to make rich private coal companies richer. Then I worked it out. Everything's fucked up. The whole world is totally absurd and filled with people doing things the way they've always been done, just because it's the way they've always been done. It was only after he died that I worked out that my da dedicated him-self to what he did because he was trying to make some kind of sense of his life.'

'But you're not.'

'No, I'm not. That's why prison never bothered me: it's just another place, just another room you're in. Except prison makes more sense than the outside world. I'm a thief: I steal things and if I get caught I get punished for it. There's nothing absurd about that. But the truth is that everyone is a thief. Everyone steals from everyone else and the whole system is run by the best thieves of them all – the ones who steal power and opportunity from you. Steal your life. You want to know the difference between prison and the outside world? The people you meet in prison are more fucking honest. If you knew—'

It was there again: something bigger, something more imme-diate and specific behind his anger, a brief shadow on the threshold. Tommy decided against sharing it and the fire in his eyes dulled.

'And you're the same as me, Lennox,' he said. 'People like us see things the way they really are because we've had the shite knocked out of us. We both see that everything is chaos and crap and we just go along for the ride. Play the game without playing it, if you know what I mean. Make the most of it.'

'And what does your sister make of it? You said she has brains too.'

Tommy smiled. 'Jennifer? Aye, she's got brains too. But she's well out of Glasgow. I used my earnings to send her to college in England. She's got a good job in London. Nobody tells our Jennifer what to do, she's her own woman. If there's one thing I'm proud of, it's that I got her the hell out of Glasgow. She has a life. A future.'

'What about you, Tommy?' I asked. 'Do you think you'll ever settle down? Get married? Have kids?'

'Never. I'd never bring a child into this evil, fucked-up world. You don't grow out of childhood here, you survive it. Or some bastard rips it away from you.' Tommy gave an awkward laugh, embarrassed at his own sudden vehemence. He took another drink. 'Sorry. I like kids. I just think they get the shite end of the stick.'

We drifted back into discussion about the foundry job and it was agreed that we'd do it a week Sunday night, when there would be the least chance of there being anyone around. In the meantime Tommy would survey the site and draw up his plans. All I had to do was act as a driver and lookout, Tommy providing the vehicle. Given the profit I was going to make, I readily agreed. After we had finished, Tommy offered me a couch for the night, but my ribs protested that they needed the comfort of my own bed and I drove home.

I had an allocated space in the parking lot outside the apartment. When I parked, I sat for a moment with the car's engine switched off, checking parked cars for silhouettes or the tell-tale red glow of a cigarette tip, then searching the shadows between the pools of pale light from the lamps in the car park and the bushes that fringed it. As I got out and crossed to the building entrance, I kept checking the three a.m. darkness for lurking goons. No one jumped me and when I got into my flat, everything was in order.

I'd already begun to stiffen up and any movement of my arms seemed to send a jolt through my ribcage, making getting out of Tommy's loaned suit a slow, cautious process. I swallowed some aspirin and swilled my mouth with water to cleanse it of the sour taste of Scotch and violence.

Easing myself into bed, I closed my eyes and tried to sleep, but my ribs ember-glowed with a malevolent ache and the events of the evening kept running like an endless film loop against the screen of my closed eyelids. In a city where violence was common and generally senseless, I couldn't understand why I was struggling so hard to make sense of my ambush.

The birds had already started singing by the time I fell asleep.

# 6

I spent the next two days recuperating. Irene and I had made no arrangement to meet because, it being the weekend, she was playing the role of mother and wife. In any case, the stiffness I was feeling as a result of my encounter with pavement and boot was not the kind of rigidity that would have been of any use to Irene.

By the Sunday, the pain had dulled into a persistent but manageable ache, but when I removed the strapping to soak my battered torso in the bath, I saw that both sides were covered with livid blossoms of purple, maroon and black. Amateurs or not, I'd taken a kicking all right. The bruise blooming out from my hairline onto my forehead was also diffusing into a fudged rainbow, and I was already planning out my Monday morning explanation for Archie, whose seemingly slow, dull, watery eyes missed nothing.

I hadn't slept well either night, small electric jolts in my ribs wakening me regularly. When I had managed to find some sleep, it had filled with vivid dreams, including the one that had haunted me so often: a terrified face that was more boy than man desperately begging me. In German. The same dream that seemed to re-emerge every time I'd gotten myself into a fight, like some kind of echo reminding me how hollow I had become.

I eased myself gingerly into the day. I knew I had to be by the 'phone at one p.m. to take McNaught's call, but first I wanted to pick up the newspapers and a supply of cigarettes. As the sun was making an unaccustomed appearance, I decided to walk instead of drive, thinking the activity might loosen me up. So, once I'd done my best to strap my ribs up tight, I headed out into the sunshine and down Great Western Road. The Glasgow sky rewarded my spirit of endeavour by clouding over before I had reached the newsvendor outside the Gaumont Cinema, which for some reason the locals still called the Ascot. I could hear him from half a mile away, shouting out '*Heeeeauheennyoooos! Geayty-ooheeeeauheennyoooos*' in that near consonantless language of newsvendors that was unintelligible everywhere, but in a Glaswegian accent was doubly encrypted.

Tucking the papers under my arm, I nipped into the foyer of the Gaumont: I'd been cultivating the redhead who worked the tobacco kiosk and while I picked up some cigarettes I shot her a line or two. It was less of an angling trip and more of a fish-shoot in a barrel and I got a note of her days off. She was cute enough all right, but had a smoked-deep voice and a grit-and-glass accent that made me hope desperately that she didn't get vocal at times of passion. Generally, I found it off-putting for Finlay Currie to come to mind during intimacy.

'Ah'm no' on the phoan, but,' she rumbled. I assured her that I'd call by the kiosk later in the week to make final arrangements.

I was back in my flat by twelve-thirty and, at exactly one p.m., my 'phone rang. I recognized the voice right away as belonging to my new friend with the lopsided face.

'Have you fixed a schedule for what we discussed?' he asked without preliminaries.

'Next Monday, one a.m.,' I said.

'And you can rely on your associate to stick to that time?'

'I can,' I said. 'I'll be taking him there.'

'Good. This is an important mission. I was hoping you would personally supervise it.'

'How do I contact you to arrange delivery and payment?' I asked.

'You don't. I'll 'phone you again after that date to arrange collection of the information and payment of the rest of your fee.'

He hung up. I guessed we weren't going to be close.

Tommy Quaid's two-day-old, chicory-flavoured assault on my palate had haunted me almost as much as the kicking my ribs had taken, so after I'd spoken with McNaught, I fixed myself a proper coffee. I'd recently picked up a new recording at the record store in Sauchiehall Street and put the long-player of Brahms' first piano concerto on the radiogram; I may have been accused of being a thug and worse at various times, but at least I was a cultured thug. While Leon Fleisher arpeggiated, I eased myself, stiff-backed, into the armchair by the window and read through the news.

There was nothing of any note: mainly the usual crap about the forthcoming Empire and Commonwealth Games – but as headbutting wasn't a scheduled event, I didn't expect a strong representation from Glasgow in the Scottish team. The only thing that caught my eye was a three-column-inches mention of the incident I'd witnessed from my office window while Mr McNaught had been making his unobserved way up the stairwell. Headed CENTRAL STATION ACCIDENT VICTIM STILL UNIDENTIFIED, it explained that the body was of a young male who had apparently wandered onto the tracks somewhere between the Broomielaw, where trains crossing the bridge over the Clyde began slowing as they approached the terminus, and the station platforms. The police had given no further details other than that the deceased was not a railway employee and that they were not treating the death as suspicious.

I closed the papers and drank my coffee, watching nothing through the lounge's bay window.

For a sliver of a moment, I wondered why, if the dead man had been between the platforms and the Broomielaw, they had gone in through the main concourse and brought the body out the same way. That was all I thought about it.

At the time.

## 7

As we had agreed, a week later, an hour after Sunday had become Monday, Tommy and I met to do the foundry job.

At least I looked the part: I had dressed in a pair of dark cavalry twills, a black sweater the neck of which covered up my shirt collar, and a pair of rubber-soled, black suede desert boots. Examining the figure I cut in the full-length hall mirror, I couldn't help but laugh: all I was doing was driving Tommy and keeping an eye out for night watchmen or strolling coppers, yet I'd dressed as some kind of Hollywood movie-version diamond thief. At least if we got caught I'd have a Cary Grant mugshot.

Leaving my apartment building as quietly as possible, I eased the Alpine out of the car park onto Great Western Road and headed west. At the best of times, Glasgow at one in the morning was a haunted-looking place; the streets blank and silent, blind between the pools of street-lamp light. Tonight, one-in-the-morning Glasgow was especially haunted-looking under an uncharacteristically cloudless sky. The third-quarter moon had withdrawn into a sliver of crescent, giving up the night to the sparkle of stars. The next full moon, Tommy had informed me, would not be until the thirtieth. 'No point in putting on a shadow show,' he had said in the pub when we had planned the break-in. 'The full moon's like a spotlight – you become a silhouette up there on a rooftop and you'd be as well doing a dance routine for the coppers. Always best to go on a cloudy, moonless night.'

The only car on the streets, I got all the way past the Maryhill canal locks without spotting a soul, but as soon as I turned into Maryhill Road I saw a copper on foot patrol watch me as I drove past. I gave a small wave and he saluted – driving a new Sunbeam Alpine in Glasgow gave me salutable status – but I still checked my side and rear-view mirrors to make sure his hand didn't fall from the salute onto his notebook pocket. It didn't and he walked on, continuing his patrol through Maryhill, where he'd find nothing else that night to salute.

Tommy's instructions had been clear: I turned off Maryhill Road at Bilsland Drive and pulled over, leaving the parking lights on, a hundred yards from the junction. I scanned the tenement-flanked street on both sides and in both directions, but could see no sign of Tommy, or anyone else. A disconsolate-looking dog, some kind of black-and-white mongrel, trotted along the middle of the road and passed the car without looking in. I cricked my neck to watch it head back towards the junction, and also again to check for any sign of Tommy; there was still none. I was turning back to face front when the passenger door opened and Tommy dropped into the seat.

'How the hell did you do that?' I asked, genuinely impressed. 'Where did you come from?'

'Trade secret.' Tommy grinned and tapped the side of his nose with his finger. 'Speaking of trade secrets . . .'

I nodded and pulled out from the kerb. Tommy told me to keep heading along Bilsland Drive. Past the smoke-blackened brick of the railway arch, the tenements to our right gave way to the bush- and tree-edged Ruchill Park, dark and dense in the night. We passed the Elizabethan gables of the gatehouses of the infectious diseases Ruchill Hospital, the black silhouette of the hospital's baroque tower, the highest structure in Glasgow, a darker looming against the starry sky.

Eventually, Tommy directed me into a dead-end street that, like almost all of its neighbours, was empty of cars. Empty except for a scruffy old Fordson works van, green paintwork and red wheels faded and grimy, garage livery on the side barely legible. From its styling I could see it was a pre-war model; from its condition I wondered if the war it had been pre- had been the one we'd fought with the Boers.

'We can't take your car to the job. It's far too flash and we don't want anyone remembering it or some keen-as-mustard new bobby noting down the number. Park between the street lights.' Tommy pointed to a spot in the street where the car would be in the least light. I did what he asked, deciding now wasn't the time to tell him about the patrolman saluting me on Maryhill Road. We got out and I locked up the Alpine.

'I managed to borrow this.' Tommy spoke quietly as he led the way to the parked van. Spoke and moved quietly: he seemed to be able to walk without sound, as if he made no real contact with the ground. 'If we bump into any coppers, we can maybe convince them that we're mechanics called out to an emergency breakdown.' Scanning the dark eyes of early-hours tenement windows to make sure we hadn't awoken curiosity, Tommy donned a pair of gloves before unlocking the van, reaching in and handing me out a dark-blue boiler suit and another pair of gloves. 'Best put these on before you get in.'

He took out a matching pair of overalls for himself and wriggled into them.

'I'm guessing from the gloves that the van owner isn't aware he's loaned you the van?' I asked.

Tommy grinned, handing me the keys. 'I'm sure he'd be fine with it – I just didn't want to trouble him by waking him up and asking. I'll get it back before it's noticed missing in the morning.'

'Isn't this a risk?' I asked as I got into the driver's seat. 'You said yourself the job itself's reasonably risk free. It'd be a real pity to be pinched for stealing a van.'

Tommy shook his head. 'We're only ten minutes away from the ironworks so we'd be really fucking unlucky to run over a copper in the time it takes us to get there and back. And any-way,' he made a sweeping gesture with his hands to take in the van, 'who'd want to steal a piece of shite like this? The coppers wouldn't give it a second look, even at this time of night.'

'You're the boss . . .' I turned the key in the ignition and the Ford gave a rheumy cough, but didn't start. I looked at Tommy meaningfully; he caught the meaning.

'It just needs a bit of choke.'

I pulled the choke halfway out and tried again. The engine lurched into life and I three-point-turned the van and headed out of the street.

'By the way,' I said as we headed towards Possilpark. 'Thanks again for the loan of the suit – I'll get it back to you, but I'll have it dry cleaned first.'

'Thanks. How are the ribs?'

'Fine.'

'Any more ideas on why those monkeys jumped you?'

'None.'

In nine minutes we were in Possilpark: an artificial settlement built with only one purpose, to house workers for the Saracen Foundry. The original works in the Gallowgate's Saracen Lane had given the foundry its name, but demand had outstripped capacity and the decision had been made to find a dedicated out-of-city site. The fields and copses of the bucolic Possil estate had been bought, bulldozed and built over. Possilpark, a sprawling grid of four-storey red-sandstone tenements, now sat smirched greasy black by a century of smoke and soot from the massive, fourteen-acre foundry that formed its dark, smouldering heart.

'Look at this place.' Tommy's thoughts obviously paralleled mine. 'You notice there's a pub on almost every third street corner? Mass anaesthesia. Keep the poor fuckers stupefied.' He shook his head as if bemused. 'Wait until this place goes bust – and it *will* go bust – then there'll be generations of waste.'

There were tenements almost right up to the foundry's main entrance on Hawthorn Street; but the huge site was surrounded at the sides and back by areas of waste ground, all rubble and bare earth, as if scorched by the foundry's toxic presence.

The vast, arched double doors of the main entrance, like the gates of a prison, were flanked by two smaller but still huge gates; an ornate, stepped dome, something like a basilica, rose above the central doors. Everything wreathed in ornate iron-work. A high wall ran all the way around the foundry and the night sky above was pierced by the stretched spindles of tall, slender brick chimneys, one at each corner of the site and each topped with onion-dome ironwork, making the chimneys reminiscent of minarets.

'It's best we avoid passing the main gates,' said Tommy. 'Swing round next left and park at the side, near the back corner.'

'You going in through the side entrance?' I remembered McNaught's layout plans had indicated the various gates and where the drawing offices were.

'No, there's a less-used gate at the rear.'

I followed Tommy's directions.

'Pull up here,' he said eventually. To our right was the side wall of the foundry, an area of waste ground to our left. I reached down to switch off the engine but he laid a hand on my forearm to stop me. 'Leave it running.'

I'd expected Tommy to swing immediately into action but instead he sat staring out through the windshield of the van, his expression as he looked at the dark brick shoulder of the iron-works suggesting he'd been presented with something alien, surreal. I'd seen that expression before, mainly in Glaswegian restaurants when vegetables were served.

'You going in?' I asked when Tommy still made no sign of moving.

'I still think this is all very strange,' he said eventually. 'I mean, it just doesn't make any sense.'

'You want to pull out?' I asked without rancour. If Quiet Tommy Quaid had a bad feeling about a job, I had to take it seriously. After all, I was on the job with him. An accessory. My flimsy disguise of boiler suit and car mechanic's van wouldn't stand up to even a Glasgow copper's scrutiny. All they'd have to ask me to do was change a spark plug.

Tommy shook his head. 'That would leave you in a fix. The bloke who gave you this job sounds like he doesn't take no for an answer.'

'I can handle that. I'll tell him we were spotted and had to call off. I can arrange something for another time.'

Again Tommy stayed quiet for a moment. And again it worried me that he had to think it through: he had said himself it was as straightforward a job as he could get, yet his thief's instincts seemed to be echoing in the pit of his stomach every bit as much as McNaught's threat was in mine.

He took a sharp breath in and in a decisive gesture pulled on a tuque hat to hide his copper-coloured hair. 'No . . . I'm just getting jittery in my old age. Wait here . . . leave the engine running, I don't trust this rust bucket not to pack in if it's switched off.' He opened the door to get out. 'It's quarter-past one. I should be in and out in twenty minutes at the most. If I'm not, it means either I've had to duck down and wait it out because some bugger's in my way, or because I've been nabbed. If I'm not back by twenty to two, drive around the block a couple of times, just in case I've had to take another way out. But no more than twice – if there's still no sign of me by ten to two, then take off. Dump the car, but not within a mile of where yours is parked.'

'Christ, Tommy,' I said. 'If you feel that we have to—'

'Normal precautions. I usually fly solo, but when I work with someone else, we always plan it out like this. Things go south and sometimes you get separated, but it doesn't mean one of you's been pinched. You've no idea how often the polis use getting separated to get you to stitch yourself up or give away who was on the job with you. If I don't make it back to the rendezvous, clear out and keep your head down. And you know what to do if you see a copper or anything else?'

'Yep. Drive off and give two long blasts of the horn when I'm around the corner.'

Tommy nodded. 'This time of night the sound'll carry. If needs be, I'll lie low for as long as it takes.' He looked at me and smiled. 'But don't worry, Lennox, old chum. It'll be a piece of cake.'

I watched him in the side mirror, walking close to the blackened brick flank of the foundry, a shadow becoming lost in a darker shadow. I switched off the parking lights but left the engine running, constantly scanning the street front and back for any sign of an approaching police car or foot patrol. There was something about the situation that put me particularly on edge and I couldn't work out what. Maybe, I thought, it was just that it reminded me of those older, wartime playtimes in the dark. I fumbled beneath the overalls and found my cigarettes and lighter. After another check to make sure there was no one around to see the hand-shielded flare, I lit a cigarette and took a long, deep pull. It did a little, but not much, to relieve my nagging unease. All I could do now was sit it out.

## 8

Tommy didn't come back after fifteen minutes. Or twenty. Or half an hour.

The jangling in my head and gut had by now become alarm bells and klaxons. I hadn't driven off as Tommy had said, instead waiting for him to find me where he'd left me. But he had told me that his way out of the works might have to be different from his way in, so I drove slowly around the whole site, including the main Hawthorn Street entrance, twice. No sign. I couldn't risk passing by the manned main gates again, but instead of following Tommy's instructions to quit the area in the hope we could regroup later, I pulled up back at the same spot I'd been parked before. I broke another of Tommy's rules by switching the engine off and locking up the van before retracing the steps I'd seen him take before he'd melted into the shadows.

I couldn't really explain why I felt the need to put myself at unnecessary risk by going to look for Tommy, but it had a lot to do with what you went through in wartime: the instinct not to leave a man behind. And now all of my instincts were telling me that something had gone very badly wrong.

I reached where the wall turned ninety degrees, its corner curved like the shoulder of a battlement, rather than sharp angled, and I found myself making my way along the back of the foundry. The wall broke for an entrance to the works – a high railing gate with a wooden gatehouse like a garden shed set just inside – and I pressed in against the greasy, black brickwork. This had been on the plans and I knew it wasn't the main rear entrance. Because the foundry covered a fourteen-acre site, it had many entrances for different purposes: the main gates were used for the bulk of the workers at shift change, as well as for larger lorries, but there were several smaller entrances for deliveries and access to specific worksheds. This, I knew, was a minor entry and the one Tommy had planned to use. According to McNaught's timetable and confirmed by Tommy's own surveillance, the night watchman didn't occupy any of the gatehouses for any length of time but just called by to make sure each of the gates was secure. Another night watchman was on stationary duty at the main gates.

The door of the watchman's shed was open, but the interior was in total darkness, suggesting there was no one inside, so I eased forward, grateful that I had put on the rubber-soled desert boots. I was no Quiet Tommy Quaid, but I reckoned I could scale the metal gates without too much delay or noise, so I moved towards them.

A second earlier and I would have been spotted. I was in front and slightly to the side of the gates when I heard a rumbling, rheumy cough from inside the shed, followed by a deep-throated racking before the concealed watchman spat out onto the cobbles. I could hear his breath wheezing before the cavern of his post glowed red for a moment as the tubercular watchman soothed his lungs with a drag on his cigarette. Fred Astaire would have admired my silent-tap sidestep as I dodged obliquely and into the wall beside the gatehouse. I would now only be a matter of feet from the watchman, separated by the gate edge and wooden sidewall of his shed.

Again I'd been in very similar situations before, but if I were rumbled here I couldn't resolve it with a Fairbairn-Sykes fighting knife through a sentry's windpipe. In any case, from the sounds of it, the night watchman had found a much more efficient way of suffocating to death.

In Glasgow, elderly could begin anywhere from fifty onwards, but the stooped man who emerged from the shed looked as if he could remember the Relief of Mafeking, probably because his son had taken part. He had his back to me as he waddled out and I could see he wasn't much over five foot tall but was nearly as wide. The shapeless jacket of dense, dark tweed he wore was separated from a flat cap of the same cloth by a roll of thick, pallid neck. His dark trousers were baggy, adding to the squatness of his figure. Standing there with his back to me, he looked as if paused in thought, his hand hanging at his side, the last half-inch of a roll-up cigarette pinched between thick finger and thumb. Taking a final draw from his meagre smoke, he flicked it away to bounce on the cobbles in a firework shower of red embers. He took a battery torch from a cavernous pocket and thumbed it on. Then, like the *Queen Mary* announcing its departure from dock, he let out a low, rumbling fart before continuing his waddling patrol of the foundry.

Watching the old guy wobble back into the body of the works, it struck me that the owners didn't feel unduly besieged by the forces of crime; if they had secret designs or patents, they sure didn't seem to think they needed robust guarding.

Once the elderly watchman was out of sight and earshot, I again examined the gate. If the shed was able to bear my weight, then climbing over the gate and coming down onto its roof was probably my best way in. I took a moment, though, to assess my options. For all I knew Tommy had found his way back to the van, only to find it locked up and empty. He certainly wouldn't have appreciated my cack-handedly amateur efforts at breaking in. But those old instincts were jangling again, telling me that something wasn't right. I thought back to Tommy's own hesitation, and his question about whether or not I thought that everything was kosher with this job.

The gate rattled more than I had anticipated and I was glad to swing over the top and get my feet onto the roof of the watchman's shed. I eased myself down and headed in the same direction the old guy had taken. During the war I'd become used to reading maps and plans, often in a hurry, and McNaught's schematic of the works had stuck in my mind. Almost all the foundry's site was built up with tight-packed, side-by-side worksheds: each brick-built and thirty feet wide and the same height with a pitched roof. Each workshed was stretched out long, some were three-quarters of the total width of the site and the only source of light came from the tented skylights along the roofs.

Following the route along the ground that mirrored the one Tommy would have taken at roof level, I found myself in a narrow section that ran almost like a street between the blank brick sides of the worksheds. I could hear the sounds of heavy industry, but distant and muffled, and all of the sheds at this end of the foundry were silent and dark. Pulled back into the shadows, all my senses stretching out into the works, it was strange to listen to the dull throb of the place, like it was a living being. Every now and then the rumble would be punctuated by a bang or a clash of metal ringing out, muffled by the baffle of the foundry's walls.

The lighting was pretty meagre and widely spaced, affording me plenty of shadows. The odd thing was that what light there was came from the kind of lamp-posts I associated with Parisian boulevards: richly ornate iron standards with barley-sugar twists in the shaft and elaborate filigree brackets holding the lamp – itself a high-power bulb rather than a modern sodium light. I realized these lamps were more for display – examples of the foundry's craft – and I reckoned they must have been here for forty years or more.

The street between the sheds opened out suddenly into a large, better-lit square. Like a surreal arena in the midst of the industrial sheds, it had a massive bandstand at its centre. Iron looped and spiralled, burst into ferrous blossoms and arced up into the huge dome of the bandstand, which in turn rose above the tented rooftops of the foundry. The bandstand wasn't alone: a few yards to its right was an equally impressive, if waterless, fountain; to its left, between two stone stanchions that were connected to nothing else, massive Art Deco gates stood guard over nothing. And all around these central exhibits were drinking fountains, pagodas, canopies, even French-style urinals, and, of course, telephone boxes – all ornately shaped out of iron. This was the foundry's sales floor, where customers from across the Empire and around the world would examine the massive samples and place their orders for their parks, municipal spaces, rail stations or presidential palaces.

Tommy had been right, this was a museum: the kind of grandiosity that belonged in the past, to an empire now dissolving, and probably to the time when Albert was still making Victoria go bug-eyed. But this was a new age of brutalist architecture and modernist lines: no one sought out the ornate any more; the shape of the future was being cast in concrete, not wrought in iron. Again the thought nagged at me: what kind of advanced technological or production secret could this place possibly be hiding from the world?

I made my way along the edge of the display area towards the drawing office. It loomed up suddenly: a six-storey block, flat-roofed and the only new addition to the largely Victorian architecture of the foundry. The lighting was once again meagre and I understood why the elderly watchman made his rounds carrying a flashlight. Stumbling over an uneven cobble, I cursed out loud and nearly fell. I paused for a moment, annoyed at my own clumsiness, then made my way forward, keeping a steadying left hand on the wall. My reasoning was that if I made it to the main door of the building holding the drawing office, I could perhaps find my way in and up to find out what the hell had happened to Tommy.

I almost missed it.

There was a dull thump about fifty yards ahead of me. I didn't see the object fall, nor hear any sound as it fell – just the noise of impact. To start with I thought it was a heap of empty sacks – a dark bundled shape on the cobbled yard, no more than three feet out from the wall – but the instinctive lurch in my gut and chest told me that it wasn't. I looked up to the roofline but couldn't see anyone, just the black silhouette of the building against the stars, like cut-out stage scenery; no sound except the brick-muted throb and rattle of the foundry. I ran across to where the bundle had landed.

I knew before I got to it, before I could make out its shape as human, that the object on the ground was Tommy. When I got to him I could see right away that he was dead: his eyes were open and lifeless, a halo of blood blooming black on the cobbles around his head, his hair and the injury still concealed by the dark woollen tuque. I didn't need to check for a pulse: unless Tommy had been preternaturally double-jointed, I could tell instantly that his neck was very definitely broken. I again looked up to where he must have fallen from, but there was no sign of anything or anyone untoward.

My mind raced. Unusually for me, I didn't have a clue what my next move should be but I was prompted into action by a horn sounding somewhere inside one of the halls, presumably announcing a refreshment break or change of shift. About three hundred yards away, double doors opened, flooding the cobbled yard with light and workers. I shrank back into the shadows and started to trace my way back to the side gate, hugging the wall and keeping an eye out for the geriatric night watchman. I got to the gate and hoisted myself onto the roof of the shed, then hauled myself up and over the iron gates, dropping clumsily on the other side. I landed badly and was rewarded with perfectly synchronized sharp twinges in my left ankle and in my ribs, which had been slowly easing over the last week. Limping off towards where I'd left the van, I realized that nothing was broken and the sprain was a mild one – it wouldn't cause me too much trouble, so long as I got back to the van and got my weight off that ankle as soon as possible.

I got clear of the gates and made my way back along the rear perimeter wall. I stopped before I got to the corner and looked back to make sure no one was following me. They maybe even hadn't found Tommy's body yet, and if they had, there would be a lot of confusion about who he was and how he'd ended up broken and dead on the foundry yard. Searching for an accomplice wouldn't come to mind.

Quiet Tommy Quaid was dead. He was dead and had been killed pulling a job for me.

It was a fact: a brutal, sudden fact that I would have to come to terms with. But later. For now, my instincts were telling me to get as far as possible, as quickly as possible, from the foundry and Tommy's body, but I knew I would be doing a lot of reckoning afterwards.

Pulling the ignition key from the pocket of my overalls, I came round the corner and saw the van; I also saw a black police Wolseley pulled up alongside it, two coppers examining it, one cupping his eyes with his hands as he peered through the driver's window. I ducked back around the corner and pressed my back against the greasy brickwork while I considered how famously my night was going.

I tried to work out how the police could have cottoned on to the van so quickly; perhaps my slow drive twice past the main gates had aroused suspicion, but I doubted it. I tried to think it all through: there was no way of getting back to the van, but at least the coppers wouldn't find anything to link me to it – unless they caught me with the key in my pocket. I had no choice but to hoof it back to where I left my own car. A dull throb in my ankle reminded me of my haste in dropping down the side of the gate and that the walk back to the car, assuming I could get away from the foundry without detection, was going to be an uncomfortable stroll.

I stole a glance around the corner again: the coppers were still there and looked like they had no intention of moving off. The van was of interest to them; again, something I couldn't understand. Tommy was meticulous in his planning and if he had said that the van wouldn't be missed until morning, then it wouldn't be missed until morning. And there was no way these coppers could already know about Tommy's death in the foundry.

Tommy.

His face flashed in front of me again, the eyes open and dead, his mouth loose, his head at a sickening angle to his shoulders. I had been right to have that foreboding; all of that thinking back to the war. It had been like that then, too: you got to know someone, to get inside their head; you got to like them. Then one day you'd end up looking at them when they were nothing more than lifeless meat.

I had to get away.

I reckoned I had a good half-hour walk to get back to where my car was parked, but the cops were in my way and if I went back the way I'd come I'd have to pass the side gate again. My only option was to take a roundabout route that would put a block of tenements between me and the foundry.

Crossing the road behind the works kept me out of sight of the coppers at the van but potentially not the rear gatehouse, but if the elderly watchman had headed back in that direction, he would be occupied with Tommy. Once I was across, I headed up a side street between tenements, effectively in the opposite direction to where I wanted to go. I dropped the van's ignition key down the first storm drain I could find, severing my connection with one object of police interest. Memorizing every right and left turn to try to keep my bearings, I navigated what I thought would be a route to take me all the way around the foundry. I came out on a main road and for a moment my sense of direction was confused. Then I realized that across the street was the edge of Ruchill Park. I decided to follow the fence until I found a pedestrian gate into the park, but I'd only gone a few yards when I saw two sets of headlights, one behind the other, come around the corner at the far end of the road. They were moving quickly and I guessed they were more police cars; at this time of night, with the roads to themselves, there was no need for them to sound their bells. With shenanigans at the foundry there was no way they wouldn't stop to question a Canadian in overalls limping along in both the middle of the night and the middle of nowhere. I knew I had to get out of sight quick. The park fence to my right was too high for me to climb and I wouldn't have enough time to get back across the street. Ignoring the pain in my ankle, I sprinted towards the approaching lights, hoping I would find some way into the park. I realized it would only be a matter of seconds before they saw me and I was short on credible explanations for my presence.

I was just about to fall into the range of the first car's headlights when the fence dropped to waist height, with a turntable gate for pedestrians to enter the park about fifteen yards ahead. I didn't have enough time to reach the gate so I vaulted the fence and thrashed into the shrubbery beyond. I pushed down into the soil and hoped I hadn't been spotted. I would have been pretty pissed if I'd gone through all of that for a couple of goods lorries, and was almost relieved when I turned just in time to see the vehicles pass: another police Wolseley, followed by a Black Maria, clearly on their way to the foundry.

They must have found Tommy and called it in.

I lay for a while, tangled and breathless in the bushes, gathering my composure and reflecting that Cary Grant had never had to put up with this kind of thing. I had planned to lose the overalls as soon as I could but was grateful for the extra protection against thorns and dirt they'd afforded me. It was entirely possible that the occupants of the first car had seen me, so I stayed very still until I was sure that the coppers weren't going to pull up or turn around. Then, pushing through the bushes, I slipped into the darkness of the park. My ankle was throbbing but still able to take my weight: I seriously considered finding a park bench to spend the night, allowing my swelling ankle and the reawoken protesting from my ribs the chance to subside, but my instinct was still to get as far away as quickly as I could. Added to that, I was less likely to be spotted retrieving the Alpine at night than during the day. There were lamp standards along the park's tree-lined footpaths, splashing pools of light on the pavement, so I made my way directly across the grass and darkness, hoping like hell I didn't fall into some ornamental pond. As it happened, my trajectory brought me into a thick swathe of trees and bushes and I had to trace my way around them, first of all stripping off the overalls, bundling them up and stuffing them as deep as I could into the bushes, hoping they'd be as concealed in daylight as they seemed at night. Eventually I saw the street lights on the far side of the park.

I came out onto the street and again it took me a while to get my bearings. When I did, I walked as briskly as my ankle allowed until I found myself again on Bilsland Drive. I turned up the dead-end street and was relieved to see no policemen waiting by the Alpine. Of course it would have made no sense for there to be any; but nor had it made any sense for there to be any waiting at the van Tommy had stolen.

I got into the Alpine. Sitting in the warm leather had never felt so good. It had taken me fifty minutes to make a journey that should have only taken twenty-five.

I was startled by Tommy's voice. He said, just as he had in the bar that night: *'I trust you, Lennox. You know that, don't you?'* I turned, smiling, ready to congratulate him on fooling me again, the way he had on the way to the job when he had appeared out of nowhere. But I was alone in the car. Tommy was still dead. Still lying broken on an ironwork's cobbles.

I sat for a moment, partly again to gather myself but also because a light had gone on in one of the upper tenements. Once it went out I drove off, retracing my route from earlier and hoping not to earn any salutes on Maryhill Road.

'I trust you, Lennox . . .'

As I drove, my thoughts were filled with Quiet Tommy Quaid. Most of all, I thought about one thing – something that nagged and worried at the frayed edges of my exhausted mind. I reflected on how Quiet Tommy had lived up to his name until the very end. How he had fallen from a six-storey rooftop to his death without making a single sound.

No matter how I thought about it, Tommy Quaid's quiet death made no sense to me at all.

# Part Two

Part Two

# 1

By the end of the week I began to breathe a little easier.

I'd picked up a divorce case and was purposefully giving it my full-time attention: not that there was any real detective work involved. Divorce in Scotland was a pantomime involving staged, often fully clothed, mock-infidelities, bribed hotel staff and a mountain of statements. Scottish society at all levels remained censorious about divorce and I liked to think that I was doing a public service by helping the unhappily coupled de-couple, navigating them through a largely hostile legal system. The fact that I came out of it with better-lined pockets was all to the good.

All of the divorce cases I landed were sent my way by two Glasgow legal firms, both of whom trusted me to be efficient and prompt in 'gathering' evidence. Everyone knew that I booked the rooms, arranged the times for the soon-to-be-ex-spouse and often professional co-respondent to lie fully clothed in the bed while two members of hotel staff, both of whom I also paid for their services, entered the room and witnessed the 'infidelity'.

It was all a very Scottish affair – a dry, emotionless, clinical business. Often it was kept dull to avoid the interest of the press, should the plaintiff or appellant be in the public eye, which they hardly ever were. My job was to make sure there was never anything titillating or salacious in the evidence: no talk of

Roman orgies in Rutherglen or transvestism in Teuchar; no photographs of Mr A bent naked over the knee of Madame X and having his bottom spanked with a rolled-up copy of *The People's Friend*.

So I applied myself diligently to arranging the evidence in the case of *Murray v Murray*. I even turned down Archie's offer to lend a hand – Archie, being a suitably dour-looking type and an ex-policeman without a stain on his record, made a particularly credible witness. My credentials and background did not stand up so well to scrutiny, so I had tended to avoid presenting evidence in court. But as this was a case where both parties were solely interested in parting company, my evidence would be unchallenged.

The main reason I'd devoted myself to the divorce case was really because I was trying to put that night and what had happened to Tommy out of my head. It was a fool's errand: Tommy would flash into my mind whenever I wasn't otherwise mentally occupied and frequently when I was. I'd see him lying there, twisted and broken, his open eyes dulled. And all of the questions I struggled to ignore would crowd in on me whenever I tried to get to sleep: like the fact that Quiet Tommy Quaid was the best roof man in the business and could tightrope-walk his way with arrogant ease along the ridge-piece of a ten-storey-high roof apex; so why had he fallen over the edge of a flat-roofed building? I also found myself wondering why I had heard nothing from McNaught, who had been so very clear in his threats about failure to deliver. What trade secrets could a failing foundry have that would be worth stealing? And what brought the police to the parked van? A parked van I was supposed to be sitting in?

And then there was the biggest puzzler of them all: why had Tommy not cried out, made any sound at all, as he fell to his death?

I wanted to push them all out of my head. My main aim was to keep out of the whole thing. Whatever the whole-and-nothing-but about that night turned out to be, I was best left well out of it. There had been more than enough in my past, both before my time in Glasgow and during it, that was best kept beyond police scrutiny.

There were plenty of people who knew I was friendly with Tommy; there were one or two who even knew of my occasional employment of his services. It was a connection I didn't want made: if the coppers took that much of an interest, they could perhaps trace sightings of the stolen van back to where it had been parked and a Sunbeam Alpine convertible, a rare sight in Glasgow, had shown up. From there it would be only a small step away from a particular patrolling bobby remembering a particular salute. Sometimes I could be too flash for my own good.

For most of that week, I half expected a visit from the police. My sleepless nights had been spent working out strategies, the best of which was straight denial: I couldn't see them having any clear evidence of my presence, other than a car like mine being seen in the small hours in Maryhill. I'd brazen it out, I decided.

But I never did get a visit.

## 2

I needed to establish a chronology: for someone to remember breaking the news to me about Quiet Tommy's death. It was time for me to call into the Horsehead Bar.

The Horsehead was just around the corner from my offices and I'd been a regular there for most of my time in Glasgow. I visited the Horsehead less often now, and never at a regular time. I'd changed my habits mainly because, in the past, people had known about my 'double office hours': if you were an ordinary Joe and had something legal, or at least semi-legal, you wanted me to do for you, you called into my regular office; if you were one of the Three Kings, worked for them, or you were otherwise feloniously employed and you needed something 'looked into', everyone knew where to find me. It had been a well-known fact that I'd be at the Horsehead Bar between seven and eight most nights. It was a routine I had very purposefully broken to send out the message that, like Doris Day's, my virginity had been restored.

It hadn't been until after six months of being on the comparatively straight-and-narrow that I heard Jock Ferguson – who was one of the few coppers in the City of Glasgow Police I liked, and the only one I trusted – had turned up regularly at the Horsehead during my former consulting hours to make sure I wasn't there. It was shortly after that that Ferguson had recommended me as security for the bank run. It was an act of faith I hadn't forgotten.

The Horsehead always bustled, but was bustling a little less despite it being a Friday night. There was a crew of three behind the bar: hard-faced, tough-looking types whose demeanour indicated they were no strangers to trouble and could handle anything anyone threw at them. And two of them were barmaids. The third was in charge: a huge bear of a man whose heavily tattooed forearms could have been the model for Popeye's, had they not been too big.

When he saw me arrive, Big Bob the barman greeted me warmly, as he always did. Bob seemed to like me – more importantly, he seemed to have some kind of respect for me – which I always took as a compliment. From Big Bob's position behind a Glasgow bar, he would have seen the worst of people. The paradox of booze was that the cleverer it made you think you were, the more stupid you sounded. Alcohol was a mental laxative, opening emotional bowels and releasing a torrent of verbal shite and Bob would have heard it all, seen it all. I'd probably had more than the occasional bout of vocal incontinence myself, but it seemed to have done my standing with Bob no harm. And he had liked and respected Quiet Tommy Quaid as well; maybe even more. But there again, I had seen Quiet Tommy tie one on more than a few times, and the booze never seemed to have any visible effect. I had always put it down to his equanimity being thoroughgoing, but of late I had begun to wonder if it was simply that he kept everything locked up tight. I'd always kept a 'there's less to me than meets the eye' thing going, particularly around coppers; maybe Quiet Tommy had outmastered me at it, and had depths and dimensions and secrets that no one ever got to see. The closest had been, I realized, the passing shadow in his expression the night after I'd been jumped.

My visit to the Horsehead had three specific purposes: it would establish a credible chronology for me, would allow me to gauge how much suspicion there was about Tommy's death, and whether anyone had made a link between me and the thief's demise. Bob, more than most people, knew that Tommy and I had been friends.

Big Bob's smile faded and he asked me if I knew about Quiet Tommy. I feigned ignorance and he broke the news to me. And with it my credible chronology was established: any longer than a week after the fact and I would struggle to claim I didn't know what had happened to Tommy, but would have to explain how I found out. Now I could say I'd heard about it six days later from Big Bob at the Horsehead. All perfectly credible.

'You an' Quiet Tommy got on, didn't you?' Big Bob asked.

'Sure. I really liked Tommy. I guess everyone did . . .' I said. 'It's terrible news.'

Big Bob poured me a Canadian Club on the house and I realized I hadn't really been feigning. There had been something about discussing Tommy's death with another person for the first time that shifted it from a bad dream into reality, and the shock of the transition must have shown in my face.

'Anybody know what happened to him?' I asked.

Big Bob shrugged. 'Slipped an' fell, the poor bastard. After a' them years clambering about on roofs in the dark, it was bound to happen, I suppose. What the fuck he was doing breaking into the Saracen Foundry is beyond me. It's a real shame, though. You'd struggle to find anybody to say a bad word about Tommy Quaid.'

'You would that . . .' I said gloomily as Bob excused himself to serve a customer further down the long sweep of the curving bar.

I drank another three whiskies before saying goodnight to Bob. There had been no more discussion of Tommy and I had accomplished my mission.

There was another fine drizzle hanging in the limp, tepid Glasgow air when I came out of the Horsehead. This time I valued my security over my tailoring and, as I made my way back to my car, I checked every doorway and every corner with a vigilance that would have made John Wayne leading a wagon train of virgins, whiskey and guns through Apache country look relaxed. There were no lurking ambushers.

But that had been another question that came back to haunt me during that week: I still could not work out why the two amateur heavies had jumped me that night outside the bar in the West End. Everywhere I went, just like when I came out of the Horsehead, I still kept an eye out for them, or any other likelies, as I went about my business. Because I had been on the clinically paranoid side of watchful, by the middle of the following week I could be sure that no one was watching me, tailing me or otherwise showing undue interest in my movements.

But that bothered me in itself: no one now seemed to be looking to jump me. Thinking it through – and remembering the similarity in our height, build and sartorial taste – brought Tommy's suit back to mind. I had dispelled the idea of the attack being a case of mistaken identity, but Tommy's sudden, unlikely and silent demise a week later cast everything in a different light. But if someone *had* broken Tommy's neck and thrown him from the roof, it was a professional job; the attack in the street certainly hadn't been.

And while I was watching out for faces in the crowd, I also

kept an eye out for a lopsided one; but Mr McNaught was conspicuous by his absence too. Maybe, I thought, he had read about Tommy's death and decided, like me, that the best thing for him and his anonymous client was to keep as clear of the mess as possible. I kept his down payment to hand, just in case.

In the meantime, I tried to get on with my life.

## 3

'Pherson's was a bit of an institution in Glasgow and a regular habit of mine. No one ever explained, nor even mentioned, the fact that the 'Mac' had got lost somewhere in the post and everyone referred to the man as 'Pherson and his business as 'Pherson's.

Old man 'Pherson himself was what would have been euphemistically described as a 'confirmed bachelor'; in his case, a *very* confirmed bachelor. He was a frail, birdlike man aged somewhere between fifty and a hundred, whose own hair was preternaturally dark and whose hands and scissors seemed to flutter around your head without making any kind of contact. He was also probably the best barber I'd ever had and I visited him every couple of weeks. After the events of the weekend before, I was doing my best to keep to my usual routine; the next day was one of my regular appointments for a trim and one of old 'Pherson's surgically close shaves.

There are places you find, places you build into your routine, that give you a strange sense of belonging. Anchor points. Places you rely on not to change, to stay constant. 'Pherson's was like that for me. It was a uniquely masculine environment: the impossibly robust leather and polished steel barber chairs – raised, lowered and tilted by unseen pneumatics and levers – were as self-evidently pieces of engineering as battleships, tanks or sports cars. 'Pherson himself wore an immaculate white mandarin-collared overjacket of the kind you'd expect a movie surgeon or a top-end-no-National-Health-patients-thank-you dentist to wear, indicating that gentleman-barbering was a science rather than an art; the radio on the shelf was tuned permanently to the Home Service; the unguent odours in the air were as much chemical as perfumes; the tiles on the wall were pastel-hued but spoke of surgical wards and were broken with calendars of pneumatic young starlets stretch-testing the tolerance of their knit or cotton tops. It was all a declaration that there was some science and robust engineering and indisputable manliness in a place which was, after all, dedicated to male grooming.

As usual, while he trimmed, old man 'Pherson chatted in the way he always did: amiable but lacking in depth. I guessed that when you were a 'very confirmed bachelor' in nineteen-fifties Scotland – a society that actively persecuted, and imprisoned, 'very confirmed bachelors' – you learned to talk a lot without saying anything. Old 'Pherson restricted himself to what was happening in the news, chirruping his way with his overly formal delivery through several of the happenings locally and nationally.

'Was that no' a terrible thing the other week with that young fellow at Central Station? Don't you have your offices near there, Mr Lennox?'

'I do . . . I saw all the comings and goings but don't know much more about it.'

'Terrible thing . . . just terrible,' 'Pherson intoned with the florid relish he reserved for really bad news. 'Young fellow like that throwing himself in front of the train. Just *terrible*. His guts and everything spilling oot like that . . . *terrible*. Did you know he wis cut clean in half?'

'I didn't. I didn't know it was a suicide either.'

'Oh yes . . . A good friend of mine saw it. Saw the whole thing. They was waiting for the train to come in and seen that poor boy standing away at the far end of the platform, nowheres near where the train would stop. That's why he noticed him. Why my friend noticed the young laddie, I mean. And then when the train was coming into the station, this young fellow simply jumps off the platform and chucks himself under the wheels. My friend says.'

'I thought it happened near the Broomielaw, not in the station. That's what it said in the paper.' I turned a little to the old man but thin, bony fingers dug into my scalp and turned me back to face the mirror. The scissors resumed their butterfly fluttering.

'No, no . . . *my friend* saw it *all*,' said 'Pherson, emphatically. 'It was in the station, so it was. Loads o' folk screamin' and cryin'. Dreadful thing. Just dreadful.'

I thought about what the elderly barber had said. It would make sense of what I saw: the body being brought out through the main entrance.

Old birdlike 'Pherson continued to twitter about other things while he tilted my chair back and shaved me deftly and assuredly with a cut-throat, before our conversation was stifled by the application of a hot towel.

I had absolutely no idea what practical purpose laying an almost scalding damp towel on my face served, but it certainly always had a therapeutic one. There was a ritual to it: the chair tilted back further, hot cloth applied, all conversation suspended while the customer was left in towelling-insulated solitude. And once the towel came off, there was no feeling like it, the skin glossy, taut and tingling.

After a while, 'Pherson kicked the chair lever and whipped off the towel as the chair came upright. There was more fluttering: tiny slaps and the cold sting of cologne; a dance of soft brush bristles on my neck. When he finished he asked me matter-of-factly if I would be needing 'weekend supplies' and I told him I would. No matter what day of the week I called in, 'Pherson always assumed the 'supplies' were for the weekend. In a Presbyterian society like Scotland, fornication seemed to be considered a strictly weekend activity – the last commodity yet to be freed from rationing.

Ten minutes later I came out of 'Pherson's into a typically muggy Glasgow Saturday, the air hanging damp, warm and sullen and muting the fresh tingle of air on my smooth-shaved and cologned skin. My 'supplies' were discreetly wrapped in the brown paper bag I carried.

I walked the block or so to the dry-cleaners. Dry-cleaning was still something of a novelty in Glasgow, home of the tenement basement 'steamie' where a history of industrial soot and grime meant clothes were traditionally boiled to destruction. The dry-cleaners I used – the Saturn Laundry – had decided to go for a space-age futuristic theme. From the decor, it was clear they firmly believed that Formica and coloured Perspex would feature as heavily as interplanetary travel in the Space Age to come. The regular woman there was Maisie: a short, heavyish sort of around forty who was just, and no more, clinging to the last vestiges of youthful prettiness, her moon-round face framed in hair that was about as naturally blonde as 'Pherson's was black. Maisie looked like she'd been around the block several times and had always given me the impression that she'd go round once more with me any time I wanted. We exchanged banter whenever I came into the shop, although we both knew that

that was as far as I'd take it, but we kept up the kidding as if I might. Just a bit of fun; one of those games you played. And anyway, experienced sailor that I was, I liked to keep a light burning in all ports in case of storm.

'Just come from the barber, Mr Lennox?' she enquired, looking pointedly at the brown paper bag that I carried instead of at my haircut. 'It was just the two suits, wasn't it? No lipsticky shirts this time?'

'Just the suits, Maisie.' I smiled. 'I'm leading a morally reformed life.'

'Aye . . . and I'm Audrey Hepburn's twin sister.' She returned with the suits – a dark blue of mine and Tommy's Prince of Wales – on hangers in the same bag.

I thanked her and turned to leave when she called out to stop me.

'Oh aye . . . I forgot about this . . .' Reaching into a drawer, she took out a Yale key with a blue tab attached to it and placed it on the Formica surface of the counter. Next to it she placed the stub of a theatre ticket. 'You left these in a pocket.'

'They're not mine,' I said. I hadn't seen the key before.

'Aye, they are,' she protested. 'The key was in the outside pocket of your suit. Maybe one of your girlfriends put it there.'

'Which suit?'

'The checked one. Prince of Wales.'

Tommy's suit. I shook my head as if annoyed with my own stupidity.

'Yes . . . yes, of course. Sorry. I'd forget my head if it weren't screwed on. Thanks, Maisie.' I snapped up the key and headed out. 'Give my regards to Audrey when you see her . . .'

# 4

I drove home with the roof down on the Alpine, trying to sustain the fresh feeling of the shave, but when I got back to the apartment building all I felt was grimy. I had a date with the kiosk redhead from the Gaumont that night and decided to take a shower.

Before I showered, I emptied the packets of condoms from the paper bag and into the bedside drawer, then took both of the suits I'd picked up from the dry-cleaners and hung them up, still encased in the bag. It made me feel like I was putting Tommy's ghost into my wardrobe but, at that moment, I couldn't think what else to do with the suit. Again it struck me that it was so very like the Prince of Wales check I'd ruined during my dance routine with Victor McLaglen and his chum. Once more I thought about Tommy's death making no sense and found myself wondering if my ambush had been a case of mistaken identity, the two goons confused by our matching tailoring. I wanted to let the whole thing go, but Tommy's death just didn't make sense.

I took the key from my pocket and looked at it. Rather carelessly, I hadn't gone through Tommy's suit when I had put it into the cleaners, assuming he wouldn't have lent me a suit with anything in the pockets. It was a Yale type key for a pin tumbler type lock. There was a blue plastic tab attached to it with the number 47a stamped on it. I remembered that that was the number on Tommy's door. That was why Tommy hadn't missed it: it was a spare key to his flat.

I dropped the key into the ashtray on the sideboard and went for my shower.

Agnes – the redhead from the Gaumont kiosk – had a bit of a busman's holiday attitude about going to see a movie so we went for a drink instead. Keen to steer clear of the West End, I drove out of the city and north to Drymen. By and large, the Scots were indoors drinkers; partly because of the shitty weather and partly because they didn't like to be distracted by scenery from the serious business of drinking.

I'd found this country pub on the outskirts of the village and, although the Scots viewed beer gardens with scepticism and even mistrust (the Germans and the English were big on them), there were a few benches outside where you could sit and take in the views. Agnes talked, although I tried to encourage her not to, and told me all about the ins and outs of running a tobacco kiosk. After about an hour, I could have told you when the Players No 5 were delivered and exactly how many ounces of loose leaf sold in an hour. All this information was disclosed in a gravelly baritone and Govan accent that were beginning seriously to blunt my ardour. But when Agnes wriggled closer to me and suggested we go back to my place, I blocked out Finlay Currie and reached for my car keys.

I was just draining my beer when a ship of a car pulled up into the pub car park. It was a smoke-grey Bentley S1 and when the doors swung open I could almost smell the walnut, leather, Axminster and new money from twenty yards away.

A medium-height guy with too-oiled hair slicked back from a too-long, slack-jawed face got out of the driver's seat and stood taking in the view. He was dressed in an expensive suit that was more flash than style and the face was dressed in the kind of smug expression you instinctively wanted to wipe off with your knuckles. He made no effort to come round and aid the woman who stepped out of the passenger seat. She was too tall and too slim for my taste and again was dressed in a way that suggested a bank balance that had overtaken a sense of taste. She would have been unremarkable-looking had it not been for the expensive silk turban-style hat and the acre of Arctic fox wrapped around her shoulders – she was obviously expecting the mild July evening to turn a bit nippy. The long gown she wore underneath the pelt suggested she was also expecting Prince Rainier and Grace Kelly to be minding the bar.

The husband indicated the pub with a nod and they both headed into it.

'Did you no' see who that wus?' said Agnes, clearly awed.

'Who?' I shrugged.

Agnes looked at me as if I had said something profoundly stupid.

'Frankie Findlay.'

'Never heard of him.'

Agnes was now open-mouthed. 'Frankie Findlay the comedian. You know, Frantic Frankie Findlay . . . Dinnae tell me yuv no' heard uh Frankie Findlay.'

'Oh . . .' I feigned enlightenment, looking at the Bentley. I still had no idea who he was. There again, I was purposely ignorant of Scottish comedy. Scotland had much of which to be proud: it had been the birthplace and heart of the Industrial Revolution; it was a small country that had produced a truly disproportionate number of engineers, medical pioneers and inventors for its size. But that pride didn't extend to comedy: I had seen enough Scottish comedians to know that, as a nation, they should have stuck to building bridges. Scottish music hall comedy, which had now filtered into radio and TV, was truly, spectacularly dire. Only one act I'd seen, a deadpan comic called Chic Murray, had had any subtlety or sophistication to it; the rest had been crass and moronic.

'He's been on the telly and everything,' Agnes said.

'Oh yes . . .' The truth was that in that instant the name did become familiar: I realized I'd seen it somewhere before. 'Frantic Frankie Findlay, you say.'

'Aye . . .' Another incredulous look. 'That's him.'

# 5

I didn't take Agnes back to my place. The Forestry Commission had long been an accomplice of mine in matters romantic and, taking the scenic route back to town, I pulled into a forest track off the road, far enough to be hidden by trees but not so far as to risk getting the Alpine stuck. We went through the usual obligatories and preliminaries before Agnes yielded to the inevitable. As it turned out, it was all a bit of a disappointment.

As a horizontal dance partner, Agnes was nowhere near the same class as Irene; she was unresponsive and expressionless to the point of catatonia, and I had to resist the temptation in passion's midst to check her for a pulse. I liked to think that my performances were worthy of some show of appreciation – in Irene's case usually a couple of encores. I suppose at least Agnes had remained quiet throughout the proceedings, which was preferable to having her whisper Finlay Currie sweet nothings in my ear.

After we adjusted our dress, smoked our cigarettes and drove back into town, I dropped Agnes off near her digs. She had remained quiet, almost sullen, throughout the journey. The quiet treatment wasn't anything unusual: a lot of women went like that afterwards. Some even cried, which did my ego no end of good.

I could never really understand why so many women felt guilty afterwards when we had both made the same choice, both done the same thing. I never forced my attentions on anyone, always retreating when the slightest resistance was met, and I always made sure when ascending the heights of passion that my chosen co-pilot had a licence and had already clocked up several hours of previous flight time. But the landings always seemed bumpy and a sense of shame, in varying degrees, seemed to seize them – Irene being the obvious exception. I supposed it was just another of those codes and double standards that women seemed to get the shit-end of – and the kind of thing I imagined philosopher–thief Quiet Tommy Quaid would have had a theory about.

As I drove home I thought about the over-oiled, slack-jawed comic with the flash Bentley. The name, that much to Agnes's frustration I hadn't recognized when she'd mentioned it, now sat picking away at a thread in some fraying corner of my brain.

When I got home I dug out the ticket stub the cleaner had found in Tommy's suit. I had been right: when Agnes had told me the spivvy-looking comedian we saw outside the Drymen pub was Frankie Findlay, it had rung a bell. This bell. The ticket stub was for a show at the King's Theatre, called *Frankie Goes Frantic!* and starring none-other-than. I had been right; but for some reason, the thought still picked away at the same frayed corner.

Another few days passed without any contact from the police and I found out that Quaid's body had been released and the funeral would be the following Saturday. I decided I'd go along to see who made an appearance, hopefully without drawing too much attention to myself. I stopped strapping up my ribs and reckoned that whatever damage had been done had been super-ficial and was well on the mend, so long as I didn't over-exert myself too much.

I got a call at the office from Irene, whom I hadn't seen since before the night I got jumped. In two short sentences she explained she was free for an hour and she'd see me back at my flat. I thought she sounded strained on the 'phone and I agreed, but when we went up to the apartment it became clear that her urgency was of the good old sort and she was just seizing the opportunity.

We indulged in the kind of over-exertion I'd sworn to avoid, but I rose to the challenge and my ribs held out. The vigour with which Irene performed sex was a stark contrast to Agnes. Irene was a woman who knew exactly what she wanted and took it, which probably intimidated and riled most men, but which I always found attractive in a woman. She did, however, seem con-cerned about the livid bruising on my torso – perhaps only because it could have an effect on my performance – and listened patiently and with a show of interest, feigned or otherwise, while I sketched out what had happened, deliberately erasing Quiet Tommy from the picture and being vague about where exactly it had all taken place.

When I was finished, she smiled and suggested she could kiss it all better, but either her aim or her knowledge of anatomy was seriously off, because it wasn't my ribs her lips made con-tact with. I over-exerted again.

When Irene was leaving, I noticed that, as she tucked her blouse into the waist of her grey check pencil skirt, she went over to the window and looked down, scanning the car park: something she had done a couple of times since she'd arrived.

'Is everything okay?' I asked.

She turned and looked at me blankly for a moment, as if she hadn't understood me, then shook her head. 'Aye . . . everything's fine. Why wouldn't it be?'

'You seem jumpy.'

'It's just George. He's been funny lately.'

'You said that before. But you said you didn't think he was on to us.'

'Aye . . .' She turned from the window. 'It's just that the other day I went shopping. He was supposed to be at work, but he was following me.'

'Following you? You sure? I mean, you sure it was definitely him?'

'Definitely.'

'And did he know you spotted him?'

'I don't think so. But I've been watching my back since.'

'And you haven't seen him following you again?'

'No. But it's not just that . . . he's been so moody recently. Snappy round the kids; almost sulky with me. I think he suspects I've been seeing someone, but he cannae prove it, even to himself.'

I lit cigarettes for us both. I didn't say it, but Irene's marital backstory was a complication I could do without – a potentially nuisancesome third dimension to our hitherto strictly two-dimensional relationship. I maybe didn't say it, but I guess my expression shouted it: Irene finished her cigarette and left.

## 6

The next day was the day for the bank run. The ten-thirty sun was suddenly eclipsed and the office fell into shadow. Twinkletoes McBride – whose build could indeed best have been described as planetary – had come into the office and was standing by the window, blocking out the light.

Twinkletoes was dressed smartly, as he habitually was. He wore a dark blue serge Burton's suit that I guessed had been made to measure – although he must have paid for cloth by the acre rather than the yard – and a copy of the *Readers' Digest* jutted from his jacket pocket. Twinkletoes read the *Readers' Digest* specifically for its 'Improve your Wordpower' section, committed as he was to learning every day a new word to mispronounce.

'Good morning, Mr Lennox,' he said amiably, but in a seismic baritone that probably caused china in Pollockshields to rattle on its shelves.

'How's it going, Twinkle?'

'I am in the *very-table* pink, Mr L. And you?' Twinkletoes was also courteous to a fault. I'd known him for years: long enough to know the queasy reason for his nickname. Before I'd offered him a job doing the security for wages and bank runs – his first legal employment 'with insurance stamp and everything', as he had gratefully pointed out – Twinkletoes had worked for Willie Sneddon, one of the Three Kings.

Unlike the other two Kings, Sneddon had the vision to see beyond his criminal activities. With Sneddon's gradual legitimization, Twinkletoes had become largely surplus to requirements.

But before Sneddon had yielded to legitimization and the appeal of Rotary Club and the Glasgow Chamber of Commerce memberships, he had employed Twinkle in what could best be described as something between a pedicurist and a public relations role. Twinkletoes had been tasked with dealing with anyone who had earned Sneddon's ire: those who'd been ill-advised enough to set up in competition to the crime boss, defaulters on debts, and anyone in the Sneddon empire who was thought to have a too talkative nature when in the company of the boys in blue.

Twinkletoes's nickname (or *sore-brick-ett* as he would solemnly intone) had been inspired by his method of removing his victims' shoes and socks and reciting 'This Little Piggy' as he set to work on their toes with a pair of boltcutters. It may not have seemed the most auspicious work history, but if there was one thing I could say with confidence about Twinkletoes, it was that he possessed an impeccable work ethic. In the past Twinkle may have been a merciless, inconceivably violent gangland torturer and thug, but at least he had been a *diligently* merciless, inconceivably violent gangland torturer and thug. And courteous.

And I knew I could rely on him.

The funny thing was it became very clear that Twinkletoes's heart hadn't really been that much in his previous work and I had been surprised by how grateful he had been when I had offered him a way out. As I had gotten to know him better, I found out that the thug with violence sewn into his fabric was also a devoted family man with two young kids he doted on. On the few occasions I'd been to his home, it had been the strangest thing to watch him with his children: in their presence, he became a child himself – a huge, lumbering, gentle infant, playful yet always protective. It was a sight that, for some reason, filled me with hope.

In our different ways, we were both committed to getting beyond the reach of the Three Kings. It had to be said that Sneddon, however, had not fully emerged from the shadows, and I knew better than to ask Twinkle what he got up to on his days off.

Archie ran through the usual procedures again for the bank run, but this time he made sure Twinkletoes got everything well and truly into his head. I generally left Archie and Twinkletoes to handle the bank transfers. Twinkletoes's sheer physical bulk was enough both to the bank and to deter any would-be robbers, but I'd hired him for more than that: Twinkle was known – specifically known – to have been connected to Sneddon's outfit, and that meant that the usual heist crews would think twice before having a go for fear of bringing the wrath of one or all of the Three Kings down on them. We hadn't had as much as a sideways glance since we'd been doing the run, but the bank had picked up the business of another shipyard, meaning our payload had suddenly become that bit more attractive, and that bit more worth the risk. So this week, I joined the posse.

At Archie's insistence, we had invested in a reasonably new Bedford van. Previously, we had hired a van each week for the run, but Archie put forward the case that wages runs had become the most lucrative part of our business and it would be cheaper in the long run to buy rather than keep hiring vans.

It also allowed us to reinforce the doors, locks and cargo cabin of the van. I'd gone along with it, despite my concern that we would be using the same van all the time: hiring vans meant we could change them each week to further camouflage our activity.

Archie had brought the van in with him: it was kept at his house and he used it for other work when his antique Austin let him down, which it frequently did. There had been talk about Twinkletoes keeping it between jobs, but one thing I had found out about the Gallowgate giant was that he was really rather snobby about the cars he drove, or more particularly those seen parked on the street outside his tenement flat.

We arrived at the bank bang on time. Both Archie and Twinkletoes were armed with coppers' truncheons: fifteen inches of iron-hard lignum vitae that, strictly speaking, it was illegal for us to carry, but to which the police turned a blind eye. It was more for show and to reassure the client: most bank robbers came armed with sawn-offs. Personally, I carried a concealed, lead-filled leather sap – a slim blackjack that sat nicely in my inside pocket without ruining the line of my suit.

We made the pick-up in the usual way. Twinkletoes, bless him, had a face that any self-respecting Neanderthal would have considered primitive. It was all brow and busted nose and over the years the other features had been jumbled about by repeated contact with fists, bottles and Christ knows what else. His bag-of-spanners face, combined with his intimidating physical presence, made him the ideal deterrent: so while Archie and I pass-the-parcelled the canvas cash bags into the van from the bank's rear door, Twinkle stood guard, baton in meaty fist, watching the street and scowling passers-by over to the other side of the street. I could have sworn I even saw a couple of birds change flight path too.

Once we were loaded up, Twinkle climbed into the back of the van with the cash, hunching his massive shoulders and sitting stooped on the bench, his truncheon braced on his knees. I sat in the front and Archie drove.

As a trio, the difference in backgrounds was odd, funny almost. And as we had filled up the van with the heavy canvas-and-leather cash bags, I caught Archie, the ex-policeman, eyeing me and Twinkle in a way that suggested he sometimes worried that our not-too-distant pasts, plus the temptation of several thousand pounds in portable cash, might awaken the recidivists in us.

I think that the extra cash made us all a little jumpy – even poacher-turned-gamekeeper Twinkletoes had seemed edgy – and I was relieved when we made our first delivery of the day. My reasoning was that if anyone knew about our newly bountiful cargo, they would have hit us when we'd had a full load.

There was a strange Gothic beauty to the working Clyde – a beauty I daresay completely eluded the poor schmucks working in its yards and worksheds. But it was there all the same and I reflected on it as we headed out of the first shipyard. A forest of latticed iron cranes, interlaced with a web of cables and lines, bristled along the waterfront and pontoons, rising over and huddling around the dark hulks of forming ships, the ale-dark, oil-sleeked waters of the Clyde beyond. They looked like impossible, giant insects at work weaving and cocooning their offspring.

Twinkle banged on the panel that divided the cargo and driver's cabins, and I slid open the door of the face-sized hatch between them – or it would have been face-sized if it had been anyone other than Twinkletoes on the other side.

'What's up?' I asked.

'I don't mean to cause any undue *trepp-er-day-shun*, Mr Lennox, but there's a blue works van behind us. It could be followin' us . . . I think it was there before we made the first drop-off.'

I looked to Archie, who was already checking his side-view mirror. 'I see him. Driver and front passenger. There could be others in the back but I can't see. I'll make a couple of unscheduled turns and see what he does.'

'You keep an eye on them too,' I said to Twinkle and left the panel open.

We were in the heart of the shipyards, the road flanked on one side by the river with its quays and cranes and on the other by soot-blackened worksheds. This was no residential area and Archie struggled to find a side street to deviate from his route. There were, however, entrance gates to the various factories and yards. I hoped that our chums were innocent workers and would turn off into one of them.

'They still there?' I asked through the hatch.

'Aye,' rumbled Twinkletoes. 'They're still there.'

Ahead of us, to our right, there was a break in the industrial architecture: a wasteground square of rubble and scrub grass with twisted fingers of rusted metal pointing to the sky, probably in accusation at the German pilot who'd cleared the site with a bomb more than a decade before.

I indicated the section with a jut of my chin. 'If our chums behind are after our cash, that's where they'll do it. We'll be out of sight for fifty yards.' I turned to the hatch. 'Twinkle, get ready to dance.'

Archie suddenly swung to the right and into the entrance to one of the yards. It had a gatehouse manned by a uniformed security man. Archie pulled up at the gatehouse and jumped out of the van. I followed suit, first telling Twinkle to stay put with the doors locked.

Archie and I watched the blue van make its way along past the stretch of waste ground. By the time we were out of our Bedford, it was too late to get any kind of look at the driver. The blue van didn't slow down or show any sign of stopping. There was no hint that they had any interest in us whatsoever. Archie and I watched until it was out of sight. The security man, a tall, heavy man of about sixty, came over to us.

'What d'you think you are doing?' he lilted with a Highland accent. 'You can't be blocking the entrance like that – Oh, it's you, Archie.' He pronounced it 'Erchie'. 'What are you doing here?'

Archie obviously recognized the older man as a former colleague. The City of Glasgow Police compulsorily retired all its officers at age fifty-five; the pension was good, but most retirees ended up doing security work. Archie explained about the wages run and the van, and the security man went back to his gatehouse, picking up the 'phone. After a while he came back out and spoke to Archie.

'I telephoned along to the next gatehouse – remember Harry MacTavish? He's on the gate at the Merchiston yard now. He said he did see a blue van pass his gatehouse chust now but it drove on westwards. Could you not have been mistaken, do you think? I could telephone the station and get a car down.'

Archie didn't answer for a moment, still watching the road. He was bareheaded and his bald scalp domed pale in the daylight. After a moment he said, 'No need, thanks, Geordie.' When the watchman returned to his gatehouse, Archie turned to me. 'What do you think?'

I shrugged. 'Just workmen going into one of the yards, probably.'

We got back into the driver's cabin, 'It's all right, Twinkle,' I said through the hatch. 'False alarm.'

We were a couple of minutes late for the wages drop-off at the second shipyard. It was enough to have riled the pay-office manager – not that he was an undue stickler for punctuality, but that each wages office had strict instructions to 'phone the police if we were more than five minutes behind schedule.

The third drop was a shipyard further down the Clyde, out towards Dumbarton. As we drove, I noticed Archie checking the side mirrors.

'See anything?'

He shook his head.

'How about you, Twinkle?' I asked through the hatch.

'All clear, Mr L,' he replied in his usual rumble and I could have sworn the metal of the van vibrated.

We reached the shipyard. I was still puzzled as to why I felt so relieved. It had happened before: some innocent motorist had just happened to follow the same route, or perhaps had lacked the confidence to overtake the slower-moving van. But there had been something different about that day. Something different about the feeling I'd got.

We made the drop and headed out the main gates and back towards the city. It was almost as if I could physically feel the lightening of our burden with the last of the cash delivered.

'Mr Lennox . . .' Twinkletoes's baritone was infused with a warning.

'It's okay, Twinkle,' I said, looking in the wing mirror at the blue van following us. 'I see him . . .'

## 7

We were back into the outskirts of Govan, the Clyde's dark industry still pushing sooty fingers through where people lived, repair sheds now grudgingly sharing the landscape with workers' tenements. It was the same shit deal as Possilpark – drone hives huddled close to their place of toil; lives subordinated to industry's need.

Not that I was paying much attention to the scenery: I was too preoccupied with the blue van following us. I could see Archie watching in his wing mirror too.

'What do you think his game is?' he asked. 'He was tailing us earlier and must know we've offloaded the cash.'

'Maybe we've got the dumbest armed robbers in Glasgow.'

'Or maybe they're casing us out – checking out our routine so they can plan when and where to hit us on a future run.'

'Could be.' I leaned into the hatch again. 'Twinkle, can you see if you can get the registration number?'

'Sure thing, Mr L.' Twinkletoes's voice rumbled in the cargo cabin.

'What do we do?' asked Archie. 'I could detour a little again and see if they stick with us.'

'Do it. See if you can lead them into somewhere they can't pass us.'

'You thinking of having it out with them?' Archie's tone suggested he thought it was a bad idea bordering on idiotic.

'Maybe.'

'And what if they've come tooled up?'

'Then we put our hands up and let them rob an empty van . . . Twinkle, you set?'

'Ready when you are, Mr Lennox . . .'

'As soon as we stop, get out of the van.'

'I thought I was to stay in here, no matters what,' he rumbled doubtfully.

I sighed. 'No, Twinkle, that's only when there's cash *in* the van with you. It's empty now.'

'Righty-oh, Mr L. My *faw-pass*.'

'If our chums come after us, be ready to get handy. But if they've got guns, don't do anything. There's nothing for them to take.'

I checked the mirror again. It was still there, trying to skulk behind the scant cover of the car it had allowed to get between us.

Archie was scanning the soot-dark topography of tenement and cobble with his watery, Alastair Sim eyes. 'I used to patrol here when I was in uniform,' he said casually, as if being a beat bobby in Govan didn't make being a Christian sharing the Colosseum with lions sound cosy. 'There's a street up ahead I can turn into. One way in, one way out.'

I reached into some Savile Row and pulled out the blackjack. I rested my other hand on the door handle. 'Okay.'

Just as he'd done at the factory gates, Archie didn't slow down or indicate we were turning and the tyres squealed in protest as we swung into the alley. The van tilted as it turned and for a moment I worried about Twinkletoes's bulk shifting too suddenly and toppling us over. Archie slammed on the brakes and the Bedford slipped wetly on greasy cobbles. I was out before the van stopped moving. By the time I got around to the back, Twinkletoes had burst out of the rear door. The overhang of his brow had lowered even more over his eyes and he bared his teeth in a grimace. Again the police-issue truncheon looked small in his fist. Not for the first time, I was glad we were on the same side.

Archie was out too, flanking Twinkle on the other side. We stood with our backs to the van, its engine still running, watching the mouth of the alley.

Nothing.

'Could they have gone past?'

'Doubt it,' Twinkle growled. 'I was watching it till we made the turn.'

We stood for a few seconds more in expectant silence. I braced when I heard a motor, but it turned out to be a grubby coal truck – a moving darkness against a dark landscape – and it passed by the mouth of the tenement alley without stopping. I took in our brick and cobble redoubt. Banners of washday linen, hanging on lines looped between the windows, were the only brightness against Victorian tenements grimed black by a century of industrial toil; even the broken-paved street seemed sleeked with a sooty grease. It was a darkness that seemed to suck the light of the unreflected sun out of an otherwise bright day.

I realized we had attracted a small audience of children. Four boys and a girl, all maybe nine to eleven – although Glasgow kept its children small and they could have been older – stood mutely watching us, their faces, hands and clothes smirched from play in the grimy street, as if the darkness that surrounded them had already begun to claim them.

I turned to Twinkletoes, then nodded in the direction of the main road. He nodded and headed off to the road end, looked in both directions before turning back and shaking his head.

As Twinkle made his way back towards us, one of the kids who'd been watching us impassively made his way over to me. He wasn't the biggest of the boys but was clearly the leader of the sad little group. Again I cast a nervous eye towards the road end: the last thing I wanted was for kids to get caught up in it if things went south.

Still no van appeared at the road end.

'I got the number, like you said.' Twinkle held up a small notebook. 'SLR 882.'

'You sure you got it right?'

'Sure, boss. SLR 882.'

'Good work. Thanks, Twinkle.'

I felt the tugging of small fingers on my sleeve and looked down. The boy's face, topped with a sprout of unbrushed, black hair, was so pale that the dirt from his playing stood out like dark bruises.

'Excuse me, mister . . .' he said. 'Are you the ice cream van?'

'No, sonny,' I said, smiling. 'Sorry.'

'You're definitely no' the ice cream van?'

I shook my head.

'Oh . . . Well if you're no' the ice cream van,' he said without changing tone, 'then why don't yous fuck off.' A sharp pain jabbed through my ankle – the same ankle I'd injured the night of Tommy's death – as he kicked me hard and ran off, he and his pals laughing raucously as they did so. He turned just before he and his pals were swallowed up by the black mouth of an entrance to tenement close. 'Yah bunch o' fannies!'

The loud roaring laughter of his playmates echoed in the china-tiled close.

'Little bastard . . .' I muttered, rubbing my bruised ankle.

'From small acorns . . .' said Archie.

'Let's get out of here,' I said and climbed back in the van.

## 8

I couldn't work out what would have been more suspicious: for me to go to Quiet Tommy's funeral or if I stayed away. The truth was that the police had shown no interest in me – and very little in Tommy's death, for that matter – and there was nothing to link me to the events of the night of his death.

But my paranoia was not totally unfounded: Quiet Tommy Quaid had, in his own words, been a craftsman; a craft which had been employed at one time or another by each of the Three Kings, and anyone else who had something they wanted liberated from the inconvenience of lawful ownership. There was always the chance that Tommy's funeral could see a turnout of the great and bad from Glasgow's underworld, which also meant the City of Glasgow Police would make the effort too. Liked as Tommy was by his opposite numbers in blue, the constabulary's interest in his funeral would be more than a paying of grudging respect. The police would want to see who turned up; again, that interest wouldn't have anything to do with how the thief had met his end, but what connections could be made between funeral attendees. There was also the chance that the odd outstanding warrant could be discreetly executed at the cemetery gates.

Given Tommy's atheistic leanings, it didn't surprise me at all that there was no church service, nor any clergyman at the interment. Someone had coughed up the funds, however, and Tommy was brought to his final resting place in the Glasgow Necropolis by the Co-operative's finest. The polished and waxed coachwork on the Austin Sheerline hearse gleamed and sparkled in the bright July sunshine – the same sunshine that forced me to wear sunglasses and nagged me to take off my jacket. I couldn't help but think that Tommy would have appreciated the weather's complete lack of funereal tone.

I could tell from the cars lined up outside the cemetery that there was a good turn-out for Tommy: two Bentleys and a Jaguar, all new and polished to a mirror sheen, declared the regal presence of all Three Kings. A lot of Tommy's former associates had clearly turned up, and the fundamental flaw in the whole crime-doesn't-pay thing was highlighted by another Jaguar, two Rovers, a Daimler and an Armstrong-Siddeley Sapphire parked at the cemetery gates. Parked among them was a battered old Morris Oxford and a two-tone, light blue over cream Ford Consul. At the time, I had no idea that I would later have good cause to remember the Consul in the ice cream colours.

I decided against watching proceedings from a distance: I had noticed Jock Ferguson and a couple of younger CID guys taking up that position as I had come in through the main gates with the other mourners. I had been expecting the police, of course, but I was surprised that Jock had taken a personal interest. He looked in my direction when I arrived; I deliberately smiled and gave a small nothing-odd-about-me-being-here wave, which he returned with a nod.

Funerals are the oddest occasions at the best of times, but I found Tommy's send-off stranger yet. Quiet Tommy Quaid had been liked by everyone, but known by few – and even those few, in which I included myself, had enjoyed only restricted knowledge of the man. But Tommy had somehow managed to create the illusion of intimacy: he was the kind of guy who knew everyone's name, who passed the time with anyone he encountered, with whom you could spend a whole night drinking, exchanging deep secrets and universal truths, only to realize the next day that he hadn't really said anything at all. I calculated that there was something in the region of sixty mourners at the funeral, and I guessed that most of them genuinely felt they had known Tommy. Maybe it would be only now, with his death, that they would question whether they were mourning a friend or a complete stranger.

I positioned myself far enough back from the graveside not to be conspicuous, close enough to watch proceedings – and keep an eye on a cutie in a black skirt and bolero jacket I'd noticed at the centre of events.

It was a strange thing to watch the mourners: the actors and backstage hands in the playing out of a man's life. I recognized many of them, but as many were strangers to me. Tommy's life had been a drama of many acts, and I hadn't been in the audience for them all.

The Three Kings were all there. Handsome Jonny Cohen wore a dark Italian suit and sunglasses, as always looking more like a movie star than a gangster. Hammer Murphy did his best to look sombre, but was his usual fizzing ball of barely contained aggression and looked at his fellow mourners, the sky, the world as if challenging them all to a fight. There again, he always looked like that. Murphy too had pushed the boat out on his tailoring: bespoke and expensive, his black suit vaguely glossy in the sunlight. Mohair, I guessed. But where Cohen looked classy, Murphy just looked spivvy: you can wrap a turd in Christmas paper and a silk bow; it doesn't stop it being a turd.

That Willie Sneddon had also turned up surprised me: Sneddon was doing his best to keep his criminal connections out of sight and he wasn't the kind of person to fulfil moral or personal obligations. He was there, I reckoned, for a reason.

I checked out the other mourners: Tommy's professional circle was well represented and I counted eight housebreakers, two of Glasgow's most successful pickpockets, three armed robbers and four petermen, including the retired Tony the Pole Grabowski. I sensed the dead beneath my feet clutch bony fingers protectively around whatever valuables had been buried with them.

One of the attendees I hadn't seen before was a man of about forty. He was small and wiry and I noticed him mainly because his movements had an electric jumpiness about them. Combined with his small frame, they made him seem vaguely rat-like. Watching him, I got the impression he was trying to avoid being noticed, always folding himself into the crowd or half behind a memorial stone. The more casual he tried to appear, the more shifty he looked. He darted eyes across the assembled mourners and I could see he was searching for someone. Given the professional circles Tommy Quaid had moved in, I thought it entirely possible that the little man was checking out the best pockets to pick.

Another stranger I noticed was a woman of about forty, with dark hair unfashionably short and wearing a black skirt suit that was even less in mode. I noticed her because she looked unlikely as someone Tommy would have been involved with. Yet I could tell, even from a distance, that she was genuinely upset: something about her movements and the way she stared dully at Tommy's coffin. There was no dabbing of eyes or bowing of head: hers was a tearless grief; a grief muted by shock.

In the absence of the usual religious master-of-ceremonies, I wondered if there would be some undignified confusion about when Tommy should be lowered into the ground, but the attractive young woman who'd bleeped on my usual radar seemed to be the principal mourner and very much in charge of things. She had dark blonde, almost copper-coloured hair and was tallish and slim, but despite the black formal dress and bolero jacket she wore, I could see she had curves in all the right places. It was the hint of copper in the hair that told me who she was and why she was in charge: Tommy's sister, the one he had been so proud of getting out and away from Glasgow. She nodded curtly to the undertaker and the coffin was lowered into the ground. No eulogies, no graveside words of remembrance. Quiet Tommy Quaid's burial, like his death, lived up to his name.

'You should be ashamed of yourself,' someone said in low tones, close to my ear.

I turned round; Jock Ferguson and a too-youthful detective companion were standing behind me. The younger man looked at me with deep suspicion. I knew not to take it seriously: it was the mask rookies pulled on to conceal their inexperience; the younger the cop, the deeper the suspicion.

'Me? Why?'

'Tommy Quaid's funeral isn't the place to eye up his sister as a potential conquest. I saw you looking at her.'

'I could say that a funeral isn't the place to run a warrant round-up. I'm sure you're not here out of your fondness for Tommy.'

'Let's just say I was interested to see who showed up. You I get – you and Tommy got on. But Sneddon?'

'I was thinking that myself.'

'But there's someone conspicuous by their absence,' said Ferguson.

'Who?'

'Jimmy Wilson. You know him?'

I thought for a moment then shook my head. It was an automatic reaction whenever a copper asked me if I knew someone. In this case it was true; I'd never heard of Wilson.

'He's a small-time peterman and housebreaker. We've heard that he helped out Quiet Tommy from time to time and thought he might turn up here. We've an outstanding warrant.'

'Tommy never mentioned him to me.' Again it was true. Tommy may have waxed philosophical to me now and then, but he played his professional cards close to his chest. I hadn't heard of Wilson and I was hoping that Wilson hadn't heard of me.

I jutted my chin in the direction of the small, wiry-looking man, who was still trying to camouflage himself in the dark foliage of other mourners. 'You know him?'

'Nope,' said Ferguson. He turned to his taciturn junior officer who shook his head. I guessed he must have been a laugh a minute to work with.

The copper-blonde passed us and her eyes briefly caught mine. I was about to express my condolences, but she passed on by, purposefully.

'How do you know she's Tommy's sister?' I asked Ferguson as I watched her make her way through the gates.

'She came in to see me,' said Jock. 'Asking where we were with the case. If we thought there was anything suspicious about Tommy's death.'

And there it was: that combination of words I had dreaded hearing. 'Tommy's death' and 'suspicious' in one sentence, and in a copper's mouth, sent a chill through me despite the early August sunshine.

'And is there?' I hoped my nonchalance was convincing.

Suddenly I worried that the younger cop's suspicious gaze seemed more than a youthful guise.

'I doubt it.' Jock shrugged bony shoulders in a cheap Burton's off-the-peg. Charcoal grey rather than black. Jock and I, mainly because of our wartime experiences being of the same kind – the shitty kind – had a lot of things in common. Dress sense wasn't one of them. 'I told her the case was closed. Tommy got sloppy, that's all. If you spend your life dodging about on factory roofs in the middle of the night, all it takes is one foot put wrong and . . .' He finished the sentence with a gesture indicating the burial grounds.

'But the Saracen Foundry?' Emboldened by Jock's lack of interest, I decided to push my luck. 'Have you any idea why he would want to break in there?'

'Beats me – maybe he'd been tipped off there was cash in a safe or something. The foundry says not, though. Nothing worth stealing at all.'

I did my best not to give a sigh of relief: coming to the funeral had been worthwhile just to hear Jock express his lack of interest. I was in the clear.

Admittedly I was a little surprised: Jock was a smart guy, and an instinct-driven cop who let little get past him – but he clearly was frying bigger fish than the death of a burglar. Maybe he did suspect Tommy's death wasn't as simple as it seemed; the simple truth was, I could see, that he didn't give a shit either way.

'So she accepted that? The sister, I mean?'

Jock shrugged and nodded. 'Seemed to. She was a bit annoyed that there was no fatal accident inquiry, though. To be honest, it surprised me too.'

'Should there have been?'

'Maybe not. I suppose the cause and manner of death's quite

straightforward. But the odd thing is that there was supposed to be an inquiry – it was originally scheduled but the procurator fiscal cancelled it. He's said he's satisfied that Quaid's was a death by misadventure during the commission of a crime.'

'I see,' I said. Scotland had its own way of doing things: there was no such thing as a coroner's court in Scotland, no inquests before a jury. Instead most sudden deaths were investigated and signed off by the procurator fiscal, the public prosecutor in Scotland. Fatal accident inquiries in front of a sheriff – the Scottish equivalent of a magistrate – and without a jury only took place when there was a public interest or where specific circumstances surrounding the death required further scrutiny. I suddenly felt a cosy glow of appreciation for the Scottish legal system.

People started to drift away from the graveside. I saw Jonny Cohen look pointedly in our direction as he headed out of the cemetery. Cohen and I got on well, better even than I had gotten on with Tommy, and he had gotten me out of a few sticky situations, including once when he very definitely saved my life – but he was what he was, a gangster, and I had pretty much avoided him of late. I could sense his disapproval at what he'd see as my cosiness with the police.

'The funny thing . . .' said Jock absently as we headed towards the gates, 'is that it's the second cancelled inquiry that I've been surprised about.'

'Oh . . .'

'Aye . . . you know the young laddie who threw himself in front of the train near Central Station?'

'I read about it, yes.'

'Well the fiscal cancelled that one too.' He shook his head. 'Now that's one I thought should have had a hearing. But it's been chalked up as a suicide. Bloody shame. Nineteen years old, apparently.'

We reached the cemetery gates.

'Jock, can I ask you to do me a favour?' I asked.

'That depends . . .' Jock glanced meaningfully at the young copper at his side, who still regarded me with deep suspicion. I got the message: if my favour involved any bending of rules, then it was not a request to make in junior's presence. I smiled and shook my head.

'It's straightforward, Jock. I just need a registration number checked out.'

Ferguson arched an eyebrow. 'And exactly why should this confidential police resource be made available to you?'

'Don't worry, Jock, it's on the up-and-up. Last bank run we did, this van was sticking to us like shit to a shirt tail. What I can't work out was why they followed us both ways – when we were full and when we were empty.' I reached into my jacket pocket and handed him the slip of paper on which Twinkle had written the number.

'Casing you?' Jock took the note.

'Could be. Archie thought they might be. Inexpertly done if they were.'

'Okay, I'll get it checked.'

# 9

Sometimes you get an itch in your brain. Some splinter of an idea in the back of your mind that prickles insistently, demanding you pay attention to it. Sometimes you know what it is, mostly you don't. The itch in my head was incessant, but I promised myself to ignore it. For once, I knew exactly what it was that was causing the irritation and I was determined not to scratch it.

A suit so very like mine hanging in my wardrobe.

A ticket to a show Tommy would have had no interest in.

The body of my sure-footed and quiet friend lying broken and dead from a silent and unlikely fall.

All of my instincts were telling me to leave well enough alone. *Conspiracy to open a lockfast place with intent to steal* maybe didn't sound like the crime of the century, but it was enough to put me in prison for a couple of months and end my career as an enquiry agent. I had conspired, I had driven Tommy to the lockfast place, I had sneaked my own way in. No one was looking into Tommy's death, and that meant no one was looking for me.

But those same instincts were telling me that included in the no one looking for me was Mr McNaught, who should by now have been demanding – with promised menaces – the plans he had wanted stolen, his down-payment cash, or both.

And that didn't make any sense at all.

Summer nights in Scotland never got truly dark, the ghost of the old day lingering until the infant light of the new took hold. The night of Tommy's funeral was muggy to boot. I lay sleepless in bed, smoking and staring at the darkened bedroom ceiling, and an idea that had been floating about half-formed for weeks began to coalesce in the drifts of cigarette smoke.

It had all been a set-up.

For some reason, Quiet Tommy Quaid had been set up for a fall, in the most literal way. Someone had been on the roof waiting for him; the reason Tommy hadn't made a sound was because his neck had already been broken before he fell. As I had learned only too well during the Grand Tour of Europe organized on my behalf by the First Canadian Army, killing a man doesn't need to be a complicated business. Whoever had planned Quiet Tommy's demise had gone to a lot of trouble to make it look like an accident. But even that didn't make sense either. Stabbings and beatings-to-death were commonplace in Glasgow and, after all, Quiet Tommy Quaid was a member of the city's underworld, where grudges and rivalries often turned deadly but difficult to trace. Even a hit-and-run with a truck would have been simpler.

Instead, Tommy's killers had gone out of their way to make it all look like an accident – and a perfectly plausible accident. Its elaborate staging meant Tommy was involved in something, or knew something, big, and whatever it was, they didn't want the police looking for a reason for Tommy's death.

And I had been the patsy in the set-up: there had been no plans to be stolen, no trade secrets, no client behind McNaught. The break-in could have been anywhere, but the Saracen Foundry was an out-of-the-way, low-security place where Tommy's killers could, as I had done, get in and out without detection. And when they had, they'd called the police anonymously to report a suspicious-looking van parked at the side of the foundry. I was supposed to have been found waiting in the van and would have told a story about trade secrets and roof-top break-ins. The fact that the police would never track down the mysterious – and probably pseudonymous – Mr McNaught would simply be put down to him having the sense to get out of Dodge.

But that hadn't been my main purpose as a stooge. The thought stung that McNaught – or whatever his real name was – had used me because, if the job came through me, Tommy would have trusted it. For whatever reason, they had known a direct approach to Tommy would have been seen through.

That was why Tommy had seemed so different, so edgy. Shit – Tommy *knew*.

But why? What importance could a minor if not petty criminal have that warranted an elaborate luring to his ambush and murder?

Sleep had given up on me, so I decided to make it mutual. Pulling my dressing gown on, I went through to the dining room and poured myself a rye whiskey. The French windows opened out onto a narrow balcony, so I took my whiskey and my two-in-the-morning thoughts out into the night air.

The silk-streaked sky above the city wasn't as clear as on the night of Tommy's death, but the brighter stars were visible above the street-light glow of the city. I lifted my glass in a silent

toast to Tommy and was immediately angry with my own maud-
lin sentimentality: Tommy wasn't looking down on me; Tommy
didn't exist any more; Tommy's light had been snuffed out by
someone with a bigger plan. And I would never have an excuse
to dig into what that plan was.

But that was all about to change.

# Part Three

Part Three

# 1

Two days later I got my excuse to start digging into Quiet Tommy Quaid's death: a legitimate excuse to ask questions out in the open. An excuse that came wrapped up in a very appealing package.

Glasgow was a city of fast-changing mood and the weather had cooled right down: August guising itself as another, later season. It was nine-thirty when Jennifer Quaid came into my office. She was wearing a light tweed jacket and skirt in pale grey with a white knit top beneath. An expensive string of pearls looped around her throat. Everything she wore was quality without being ostentatious, and it was clear she had the same innate good – and expensive – taste as her brother.

Sometimes seeing a woman up close lets down the promise from a distance. It was the reverse with Jennifer Quaid: she had the same kind of misplaced nobility that Tommy had had; fine, well-proportioned features and large, intelligent, blue-green eyes. There was something of the pre-Raphaelite about her: a natural, classic, easy beauty. Her copper-blonde hair was longer than the usual style, but still short of her shoulders, and the soft waves in it looked natural and unaided by heat or permanent lotion. Her skin was pale and flawless, her lips were full without being fleshy and lipsticked pale coral, and I had the strongest instinct to smudge them.

All of this I noticed before wondering what could possibly have brought her here to my office. I had it bad. Bad, deep and instant.

While I scanned the office for a lurking winged cherub toting a bow and arrow, I let her go through the formality of introducing herself and thanking me for attending Tommy's funeral. I returned by expressing my sorrow for her loss. Suddenly, my office seemed strangely inappropriate for our conversation.

'Why don't we go around the corner,' I said. 'There's a tearoom.'

She nodded. I let her lead the way down the stairwell to the street and enjoyed the view: she had been very well assembled.

The tearoom was half a century out of date with a heavy-handed Art Nouveau feel to it, yet it was a style oddly in keeping with my companion. We were led to a window table by a waitress so elderly I worried she'd survive the trip, and so frosty she made Heinrich Himmler look like he had people skills. Only one other customer had found the waitress's charm irresistible, but he sat over at the far side of the tearoom and I felt we were reasonably free to talk. I ordered a coffee for myself and a pot of tea for Jennifer; our unsmiling geriatric attendant shuffled back across the tearoom and potentially off this mortal coil.

'You and Tommy were good friends, I believe,' she said.

I nodded thoughtfully. 'I guess you could say that. Tommy got on with most people, but I don't know if he ever let anyone get that close. But yes, I like to think that we were friends.'

'Well, I can tell you Tommy certainly regarded you as someone he trusted and respected very much. His trust and respect were hard to earn. Harder than his friendship.' She spoke with the restraint of the recently bereaved, stumbling over the mention of Tommy's name, struggling with the strange novelty of referring to him in the past tense, trying to keep a lid on her grief.

'Tommy told me you live in London,' I said to break an awkward silence.

'At the moment, yes.'

'You thinking of coming back to Glasgow?'

'God no – but I am thinking of getting out of London. It's as bad as here: filthy, grimy, crowded, full of slums. But at least I had a chance to become something down there. And that was all thanks to Tommy.'

'So where do you think you'll end up?'

'I don't think I'll ever come back to Scotland. But I'd like to move to a smaller town out of London. Maybe something on the south coast. I'm a teacher so I can work anywhere there are children.' There was no Glasgow or Lanarkshire left in her speech; she had a soft, educated Scottish accent that you couldn't pin down to any region, but its clarity had become slightly fudged by southern English non-rhoticism, the occasional 'r' getting lost in the post.

There was a pause: that conversational punctuation that tells you the small talk is over. I made an open gesture with my hands. 'What can I do for you, Miss Quaid?'

We paused as Methuselah's mother wordlessly and unsmilingly served us with our tea and coffee, placing one of those bone china high-tea stands, laden with unnaturally brightly coloured cakes, on the damask-covered table between us.

Once the waitress was gone Jennifer asked, 'Do you believe Tommy's death was an accident?'

And there it was.

I shrugged. 'The police seemed to be satisfied it was.'

'That's not what I asked. I asked if *you* believe it was an accident.' She held me in a penetrating blue-green gaze, as if ready to see through any falsehood or subterfuge.

'I take it you don't.'

She sighed, clearly annoyed at my evasiveness. 'I *know* it wasn't.'

'And how do you know that?'

'You still haven't answered my question. Do you believe Tommy was killed in an accident?'

It was my turn to sigh. 'As a matter of fact, I don't. Tommy was too professional, too careful, to fall off a roof like that. But the fiscal has already signed it off as a misadventure during the commission of a crime. I have absolutely nothing to prove otherwise.'

'What if I told you that Tommy knew he was in danger? That his life was threatened?'

That hit a nerve. Memories of Tommy's strange mood after I'd been jumped in the street, uncharacteristic uncertainty the night of the job, flashed through my head. I leaned forward. 'He said that to you?'

'That's why I'm here. That's why I've come to see you. Like I said, Tommy thought a great deal of you and told me that if anything happened to him, you would know what to do.'

'I don't—'

She cut me off by reaching into an expensive ivory handbag and handing me a thickly wadded envelope. The envelope was sealed, but it didn't stop my old Pavlovian response. So many people had given me cash-stuffed envelopes of late I could almost guess the value by heft.

'What's this?'

'Two hundred pounds. Tommy said if anything happened to

him, I was to come to you and give you this. If he were to die suddenly, he told me you would be the person to take care of things. To make sure that I was safe and that you would find out who killed him and you would know what to do.'

I shook my head and pushed the envelope back across the table. 'I can't accept this.'

'You won't look into what happened to him?' She looked genuinely surprised and upset, as if I'd let her down. I'd known her for less than twenty minutes, and already the last thing in the universe I wanted was to let Jennifer Quaid down. I was usually the unsmitten type and immune to romantic foolery, but Tommy's sister had done a hell of a lot of smiting in those twenty minutes.

'I didn't say that. What I said was I can't take the money. I won't take the money. Tommy was my friend.'

'He wanted you to have it.'

I looked at the envelope for a moment then picked it up and slid a thumb under the sealed flap. Taking a single twenty-pound note from it, I pushed the envelope with the rest of the cash back across the table.

'This is all I need,' I said, holding up the twenty to let her see. 'When I get back to the office, I'll write you up a receipt for this. And all I need this for is to prove to the police that you have officially retained me to investigate Tommy's death.'

'And why do you need that?'

'The police and the procurator fiscal's office get very antsy when someone suggests they didn't do their job right. I need to keep this all official – that I'm investigating professionally on behalf of a client and not just sniffing around as Tommy's friend.' It was true I had to prove a genuine professional connection to the case – but I didn't mention that connection was more than a friend's sense of duty and more to do with having been Tommy's Cary Grant-outfitted accomplice on the night he died. 'I have to warn you that even if I do get to the truth and find proof that Tommy's death wasn't an accident, it's still highly unlikely that anything will change. At the end of the day, the police and the fiscal's office are bureaucracies. Not the most imaginative or energetic people. All Tommy was to them was paperwork that's already been stamped and filed.'

'I know the police aren't interested. I talked to them. I spoke to the policeman I saw you with at the funeral and he told me the case was closed. Tommy said that if anything happened to him, you'd know the right thing to do. Not the police – you.'

'I can ask around but, if I'm honest, I don't have anything to go on. Tommy was vague even when telling you he was in danger.'

Again she reached into the handbag, this time placing a key on the table, next to where the envelope still lay. I noticed the key had a similar tag on it to the one Maisie, my perpetually willing dry cleaner, had found in Tommy's suit, but now was not the time to mention it being in my possession.

'This . . .' Jennifer pointed to the key. Her hands were slim, pale and porcelain delicate. ' . . . is for a lock-up somewhere down by the Clyde. Tommy wrote me that it was totally secret, that no one knows about it. It was one of the places he used to store his—'

'Stuff . . .' I said, helpfully diverting her from the word 'proceeds'.

'Exactly. But he said in his letter there was something there that would explain everything if anything were to happen to him. He said you'd know it when you found it. Here's the address.' She pushed a note across the desk.

'Do you still have the letter Tommy sent you?'

She shook her soft waves. 'I burned it. Tommy told me to burn it after reading it. He also told me that if anything happened to him, after I gave you the key, the address and the money, I was to get out of Glasgow and back home as quickly as I could. Whoever he was afraid of, he obviously thought they were very resourceful and had a long reach. As soon as I got the letter I 'phoned him. I was so scared for him. He told me not to worry, that nothing was going to happen to him, but it was just a precaution. But if anything *did* happen to him, I was to trust you completely.'

'In either his letter or when you spoke to him, did he give any idea who would have wanted him dead? Or the reason why?'

Another shake of curls. 'Not directly. He said he had stumbled onto something. That he had something in his possession that didn't belong to him—' She stopped, reading my look. 'No, that's not what I mean. Not just the usual stolen property – or maybe it was – but it was more significant than that. Worth more than money.'

'He said that?'

'Not in so many words, no. But that was the impression I got. He said there were people who would do anything to get their hands on what he had.'

'And these people were after him?'

'No . . . or at least not then. They would have been if they had known who they were looking for. He said that he had stumbled across something – had discovered it by mistake, by pure accident. He said he didn't think he was in immediate danger because these people didn't know he was the one who had found it. He told me not to worry because he was safe as long as no one linked it to him. But if anything *did* happen, I was to come and see you.'

'And that's all? He didn't say what this *thing* was?'

'Whatever it is, knowing about it obviously places you in danger. He didn't want me placed in that danger.'

'What about the people who want it back? Any ideas who they might be?'

'Listen, Mr Lennox, I have no illusions about what Tommy did. I know exactly how he got his money and I know that a lot of it went to getting me out of Glasgow and into a better life, so I'm in no position to judge him. I'm grateful for what he did for me and always will be. But I also know that in the kind of life Tommy led, there are a lot of very dangerous people and fall-outs and grudges are common. But I got the feeling that this wasn't about that – that there was more to the threat than gangsters or criminals in the conventional sense.'

'What makes you say that?'

'Tommy used to 'phone me every week. The last few times he seemed odd. Preoccupied. It was maybe a month or six weeks before he died that I noticed it the most. Later, when he told me that he'd "discovered something", I thought back to that earlier 'phone call. I think that must have been about the time he found out whatever it was he found out. He was so distracted. And he said funny things.'

'What kind of funny things?'

'Bitter things. And you know Tommy was never bitter. He started to talk about the people in charge being the most corrupt of all. About the whole system being rotten. More rotten than anyone could imagine.'

'And that's why you think the threat to Tommy came from outside his usual circle?' I asked, remembering him expressing similar sentiments to me.

She shrugged. 'It's just a feeling.'

'So have you any idea as to who else could have wished him harm?'

'Not from anything Tommy said, no.'

'But you have your own ideas . . .'

'Not really, or only the vaguest ideas, and that's just because I've been racking my brain.'

'In the absence of any other kind of idea, vague is good . . .'

We had both left the garishly-coloured cakes alone and I took out my cigarette case, offering her one. She leaned close while I lit it for her and for a second her scent fumed with the cigarette smoke.

'What do you know about Tommy's war service?' she asked.

'Nothing much. I knew he'd been a commando and I got the idea from a couple of things he said that he'd had a rough time of it. We both had. Neither of us really talked much about it.'

'So you didn't know Tommy was in prison at the start of the war?'

'No . . . no, I didn't.'

'Tommy kept quiet about his record. Or at least he fudged it a little. He let people think that he'd done a year of prison time here, a few months there, but it wasn't like that. Tommy was sentenced to eighteen months when he was still a teenager, but got out early for good behaviour. They arrested him God knows how many times after that but could never get enough for a conviction. Then, just at the start of the war, he broke into the house of Sir John MacIlwain.'

'The shipyard owner?'

'Yes. MacIlwain also owned the mining company our father had worked for. I think Tommy thought he was collecting dues. He struck it rich that night all right: it was estimated that he got away with fifteen thousand pounds' worth of cash and jewels – although Tommy swore that MacIlwain exaggerated the loss for the insurance company. If Tommy had stuck to the cash, he'd have been all right, but the fence he'd done a deal with for the jewellery was caught and through him they got Tommy. Because the value of the cash and goods recovered didn't match the claim, they really threw the book at him. That and the fact that there was a war on and the MacIlwain yards were seen as essential to the war effort. Suddenly, stealing from a multimillionaire became unpatriotic. Tommy got fifteen years. Truth is that I think he really did keep some of the proceeds back. I think that was what paid for me to go to an independent school.'

'He obviously didn't serve his whole sentence,' I said.

'He'd done less than two years when the army came calling. They made Tommy an offer – from what he could work out, they had offered the same deal to a handful of other burglars and safecrackers. The offer was that they would wipe Tommy's slate clean if he agreed to serve in the army for the duration.'

'The commandos.'

'Actually no. Or not at the start. According to Tommy, they said he would be with the Royal Engineers, but that he might have to do dangerous work behind enemy lines. It was obvious that the military wanted people who were skilled in breaking into places. It was a gamble for Tommy: for all he knew the war could have gone on for longer than his fifteen year sentence, and he seemed to have adjusted to prison life, but he said yes.'

I thought about what she had said. I knew the army had effectively offered freedom for service to a small number of convicted felons with special skills. The kind of skills valued in wartime but criminal in peacetime.

'So why would you think his war service might have something to do with his death?'

'I don't know. Before the invasion, Tommy was transferred to the commandos. A special unit. You know Tommy – he was tight-lipped at the best of times and that's all I know. Except that, after the war, he never had anything to do with anyone he served with. I can't say if there was any kind of fall-out, or whether Tommy just wanted to put everything that happened in the war behind him.'

'The war was a long time ago. What makes you think that old comrades could be involved in his death thirteen years later?'

'Nothing . . .' She shook her head as if annoyed at the foolishness of her logic. 'It was just that, at the funeral, there was a man – there was something about him that I didn't like. He had travelled up from England to come to the funeral. He said he had served with Tommy during the war. That's what made me think of him.'

'What did he look like?' I asked, braced for a description of a big, burly military type with a lopsided face.

'He wasn't very tall. Or very well-built. Almost slight. And he seemed, well, *shifty*.'

'I think I saw him,' I said. 'I thought he was maybe one of Tommy's criminally connected friends, but Inspector Ferguson didn't know him either. And yes, there was something shifty about him. But he was maybe just there to pay his respects.'

'You're probably right, but it's a long way to come up from England when there wasn't even a funeral service. I wanted to have one, by the way, but you know how Tommy had funny ideas about that kind of thing.'

I nodded. 'Did you speak to him?'

'Only briefly. And that was what made me start thinking about Tommy's war service maybe having something to do with what had been troubling him before his death. You see, all

Baines seemed to be interested in was if Tommy had seen any of his old unit recently.'

'Baines?'

'That was his name. He told me his first name, but I've forgotten it.' Something seemed to strike her. She reached down and picked up her handbag again. 'Speaking of names, I thought this might be useful.' She took an expensive-looking notebook, bound in burgundy leather, from her handbag. 'It's Tommy's diary and address book. I found it among his stuff. I thought it would be useful.'

'It definitely will be,' I said encouragingly and slipped the notebook into my pocket, although I guessed Tommy would hesitate to commit his more interesting contacts to paper. I certainly hoped he hadn't pencilled in his professional engagements – *Sunday, breaking into Saracen Foundry with Lennox.*

'I'm afraid that's everything. I've given you as much as I can for you to go on. I'm sorry it's not much. I'm guessing that whatever is in Tommy's lock-up will give you the answers.'

I looked at the key to a lock-up on the Clyde – and to Pandora's Box. If I found whatever it was he'd hidden there, then I would be in the same position Tommy had been in. I knew I'd go and look: but I vowed in the meantime to avoid rooftops and even high pavements.

I took the blue-fobbed key and slipped it into my pocket. The envelope with the cash remained untouched on the table; I picked it up and handed it to her. 'You'd better get that into a bank. If our charming waitress sees it she might think it's a tip for her wonderful service.'

She looked at the envelope, her expression worried. 'Tommy said I was to give you that. He insisted.'

'Listen, Jennifer, I'll do what Tommy asked. I'm just not going to take money for it. I'd rather you kept it.'

'Believe me, Tommy's taken care of me financially—'

'All the same . . .'

She put the envelope back in her bag.

We talked a little more, I being mindful of the fragility of Jennifer's grief, she pulling a veil of politeness over it. I arranged to keep in touch and, before heading back to my office from the tearoom, I got the details of the hotel she was staying at, walked her to the taxi rank at Central Station and saw her into a cab.

As I watched the taxi make the turn into Waterloo Street, I thought about the face I'd sat opposite in the tearoom. It had been a long time since I'd spent time with a woman I really wanted to get to know, to get to understand fully, to share something of each other – rather than my usual base instinct just to nail her.

But, of course, I also really, really wanted to nail her.

## 2

I tried not to look too surprised – or guilty. Coppers have an instinct for that kind of thing: reading first reactions. Or maybe they teach it to them at basic training along with masonic hand-shakes and how not to leave bruises on suspects.

When I got back to my office, Jock Ferguson was sitting very comfortably at my desk, chatting to Archie. That was another thing I'd noticed about coppers: they were very good at making themselves at home.

'Hello, Jock,' I said casually. 'Have you decided to join the private sector?'

He smiled his usual half-smile: the other half, I had always thought, must have gotten lost in the war.

'Divorce cases, lost dogs and bank runs? Such dizzy heights are not for me, I'm afraid. I was just passing and I thought I'd let you know that I checked out that van registration you gave me.'

'Oh . . . stolen?'

'Not quite . . .' He stretched the words out contemplatively. 'Are you sure you wrote down the right number?'

'I didn't – it was Twinkletoes who noted it down.'

Ferguson made an ah-that-explains-it face. 'Then he wrote it down wrong. It doesn't belong to any registered vehicle that we can trace, stolen or otherwise. But the number sounded wrong anyway.'

'Wrong how?' asked Archie.

'SLR 882 – the SLR prefix makes it a London-registered vehicle. I mean, that's not impossible, but it's unlikely that crooks would fake a number plate that would be so obviously out of place in Glasgow.'

'But if the number can't be found,' I said, 'then surely that means exactly that – that they're fake plates.'

'Let's face it, Lennox – Twinkletoes McBride isn't famed for his intellectual prowess. I'd say it's the safest guess that he wrote the number down wrong.'

'I guess . . .' I said. The truth was Twinkle may not have been the sharpest knife in the cutlery drawer, but he was diligent. I had asked him at the time if he had been certain that he'd gotten the right number, and he had assured me he had. Whether the number was genuine or not, listed or not, I trusted Twinkletoes that that was what had been on the van's plates.

And there was something else that wasn't ringing true: Jock Ferguson had come to tell me in person that Twinkle's note-taking was below par, something that he could easily have done over the telephone. I was probably reading too much into it, but it was almost as if he needed to see me convinced.

Picking his hat up from the desk, Ferguson rose from my chair. 'Well, I'd better let you get back to your divorces and lost dogs.'

'Actually, while you're here . . .' I said, and Ferguson responded by doing his eyebrow-arching thing. 'Was there anything suspicious noted about Quiet Tommy Quaid's death?' I asked.

'Why? What's it to you?'

'I'm officially on the case,' I said, trying not to emphasize the word *officially*. 'Tommy's next of kin has hired me to look into his death.'

'Next of kin? You mean that sister of Tommy's you couldn't take your beadies off?'

'My interest is purely professional. Was there anything odd about Tommy's death?'

'Like I told you at the funeral: occupational hazard. If you clamber about on roofs in the middle of the night, then there's always the chance you're going to take the quick way down. What are you getting at? That it could be something else? Murder?'

'I just asked if there was anything odd you'd picked up.'

'Well . . . the only thing is that Tommy clearly got to the place in a stolen van – we found it locked and abandoned outside the foundry. We couldn't find the van keys on Tommy, or anywhere near him; that kind of points to an accomplice. A driver. Maybe someone who was up on the roof with him. If you're trying to suggest murder, then the missing van driver would be your only suspect.'

I tried not to swallow too hard. 'Any ideas who Tommy's accomplice might have been?'

'Not really.' Ferguson shook his head. 'If there was an accomplice. But the only other odd thing is that we haven't been able to find Jimmy Wilson. Remember I said he sometimes worked with Tommy?'

'Yes . . .'

'Well, we can't find hide nor hair of him. Dropped off the planet completely. So maybe he was with Tommy. But even if he was, and he was up on the roof with Tommy, there's no way that Jimmy would have pushed him off. Like Tommy, Jimmy Wilson isn't the violent type. Anyway, what possible motive could he

have? My money is on him having seen Tommy fall and pan-
icked . . . if he was there at all.'

I shrugged. 'All I know is that, of all the roofs for Quiet Tommy
Quaid to fall off, that wasn't a likely candidate.'

'You know the foundry?' asked Ferguson. I tried not to let my
mental *oh fuck* show in my expression.

'I checked out where he's supposed to have fallen from.' The
secret to a successful lie is to lie without hesitation and not to
look for hints of belief in your interrogator. 'You know Tommy
was a pro. One of the best. I can't see him taking that fall.'

'It happens, Lennox. You can drown in a tumbler of water, or
break your neck tripping on a kerb. God knows the number of
times I've done someone for murder or manslaughter when a
single punch has turned out fatal.'

I nodded. It was time for me to let it drop. My first priority, I
knew, was to get to Jimmy Wilson before the coppers did. I also
had to get out to the Saracen Foundry to make true my claim to
Ferguson that I'd seen the scene of the 'accident'. It would also
give me a chance to check if anyone had spotted anyone else
around that shouldn't have been there. Including a limping
man in a Cary Grant burglar outfit.

I spent the rest of the morning going through the paperwork of
the divorce we were working on. Just before lunch, Archie went
out to get witness statements and I was left alone in the office. I
took out the two keys, each attached to the same type of blue
plastic fob, and laid them on the desk. Funnily enough, staring
at them didn't get them to give up their secrets, but it allowed
me to get my thoughts into some kind of rough order. Two keys,
both given to me indirectly by Quiet Tommy Quaid. One key to
his home, the other to a location he'd kept secret and which, if

what Jennifer had said was right, contained a secret that was important enough to kill for.

I hadn't, of course, been totally truthful with Jennifer Quaid when I said I had nothing to go on. After all, I'd been with Tommy the night he had died; worse still, it had been me who had, albeit unknowingly, sent her brother to his death. And I knew about Mr McNaught. I was the only one who knew about Mr McNaught. I also didn't tell Jennifer about the key I had to Tommy's flat, or the ticket stub for the Frantic Frankie Findlay show.

I checked the address and directions to the lock-up again, slipped the keys back into my pocket, and headed out to where my car was parked in Argyle Street.

I drove towards Clydebank, following the course of the river. Again the shore bristled with loading cranes and just like on the shipyard wages run, there was no doubt I was in a landscape of labour, of industry. It was maybe because of the bank run experience, or maybe because of my post-McNaught paranoia, that I checked my rear-view mirror more than normal. Right enough, I became sure I was being followed. No blue van this time, and whoever was stalking me was taking more care about it. A lot more care.

About three cars back, there was a Ford Consul – one of the new models – the coachwork two-tone, light blue over cream. What troubled me was I was pretty sure I'd seen it before – or at least the same model and same colours – parked outside the cemetery gates among the Bentleys and Jags the day Quiet Tommy Quaid was planted for eternity.

I made a couple of turns, indicating well in advance, to see if the Consul would follow. It did. Unlike Archie's evasions, I made sure the turns I made weren't sudden or obvious and didn't take me too far off course. After a couple, I lost sight of the Consul and headed back towards the riverfront. He was there again, further back, maybe four cars behind. He was good; better than me. This time, I was being tailed by a pro.

I reached the entrance to the lock-ups: serried ranks of large wooden storage sheds dark-varnished almost black. I knew they were rented out mainly to companies involved in shipbuilding, as well as tradesmen, a few private individuals and, as I now knew, the odd career thief. I drove past without turning in.

And when I did that, the Consul took the next turning off the main road and disappeared. Either I had been wrong and the presence of the car was a coincidence, or chummy had turned off to convince me that he hadn't been tailing me after all. What bothered me was that if he *had* been following me, then he had decided to break off when he saw I didn't turn into the lock-ups.

Which would mean the location of Tommy's secret stash wasn't so completely secret after all.

Sometimes it didn't pay to be flash. My Sunbeam Alpine convertible was too conspicuous for surveillance work – and as I found out the night of the foundry job, it was even too flash to drive down Maryhill Road in the hours of darkness without attracting a copper's attention. Probably in the hours of daylight, too. So when it came to dodging others who were surveilling me, driving about in it was a positive liability.

I decided to leave the lock-up until after dark. I stopped at a telephone box and called Archie at the office, explaining I had a couple of things to do and wouldn't be back for the rest of the day. Truth was, I had lost my tail and didn't want to pick it up again by going back and parking near the office.

I had places to go and people to see; what I needed was

something less conspicuous for a few hours. I had a contact who ran a garage in Maryhill, and I arced up along the south and east sides of the city. They rented out cars to me on an informal basis, as and when I needed something inconspicuous. The Wishart brothers not only repaired, bought and sold cars, they had unravelled a mystery of physics that had eluded Einstein and his buddies: the reversal of Time itself. When a car left their garage, the cars they sold always had considerably lower mileages on the clock than when they had bought them.

Willie Wishart wore the suit and his brother Bobby the overalls, and when I arrived at the garage, Willie was laying it on with a trowel to a worried-looking young couple. I gestured to him that I'd wait in the 'sales-office': an ancient, battered old shed, the wooden clapboard looking like it was held together by the layers of creosote that had been lathered onto it over half a century. A sign above the door promised DOUBLE THE CAR AT HALF THE PRICE, which I had heard was a promise the Wisharts regularly lived up to: the cars they sold were often the welded-together undamaged halves of insurance write-offs.

The odd thing was that Bobby Wishart was an excellent mechanic and whenever I needed the Alpine serviced and tuned, it was the Wisharts who did it for me. When Willie finished with the customers, I told him I needed something reliable, but which would blend into the background. He gave me the keys for a black forty-eight Vauxhall Wyvern. It was inconspicuous and reliable all right, but I wouldn't have wanted to have gotten into a car chase with it, given that the only thing it was capable of outrunning was a pushbike.

'I'll need it for a few hours,' I told Willie. 'Maybe overnight. Can you valet and wax the Alpine while it's here? Garage it overnight?'

Willie said he would and I took the keys of the Wyvern.

I sighed when I climbed in behind the wheel. I had a bad feeling about where I was heading – and not just because I was going to Govanhill, which was enough to depress me at the best of times. Over the last three years I had made a real effort to stay on the vaguely legal side of the business. I had risked cashflow and physical wellbeing by turning down work from the Three Kings – other than the odd and mainly legal job. I knew only too well that my copybook was never going to be spotless, but I had done my best of late to keep my slips to smudges, rather than blots.

And now I had screwed it all up by getting greedy and taking part in a break-in for a complete stranger. But Quiet Tommy Quaid had been killed and that just wasn't right, and I had to do something about it.

If there was one positive aspect of my previous life, it was that if I were ever in a fix, then I had a host of underworld contacts I could call on. It was something I tried to do less these days, but if I needed, I knew and could call on an array of thugs, gang lords, housebreakers, prostitutes, pimps, pickpockets, fraudsters, and even one professional killer. And I knew exactly who I needed to go to now.

A greengrocer.

## 3

Tony Grabowski – also known, for obvious reasons, as Tony the Pole – had been Scotland's most successful post-war peterman. He was famed as an incomparable seducer of safes: they would yield themselves to his lightest touch, opening up for him and offering their treasures without resistance.

Like Quiet Tommy Quaid, Tony the Pole had always been very careful about with whom he worked; and also like Quiet Tommy Quaid – perhaps even more so – he had kept his own counsel wherever possible. Being tight-lipped was probably the best of all defences against detection and conviction and it had served Tony well: he had never once been caught. But the police had come close that one time too many, and devoted family man Tony had decided the risk of lengthy behind-bars separation from his wife and kids was too great: Scotland's best safecracker had retired from the safecracking business.

But in going straight, Tony the Pole had made a fundamental error of judgement: he had become a greengrocer. In Glasgow.

Selling fruits and vegetables to Glaswegians was comparable to selling kryptonite to Superman or crucifixes to Dracula, so Tony the Pole supplemented his income by moonlighting as an illegal bookie and all-round fixer. It was low-key, low-risk stuff that boosted a carefully managed nest egg from his safecracking days.

I had called Tony after I'd 'phoned Archie, and we had arranged to meet at a greasy spoon transport café near his greengrocer shop on Cathcart Road. I hadn't been to the café nor heard of it before, so I allowed extra time to find it and arrived about ten minutes early.

The café was in a new-looking large wooden shed-type building, painted an inappropriately cheery duck egg blue and tucked into the corner of a scrubby square of wasteland between darkly looming Govanhill tenement blocks. It looked to me like a cleared bombsite; I didn't know if any bombs from the Clydebank raids had ever strayed this far, but truth was anywhere in Glasgow could have a naturally war-torn look, and it was clear that there had been tenements here. The sky was a bright, pale blue, paradoxically making the setting bleaker, as if someone had sketched the buildings in gritty charcoal on pale blue-coloured paper.

Part of the site had been roughly tarmacked to allow heavy goods vehicles somewhere to park, and I manoeuvred the Wyvern next to where four or five lorries sat.

In Glasgow, as with probably everywhere else, if you saw that long-distance drivers chose a particular transport caff to stop, then you were pretty much guaranteed a clean place and decent, if none too healthy, food.

I sat in the car and smoked while I waited for Tony, staring at the tenement gable end facing me. 'Magic Moments' played on the car radio and Perry Como's mellow jollity seemed totally out of place here. The tenement gable bore evidence of its now demolished neighbour: like fossils impressed into stratified rock, the outlines of fireplaces, of wiring conduits, of floor and ceiling edges, even tattered rectangles of wallpaper, were etched in bas-relief. Six geometric impressions of the cramped living of long-gone families; six reminders that other families still lived that way in the remaining tenements on the other side of the gable wall.

I took the time waiting for Tony to go through the diary-cum-address-book Jennifer Quaid had given me. It didn't take long: as I suspected, there weren't many contacts related to Tommy's professional life and most seemed to be women; there were no entries in the diary, even cryptic, alluding to jobs Tommy did. The first thing I'd done when I got the diary was to check the Sunday night we had gone to the foundry: the pages were reassuringly blank.

One name cropped up regularly in the diary: *Nancy*. Every week either on a Tuesday or Wednesday, sometimes at seven p.m., sometimes half an hour or an hour later. The name was written out full to start with, then just appeared as an *N*, each week. I guessed that 'Nancy' was the same one listed – without a surname – in the diary's address section.

Another half a cigarette's length later, I saw a small, stocky man approach across the lot on foot. He wasn't wearing a hat and his bald head – the ring of remaining hair trimmed so short as to be almost shaven – gleamed bullet-like in the sunlight. I got out and waved to him.

'Hi, Tony . . . whaddya hear, whaddya say?' The Cagney line from *Angels with Dirty Faces* had been our way of greeting each other since our first meeting, Tony always getting a kick out of what he considered my 'American' accent.

'Hey, Lennoggs, yah ould bazzdahrd. Vaht dayah hear? Vaht dayah zay?' And there it was, Tony the Pole's trademark: a blend of Glaswegian dialect and the thickest possible Polish accent. It was like listening to the love-child of Harry Lauder and Bela Lugosi. 'Vaht aboot a vee cuppa govvee an' a vee blether?' He indicated the café.

'My treat.' I smiled. I liked Tony the Pole. He was continually cheerful and friendly, despite the fact that most of his family back home in Poland had been wiped out during the war; the ones who had survived now living beyond his reach behind a curtain of iron. What's more, I trusted him.

'Zere's naw need furr you to pay,' he beamed back. 'Zizz vun vill be oan ze houze . . .' He led the way into the transport caff. The air inside was thick with cigarette smoke and the odour of hot meat, more than half the tables and booths occupied. When we walked in, the cook and the female server behind the counter waved and Tony waved back.

'On the house?' I asked. 'You mean . . .?'

'Aye, Lennoggs . . . I own ze bazzdahrd. Greengrozzer bizzinezz iz a pile o' shide. I'm keepin' it going, but zizz iz verr money iz.' As we passed a lorry driver seated at a table and bent over his plate of sausages, eggs and bacon, Tony slapped him on the back. 'Hey, Boaby – hooz it goin'?'

There was an exchange of banter and we moved on, Tony the Pole joking, laughing and waving to customers in acknowledgement as we passed them: it was clear that the café had already built up a regular clientele and I guessed that Tony's huge personality and good-naturedness played a big part. He led the way to a booth by the wall.

The inside of the café was spotless, the wood-panelling painted in pale pastel blues and greens and yet to pick up its final permanent nicotine glaze. The booths along the walls were fitted with Formica-topped tables and red leatherette benches; the freestanding tables and chairs in the middle of the café were of matching materials and design. The linoleum floor was clean and brushed and had picked up only a few scorch marks from ground-out cigarette stubs. I could see Tony hadn't skimped on decor.

'Lorry driverz iz bazzdahrds for everyzink tip-top . . .' Tony read my mind. 'Venn you dinnae get it right, venn ze food iznae up to zcratch, or ze place iznae clean enough, zay no' come bagg. And ze toilets! You'd zink zay vuddnae be fussy, zat ze big hairy-arzzed bazzdahrds vould shide in a bucket, but naw – ze toilets muzz be zpottless. I'm delling you, Lennoggs, zey're mehr vugging choosey zann Egon vugging Ronay. Vaht you vant? You vant bacon an' eggs? Zome zquvare zauzage?'

'No thanks, Tony, just a coffee.'

'Okay-dokey . . .' Tony turned round in his seat and yelled to the woman behind the counter. 'Hey, Senga dahrlink . . . go an' geez uzz two govvees . . .' He turned back to me, smiling. 'I'm taking it ziss izznae a zocial call . . . Vaht can I do vorr you, Lennoggs?'

So I told him. If there was one danger about Tony the Pole, it was that you told him too much: he was one of those people who invited confidence to the point of carelessness. There was something about the broad Slavic smile in the broad Slavic face, and the broader – and I suspected hammed-up – Slavic accent that broke down your guard and made you feel like spilling every bean you had ever had to spill. It was like when you were a kid talking to your favourite uncle – the one who was like your dad but not your dad and who you could tell things that you couldn't tell your dad. If, that is, your favourite uncle was a bald, Glaswegian Bela Lugosi.

Leaning forward with my elbows on fresh-wiped Formica and dropping my voice under the café's buzz so that only he could hear me, I told Tony more than I had told anyone else, which wasn't difficult. I didn't tell him everything, of course, leaving out the pretty essential facts that I had hired Tommy, that I had been riding shotgun on the job the night he died, and that a spook with a lopsided face called Mr McNaught had orchestrated the whole thing and had since dropped off the planet.

But I did tell Tony that I was sure Tommy's death was no accident. I told him about Tommy's sister and what she had said about his wartime service and his post-war avoidance of his commando buddies; about the night I had been jumped in the street for no reason and had started to suspect it was because I had been mistaken for Tommy; I told him about the blue van following us on the bank run and that I'd swapped my car for the Wyvern because of the Ford Consul persistently in my rear-view mirror.

The good humour fell from his face and Tony listened solemnly as I spoke. We paused when Senga, the waitress, brought over our coffees, squinting against the smoke from the cigarette angled between her thin, bright crimsoned lips. Senga was stick-thin and aged somewhere between fifty and a thousand, with a wrinkled complexion a vampire would have described as 'pasty': a pallor accentuated by her artificially red hair. She obviously shopped for hair dye in the same place as 'Pherson the barber. As she placed my coffee on the table, I could have sworn she winked at me, but it was maybe just the smoke in her eyes.

'Bad bizzinezz.' Tony shook his head. 'Quiet Tommy waz good boy. Good boy. Zo vaht you vant from me? I do anyzing to help.'

'Listen, Tony, I know you keep your cards close to your chest and you've never talked about the jobs you did. But I'm lost here. I believe Quiet Tommy Quaid was killed on that rooftop and pushed off to make it look like an accident, but I've got nothing to back that up. I've been asked to make sure the right thing is done by him, but I'm struggling. You were the best peterman in Scotland and Tommy was one of the best planners and roofmen. I'm guessing that you probably worked together on more than one occasion. If there's anything – *anything* – you can tell me that would help, then I'd owe you a huge favour. I'm also guessing that there's a chance you were offered the same kind of deal as Tommy during the war and you can maybe give me something more to go on. And I know you know Jimmy Wilson, who I've heard worked with Tommy sometimes and I guess worked with you. Jimmy has disappeared off the face of the earth and I think it's got something to do with Tommy's death – or at least his disappearance coincided exactly with it. Anything you can tell me to point me in Jimmy's direction would be a huge help.' I stopped, leaving it all laid out on the table between us, waiting for Tony to respond. He sat quietly for a moment, his lips pursed while he thought through what I had said.

'Okay – let's take ze zing viz Jimmy virst. Ze problem iz zat you zay you'zz bein' followed. You could lead whoever'z following you right to Jimmy.'

'So you know where he is? And why he's hiding?'

'Naw – I didnae zay dat. But I could maybe tell you who does.'

I made an open-handed gesture. There were no guarantees I could make, but Tony knew me well enough, I hoped, to trust me to be as discreet as possible. He took a small notepad from his pocket and scribbled something into it, tearing out the page and handing it to me.

'Zat Jimmy's brudder. He runs garage in ze Gallowgate. Ozzer name iz Jimmy's bezd pal. Bit of a pizz-hied, if you ken vaht I mean. But I don't know how much zey be of uze to you. If Jimmy vahnt to ztay hidden, he ztay hidden.'

I thanked Tony, but made another gesture, inviting more. He sighed, then started to answer my questions. As he spoke, I noticed he toned down a little both the Glaswegian patois and the East European accent. It was still thick, but I started to suspect that Tony played a part – adopted a character. The strategy of the immigrant wanting to be liked, to find acceptance.

Tony explained that he had never been approached to do the same kind of war service. He had never been convicted of an offence, so there was no evidence of illicit skills. In any case, he'd already been in the Polish Free Army when he arrived in Scotland in August nineteen-forty, one of thirty thousand Poles who, after their own homeland had fallen, had come to Scotland to protect it with their lives from an expected German invasion launched from Norway. The relationship had been so close that many of the Polish Army units had adopted Scottish motifs into their insignia. After the war, many – like Tony – had stayed on in Scotland. Now, the Polish-Scot, like the Italian-Scot, was an accepted part of Scotland's culture. It seemed that the Irish – their closest cousins – were the only immigrant group the native Scots struggled with.

'But I did know of zuch units,' Tony explained. 'Laycock vent about recruiting zafecrackers and burglars vor his new commando zervice. I knew Tommy vaz in von, but you knew Tommy, he not talk much about zuch zings.'

And I had known Tommy. I guessed Tony was telling the truth and that Tommy had confided in him no more than he had in me.

'But you did do jobs with him?' I asked.

'And you know zat I don't talk about zuch zings.'

There was a silence and I let it ride.

Eventually Tony gave another sigh and said, 'I'm no' zaying vee did, I'm no' zaying vee didnae. But Tommy vaz good, really good. Ze best at vaht he did. Naebody dezerved the name "cat burglar" like Tommy – zat vaz vaht he vaz like on a roof – like a cat. Zere's no' vugging way he vell ovv that foundry roof. Tommy vaz too careful.'

'Did he ever talk about other people he was involved with? Or even his wartime buddies?'

'Not him, no. But I know he do lot of vork for Hanzome Jonny Cohen. More than for ozzer Kings. I did hear zomezink else vonce,' he said, 'a rumour about Tommy . . .'

'What kind of rumour?'

'You know ze vay it goes viz crooks, Lennoggs – zay have zere own legends and myths. Zere vaz a rumour about Tommy: zat he had a pile of treasure zomewheres – zat venn he vaz commando hiz unit steal big pile of Nazi loot.'

I remembered what Jennifer had said about Tommy's 'special' unit, and suddenly the memory came to mind of the small, wiry mourner with the rat-like movements at Tommy's funeral.

'Was the rumour that Tommy had this Nazi loot stashed?'

'Zome zaid he had it buried zomewhere. But you know zeze zings – stories crooks tell each ozzer to pass time in prison. All just pile of shide.'

'Thanks, Tony. Could you ask around? At least keep an ear to the ground and let me know if you hear anything about Tommy or of Jimmy Wilson's whereabouts?'

He nodded. Then the seriousness left his face and he beamed a smile at me, held his arms out to indicate our surroundings.

'Zo, Lennoggs – vaht do you zink of my new plaze?' The accent and the volume were fully restored. It was a signal that our exchange of confidences was over.

'It's fine, Tony. It's really fine.'

## 4

The Scottish summer frustrates larceny and generally any shenanigans that demand the cover of dark: the night comes
late – in August, daylight lasts nearly seventeen hours – and
when night does come its presence is half-hearted.

I was hoping for a blanket of cloud, but the still-bright afternoon
sky remained clear of cover and I could see I was going to have to
wait until near midnight before doing any serious skulking.

In the meantime, the imagined urgent weight of the two Yale
keys in my pocket – one to Tommy's apartment, the other to the
lock-up – nagged at me. But I knew I had to be patient: if my tail
was waiting to pick me up again, then it would either be at one
of those locations or outside my office.

Even though I was driving the Wyvern, I kept checking my
mirrors for the Ford Consul or any other persistent presence
behind me. There was none that I could see, but I still kept my
guard up.

Burdened as I was with the curse of the migrant or displaced
person, there were the odd fleeting times where I lost my bearings. Sometimes the weather, the light, would play tricks on me,
mixing moment and memory and taking me back to a different
place, a different time, a different me.

Because of the length of summer days in Scotland, sunsets were often gradual, lengthy affairs. That evening, the gold-tinged sky was mimicking a different season and a different continent. I found myself remembering fall sunset evenings before the war, growing up on the shores of the Kennebecasis River.

Unlike here in Glasgow, where the distinction between the times of year was fudged, I'd grown up in a markedly four seasons climate: New Brunswick winters were long, lasting through March, and were perpetually snow-muffled, but punctuated with blue-sky days of snow-reflected brilliance; springs came late and were short, the ground burnt brown once the snow finally disappeared. For me, the only enduring memory of Canadian springs was the relief from snow and the taste of fiddleheads and maple syrup. The summers were intense: a heat stretching into September, far hotter than anything in Scotland. But above all it was the falls I missed: fall in New Brunswick was bright and mellow with the forests around Saint John exploding with colour. But it was nature aided by industry: the high-altitude drift of pollution from the Rust Belt – the US industrial heartland of Michigan, Illinois, Ohio, Indiana – was swept up by the jet stream and scattered across the New Brunswick sky, invisible except at sundown. The result was the most spectacular sunsets.

And sometimes, like now as I stood staring dumbly at the sky when the evening sun shone in the middle of a Glasgow summer, the light and the air reminded me of autumnal evenings back home and tended to provoke a dull melancholy in me. But this time, the vague homesickness and gloominess were tinged with something else.

Maybe it was thinking about the pre-war me that did it, the

bright-eyed Kennebecasis Kid who was yet to be fucked up by a war on another continent. If I were honest, I had felt pretty sorry for myself during and after the war, blaming all my subsequent wrongs and woes on being dragged into a conflict where I would see all that was bad in men and all that was worse in me. Everything I had done wrong since, I blamed on the world, not me.

But the truth was that I'd had it pretty good before the war: I had been brought up in comparative wealth, in a big century home, and educated at the Collegiate in Rothesay, which was as upper as the crust came in Maritime Canada. I'd had a happy childhood and youth, had had a promising future. A lot of men had started with less than me, had gone through the same as I had, and had come back from it to fulfil the promise of their futures.

And whenever I thought about Quiet Tommy Quaid, my excuses to myself just didn't fly. He had had a tough war too. But Tommy had had a tough peacetime before it; an unjust background of deprivation and want. He had forged his way in a world much more challenging than the one I had known.

The simple fact was that Tommy was a better man than me.

Only one of us beat men half to death when his anger was sparked; only one of us treated women as disposable assets. Sure, Tommy had been every bit the bedroom swordsman I was, but his attitude to women had been different. One evening out on the tiles, when we were perhaps only halfway into our cups, Tommy had explained his attitude to women. He liked them. Not just in the usual way – not just in the way I liked women, and I had done a lot of liking. I was yet to see his book collection, but there had been a hint of Tommy's erudition that night. He had asked me if I knew the works of Stendhal, and told me that the French author was famed for both the extent of his womanizing and the strength and depth of the female characters in his writing.

'Stendhal *liked* women,' Tommy had explained. 'They interested him, he valued them. He listened to them. In many ways
he thought them superior to men. A true ladies' man, in every
sense. I sometimes think I've got a bit of that going. I enjoy being
with women. Spending time with them.'

'So you go out with women because of their minds?' I had
laughed, knowing Tommy's reputation.

'I go for the whole package. The works. Not always, of course,
but life's too short to spend with people who don't interest you.
And as for brains . . . I'm telling you, Lennox, there's nothing
sexier than an intelligent woman.'

Something fell into place.

The memory of that conversation with Tommy made me
scrabble about in the glove box of the Wyvern, where I'd put his
diary to stop its weight ruining the line of my jacket.

Having only given it a cursory glance while I had been waiting
for Tony the Pole, I now took the time to go through the diary
more thoroughly. There were a couple of names in the address
section that I didn't recognize, but most were female acquaintances of Tommy's – including a barmaid I had acquaintanced
myself on more than one occasion. I considered contacting her
to see if it yielded anything useful about Tommy, but I guessed
it wouldn't, nor would most of the other women in the book.
Gynophile or not, I didn't see Tommy confiding anything of
value to a barmaid or cinema usherette.

I found what I was looking for in the back of the diary: the
address entry brought to mind by my memory of what Tommy
had said that night. It was headed 'Nancy', without a surname,
and was in the west end of town, near the university. This was

the N Tommy had visited every week. I decided not to 'phone the number listed, but instead to call in person: it was always easier for someone to hang up on you than to close the door in your face.

I fired up the Wyvern and lumbered along Great Western Road, still checking my rear-view.

The address was that of a ground-floor flat, midway along a four-storey-plus-basements blond sandstone terrace in Cecil Street. There was only a handful of cars parked along its length and I guessed most of the occupants were either staff or students who mostly walked or cycled between home and the nearby university.

I recognized her as soon as she opened the door. She was the woman of tearless grief I'd seen at Tommy's graveside. In her early forties and tired, her eyes were shadowed and her face pale. It was difficult to tell if she was simply weary from the labours of the day or from the travails of life in general, but I guessed that the sudden absence from her life of a quiet, handsome man had something to do with it.

Just as I remembered from the funeral, her hair was dark and cut unfashionably short. She was dressed in a knit jumper and tweed skirt that suggested when it came to choosing her wardrobe, functionality always won over fashion. Despite the unflattering clothes, I could see her figure was still slim and good and the ghost of a pretty, happier girl lingered. Her face was naked of make-up and full of character and I could see she was a handsome woman with a special kind of attractiveness. Her unlikely connection with Tommy started to seem more likely.

I had practised my opening gambit on the way from the car; being a stranger at the door was always an obstacle to overcome;

revealing yourself to be a professional snooper often turned that obstacle into a drawbridge. I had decided to keep things personal rather than professional, introducing myself as a friend of Tommy's, not an enquiry agent, and then explaining that his sister had asked me to look into his death.

'I've been expecting you,' she said dully, before I had a chance to say anything; then, standing to one side, 'You had better come in, Mr Lennox.'

I followed her mutely into the apartment, leaving my unwrapped opening gambit on the doorstep. The walls of the narrow hall were decked with modern art prints and politically themed posters for the CND and the Communist Party of Great Britain, a framed cinema poster for *Battleship Potemkin*, as well as an ugly, modernist one for Bertolt Brecht's *Mother Courage and her Children*. By the time we made it to the living room I had worked out she wouldn't be joining the local branch of the Women's Institute any time soon.

'You know who I am?' I asked.

'Tommy told me about you.'

'And you were expecting me?'

'He said there was a chance you would come. If anything happened to him.'

'He told you he thought something would happen to him?' This was getting interesting. Whatever else had been going on between them, Tommy – who confided in so very few – had trusted this unlikely confidante.

'He said he was mixed up in something dangerous. That there were people who might wish him harm. He told me that if anyone ever came asking about him – including anyone *official* – I was to plead ignorance. Except you. He told me that you were to be trusted.'

'How did you know it was me? How did you recognize me?'

'Tommy described you. He said you were a good man – someone I could rely on – but you looked bad. A little like the actor Jack Palance. It's not that common a look in Glasgow.'

I shrugged. Comparisons with Hollywood stars were indeed rare in Glasgow. Although I thought I'd spotted Lon Chaney a couple of times.

'I don't know your name,' I said. 'Other than you're Nancy.'

'Nancy Ross,' she explained. 'I'm a lecturer at the university.'

'Did Tommy say who he thought might wish him harm?'

'He was vague about that. Specific enough to scare me, but vague enough to leave me in the dark. But he said they were powerful people. Not criminals – or at least not the accepted kind of criminals. He said these were people in positions of real power.'

'What kind of positions?' I asked. 'Military . . . army?'

'Like I told you, he was vague about them. He never said anything specific enough to make me think they were military. But he said I should understand what he meant. Can I get you something to drink?'

'I don't want to put you to any trouble,' I said, but she was already over at the sideboard on which there was a tray with tumblers and bottles of sherry, whisky and gin. I obviously wasn't going to be offered tea or coffee. She poured herself a heavy-handed measure of gin, only letting it get a sniff of tonic. She waved the gin bottle at me but I shook my head: I was an Olympic-level drinker, but I'd learned from experience not to drink with those who use alcohol to self-medicate. It was clear that booze was the anaesthetic Nancy Ross used to blunt the sharp edges of her loss.

She indicated an aged leather armchair and invited me to

sit; I took in the room as I did so. The side table beside the armchair was heaped with magazines and periodicals, topped with
the current issue of *Tribune*. Two of the walls were filled with
floor-to-ceiling bookcases and there were books anywhere else
there was a free surface: philosophy and political textbooks
mainly, with heavyweight-looking fiction dotted through them,
some in the original French or German. Like her non-membership
of the WI, it was clear that Nancy wasn't the Agatha Christie or
Barbara Cartland kind of girl either.

'What do you think he meant when he said you should know
who he was talking about?'

'My subject is political philosophy. My whole life is devoted to
the study of the acquisition and use – and abuse – of power. I
suppose that's what he meant. If it was, then it suggests people
in all kinds of positions – people who are part of the Establishment. Maybe people in direct political power. Whoever they are
and wherever they are, Tommy had something on them. And
whoever they are, they have a long reach.'

'What makes you say that?'

'Tommy left something for you. A sealed envelope. He told me
not to open it, for my own safety, but to keep it for you. It felt
like there were documents and other stuff in it. The strange
thing is he told me not to get in touch with you. You had to
come to me. If you hadn't found your way to my door within
three months of anything happening, I was to put the envelope
unopened into another one and send it to the editor of the *Glasgow Herald*. But he said that wouldn't really do much good.
Whatever I did I was to make sure the envelope couldn't be
traced back to me.'

'And you didn't open it?'

She shook her head. Another gulp.

'Well . . .' I said somewhat impatiently. 'Can I have it?'

'No.'

'Why not?'

'It's gone. Disappeared. Two days after Tommy died, my flat was broken into while I was at the uni. Broad daylight.'

'You reported it to the police?'

Her laugh was almost a snort. 'The police? The police would love a chance to have a sniff around my stuff. The *other* police. The *secret* police. The kind of police we're not supposed to have on this sceptred isle. Do you know I had someone from Special Branch at the door only a couple of months ago? He sat right where you're sitting and questioned me about all my trips abroad. He knew everything about me. Every academic contact I had in Europe, every man I had ever been involved with. Other things . . .' She lowered her eyes for a moment, then took another swallow of gin. 'Anyway, there was no point in me reporting the break-in.'

'Why?'

'Because only I could tell there had been one. Whoever it was, they were very professional, very clever. The only thing that had been taken was the envelope Tommy had left for you.' She walked over to the bookcase behind her and pulled a volume from the shelf. Holding it out to me, she opened the cover to reveal it was a dummy, the inside a box. 'This is where it was. They must have gone through everything, taken every book from the shelves, before they found it. It must have taken hours.'

'Maybe they knew exactly where it was hidden.'

'No, they didn't. That's how I knew someone had broken in.' She waved an arm at the books on the shelves and scattered on tables and the desk by the window. 'All this looks like chaos to you, to everyone, even did to Tommy – but I have this weird memory for books, where I put them. They tried to put everything back the way I had it, but I could see where one title was out of place here, another there. And there were other, tiny hints that someone had been in the flat.'

I thought about what she had said. If she was right, whoever had broken in had had skills very similar to Tommy Quaid's. 'But the only thing missing was the envelope Tommy had left for me?' I asked.

'Yes. I think you can see why I didn't report it. At best I would sound like a paranoiac. And anyway, I'm not at all sure it wasn't Special Branch themselves who broke in.'

'You said this Special Branch guy knew all the men you've been involved with. What about Tommy? Was he mentioned?'

'No. Tommy was the only one who wasn't. I felt he was conspicuous by his absence.'

'What did Tommy say about the visit from the Special Branch?'

'He told me not to worry, but I could see he was shaken up by it. And you know Tommy, very little had the power to shake him. He told me to forget all about it.'

'Why would Special Branch have a particular interest in you?'

'I was a member of the Communist Party when I was a student, but I quit years ago. Since then I've been a member of the Labour Party, but very much on the left. But I wouldn't be flavour of the month even with Labour Central Office. I'm a Bevanite. That's not a problem up here in Scotland, but the Labour Party down south prefers pink to red. I hate Gaitskell and what he's done to the party. A Tory in socialist clothing. Special Branch think the rest of us get our orders direct from Moscow.'

'But that's not enough for them to make house calls – either openly or surreptitiously.'

'One of the men I was involved with, before Tommy . . .' She lowered her eyes. 'He was a Czech. He was over here on a university exchange and we got involved while he was here. He was only interested in people who were communist party members and I think I was pretty naive not to pick up he was more than an academic. I've been . . . *scrutinized* ever since.'

'Where does Tommy fit into all this?' I asked. 'What was he to you?'

'You mean what was I to Tommy? You're struggling to see what someone like Tommy would have to do with someone like me?' There was no bitterness in her tone or in the dully frank way she looked at me. It was blank, disinterested, detached.

'I'm just trying to establish how well you knew him.'

'We were lovers. For the past four years. Tommy would come into my life for three to four hours, one evening a week. And during those three or four hours he would make me feel like there was no one else in the world who mattered to him. I know Tommy was involved with a lot of women, but I think – or I like to think – he was closer to me than any other woman he was involved with. I think I knew him better than anyone. Which means hardly at all.'

I knew exactly what she meant.

'How did you meet?' I asked. There was a sofa facing me – or at least the shape of a sofa beneath a draped candlewick spread – and she sat down on it, balancing her gin on the arm.

'The Mitchell Library, of all places. Tommy was looking for the same book as me. I bet you didn't know he was interested in political philosophy?'

'No I didn't, but it doesn't surprise me in the least. There were a lot of things I didn't know about Tommy until recently. Tommy had depths. I don't think any of us who knew him knew him completely. He was a clever guy. A clever man born in the wrong place at the wrong time.'

'Was he? Tommy would argue he was who he was exactly because of his time and place. But yes, he was one of the brightest people I have ever known.' Her voice shook a little; the gin was losing the battle to keep her grief contained.

'Apart from his interest in political philosophy,' I asked, 'did Tommy ever express political leanings? I mean, did he share your views, for example?'

Nancy Ross snorted. 'Tommy hated state socialism almost as much as he did the Tories. He said we were out to control everyone's lives just as much as they were. You know the saying "absolute power corrupts absolutely"?'

I nodded.

'Well Tommy believed that *any* power corrupts. He believed in direct, not representative, democracy. He said as soon as someone has a position of influence or power, they instantly abuse it to one degree or another. So no – he hated all politicians and authority figures equally. If I were to give Tommy's political views a name – which he never would – then I would say he was an anarchist. An anarcho-syndicalist. Or maybe just bitter. His contempt for those in authority seemed to get much worse shortly before he died.'

'Any particular reason?'

'Oh yes – there was a particular reason all right. I could see that. But Tommy being Tommy, he kept it all locked up and to himself.'

She took another sip of gin. 'Are you sure you don't want a drink?'

I shook my head. 'Did you and Tommy ever go to the theatre together?'

'We didn't go out much. Tommy would come here and we would stay in, mostly. Talk. I did take him to the Citizens a couple of times. Brecht. The truth is Tommy found theatre pointless, frivolous. He said we already lived in an acted-out fantasy.'

'Did he ever suggest he'd be interested in variety shows? At the King's or the Alhambra? Frantic Frankie Findlay?'

Nancy laughed and looked at me incredulously. 'What on earth would make you think that?'

I told her about the ticket stub. Her bemusement was genuine.

'It's probably of no significance,' I said. 'It could have ended up in Tommy's possession any number of ways.'

She went over to the sideboard and generously refilled her glass before sitting back down.

'Is there anything else you can think of that struck you as strange?' I asked. 'Anything that happened in the weeks leading up to Tommy's death that was out of the ordinary?'

She returned to the sofa, her tumbler refilled. She shrugged. 'Not that I can think of.' She took another sip, smaller this time. 'There was one thing, but I don't know if it really has anything to do with anything . . .'

'What?'

'Tommy seemed to get upset about something that had nothing to do with him. You know what he was like – nothing ever seemed to faze him, especially anything that was unconnected to people he knew – but this seemed to get to him. You maybe didn't hear about this, but maybe a week or so before Tommy died, there was this young fellow who threw himself in front of a train at Central Station.'

'I remember it.'

'Tommy got very low when he read about it. There was no

name given in the paper, but Tommy seemed to have an idea who it was. It was about that time that he began to get really bitter about "the powers that be". Your guess is as good as mine as to whether the two things were connected or not.'

'Did he discuss it with you?'

She shook her head. Mine was buzzing with connections and coincidences. We fell into an awkward silence. I guessed it was time to go.

'What's your interest?' she asked as I stood up. 'I mean, you don't strike me as someone who is easy to read – maybe easier than Tommy to read, but that allows a lot of scope. I just don't get how Tommy had the measure of you to the extent that he could predict you would come calling.'

'He asked me to. Or he left instructions for his sister to ask me on his behalf. He felt I would make things right – what I've to make right and how is beyond me at the moment. I guess he thought he could rely on me.'

'But why? I mean why are you doing it?' She took what should have been an eye-watering gulp of gin but it didn't even register. 'Tommy's gone. Dead. The dead have nothing to do with the living. You can't let Tommy down because there is no Tommy to be let down any more; any debt you owe him died when he fell off that bloody roof. Or maybe you're the spiritual kind.' Another gulp. It really was time for me to go.

I didn't answer for a moment; not because what she had said had annoyed or offended me, but simply because I didn't have an answer for her, or for myself. I was fulfilling a duty to a dead thief: she didn't know why I was doing it; I didn't know why I was doing it. But Tommy Quaid had trusted me. He had known I would do it. Something about that made me feel better about myself.

'I'm doing it for me,' I said eventually. 'I'm doing it because Tommy was my friend. It's as simple and as complicated as that.'

Nancy Ross saw me – a little unsteadily – to the door. I knew she was going to do more drinking after I'd gone and I wanted to do something to stop her, to help. But there was nothing for me to do.

'For what it's worth,' I said from the doorstep, 'I think you're right – I think Tommy Quaid was closer to you than any other woman, than anyone else, for that matter. I really am sorry for your loss.'

She nodded her thanks, curtly, tight-lipped, her eyes glazing with tears. I left her standing at the door with a gaping hole in her life and started to think about how I had felt after Fiona White had died. How I still felt.

I didn't look back as I headed towards where I'd parked the car.

## 5

Maybe it was all Nancy Ross's talk of secret policemen and clandestine searches, but when I climbed back into the Wyvern, I could have sworn I caught a glimpse in the rear-view mirror of a two-tone Consul flash past the road end behind me, travelling along Great George Street. Waiting a minute to see if it reappeared, I took a deep breath and shook my head to free it of its itch of paranoia. It didn't make sense: I had swapped my Sunbeam convertible for the anonymity of the Wyvern – and that was a lot of anonymity. And I had expended a great deal of effort to make sure I wasn't being followed.

Jock Ferguson, having been elevated to chief inspector, generally kept normal office hours these days, but I knew he sometimes worked on late into the evening. I decided to chance my luck and stopped at a telephone box and called to see if he was still at his office. He was, and agreed, somewhat reluctantly and wearily, to see me if I came straight away, as he was about to leave for the evening.

The itch in my head was still there as I drove all the way back across the city towards Glasgow Green, constantly checking my rear-view mirror. When I parked on Turnbull Street, outside the City of Glasgow Police's St Andrew's Square headquarters, the paints seemed to have dried on the sunset and I despaired at getting any cover when I went down to the waterfront storage sheds later.

I went in through the main entrance and had to wait while a huge Highlander constable tried to book in a tiny, very drunk tramp who refused to play nice. Despite it being early August, the small man was bundled in the uniform of trampdom: a stained mackintosh fastened around the waist with cord, and a mismatched, tattered cap. I sometimes wondered if tramps rejected coats they found complete with belts.

In my time in Glasgow I had seen a great many tramps and there were, broadly speaking, two kinds: the first was the drunk who, having found the bottom of the bottle had fallen through it into a life of sleeping rough and taking care of nothing other than finding the next drink; the second was the victim of circumstance who found him- or herself homeless and indigent but refused to lose their dignity. The clean tramps – the ones who used public bathhouses and sought casual labour, many of them ex-servicemen damaged by combat and still lost more than a decade later behind enemy lines in their home town.

This tramp was the former. He was filthy. Like the sandstone building he now stood in, Glasgow had ingrained soot and grit into every exposed exterior surface: into his pores, into every crevasse, fold and crease; in his hair and unkempt bush of beard.

And I had the misfortune of being able to smell him, even from a distance. He had clearly decided to mourn the passing of the late king by not taking a bath since His Majesty's death. Approaching the desk, I passed by him that little bit too close and began to wonder if maybe it was Queen Victoria he was mourning instead.

The uniform behind the counter had a crown above his stripes, indicating he was a station sergeant. He watched the tramp impassively, elbows and stripes resting on the charge desk, with an expression of patience that a Buddhist monk would take a lifetime to achieve.

'And you're insisting this is your name?' the Highlander copper lilted musically as he took his police cap off and placed it on the desk.

'Aye. That's my name, awright,' the tramp said in a Glasgow accent as edged and harsh as the Highlander's was rounded and gentle. 'An' I'm very proud of it. I'm a Teuchter, like yersel'. You know, a big thick-as-shite, hairy-arsed, sheep-shaggin' Teuchter. That's me.'

If the invective was intended to rile the constable, it failed. 'And where do you come from?' he lilted. 'In the Highlands, I mean?'

'Oh – eh . . . Skye. Aye, that's it. Stornoway.'

'Stornoway's on Lewis, not Skye.' Still no annoyance, no impatience.

'Aye . . . that's whit I meant. Lewis. That's where wir clan is from. We're very big up there. Oh, aye, very big. Very important. You should be mair respectful.'

'Well . . .' lilted the Highlander, 'I'm from Harris and the station sergeant here is from Oban, and I can say that I have never heard tell of a clan of that name. Have you, Sarge?'

The stripes shook his head, his demeanour still one of weary uninterest. 'You are aware that giving a false name to the police is an offence in itself?' he said.

'Are you callin' me a liar?' The small tramp straightened himself up, his face theatrically indignant.

'So you're sticking with this name?' asked the constable.

'I am!' He stabbed a black stub of a finger on the charge ledger in front of the sergeant. 'Whit's mair, I insist you enter it thus!'

'I see.' The constable stroked his chin. 'Hamish MacCuntypuss?'

'That is my name, given to me by my dear old ma an' pa,' the tramp said with pride.

'In that case, Mr MacCuntypuss,' said the constable, 'would you step in here for a moment.' He led the tramp across the foyer and into a room off, closing the door behind him. I stepped up to the desk.

'My name is Lennox,' I told the stripes, somewhat abashed at the comparative blandness of my name. 'I'm here to see Chief Inspector Ferguson. He's expecting me.'

The station sergeant said nothing and, moving with studied weariness, picked up the receiver of his desk 'phone and dialled three numbers.

Across the foyer, from behind the closed door of the room into which the constable had taken the tramp, I heard several slapping sounds, followed by a cry, followed by a thud.

'There's a Mr Lennox here to see you, sir,' the station sergeant said into the telephone, oblivious to the muffled sounds of violence. From behind the closed door, someone gave a high-pitched squeal. More slapping sounds.

'You've to go straight up,' the stripes said, replacing the receiver, still deaf to the sounds from the room. 'You know the way?'

I nodded and he lifted up the table-top gate to let me through.

At that point the constable and the tramp came out of the room behind us, the policeman with the same calm demeanour, the tramp holding the side of his face, his cap askew and his gaze lowered, looking decidedly less sure of himself.

'Hugh – otherwise known as Shuggy – O'Neil, Sarge . . .' the constable said and the sergeant started to write in his ledger. 'Drunk and disorderly and urinating in a public place . . .'

*

Ferguson was in his second-floor office. To get to it I passed several uniforms and plainclothes men and it was like an inventory of my time in Glasgow: the majority didn't acknowledge me, some nodded a greeting; one was a detective I regularly bribed for information and he made a great effort not to look in my direction. Others – those who had crossed my path accompanied by Superintendent Willie McNab – viewed me with everything from vague suspicion to outright hostility. It was clear that these officers were unconvinced by my conversion to the righteous path; I reflected bitterly that they were probably the ones with the best measure of me.

Chief Inspector Jock Ferguson's office was a lot smaller than you would have expected. It had a reasonable-sized window looking out onto St Andrew's Square, but other than that was cramped and municipally bleak. Almost cell-like. For some reason it made me think again of what Tommy had said about us all being in prison, just some prisons were easier to see than others.

The other thing I noticed about it was it was painstakingly tidy. There was a pile of papers on Ferguson's desk, but it was neatly arranged, fitting with the geometry of everything else – two phones, stapler, ashtray, a wire basket filled with buff folders – on the desk. There was an uncompromising order to everything. I knew that Ferguson had been stationed out in the Far East during and after the war, one of those unlucky buggers who didn't get demobbed until forty-six. Some of these men, those who had had contact with the Japanese, had come back either hating them or bringing something of their culture back. Or both.

'What can I do you for?' asked Ferguson. He smiled, but I could see he'd had a long day and had no intention of allowing me to make it longer. He stood behind his desk, placing some papers into his briefcase. It was an attitude of departure and he made no sign of sitting back down, or inviting me to sit. 'Is this to do with your *official* investigation into Quiet Tommy's death? How's his sister?'

'I haven't seen her since we last spoke. And yes, it has. Have you found Jimmy Wilson yet?'

'No, we haven't. But we're not trying that hard, to be honest. He's hardly Glasgow's most wanted. Small-time warrant for a small-time crook. And we won't be able to make it stick: we never do. Wilson's like Quaid, smart as a rat. I'll let you know if we do find him, though. That it?'

'Not quite. I'm struggling to pin down any other contacts Tommy Quaid may have had. I wondered if you had any intelligence on known associates.'

Ferguson gave me a funny look. Suspicious, almost. 'You're asking the wrong source, Lennox,' he said. 'Tommy Quaid was a crafty bugger and kept his cards close to his chest. Our list of known associates is very short – that said, you'd be surprised who is on it. Like the odd shady enquiry agent.'

I didn't like that. The one thing that I didn't want Ferguson doing was putting any twos together with any other twos.

'Why don't you take a trip down to Newton Mearns,' he said. 'You and Handsome Jonny Cohen are also very chummy, or so I've heard.' Another dig. 'And from what we can gather, Cohen had a market for the skills Quaid had to offer. Jimmy Wilson too. A market for your skills too, if rumour's right.'

'Jeez, Jock, what've I done? Why the character assassination?'

He sighed, resting his hands on the now sealed briefcase on his desk. 'It's been a long day, that's all. And, to be frank, I stuck my neck out for you – vouching for you for the bank run. It seems you're back to keeping old company. I just hope to Christ that doesn't mean old habits.'

'Listen, Jock, I'll never forget what you've done for me and I won't let you down. I'd have kind of hoped you knew that. This isn't about me and Jonny or any of the Three Kings. This is all about Tommy Quaid. I've been hired to establish whether his death really was an accident or not. Like you, I'm just doing my job.'

'Okay,' Ferguson said, but he still didn't look convinced and that worried me. He made an open-handed 'is that it?' gesture.

'Did you ever hear a rumour that Tommy had some kind of stash from his commando days?'

'I heard something of the kind,' said Ferguson, 'but it's all bollocks. There were a lot of burglars and safecrackers drafted into Laycock's Special Brigade, Layforce, and then the commandos. The ones who survived the experience and came back home all have a stash of Nazi loot, if you believe the rumours.'

'But you've never heard anything to suggest there might be some truth in it?'

'Okay, Lennox, your time's up. If you don't mind . . .' He moved around the desk.

'Remember you said there was another case that you were surprised the fiscal didn't order an inquiry on?' I asked.

He sighed. 'The boy in the station? What about it?'

'Who was he?'

'I dunno – just some kid. Depressed, I think. Well, you don't chuck yourself in front of a train if you're having a fit of the giggles.'

'Do you have a name?'

Again, Ferguson indicated his suspicion with an arched eyebrow.

'It came up,' I said, weakly. There was no way I could justify my interest without telling at least part of the truth. 'Quiet

Tommy Quaid seems to have gotten upset about the kid's suicide.'

'Quaid? Did he know the boy?'

'That I don't know . . . until I get at least a name.'

The eyebrow arched again.

'Honestly, Jock,' I said. 'I don't know what connection there is, or if there's a connection at all. Maybe Tommy simply read about the kid's suicide and it provoked his *Weltschmerz*.'

'Quiet Tommy Quaid didn't strike me as a *Weltschmerz*-y kind of guy.'

'Nor me. Jock . . .?'

He sighed again, went back to his desk and made an internal call, still without sitting down. He asked for the details of the case and flipped open a pad. He was obviously getting quite a bit of information and he scribbled it down on the pad.

'Robert Weston. Seventeen years old. Lived for the last year in a lodging house, before that he was a boarder at St Andrew's School. It's a school in darkest Ayrshire for military kids, mainly orphans.'

'Which Robert Weston was?'

'I believe so.' He handed me the note he had taken and punctuated our conversation by switching off his desk lamp.

'I'll get out of your hair,' I said. Ferguson came around the desk to follow me out. He reached past me and took a suit on a hanger down from the hook on his office door. It was a formal dinner suit with black tie. I hadn't noticed it when I had come in.

'You moonlighting in the dance halls?' I asked. 'A shilling a tango?'

'Retirement do at the end of the week.' He looked gloomy. Gloomier. 'Chief Inspector Bob MacIntyre, a senior who's been around since Methuselah was in nappies. He got an extension on compulsory retirement. One of Willie McNab's old buddies. You remember Superintendent McNab, don't you?'

I smiled. He was being sarcastic, of course. I had taken a beating at McNab's behest, much worse than the one I'd heard dished out to the tramp downstairs.

'Black tie is a bit formal for a police smoker, isn't it?' I said. 'I didn't think you were the stripper and stag movie type.'

'Christ knows I'm not, but it would be preferable to this. It's going to be quite a do. Frantic Frankie Findlay is appearing as a special favour. An old buddy of MacIntyre, our retiring chum, apparently.'

'Frankie Findlay?'

'I know,' Ferguson said wearily. 'But I have to show face . . .'

'This may sound strange, Jock, but could you swing an invite for me?'

Ferguson managed to look dumbfounded and suspicious at the one time. 'What, you're a fan?'

'God no. It would be good to build some bridges, make some new contacts in the force.'

Ferguson's face darkened. 'For Christ's sake, Lennox, do me a favour and don't insult my intelligence. You and I are going to have problems if you start playing me for an arse. What's your angle?'

'Okay, Jock, I'm sorry.' I could see he was genuinely angry. I told him about Tommy having a ticket stub to Findlay's show at the King's and it not making sense. 'I just wanted to see the guy up close.'

'Well, you can buy a ticket to one of his shows. There's no way I'm going to let you use me so that you can snoop around at a police function. You're pushing our friendship too far, Lennox.'

I was about to respond when Ferguson's desk 'phone rang. He

scowled at me, making it clear that he would have missed the call and would have been on his way home if he hadn't been stuck talking to me. He leaned over his desk and picked up the receiver without putting down his cellophane-wrapped dinner suit or his briefcase.

'Oh, hello, Bob,' he said, and looked at me, as if I should understand his surprise. 'What? No, I don't have any direct interest, it just came up in conversation and I couldn't remember the lad's name . . .' Ferguson listened for a while, still looking over at me and frowning. After a while he said: 'No, that was all. Just couldn't remember the name.'

After he hung up, Ferguson left his hand resting on the receiver in its cradle.

'Talk of the devil . . .' he said, thoughtfully. 'That was Bob MacIntyre, the chief inspector I was talking about.'

'The one whose retirement the monkey suit is for?'

Ferguson nodded. 'He was asking me why I'd asked for details of that boy's suicide.' His frown deepened. 'What the hell has it got to do with him? I didn't think, but there was actually no reason for him to have an interest. And Christ knows how he knew so quickly that I'd been asking.'

'He didn't investigate the death?' I asked.

'God no. Not his area. But there again, we never get to hear what his crowd are into.'

'His crowd?' I asked.

'Special Branch,' said Ferguson as he steered me to the door.

## 6

This time I knew it wasn't my imagination. The light was finally fading by the time I got back to my car and I decided to take a swing by the lock-ups down by the river. I was heading towards the Broomielaw when two cars that had been behind me turned off at Greendyke Street. And there, suddenly exposed, was chummy in the two-tone Consul. I gave no indication that I'd seen him and turned into Clyde Street. He didn't make the turn with me, and I guessed he had pulled over and was waiting for some other cars to hide behind. But it was quiet at that time of night and he clearly decided he would have to rely on distance rather than camouflage; in my rear-view mirror, I saw him take the corner about a hundred yards behind me, no lights.

I guessed he expected me to try the storage shed site again, so I decided not to let him down and headed in that direction. He was doing his best not to be seen, holding back to the point of risking losing me, his thinking clearly that he knew where I was heading and could pick me up again if he lost sight.

I decided to make things interesting for him. I indicated right, before turning up a side street. Once out of sight around the corner, I floored the pedal and accelerated as fast as the Wyvern would allow, pulling up at the kerb about fifty yards along the street. I got out and locked the car and ran back up the street, seeking out some kind of cover before chummy made the road end. The street was narrow and not residential, flanked on either side by huge sandstone warehouse-type buildings and offices, all about five storeys high. They threw the street into shadow and made the most of the gloaming. The only form of illumination was a couple of wall-mounted street lamps that gave off an insipid, nauseous orange light. There were no signs of life or light from any of the buildings and I congratulated myself on my excellent choice of ambush spot.

I was running out of time, so I ducked into the only half-decent cover I could find: a deeply recessed doorway, shaded by a heavy stone lintel and pillars on either side. It was very similar to the cover my attackers had used three weeks before. Shrinking back as far as I could into the shadows, I checked the Wyvern. I'd parked it outside the main entrance to a shut-up warehouse, making it look like I had gone inside.

And there he was. The Ford Consul, its headlights now on full, turned into the street but pulled up just inside the corner, the engine still running. The driver was obviously holding back and assessing the situation. This was clearly no dimwit.

After what seemed an age the car started moving again and slowly made its way along the street; I squeezed myself into the smallest shadowed place in the doorway as the car passed and I couldn't make out the driver, or whether there was more than one person in the Consul. It slowed even more as it passed the parked Wyvern; they were checking it out.

Thinking it through, I decided I would wait until they got out of the car, hopefully only one of them and with his back to me, then I would pull the same stunt on him that had been pulled on me three weeks before.

This time, I promised myself, I would show a little more restraint. I steeled myself for action.

The car drove on. It headed for the far end of the street, turned the corner and disappeared. So much for steeling myself. I stayed put, though, just in case the car came back. And it did. It reappeared and turned back into the street, heading towards me. I quickly shifted position so that the opposite side of the doorway shielded me but, even at that, there was a good chance I'd be picked up by the Consul's headlights. But he stopped at the other end of the street, switched off his lights and sat. No one came out of the car.

After five minutes, I saw the spark and flare of a match, then the ember glow of a drawn-on cigarette. Just one. After ten minutes, I realized my ruse had worked that little bit too well, and the guy in the car was waiting for me to re-emerge from the warehouse and drive off.

I was pretty much at a loss about what to do. Another painfully slow ten minutes passed and I stayed hidden. Thankfully, the guy in the car must have gotten pretty fed up too, because he got out and headed towards my parked car on foot. I guessed that he was on his own and that there were probably no hulking, non-smoking passengers left sitting in the car. He was wearing a narrow-brimmed hat and a lightweight summer raincoat, and I could see the man wasn't too tall or robustly built. But there was something about his movements that seemed familiar.

I decided he wouldn't present too much of a danger, especially if I caught him unawares, approaching from behind. He stopped at the Wyvern and tried the door. His back was half-turned towards me and I eased out from the concealment of the doorway and made my way as silently as possible towards him.

He leaned forwards and peered into my car, cupping his hands around his eyes and against the glass. I decided to make the most of his encapsulated attention and grab him from behind.

I closed the last five yards in a sprint and seized a fistful of raincoat and jacket collar, knocking the hat from the small man's head.

It was the shock as much as the pain.

A bolt of intense pain seared through my barely healed ribs as the small man's elbow found its mark. I realized that I still had a hold of his coat collar, but he in turn had an iron grip on that wrist.

Suddenly my feet were off the ground and swinging through air, and I found myself slamming into the greasy pavement. I came down on my back and right side and my breath pulsed out of me. He had levered me clean off the ground and over his shoulder. With rat-like speed and agility, he dropped a knee onto my chest, squeezing the last of my breath from me and leaving me sucking air desperately. Just to add to the fun, the blade edge of his hand slashed across my throat, shutting off my airway for a split second.

I no longer knew where he was or what he was doing; I made no effort to defend myself further. Every ounce of my being was focused on that single existential need: to breathe. To pull air through a constricted throat into empty lungs.

I guess he had grabbed my collar and dragged me across the pavement, because when I started to breathe more easily, I found myself propped up in a sitting position against the warehouse wall. I looked up and saw the small man standing over me, his stance one of readiness, his hands balled into fists.

'You had enough?' he asked. He had one of those working-class English accents I always found difficult to place, but

I guessed somewhere south rather than north. I nodded. It had been a long time since I'd been bested in a fight and I was struggling with the etiquette of it – and with the embarrassment of having taken a hiding from someone who looked like he should be wearing jockey silks and whipping a thoroughbred around Aintree.

Two things dawned on me. The first was I remembered where I recognized the swift, rat-like movements from: he was the same small guy I'd seen at Tommy's funeral, trying to merge into the background; the one who had asked Jennifer if Tommy had seen any of his old army comrades recently. The second was that this small, slight man had been very professionally trained and could have done a lot more damage to my throat if he had wanted to. My money was on him having been a commando.

I started to ease myself up and if I had had any remaining thoughts of resistance, he put them out of my head: he reached into his coat pocket and I found myself looking at the business end of a Webley revolver.

'We'll take my car . . .' he said with a smile that was more a rodential baring of teeth, and tossed me the keys with his free hand. 'You drive.'

## 7

'Where to?' I asked with the kind of amenability that comes from having a gun dug into the side of your belly.

'You know where to go.' He sat in the passenger seat but turned sideways, facing me.

'Just tell me where you want to go,' I said wearily. My ribs hurt like hell again and my throat still felt tight and raw. 'It's been a long day.'

'The lock-ups. Tommy Quaid's lock-up.'

No big surprise there, I thought.

'So I show you the way to the right lock-up, you get the key, McNaught clears it all out and I take a dip in the Clyde – that it?'

'Just drive.'

I did, despite the sparks and flashes that still danced across my vision. I needed to think. To work out a strategy: one where there was a future in which I would still be breathing. As soon as McNaught's henchman got the key and knew which lock-up it fitted, I would become decidedly surplus to requirements.

'Your boss McNaught. Was he in the same unit as you and Tommy? Is this what this is all about?'

My passenger remained silent.

'All of that at the ironworks . . .' I persisted. 'It was all a smoke-screen, wasn't it? There were no trade secrets, nothing to be stolen. It was just a credible place for Tommy to take a tumble. Somewhere out of the way with minimal security.' A thought struck me and with it I felt a surge of anger. 'You're pretty handy when it comes to unarmed combat, aren't you, chum? It was you, wasn't it? It was you who broke Tommy's neck on that roof, nice and clean and quiet, then chucked him over the side.'

Again the small murine man stayed silent. We were getting nearer the lock-ups and with every hundred yards we drove I felt my life shorten by a year. One way or another, I would have to make my move soon. Despite my furious strategizing, before any plan took a definite form we had already arrived at the entrance to the lock-ups. And the end of the road for me.

'Pull in and stop,' he said, jabbing me in the side with the gun. 'Over by those sheds. We need to talk.'

I did what I was told, turning into the lock-ups and pulling over into the shadow between two storage sheds. Maybe this was it, here and now. Maybe it was just the key, not the location of the lock-up, that he needed. Maybe I had already outlived my usefulness.

'You have the key?' he asked. I said nothing. He jabbed again. 'The key to the storage shed?'

I would have to make my move. Now. But if I did, there was no way I could avoid being shot, and I would need all my strength, all my skills, to take him down. This time, I'd have to be ready for his fancy moves. But first I needed him to shift the gun from my side.

'I've got it. It's in my pocket,' I said. Reach for it, I silently prayed. 'Who's McNaught?' He didn't take the bait.

'What? Who's this McNaught you keep talking about?'

'You're telling me you don't know?'

'I wouldn't be asking if I did. And seeing as I'm the one holding the gun, I don't have a reason to lie about it.'

'If you're not one of McNaught's people, who are you? Why have you been following me?'

He gave an ugly, rat-like snigger in the dark. I felt another sharp jab of the gun muzzle, making me wince. 'You really don't get this whole question and answer thing being all about who's holding the gun, do you?'

I looked at him, trying to read a face almost completely hidden in the shadows. I was confused and, given the alternative, I decided to hold back on making a move. For the moment.

I answered his question. I told him who McNaught was. I told him that I was there the night Tommy died. I told him everything. I had no other cards to play.

He listened to me in silence. After I finished, after he sat small and dark and unreadable, he said: 'I'm not who you think I am. I'm going to take the gun away, but don't do anything stupid. You got me?'

I nodded, then realizing he probably wouldn't have seen me in the dark, I said, 'I've got you.'

'My name is Baines,' he said. 'You're right about one thing, I served with Tommy during the war. We became friends. Close friends. Or at least as close as Tommy could be with anyone. We were in the same commando unit for a while. We had both been picked because of our *special* talents – Tommy because he could get in and out of almost any building undetected, me because – well, I think you've seen my special talents for yourself.'

And I had. This man was a killer – a natural viciousness and propensity for violence had clearly been honed into a professional skill by the military. It all fitted – except I couldn't for the life of me imagine Quiet Tommy Quaid being close friends with someone whose principal skill was the taking of lives with ease.

Then I remembered the conversation I'd had with Tommy. He had been disturbed by my violence and talked about a murder-eyed member of his wartime unit. I remembered Tommy had said: '*Someone who called himself my friend too.*'

'There were a lot of special units about,' Baines went on. 'Commando units dropped behind enemy lines for all kinds of reasons: sabotage, assassination, intelligence gathering. We were in the last category. Our job was mainly to steal plans from the Krauts; ideally without anyone finding out we'd been in and out. But if we were disturbed, then it was my job to deal with the opposition.'

'And you were on missions with Tommy?' I asked.

'A few. The unit we were in was headed by Captain Jack Tarnish – the hardest bastard I've ever known. Maybe even a bad bastard. Tarnish was one of those men who had been born at the right time, the type who thrived on war. He was a Jock too, like Tommy.' Baines gave another rat-like laugh. 'For some reason Tarnish took a shine to Tommy, who was the youngest of us. But it wasn't a protective thing, you know? It was more like Tommy was an investment to be looked after, like Tarnish had special plans for him.'

'What kind of plans?'

'That I didn't know for sure at the time, but looking back, and with what I've found out since, I can guess. Back then, all I knew was that there was something big about to happen – some big mission behind enemy lines. But before it came off, I was trans-ferred out of the unit. Suddenly and without any reason or warning. I ended up in another unit, a sabotage outfit. I tell you, mate, I was lucky to survive the fucking war.'

'You think Tarnish wanted you out of the picture?'

'I got the impression he was handpicking the team he wanted around him. I mean, we were already handpicked, but it was like he was fine-tuning his team. Like he had something particular in mind and maybe something that wasn't strictly kosher. About six months later, after my old outfit had carried out their secret mission that I was no longer party to, I heard these rumours about a large cache of Nazi loot going missing and began to suspect that Tarnish had used Quaid in an off-the-books job.'

'This Scottish officer, Tarnish – did he have a wound to his face?' I asked.

'No. Why?'

I told Baines about McNaught, describing his build and his lopsided face.

'No . . . that's not Tarnish. Tarnish was tall and lean. Dark hair. No damage to his face. In fact, he isn't unlike you in appearance. By pure chance I saw him shortly after the war, outside a pub in London, dressed like a country gent and with a couple of tarts on his arm. No signs of any wound to his face. Anyway, it sounds like your McNaught has a totally different build. But that doesn't mean McNaught isn't somehow connected to Tarnish. And anyone connected to Tarnish is dangerous.'

I thought about what Baines had told me. I asked the obvious question: 'So what is your interest in Tommy's death? In me? Why have you been following me all over the place?'

'Like I told you, I liked Tommy. We got on. The outfit we were in was as tough as you get and Tarnish made a habit of recruiting misfits. Some of them were probably psychopathic.'

I repressed my urge to laugh or to bring up accusations of blackness by pots against kettles. Baines must have sensed my thought in the dark.

'You maybe think that they couldn't be worse than me, but some of them were. Much worse. The one thing that held them all together was Tarnish, who seemed to inspire some kind of deep loyalty in men. Me – I didn't get it. Problems with authority and all that bollocks. That's why Tarnish had me transferred, I think. But my point is this – the story that did the rounds was that Tommy Quaid was part of this raid on some top Nazi's place in occupied France. The story goes that they got what they were after – plans or documents or shite like that – but Tommy found all of this other stuff in the safe. I don't know if it was gold or jewels or something else, but whatever it was it was worth a mint. Tommy came out a lot heavier than when he went in. Rumour has it that he didn't let on to the rest of the unit.'

'And you think that they found out?'

'If they did,' said Baines, 'and if, like you say, Tommy's fall off that roof wasn't an accident, then that would make Tarnish and the others the prime suspects in his death. In my opinion, anyway.'

'So you're not here to do the right thing by Tommy, after all,' I said. 'Just like Tarnish, you're out for looted Nazi treasure. That's why you've been following me.'

'A bit of both, if you like. If it was Tarnish who killed Tommy, then I don't want him getting the loot whatever happens and I want to get even for Tommy. And if we find the loot I'll split it with you. You can do whatever you want with your half. But I want you to know that I'll get it, with or without your help.'

'There's a flaw in your logic,' I said. 'If Tarnish killed Tommy, then he must have found out first where the loot was hidden. Otherwise he would be killing the goose before it laid the golden egg.'

'Except you have the key. And you have the shed number. And even if they've already got it, I don't want them keeping it. Believe it or not, I want to help you find out who killed Tommy. Maybe there is no loot. Maybe Tarnish went away empty-handed. But Tommy Quaid was my friend and the only person I trusted in the army. At the least I want to find out for his sake.'

I was less than convinced by the nobility of his motives, but I didn't have a gun in my ribs any more, so I played along. If we did find a cache of war loot in the lock-up, then I didn't fancy my chances of walking away with half of it, or walking out alive. For the moment, I was winging it.

'Okay,' I said. 'We split what we find. My half goes to Tommy's sister, agreed?'

'Agreed.'

I started the car, switched on the headlights, reversed out and headed down the main avenue between the sheds. They all were the same design, double-doored and a similar construction to a domestic garage, only about twice the size. I guessed you could park a truck inside each. Baines reached into the glove box and took out a flashlight. Each shed had a square wooden plaque above its doors, each plaque with a number and letter. As we crawled along, he shone the light onto the numbers. I counted down until I reached the shed number I'd been given.

'Shed seventeen, row B,' I said. 'This is it.'

I killed the lights and we got out, Baines taking back his car keys and pocketing them. The shed, like the others, was varnished almost black under layers of creosote, an angular black shadow against the lighter deep blue sky. I took the key from my pocket and Baines shone the flashlight onto the heavy-gauge padlock – new and bright against the dark age of the storage shed doors it secured. 'Not much protection if he has stashed in here what you think he has,' I said. 'A tyre lever would open this as easily as a key.'

Baines, small and dark in the night behind the glare of the flashlight, said nothing.

I took the blue-fobbed key Jennifer Quaid had given me, unlocked the padlock, hooked it back onto the loop, and swung open the double doors.

'Give me the flashlight,' I said. Baines did nothing. 'The torch, give it to me. While I look, you keep a watch for someone coming.'

He handed me the flashlight and I hoped he wasn't complying just to have his hands free. I didn't like Baines; I didn't trust him; I didn't believe the whole wartime-buddies-bound-by-hoops-of-steel crap about his friendship with Tommy. For all I knew, it really could have been Baines who had killed Tommy on the roof of the foundry.

We could be a matter of feet away from a hoard of Nazi loot: maybe the light of the flashlight would suddenly be reflected by a twenty-four-carat gold bust of Eva Braun's tits or a pile of diamond-encrusted swastikas. Then my lights would go out for good.

I shone the flashlight around the shed. Shelving units, the kind garages used to store car parts, lined the walls. A very small car sat parked in the middle of the space between the shelving units: a grey Austin A40 and the last kind of car you would expect to see Quiet Tommy Quaid driving. I guessed that, like the van on the night of the foundry job, this was stolen, renumbered and ready to provide anonymity when on his next job.

Personally, the Wyvern was bad enough: I wouldn't be seen dead in something like the A40.

The shelving units were full of stuff, very carefully arranged and organized. Boxes of small items that Tommy Quaid had obviously stolen but not yet fenced: china ornaments, low-value jewellery, three television sets and a row of radios. What surprised me was the number of tools that filled some of the shelves. By the door there were five large metal petrol cans, a kerosene lamp with spare bottles of kerosene – paraffin as the Brits called it – and stacks of boxes, dozens of boxes, all neatly arranged.

'This is going to take a while,' I said to the small dark shape at the doorway. I took the kerosene lamp, struck a match and lit it. 'I'm going to have to shut the doors over or everyone'll be able to see the light. You keep watch.' I swung the doors closed but Baines jammed a foot in so I couldn't get them completely shut.

'I'll keep an eye on you from here as well,' he said.

'Just make sure you look out for anyone coming. I have to tell you that this isn't exactly Aladdin's cave – I don't see Tommy stashing stolen Nazi loot in here.'

'Just keep looking. And don't think about playing me for an arse, mate – you find anything valuable, you'd better tell me.'

I sighed and went back to searching. The boxes were full of documents and other stuff that Tommy had stolen and obviously thought might be of some future value. From what I could see, there wasn't any single thing of great value in the storeroom, but altogether there would have been several hundred pounds' worth of stuff. Still, it was a disappointment. This didn't look like Tommy's retirement fund, and there certainly was no sign of any loot, if it existed at all, from the wartime raid behind enemy lines.

But there was enough to incriminate Tommy, and I worked out that the cans of petrol weren't just there to fuel the A40: if Tommy had had to destroy evidence in a hurry, he could set the place alight in a few seconds.

I found the keys to the A40 hanging on a wall hook. Using my handkerchief on the handles – chrome was a gift to the coppers when looking for prints – I opened the car up. Other than a handbook in the glove box and a tyre lever, jack and spare wheel in the trunk, there was nothing. I tapped the panels and they sounded hollow, the way they should have; again no evidence of Teutonic treasure packed into voids. I decided, however, to suggest to Baines that we take the A40 with us when we left and take it apart.

I turned my attention to the shelving units, working top to bottom, and along the wall from the door to the far end of the shed.

By the time I had worked my way to the bottom shelf at the far end of the storeroom, I had given up hope. I still had the other wall to do, but it didn't look promising. A last three boxes had been stuffed into the corner. I took the kerosene lamp with me to see better but also to move it as far away as possible from the gap in the doors. I took the lid off the first box and it revealed nothing more than a pile of old newspapers. I was about to move on to the next box when I decided to start lifting the papers to check if there was anything underneath.

I mouthed the word *paydirt*.

Cash. Bundles of sterling banknotes neatly fastened with rubber bands. I reckoned there was no less than a thousand pounds. The second box revealed another large quantity of banknotes, probably in the region of another two thousand, and some gold jewellery.

This, I knew, should go to Jennifer. It wasn't any Nazi loot and Baines had no claim on it, but that was where things were going to get sticky. Keeping my back to the door, I replaced the newspapers into both boxes, trying to work out what I should do next.

Baines slipped into the shed, closing the doors behind him.

'Kill the light . . .' he hissed urgently.

I did what he said, turning the flame on the kerosene lamp down low, but using the flashlight to find my way back to where Baines stood. I killed the flashlight too. 'What is it?'

'Someone's coming . . .' He opened one of the doors a crack and peered out. I could hear the sound of metal on cloth and guessed he'd taken the Webley from his pocket. I was not at all happy about that.

'Can you see—'

'Shhh!' Another urgent hiss. He eased the door closed further, a vertical stripe of pale light painted on his face. I could hear footsteps outside the storage shed. Baines eased the door fully shut.

'Looks like some night watchman or caretaker . . .' he whispered. 'If he sees the unlocked padlock . . .'

I felt my heart pick up pace. The idea of some elderly night watchman didn't scare me, but the idea of him having his rounds, and his life, cut short by a blow from Baines did. My new chum struck me as the kind of man who dealt with peacetime situations the same way he had in the war.

The footsteps passed by without pausing. After a few seconds, Baines eased open the other door, again just a crack.

'He's heading off.'

'I didn't think they had a night watchman here,' I said. 'Are you sure he's gone?'

'He's turned into the next row,' said Baines. 'Stick with the torch.' He paused a moment, obviously thinking things through. 'No, it'll be quicker if you put the lamp on again. I'll go outside and keep watch with the doors shut. If you hear me knock quietly, kill the lights again. And Lennox – remember what I said.'

'I remember,' I said. The truth was I was already concealing something from him.

Once he was outside, I went back to the far end of the shed and opened up a third box. Again there were papers on top of another small treasure, jewellery this time. That was no use to me or Jennifer. It was stolen stuff and, unlike the cash, potentially traceable. But maybe that was the deal I could strike with Baines: he takes any jewellery and gold he can find and I keep the cash for Jennifer.

I set the box down on the ground beside me instead of back on its shelf. I was about to head back for Baines, still unsure of how best to handle him, when I noticed a section of the lower wooden shelf, exposed when I lifted the box out, looked different from the rest. I couldn't make it out with the kerosene lamp alone and shone the flashlight on it. Rubbing away dust with my fingers, I could feel a joint in the wood. I took out my penknife and, jamming it into the joint, wiggled and levered the section of wood up.

There was a large, oilcloth-wrapped bundle underneath, in the three-inch-deep space between the shelf and the floor. I pulled it out; unwrapping the oilcloth exposed a thick, expensive-looking leather folio case, embossed with the initials FF. I unzipped the folio case and could see it contained a thick, five-year diary and a buff foolscap envelope. I flicked through the diary and saw it contained entries for specific dates and times, each with a row of initials next to it. Nothing written out in full. I put the diary to one side and opened the envelope, tilting it so its contents, mainly photographs, spilled out. I picked up the first photograph, a large-scale print, and angled it to the light.

'Christ!' I said, despite the need to be quiet. The image burned me; seared every detail into my brain. I felt suddenly sick. Really sick to my stomach. I looked at the second picture and felt the same physical revulsion as it branded itself forever into my recall. A third picture. There were faces I recognized. Important faces. Powerful faces. What else I saw was beyond my recognition; completely beyond my belief. Things I could not accept existed.

My head spun. I still couldn't believe what I had seen. I couldn't believe it and I couldn't understand what something like that was doing in Quiet Tommy Quaid's possession. After four years of war and thirteen years of Glasgow, I thought I had seen everything, was beyond the capacity to be shocked: but what I had just seen had shaken my world to the core.

I didn't want to look at any more of the photographs, but there were some other documents and I picked one of them up. It was a list of names and I guessed the names corresponded to the initials I had seen in the diary. Names, like some of the faces, I recognized.

I stopped breathing.

A strong arm had looped around my neck from behind and my throat and neck were caught in a vice of forearm and bicep. I had been so horribly transfixed by what I had seen that I hadn't heard him approach. It was a professional job, a sleeper hold cutting off air and blood supplies to the brain. The kind of thing they taught commandos.

Through my panic I worked out that Baines had sneaked back in behind me and was now sealing the deal the way he had planned from the start. No Nazi treasure. No loot. What I had just seen had been the prize all along: the vile, evil, loathsome prize.

I was in a fight for my life, but half that life had already been squeezed from me. I grabbed and pulled at the arm crushing my neck, reached up to claw at the face, but my attacker knew what he was doing and had his face down and tight against my neck. I slammed my elbows backwards and into the body behind me, but he held me so tight that I couldn't get enough steam behind the blows.

As I started to black out, the thought that struck me was that the arm gripping me was too heavy and muscular, the body to which it belonged too big and solid, for it to be Baines.

Sparks and flashes danced before my eyes for a moment. Then someone turned out all the lights.

# 8

I drifted from one darkness into another.

It took a few seconds for me to gather up the scattered pieces of my consciousness, a process confounded by the complete darkness around me. My first thought was that I was grateful to have a consciousness at all: a little bit more enthusiasm and that expert sleeper hold could have put me to sleep for good. And it *had* been expert.

I remembered that I was in Tommy's storage shed and fumbled about for the flashlight. The next thing to fall into my mind was the memory of what I had seen: those images. As my brain slugged its way awake, I became aware I had something in my hand, something that wasn't the flashlight. And my hand was wet. Sticky.

I called out Baines's name, but there was no answer.

With my other hand I went to take my cigarette lighter from my pocket but couldn't find it: someone had stuffed my pockets with what felt like banknotes and jewellery. Eventually I dug out my lighter and the small flame dazzled me for a moment, searing into the raw nerves of my oxygen-deprived brain. I could now see the thing in my other hand was the haft of a knife. A long, slender handle and blade created out of a single piece of metal. A Fairbairn-Sykes fighting knife. A commando knife. And the wet stickiness on my hand was blood.

Using the meagre flame of my lighter, desperately relighting it every time movement snuffed it out, I eventually found the flashlight, about two feet from where I'd come to. I swapped the lighter for the flashlight and scanned the shed. There were streaks – red-black on the pale grey cement – stretching across the floor. I followed them with the beam of the flashlight until I found their source. Baines was lying propped up against the Austin A40, his back against the front tyre in almost exactly the pose he'd propped me up in to recover my breath after he'd ju-jitsued it out of me outside the warehouse.

Except Baines wasn't going to get his breath back any time soon. Or ever.

Someone had put a knife through his neck, behind his wind-pipe, and sliced forwards and outwards. It was an old commando specialty for silencing guards. You did it from behind and they died unable to utter a sound. A quiet death. I guessed that the knife that had been used was the one I now held. And that the blood on my hands was Baines's.

I heard the faint ringing bells of police cars, some distance off. More than one. And the sound was slowly increasing in pitch.

Getting closer.

Still groggy from having been strangled half to death, I strug-gled to make sense of my situation. When I did, it didn't bring me joy. I almost felt admiration for the professionalism with which I'd been framed for Baines's murder. My assailant had used a sleeper hold to make sure there was no injury with which to substantiate my claims of innocent unconsciousness. I was in the middle of a murder scene, my pockets filled with banknotes and jewellery, my hands and clothes covered in blood, the murder weapon in my hand.

The picture it painted was so convincing I almost believed it myself: me – Lennox – a known associate of Quiet Tommy Quaid and someone of dubious morals, and more dubious connections, had come with Baines to raid the dead burglar's hoard. But there had been a thieves' falling out and I murdered my accomplice. The police would surmise that I would have gotten away with it if it hadn't been for some public-spirited – but anonymous – citizen who had made a 'phone call, probably reporting the sounds of a violent fight in the lock-ups by the river.

That was the way it had been meant to play, but it's difficult to calculate just how much pressure to apply to keep someone out just long enough for them to be caught, literally, red-handed. Too much and your victim's brain is mush, or they don't come around at all. Thankfully, my assailant had erred on the side of caution, reckoning I'd still be out or just coming round when the boys in blue arrived.

I had only minutes, maybe even seconds, to get myself out of this fix. I went through Baines's pockets, taking his car keys, wallet and lighter. I checked the lock-up as quickly as I could to make sure there was nothing else incriminating. Pocketing the commando knife, I took out my handkerchief and made sure anything else I touched didn't pick up fingerprints. I rushed to the back corner to where the leather folio with the photographs lay. It was gone. Everything else lay where it had been, but the folio and its contents had been taken.

The bells were louder now and I reckoned the police had turned into the storage yard. I hadn't time to wipe clean everything I had touched: something more dramatic was called for.

Again using the handkerchief, I unscrewed the cap from the Austin's fuel tank, took some of the old newspaper and stuffed it into the tank. I tipped over the kerosene cans and one of the petrol canisters, letting them glug their contents onto the cement floor before using the two other cans to splash petrol all over the lock-up's contents, including Baines's body, the car and the paper stuffed into the fuel tank. I sat the remaining cans and kerosene bottles next to the Austin.

Running over to the doors, I eased one open and peered out. The police bells had stopped and I reckoned the policemen, now on foot, were making their way through the yard, checking each shed as they went.

Snatching the padlock from the shed door, I stuffed it into my pocket, not having time to wipe it down. I went over to the Ford Consul and put the key in the ignition without turning it. Further back in the storage site, about a couple of rows back, I could see the beams from police flashlights probing the spaces between lock-ups. It was now or never. I took the lighter I'd found in Baines's pocket, lit it and tossed it into the lock-up.

'Sorry, Baines,' I said.

The spilled kerosene and petrol ignited. I slammed shut the door to prevent the flames lighting me up for the coppers to see and ran to the car; without switching on the lights, I turned the key in the ignition. In the silence of the night, the approaching policemen would have heard the engine and I slammed the gears into reverse, careening backwards the way we had come in. I saw the dance of flashlight beams as the coppers, maybe three or four of them, came running through the lock-ups.

I flew out onto the road, still in reverse, still with my lights out, reckoning that the chances of running into someone at that time of night were pretty remote. There were two empty police Wolseleys parked at the road end and I narrowly missed one. At that point the sky lit up as a huge bubble of flame surged from the lock-up and into the night sky. The car and the fuel cans had gone up.

My guess was that one carful of coppers would be dealing with the fire; but at least one would have by now been sent running back to the parked police cars and would be on my tail any time now. I kept the lights out and gunned the engine, ripping through empty streets and hoping to God I didn't run into anything. I took several turns and detours, then headed back towards the city centre, slowing down to normal speed and switching on the lights.

I needed to get the Consul out of sight, and soon. There was a good chance that the police hadn't gotten any kind of good look at the car, and wouldn't have been able to report a make or colour – but there were so few cars on the roads at this time of night that it made it worth their while to stop any they saw. And I didn't have a good reason for being in a car that didn't belong to me, nor any kind of explanation for why I stank of petrol and kerosene.

The answer came to me a couple of blocks past the Tavern Bar on Finnieston Street, in the unlikely form of 'Chic's Car Cavalcade'. I drove past it twice, just to make sure it wasn't guarded by a night watchman or vicious dogs on long chains. The way my luck had been going, Chic probably had his own team of commandos or paratroopers just waiting for an intruder like me to practise their strangulation skills on.

Security for most of the used-car stock, however, seemed to comprise a fence and a locked gate. No night watchman, no dogs, no commandos. There were a few cars parked outside the stock compound but out of immediate sight of the road, behind what I guessed was some kind of repair garage bay. I pulled the Consul into a space between two of the cars and switched off the lights.

I checked my watch. It was nearly two a.m. I reckoned that it would be at least six or seven before anyone turned up at the garage. Clambering over the bench seat into the back of the car, I lay down and tried to calm myself.

The smell of kerosene and petrol fumed nauseatingly in the car's cabin and I opened the window a little. The pains in my neck, throat and ribs were singing from the same hymn sheet. And loudly.

I wouldn't sleep, but at least I could rest.

Strange thing was that, even though it was a mild night, as soon as I lay down I started to shake uncontrollably. Images flashed through my head, relentlessly and vividly. I had seen a man die tonight. I had thought myself near death twice and had had the life half choked out of me. Yet none of these were the events or images that flashed through my head.

What I saw in perfectly recalled, hideously sharp, searing detail were the photographs I had glimpsed in the glow of a flashlight for only a second or two.

Images that I knew would stay with me for the rest of my life.

It was already fully light when I woke.

Unlikely as I had thought sleep, I must have yielded to the intense physical and mental exhaustion resulting from everything that had happened the night before.

I jumped up with a start into a sitting position, suddenly and completely awake, fearful that I would be discovered. But when I checked my watch it was only five-thirty a.m. I scanned the used-car lot and there was no sign of activity.

In the full light, I could now see the state of my clothes. My suit was grubby, not too bad, but the cuff of my right jacket sleeve and, more noticeably, the shirt cuff were heavily stained with blood. I tipped out the contents of my jacket pockets; whoever had jumped me had stuffed items of jewellery into them and now the rear bench seat beside me was covered with bracelets, necklaces, brooches. Gold and silver gleamed; emeralds, rubies and sapphires sparkled. I counted out one thousand, three hundred and fifty pounds in crumpled twenty- and fifty-pound notes. I separated out eight notes that were stained with blood and put them with the jewels, folding the other notes and stuffing them in my trouser pocket.

Everything else – the jewellery, the bloodstained banknotes – was useless, worthless. The surest way of getting caught would be to try to fence the jewellery or to spend the spoiled notes. Whatever I recovered, I would give to Jennifer: some small compensation for the fortune Tommy had accumulated and I had set fire to along with Baines and everything else. I felt bad about Baines's body not getting a funeral. Without the car, without his watch or wallet, and with his already meagre body more than likely shrivelled to an inhuman husk, he might never be identified.

Which was exactly what I was hoping for.

I comforted myself with the thought that going up in flames with a stash of stolen goods and cash was maybe the crooks' equivalent to a Viking funeral. Maybe Baines now feasted in a thieves' Valhalla.

I reached into my jacket and took out the Fairbairn-Sykes knife. Like my right hand, it was encrusted with flakes of dried blood. I got out of the car, checking around that I was out of sight of street and tenement, and went over to the external tap beside the double wooden doors of the repair garage. I washed the blood from my hand and then from the knife, slipping it quickly back into my jacket pocket. I scooped up handfuls and washed my face and neck, the cold water like an electric energy on my skin. I cupped my hands and drank.

Taking my jacket off, I scrubbed at the sleeve, squeezing the fabric like a sponge, the water pooling pink at my feet. I did the same with my shirtsleeve, getting most but not all of the blood-stain out. Rolling up my sleeves did something to hide the dampened stain from sight.

Jacketless and back in the car, I examined the fighting knife again. It was a genuine commando piece and when I examined the haft, I found the initials TQ embossed on it. I had to admit it was a nice touch: the perfect frame, including me being found to have killed Baines with Tommy Quaid's own service knife. It would have been almost whimsical, poetic.

I gathered up the jewels and stained cash and bundled them up in my jacket, along with the knife. Then I stuffed my jacket into the passenger footwell and out of sight.

It was a bright morning but cool. Nevertheless I drove with the window down in an effort to clear the car's cabin from the stink of petrol and kerosene, and my head from the stink of something else, something worse. I reckoned I should be safe enough – or at least safer – now and I drove north and up through Milngavie and Bearsden, stopping first at a telephone kiosk in Maryhill to make a couple of 'phone calls.

I drove out of the city, north towards Strathblane, until I found the spot I was looking for: a lay-by next to the Mugdock reservoir, the huge man-made lake that supplied the whole of Glasgow with its water. I got out of the car and into the July morning light. I smoked, looking out over the flat mirror of water and at the birds that dove and swooped across its surface, without seeing any of it.

Up here I was above Glasgow. Elevated in every sense. The huddled dark mass of the city lay below me in the Clyde valley; behind me were the moors, forests and mountains of that other Scotland. Wide, clean, open spaces without the pollution of people and all their sins.

I knew what I had to do next; I knew I would have to go back into the black heart of that city and do whatever I could to put right a wrong. The most monstrous wrong I could imagine. A wrong because of which my quiet friend had died.

But, at that moment, all I had was the overpowering impulse to 'phone Jennifer Quaid and ask her to come here to me; to tell me there was a better place in the world, and then we could drive north to look for it, away from Glasgow.

I looked at my watch. It was coming up to six-thirty and it would take a while longer for the calls I had made from the telephone kiosk in Maryhill to bring help. I needed help: I needed others to bear this burden with me. To share the horror. While I waited, I smoked through half a packet, thinking through all that had happened, regaining detail that had become lost.

I thought about Nancy Ross, about her unbidden visitors, about the way Jock Ferguson's call about the boy's suicide had stirred the interest of a retiring Special Branch officer. I also thought, with gratitude, of how Ferguson had made sure not to mention it was me who had been asking. There again, I guessed he had done that more to protect himself than me. Had that really all been just last night?

And then I thought again about Jennifer Quaid and how I really, really wanted to be with her right now.

But the thing I thought about most, the small detail that had been stirred from the deep sands of my memory and had risen, bursting to the surface, was what Quiet Thomas Quaid had said to me that night in his apartment while he expertly strapped up my cracked ribs: that he would never have children; that he would never bring a child into a world as corrupt as this.

As I expected, it was Twinkletoes McBride who arrived first. Seeing me in the lay-by, he parked his impossibly brightly waxed and polished beige-over-cream Vauxhall Cresta behind the Consul, which he looked at, puzzled, as he got out and came over to me, furrowing what little forehead he had in concern.

'What's the trouble, Mister L?' he said, and I could see his worry was genuine. 'It sounds like you's in a real *pree-dick-ahrment.*'

'It's bad, Twinkle, I won't deny it,' I said. 'But if you don't mind I'd rather wait until everyone's here – saves me explaining things twice and, believe me, I don't want to repeat this more than I have to. Did you 'phone Archie, like I said?'

'I did. He'll be here.'

After another half-hour, another gleaming piece of coachwork arrived. This time it was in a completely different price bracket: a one-year-old Jaguar XK140 roadster, gleaming black paintwork with cream-walled tyres. It looked like something out of Hollywood, as did the driver who unfolded his tall frame from the driver's seat.

Handsome Jonny Cohen was followed a few minutes later by a more conservative, far more low-rent Anglia, then a Hillman.

We sat for a moment – an unlikely assembly of Twinkletoes McBride, Handsome Jonny Cohen, Archie McClelland, Tony the Pole Grabowski and me – looking out at the quiet, deep waters of the reservoir. The sky was naked of cloud and the sun grew in confidence as the morning matured. It was the brightest of all possible days to be discussing the darkest of all possible thoughts.

'I have a story to tell you,' I said, after a while. 'I'm afraid it's not a pretty story and you won't thank me for the telling of it. It's also a story that a lot of people would kill – and have killed – to stop being told. Once I tell it to you, there are things that I will expect from each of you. But, I warn you, once you hear my story, you won't be able to unhear it.'

They said nothing.

So I told them it.

I told them Quiet Tommy Quaid's story.

# Part Four

Part Four

## 1

Surprisingly, I slept like a baby: the rest of that day and all of the following night lost in velvet, dreamless sleep. It was as if in sharing what I had seen, everything I had been through, I had shifted some of the burden off my shoulders. Maybe those I had shared it with wouldn't sleep so well now.

I had asked them to take a lot on faith. I told them exactly what I had seen, but I couldn't show them a single proof of it. I told them about a crime that would never be punished, victims who would never be believed, culprits who were beyond the law and any justice other than the most natural kind. Even if I still had the evidence, which I didn't, the police were no use; the press would be too afraid.

I had explained to Jonny, Archie, Tony and Twinkletoes that I couldn't give the names of everyone who was involved, other than the few faces I had recognized and the few names I had seen listed: politicians, lawyers, businessmen, military, police – men at the core of the Establishment. I tried to describe without being sick to my stomach the content of the photographs I had seen. As I told them, as I explained the inexplicable, their expressions changed from disbelief to disgust to anger, their faces slowly setting hard like drying concrete. I could see they believed me, despite my lack of evidence. Twinkletoes McBride in particular listened with furrowed-brow intent, as if concentrating on understanding something he could never understand.

'How young?' he had asked.

'Early teens, mostly,' I had said. 'But quite a few younger. Much younger.'

'Kiddies?' Twinkle's voice had cracked as he had said it. 'Just kiddies?'

'I think they may have been from a military school outside the city,' I had said. 'I think Robert Weston, the boy who threw himself under the train, was one of them. Or used to be one of them.'

There had been a silence as we had all stood in the light of an inappropriately cheery sun. Then I told them that I had to find where the folio of documents and photographs had come from. Tommy Quaid had obviously found them during a break-in, but I had to find out where that break-in had been. And if at all possible, I needed to get my hands on the evidence again.

'I can't believe it . . .' Jonny had said. 'On that kind of scale . . .'

'It happens.' The statement surprised us all and we had all turned to Archie.

'When I was a beat copper in Govan, there was a thing. A woman I knew had told me that she thought her wee boy had been – *interfered with* – by their local priest. She had been so afraid to tell me because you just didn't go up against priests. I asked around a bit and started to get the impression that this bastard was at it with a load of kiddies. Next thing I know, the priest is transferred to another parish, still in Glasgow, and I get the heavy word passed down from a chief inspector that it had been "dealt with" and I was to drop it if I knew what was good for me. Never forgot his name though: Father Sean Sullivan.'

'*The* Sean Sullivan?' I asked. 'The one who's up to be made a cardinal?'

'One and the same,' said Archie. 'A lot of damage the accusations did his career. So I'm warning you, Lennox – you'll never get evidence against these bastards. And, even if you do, you'll never be able to bring it to light.'

'*If* I go through official channels – which is why I've told each of you. If anything happens to me the same way it did to Tommy, I want you to do right by me the way I'm trying to do right by him. And if I can get to the bottom of it all, I'm asking something big of each of you.'

'Vaddya need?' Tony the Pole had asked.

'The people involved in this include those you might call the instruments of justice. I will come to each of you later and ask the biggest thing I could ever ask of you: to become my – to become Quiet Tommy Quaid's – instruments of justice. But I will understand if any of you feel that you can't commit to that. In the meantime, the only thing you can do for me is to help me out of this immediate fix.'

It was my partner Archie I had been most unsure of telling everything. Archie was ex-City of Glasgow Police, had always done things by the book; I had always kept him away from the Three Kings and the dodgier side of my activities – yet now I had assembled him with Jonny Cohen, Twinkletoes and Tony the Pole and laid out my plans for illegal retribution.

Archie had stood in the sun, leaning against the drystone dyke that divided the lay-by from the reservoir edge beyond, and silently taken in all I had said, passing no comment, his expression unreadable. I had told him that a man had been murdered in my presence and I couldn't prove I hadn't done it; I told him that I had committed arson and destroyed evidence; I told him that the whole thing had happened because I had accepted a job on the sly, behind his back, from McNaught.

Yet, when I'd finished my story, it had been Archie who had taken over. Like a military commander, he told us all what we needed to do.

Getting rid of the Consul was the first priority. Jonny Cohen had gone back down the road to the nearest call box. Within an hour a flatbed from one of his scrapyards had arrived and the Consul, draped in a tarpaulin, had been spirited away. Cohen knew the stakes involved and had promised Archie that nothing of the Consul would be left to go back into the marketplace. It would be broken up, all serial numbers filed off, and scattered across his scrapyards.

Like the man himself, Baines's car would cease to exist.

Baines had been a long way from home. His burned body was most likely now unidentifiable, his car dismantled and dispersed. It would take the police an age and a lot of effort to identify him, and I knew they just didn't have the attention span, patience or diligence for that.

But I knew it was Baines. And so did whoever had killed him and tried to set me up for it.

Tony the Pole had taken the Wyvern back to the Wishart Brothers and settled my account with them. 'Vee'z auld neebourz, me and zem crafty vee Vishahrd bazzdahrds,' he had explained cheerily, 'but you godda count your fugging fingerz avder you zhake zeir handz, make sure you get zem all back.' And now my Sunbeam Alpine, washed and polished as promised, sat in the car park outside the apartment building.

The only hint that Archie didn't fully trust his new criminal fraternity chums had been his insistence that he dispose of the bloodstained money and jewellery. Fetching from the trunk of his car the canvas bag that held the wheel jack, he stuffed the money and the jewellery into it, adding a few stones for good measure. He walked to the edge of the reservoir and, swinging his long arms several times before letting go, threw the weighted bag as far out into the reservoir as he could.

'Just hope we don't get a drought any time soon,' he had said lugubriously when he returned.

Jonny Cohen had driven me home in his Jag sports car.

Both Tony the Pole and Twinkletoes McBride had volunteered to set up camp in my living room, but I assured them there was no reason to believe I was in immediate danger: whoever had put me to sleep in Tommy's shed would have been long gone before the uniforms arrived, and would assume that I was now sitting in a cell, enjoying the bruising hospitality of the City of Glasgow Police. It was, of course, only a matter of time before word got out about the fire and the fact that no one had been taken into custody.

The truth was, if my suspicions were correct, they had at least one high-placed contact inside the police. The same contact who had made sure a patrol car and uniforms were on hand the night of the foundry job. But I sent Twinkle and Tony home, nevertheless. I'd be putting theirs and Jonny's skills to use – much better use – but that would have to wait a while.

In any case, I had the Walther P38 pistol, along with a box of ammunition, that Handsome Jonny Cohen had given me. Jonny had also volunteered to station a couple of guys close to the telephone kiosk on Great Western Road from where they would have a view of the entrance to my apartment building. Like I had done with Twinkle and Tony, I had declined but reminded Jonny I would be expecting more – much more – from him later.

When it came down to it, I wasn't at all sure that they – whoever they were – would come after me now. I really wasn't that much of a threat. I had nothing on anyone; all I could go to the police with was my memory of the photographs I'd seen and some of the names I'd seen listed. It meant nothing and I could just as well be making the whole thing up: I didn't have the photographs any more and I didn't have the list.

For the moment, I was chasing shadows and they were chasing me back.

Having seen what I had seen, and who I had seen, I also figured that taking suspicions or even hard evidence to the police – even to a copper I trusted like Jock Ferguson – would result in nothing. Or worse: like me meeting with the same kind of tragic, fatal accident as Quiet Tommy Quaid.

Except, I promised myself, I would go anything but quietly.

My doorbell rang.

I picked up the Walther and snapped back the carriage to put a round in the chamber. I opened the door a crack, keeping it on the chain.

'Irene?'

'I've been trying to get you on the telephone.' Her expression was one of impatience. 'Come on, let me in. I havnae got long.'

'Give me a minute . . .' I said. There was a shelf at the bottom of the full-length hall mirror, and beneath the shelf a concealed drawer; I opened the drawer and slipped the Walther into it before easing the door closed, taking off the chain and opening the door to let her in. She was wearing a white collarless blouse beneath a black and white houndstooth suit – bolero jacket and a pencil skirt that was hugging her ass possessively. Irene stepped close and I could smell the mixture of perfume and her own earthy scent.

'What's with the chain on the door?' Her expression conveyed puzzled suspicion. 'And why have you no' been answering your 'phone?'

'Long story.' I had taken the telephone off the hook so I could sleep, but I didn't feel like a long explanation; in any case I wasn't in a position to give one.

'Has it got anything to do with George?'

'George?'

'George. My husband, George.' She was annoyed now. She pursed her full, lipstick-crimsoned mouth.

I shook my head. 'No. Why should it?'

'He's still acting odd. More so than ever. Still as moody as hell and looks at me all funny.' She tilted her head and smiled wickedly. 'But let's no' waste time. I didnae come here for marriage guidance.'

I stepped back when she moved even closer to me.

'What's wrong?'

'It's not a good time, Irene. I'm sorry.'

She looked past me along the hall. 'You got someone else here?' she asked. There was no anger, no jealousy; only a vague annoyance like she had turned up at the hairdresser only to find her appointment double-booked.

'No,' I said. 'There's nobody here.'

'Then what's the problem?' She smiled seductively again and took a step forward; I took a step back; we were only a couple more off a waltz. The truth was I didn't know what the problem was. A little feminine comfort would have gone a long way, but it felt *wrong*. For a moment, I stood a little dazed by the concept of *wrong*, like a caveman catching his first ever glimpse of fire.

'I think we should stop seeing each other, Irene,' someone said and I realized it was me.

'Why? What's the problem?'

The concept *wrong* became the word *wrong* and sat clumsily in my mouth, for the moment unuttered. 'I don't know . . . I just can't do it any more.'

She looked at me for a while, as if trying to work me out. 'You do know I'm not looking for anything from you, don't you, Lennox? This is just a wee bit of fun. It doesnae hurt anyone.'

'I'm not so sure that it doesn't, Irene. There's your husband, if he ever found out. Anyway, it isn't fun any more. At least not fun for me. It feels wrong.' And there it was, spilled out from my mouth.

Now she was annoyed, I could tell. She didn't say anything more, simply nodded brusquely, turned and left.

After I closed the door behind her, I thought about what had just happened: I had acted on a decision I didn't know I had made. Why I had made it was puzzling me, but I guessed it had something to do with having delved into Quiet Tommy Quaid's life. The thing I had found about good men, living or dead, was that they had an irritating habit of infecting you with their sense of right and wrong.

There was that, and the fact that I seemed unable to stop thinking about Jennifer Quaid. Whatever the reason, I strangely had no regrets about ending my relationship with Irene. Well, perhaps one: when I thought back to her houndstooth-hugged ass as she'd turned and left.

I 'phoned Jennifer at her hotel. There was something about the sound of her voice – even with the concerned tone it carried – that seemed to ease me. I told her to check out of her hotel and

I would pick her up there in half an hour. She began to ask questions, but I told her to do what I asked and I would explain it all when I collected her.

I took the Walther and Tommy's Fairbairn-Sykes knife from the hidden drawer under the hall mirror, tucking the pistol into my trouser waistband, at the small of my back. There was nowhere convenient for me to carry the knife without it jabbing through fabric or into my flesh, so I wrapped the blade in a makeshift sheath of two handkerchiefs and placed it in my jacket outer pocket.

I slipped on my suit jacket and looked at myself in the full-length mirror, not seeing myself but thinking about how the weapons I was carrying were enough to put me in prison for a long time. And I was carrying them with a willingness to use them.

Then I did see myself in the mirror. It made me think back to what I had said to Quiet Tommy Quaid about watching Saturday matinee Westerns at the Capitol picture house in Saint John. Cheering the good guys, booing the bad.

The guy in the mirror was a good-looking, bad-looking man with raven-black hair and a face that was all sharp angles. The Jack Palance look. Jack Palance acted in Westerns.

And he never played the good guy.

For some reason, I acted on another decision I didn't know I had made: before I stepped out through the door, I took the gun from my waistband and the knife from my pocket and put them back in the drawer.

# 2

Jennifer's hotel was in the West End, so it wasn't far from my apartment. As I drove my distinctive Sunbeam Alpine along Great Western and down Byres Road, I still checked to see if I was being followed, but not as often as I had before. I now knew that the people I was dealing with were pros, all right, and I guessed if they wanted to find me, they'd find me. In the meantime my priority was to get Jennifer to safety.

She was waiting in the foyer. Dressed in a floral frock with a tight bodice and a pleated skirt, she had her hair up and fixed with a clasp. I felt a strange sensation in my chest when I saw her, which was anatomically considerably north of where a pretty girl usually provoked a reaction.

'You look terrible,' she said. 'Are you all right?'

'It's been a tough couple of days.' I picked up her suitcase. 'Let's go get some lunch.'

I took Jennifer to a tearoom whose decor, menu and waiting staff looked like they'd remained unchanged since Violet Gibson had taken a potshot at Mussolini's nose. But unlike our last venue, this was a friendly place, and I chatted to Jennifer about the weather, about how it was different where I came from in Canada, about how much better this tearoom was than the last one we'd been in, about a place like it in Saint John I used to go to with my folks when I was a kid . . .

As she listened to me rattle on from one inconsequence to another, her frown and her confusion intensified.

'What's going on, Mr Lennox? Why did I have to leave my hotel so suddenly? And why do you look like you've been through the wars?' Her tone was insistent: these were demands for hard facts, not expressions of idle curiosity.

I sighed and looked out of the window. We were that little bit out of the city and everything looked brighter, cleaner, the colours more vivid. There was a small, immaculately ordered and tended garden beyond the window, the grass neatly cut, roses and rhododendrons parading with military precision. Years past of tending for the years to come. It was the badge of a normal life where you plan and plant for a future season. At that moment, it struck me as exactly the way people should live their lives. Exactly the way I should have lived my life.

'Lennox,' I said, turning back to her.

'What?'

'Call me Lennox. Not "Mr Lennox". Everybody calls me Lennox.'

'What about your first name?'

'I lost it. Dropped it somewhere in the war. Like I say, everybody here just calls me Lennox.'

'Okay, *Lennox* . . .' I could tell from her tone that she was losing patience with me. 'What about answering my questions?'

I looked at her. The light was catching the hints of bronze and gold in her hair, tracing the soft curve of cheek and jaw, dropping a sparkle into the blue-green eyes. She looked back at me frankly, but just like the first time we had met I thought – I hoped – there was a hint of something else there.

'I'll tell you,' I said. 'But first, can we just have lunch together and pretend for a moment we're regular, ordinary folks?'

She must have seen something in my expression or in my eyes – the terrible weight of it all – because she smiled and nodded.

So I talked and she talked back. We talked all through lunch. We got to know each other at the same kind of accelerated rate people had during the war, when tomorrows were uncertain and time was precious. Maybe it was the tragedy that had brought us together and the danger that bound us, but we each opened up our lives and laid them out for the other to see. It was the oddest of things and in that unexpected blossoming of intimacy we genuinely forgot how and why we had first met.

As our lunch drew to a close, I told her I would like to get to know her better and asked her, when this was all over, if it ever were to be all over, if she would consider seeing me again. She smiled more and said she would like that.

Afterwards, sitting in the Alpine in the car park, I told her what she needed to know. She cried for a while and I comforted her.

'I was forced to burn down Tommy's lock-up,' I explained. 'Whoever attacked me and killed Baines took the folio with the evidence in it. There may have been other information there that could have led me to Tommy's killers. I'm sorry, but I had to do it.'

'I understand,' she said. 'They were trying to frame you for Baines.'

'There's more – there was several thousand pounds in there. Money Tommy had saved and that should have gone to you. It went up in the blaze as well.'

'That doesn't matter to me,' she said. 'You did what you had to do. The important thing is you got away free and clear.'

I reached into my inside pocket, took out an envelope and handed it to her.

'What's this?'

'There's a little over a thousand pounds in there. It's all that I got away with. Actually, my chum with the beefy arms must have stuffed it into my pockets when I was out for the count – another part of the frame-up. So I can't even claim the credit for rescuing it.'

Jennifer looked at the envelope as if it were something contaminated, then handed it back to me. 'I don't want it.'

'This is Tommy's money. It belongs to you.'

'It's stolen money. And it's blood money. I want nothing to do with it. I'm glad the rest went up in flames.'

I could tell she meant it. I slipped the envelope back into my pocket. 'I'll keep it for you, in case you change your mind.'

Then she asked the question I hoped she wouldn't ask. 'The photographs. What was in them that was so terrible?'

So I told her. I sat staring out of the windscreen, not looking at her, and told her exactly what I had seen. Once more Jennifer cried and I comforted her.

When she was finished, I started the car and we drove down to Newton Mearns.

In keeping with Handsome Jonny Cohen's movie star looks, he lived with his wife and kids in a huge, modernist sprawl that would have looked more at home in Hollywood than Newton Mearns. The house – designed by some London architect who had since become a 'name' – sat elevated with a view out over its neighbours and the countryside beyond. It certainly was a lot of real estate and as I swung the Alpine up the long, sweeping driveway, I reflected on how I was going to have to break the whole *crime doesn't pay* thing to Jonny.

The man who answered the door was tall, dark-haired, with a cleft in his chin that would have made Cary Grant feel inadequate. Jonny Cohen really was absurdly handsome and, despite being a crime boss and erstwhile armed robber, he had the kind of look you instinctively trusted.

His wife joined him and they both beamed a welcome at us. I did the whole introductions thing for Jennifer's benefit. It was all very suburban and our conversation was light and unburdened by the weight of what we were really doing there. The only hint of something other than a social call had been the couple of Jonny's heavies we'd passed on the drive who did their best – which wasn't that good – not to look conspicuous.

Jonny and his wife left Jennifer and me alone in the marble-floored hallway while I took my leave of her.

'You'll be safe here,' I said. 'Once I get things sorted out, we can get you home, or wherever you want to go.'

'Wherever I want to go?'

'You said you were thinking of moving out of London. Maybe now's a good time for a change of address.'

'I think a change of address is something you should think about too,' she said. 'This is all too dangerous. If I'd known, I would never have got you involved.'

'You didn't get me involved: I was already involved. I was set up for this long before I met you. And anyway, I'm doing this for myself, for Tommy.'

'Are you sure you can't just go to the police? That's their job. That way at least you wouldn't be putting yourself at risk.'

'There are coppers involved in this. Probably at a high level. Going to the police would only put me at more risk not less. I'll be fine. The Cohens will look after you. They're good people.'

'Didn't you say he was an armed robber?'

'And Tommy was a thief, but still one of the best men I've ever known. These *are* good people. The people I'm up against, the people who arranged Tommy's killing, are the ones who are supposed to be good. The ones we're supposed to look up to and trust. Tommy was right: the world is absurd.'

'Look after yourself,' she said.

I looped my arm around her waist, pulled her to me and kissed her. It took me as much by surprise as it did her. Then she kissed me back.

She was still standing in the doorway as I headed back down the drive, passing two Jewish thugs in forty-guinea mohair suits, pretending to be gardeners.

It was another Clydeside summer's day sketched out in charcoal against a bright sky. Oblivious to the sunshine, the dark finger of pier stretched out into the even darker Clyde. Jock Ferguson was waiting at the end, as I had asked him to. He was staring down into the river and when I came to stand beside him I followed his gaze. The stone pier sank into water dressed in a dark rainbow sheen of slicked engine oil; a scurf of brownish-white froth marked where greasy stone and greasy river met and outlined boat-washed tangles of floating, half-rotted wood. The skeleton of something iron-framed jutted rust-boned out of the water.

'It never ceases to amaze me,' he said without greeting.

'What does?'

'The stuff that finds its way into the river. Do you see it?'

'What? That rusting metal thing?'

'No, next to that, just under the surface. You can just make it out and no more . . .'

I leaned forward and peered into the water. The sunlight bounced off its oil-sleeked veneer. 'I can't see anything, Jock.'

'Look . . . there . . .' he said impatiently and pointed.

I saw an indistinct shape, angled in the water. It took me a while to make sense of its dark geometry, but attached to it further down, barely perceptible and streaked with grime and algae, I made out the vague pattern of a keyboard.

'Shit . . .' I said. 'An upright piano?'

'Like I say, it never ceases to amaze me what gets dumped in the Clyde. All kinds of secrets.' Ferguson turned to me pointedly. 'You're someone who has a lot of secrets. I sometimes wonder how many of them you've dumped into the river. I tell you now, Lennox, this had better be good. And why all this cloak and dagger shite?'

'I need you to get me into that police smoker.'

Ferguson made a point of looking startled. 'You amaze me, Lennox. You really have the brass neck to ask that again? I gave you my answer and I gave it to you pretty clearly, as I recall.' He turned and started back along the pier.

'I'm not asking, Jock,' I said. 'I'm telling you I need you to get me into that smoker.'

He turned, his face suddenly stone-dark like the pier. 'You fucking what?'

'I need you to listen to me, Jock, because I'm not going to say this again. You'll either help me or you won't. I am keeping you in the dark about something – but I'm not keeping you in the dark because I'm up to something shady, but to keep you safe. I know you suspect I'm halfway crooked and most of your colleagues think I'm all the way crooked, but I'm telling you I really am on the side of the angels with this one. Whatever suspicions you may have about me, you must have seen something worthwhile to recommend me for the bank run. I'm asking you to trust me again.'

His expression changed and he came back to stand beside me. 'What have you got yourself into, Lennox?'

'Something big and something that stinks. Something rotten. And there's a good chance I'll not come out of it breathing.'

'Has this something to do with Quiet Tommy Quaid?'

'The less you know the better, trust me. I'm asking you for a favour, Jock. Maybe the last I'll ever ask you. I need you to do me this favour and answer a couple of questions. After that I need you to forget everything I asked of you. The favour I need is for you to get me into that police smoker.'

'And your questions?'

'Okay . . . I'm guessing me telling you that I'm into something big isn't news to you – you already know I've attracted heavy attention. I need you to tell me the truth, Jock: when Archie and Twinkletoes do the bank run again this week, they don't have anything to worry about with that blue van that followed us last time, do they? You know damned well it wasn't full of armed robbers.'

Ferguson looked at me for a moment, his expression unreadable. 'Yes. Yes I do.'

'Special Branch?'

He shook his head. 'Not our lot. But it was a Home Office registered vehicle. Like I said, London. I got a shout from upstairs demanding I explain why I was asking about that registration number. I had to tell them the truth: that it had been spotted following a cash van and was suspected of carrying armed robbers. I was told in short order that there was nothing to worry about and to drop the subject pronto if I knew what was good for me. They didn't exactly give me the "matter of national security" shite, but it was implied.'

'Trust me, Jock, this has nothing to do with national security.'

'Then what has it to do with? You asked me to trust you, why don't you trust me?'

'Because you're a good man. The same way Quiet Tommy Quaid was a good man. The problem with you good men is that you always try to do the right thing – or worse, the right thing in the right way – and that could very easily cost you your career or even your life. I'm afraid the only type of man who can deal with this is someone who is a little bit rotten inside. Someone who can do the right thing in the wrong way. We both know that's me. And if it turns to shit . . . well, let's face it, I'm not that much of a loss to the world.'

'For Christ's sake, Lennox—'

'Can you get me into that smoker or not?'

'What are you going to do there?'

'Don't worry, nothing dramatic. I'm just going to be there. Show face. Trust me, that'll be enough.'

'Okay. I'll get you in. Do you need anything else?'

I handed Ferguson a note with a date on it: it was the same date as the show for which Tommy had had a ticket stub.

'I need to know if there were any break-ins that night,' I said. 'Either private residences or commercial premises – but you can ignore anything low-grade. I'm talking about something worthwhile being taken or the victim being someone important.'

'So this *has* to do with Quiet Tommy Quaid?'

'Will you check it out for me or not, Jock?'

He looked at me in that odd blank way of his, then nodded. 'Anything else?'

'There's a guy calls himself McNaught – although if that's his real name mine's Mitzi Gaynor. Military type, probably ex-officer. Built like a brick shithouse. The most noticeable thing about him is he has a facial wound, probably picked up during the war – makes his face look lopsided. Ring any bells?'

Ferguson thought for a minute. 'None. Do you think he's police?'

I shook my head. 'If he is, he's of the secret variety.' I found myself using the same vocabulary as Nancy Ross. 'But again not local Special Branch. I suspect he's connected to my pals in the blue van. But I get the odd feeling he is unofficial – some kind of independent dirty-tricks contractor, but he's tied in with the powers that be, that's for sure.'

'Is that what you're telling me? That your opposition in all this is "the powers that be"?'

'People connected to them, yes. But I need you to believe me that I'm the cowboy wearing the white hat here. Crimes have been committed, Jock. A series of the worst kind of crime you can imagine – crimes that *are* punishable under the law, except they'll never see the light of day. And it's people in positions of authority who have committed them. They're beyond your reach. Beyond the law.'

'Nobody's beyond the law.'

I gave Ferguson a you-really-can't-be-that-naive look and his assurance withered under it. He stood silently watching the oily rainbow swirls on the water for a moment. 'Are you telling me there are City of Glasgow Police officers involved?'

I sighed. 'You don't want me to answer that. I won't answer that.'

Again he stared silently down at the water.

'Looking for the rest of the orchestra?' I asked.

'No – just for what'll be left of my career if you screw up.'

'I wouldn't worry, Jock,' I said. 'If I screw up, I'll be down there keeping it company.'

## 3

Sometimes it's the silences, the spaces between the words, you have to listen to. A cold shiver had run through me when Jock Ferguson had talked about secrets I might have dumped in the Clyde: there was one for sure, a big secret from a couple of years back, and I wondered just how much Ferguson knew, or suspected, about that sunken secret. The main thing was that he hadn't challenged me about, alluded to or otherwise mentioned the fire in the lock-up and the done-to-a-crisp remains found inside. It wasn't there in his words and it wasn't there in the spaces in between.

The fire and burnt corpse down by the Clyde were an obvious connection for him to make, but only if ownership of the storage shed could be traced back to Tommy Quaid; knowing Tommy I guessed that, when he had rented the storage unit, he had made sure to brush his footsteps very thoroughly from the sand.

Ferguson was a difficult man to read. I trusted him – but I trusted him only as much as I could trust a policeman, and it worried me what his copper's instincts would do with the vague ghosts of truths I had given him. I was testing his loyalties: he had worked out that there were police officers involved, but knew they were involved in something so corrupt that I was prepared to risk my neck over it. Whatever happened, I just hoped Ferguson had the sense not to stretch his own neck out too far.

Despite it now being the start of August, Glasgow, as was its wont, had grown bored with summer and decided to try out a different season. It became suddenly cooler but remained muggy, and Glasgow's sky took on its customary pallor: a sheet of pale grey in which clouds had no individual form was pulled over the city like a shower curtain. Every now and then, thick globs of viscous rain were spat against the Alpine's windscreen.

At least, I thought as I drove out of the city and southwards into Ayrshire, the weather is becoming more sympathetic to my mood.

Sometimes, if you wanted something to happen, you had to give the world a bit of a helping hand; give a little push to get things rolling.

It was time to let the dog see the rabbit.

St Andrew's School was about twenty minutes south of Ayr on the coast road. It sat on the edge of a bulge of land that shouldered its way into the sea. The drive had taken me an hour and a half and would have been pleasant if the weather had been in the same mood of only a day before. As it was, the greens of the Ayrshire coast and the blues of the sea had been muted to greys by the opaque sky and a thin coastal fog.

The school was set against the backdrop of the Firth of Clyde and the distant, southern tip of the Isle of Arran. That should have made it an appealing locale, but it was set against a backdrop of the Firth of Clyde and Arran in the same way Castle Dracula was set against a backdrop of peaceful mountains and woodland. The dark grey building looked more than forbidding: it was as if its Victorian architect had been briefed to scare the bejesus out of any poor kid unfortunate enough to be sent there. Five storeys high with baronial-type towers at each corner, the school sat square and fort-like, with its back turned to the rippling grey shield of sea; I couldn't work out whether the imperative had been to keep strangers out or keep its inhabitants in.

The school was poised on an oblong hillock that looked unnatural, like some huge burial mound. A broad expanse of playing fields sat on the flatlands to one side; on the other side scattered copses of meagre trees stood unconvinced between rolling, grassy dunes, as if considering moving inland where their roots would find more substance to hold on to.

There were only four other cars sitting outside the main entrance, suggesting there must be a car park for staff somewhere out of sight. The school was five miles from the nearest settlement in either direction, its only near neighbour the broken-toothed ruins of a coastal castle, and I guessed that most of the school's staff would probably live in during term time.

Before I got out of the car I took a leather satchel briefcase out from where I'd stuffed it under the passenger seat: having it gave me a more official look, added to which was that I had a couple of things in it I didn't want to leave unattended.

Standing outside the car, I could smell the ocean's ozone breath in the air. It was a smell I associated with the sunshine of childhood summer days on the Bay of Fundy and it seemed completely out of place here, as I looked up at the grey fortress of the school against the insipid sky.

I felt suddenly isolated and despondent, as if I was suddenly a thousand miles from civilization – although I put a lot of that down to being in Ayrshire.

The main entrance opened into a large hall that, in true Scottish institutional style, managed to combine the baronial with the municipal. It was empty of people and I had to scan the signs on the burgundy-varnished oak doors before I found one that said *SCHOOL OFFICE*. I knocked and went in. A pair of horn-rimmed glasses scowled at me.

'Hello,' I said with my disarming Canadian cheeriness, 'I'm here to see Mr Moncrieff, the headmaster.'

'Is *Major* Moncrieff expecting you?' She had short curly hair, and the horn-rims sat on a nose that was on the pug side of retroussé. In her late forties, she exuded all of the furious sexual repression of the eternal Miss.

'Yes,' I smiled. 'Yes he is. I have an appointment. I'm *Captain* Lennox.'

She scowled at me again, or maybe it was just the same scowl from a different angle, turned on her heel and disappeared into the hall.

A couple of minutes later she reappeared. 'Follow me,' she said dourly, and led me briskly along the hall, rapping on another door.

She swung the door open on command and held it for me to enter. Moncrieff welcomed me with one of those weary 'I've got much more important things to do than talk to the likes of you' smiles – and shook my hand. A small, balding, overweight man of about fifty with a military-style trimmed moustache, there wasn't much of an academic air to Moncrieff. Despite the military tache and title, he didn't much look like a man of action either and I reckoned him for the type who'd seen the war out from behind a desk.

I examined him closely to see if he corresponded to any of the images seared into my brain during its brief exposure to the photographs. He didn't; but that didn't mean he wasn't involved.

'Please sit down, Mr Lennox.' He sat behind his huge desk and I sat opposite him. 'It wasn't very clear from your telephone call . . . what exactly is your interest in Robert Weston?'

'Robert was a pupil here, I believe. A boarder.'

'That's correct. We have no day-boys or -girls here; everyone boards. But Robert left St Andrew's over a year ago.'

'Do you know what happened to him – after he left, I mean? Where he was living and what he was doing?'

'We take great care to make sure all our former pupils are placed. Most, it has to be said, follow our advice and go into the services. It is my belief that the forces can offer a true family to those who have lost their own. But Robert didn't want that. He was living in lodgings in Glasgow and we found him a place at a technical college there. Architecture, I believe.'

'Have you any idea what could have driven him to do what he did?'

'As I said, Robert left a year ago and, tragic though his accident was, it really has nothing to do with St Andrew's. Anyway, you haven't answered my question, Mr Lennox: what is your interest in young Robert?'

'Suicide.'

'What?'

'You said Robert Weston's death was an accident. It wasn't: it was suicide. And my interest is because I'm investigating another suspicious death and there's a chance the two may be linked. In fact I'm pretty certain of it.'

'Oh? In what way linked?'

'That's exactly what I'm trying to establish. And it's also where you can perhaps help me.'

'I don't really know how I can.' He frowned. 'You said that you were looking into *another* suspicious death. Surely, tragic though it was, there can be nothing suspicious about Robert's suicide?'

'Robert committed suicide, all right. There's no doubt about that. What interests me is *why* he killed himself. What, and who, drove him to it.'

'You think someone drove Robert to take his own life?'

'I'm sure of it. What I'm trying to understand are the circumstances surrounding his death: the people and events. The other death I'm investigating is tied into those circumstances.'

'If there's something suspicious about either of these deaths, shouldn't the police be involved?'

'Oh, the police are involved all right. The authorities. Let's just say I'm assembling a case that may be of interest to the appropriate parties.' I let it sink in for a moment. 'What can you tell me about Robert? What kind of boy was he?'

'There's not much to tell, if I'm honest. We never had any trouble with him, if that's what you mean. He was quiet. Kept himself to himself but otherwise contented. We never had any cause for concern – either about his behaviour or his mental wellbeing. It has of course to be said that Robert was an orphan and that in itself can lead to a profound sense of isolation. Ultimately depression. But a great many of our pupils are orphans and we are experienced in dealing with the problems that can attend. As a former pupil and outside the school, poor Robert was also beyond our pastoral care. Perhaps if—'

'Did he have many visitors?' I cut Moncrieff off and his expression conveyed that he wasn't used to being interrupted.

'As I explained to you, Robert was an orphan. He had no other family, immediate or otherwise, as far as I am aware.'

'That's not the kind of visitor I'm talking about. Did anyone else ever have any kind of – I don't know – any kind of *interest* in Robert?'

'I'm afraid I don't quite—'

'Any benefactor, or any other adults with an interest in him.' I now didn't just have my head above the parapet, I was standing on top of it, waving red flags and shouting *come and get me*. Moncrieff was trying awfully hard not to understand my meaning, but, as someone unused to having his authority challenged, his dissimulation was clumsy.

'No. Robert never received any other visitors.'

'Did he ever go on trips out of the school?'

'Trips?'

'Oh I don't know . . . to Edinburgh. Or Glasgow. Places where he might have met with other people. Maybe a school outing with other pupils. Theatre outings, perhaps.' I paused. 'Comedy shows . . .'

'No.' It wasn't an answer; it was intended as a punctuation mark. A full stop.

'I see.' I leaned back in the chair and rode the silence for a second.

'Well, Mr Lennox, if that's everything.' Moncrieff started to rise; I stayed glued.

'It's just that I thought he might have had other visitors. Or maybe he was close to a particular member of staff. Your pupils come mainly from military families, is that right?'

'That's correct.' Moncrieff was standing now, making no sign of sitting back down. 'We don't charge fees and are funded principally by a joint-services charity. A benevolent fund. We get some funding from the churches as well.'

'Your staff also generally have army backgrounds, I believe.

You don't by any chance have a member of staff by the name of McNaught?'

'We do not.'

'I've maybe got the name wrong. A burly chap, ex-military type. He has a war wound on his face, makes it a bit lopsided. Does that sound like anyone you would know?'

'No, Mr Lennox, it doesn't. Now I don't want to be rude, but I am very busy.'

I stood up. 'Well, thanks for your time.'

'Sorry I couldn't have been more helpful,' he said, singularly unapologetically.

'I wouldn't say that.' I smiled.

To make the point he walked me out of his office, along the hall and out of the front door. Behind us an electric bell trilled harshly and there was the echoing sound of many feet in transit. I noticed it was unaccompanied by the usual raucous noise of temporarily released youth.

'Your pupils seem very disciplined,' I said as I put my hat on.

'It's a virtue we impress on them,' Moncrieff said. 'We try to engraft the values of both collective and self-discipline. As you pointed out yourself, we are very much of a military tradition at St Andrew's. Good day, Mr Lennox.'

'Kids like that,' I said thoughtfully, looking up at the grey milk sky, 'I guess they don't like to complain. Good at following orders – I suppose they'll do pretty much anything their elders and betters tell them.'

Moncrieff said nothing.

'That must make them pretty easy to control. And I would imagine make things very easy for you, Mr Moncrieff.' I opened the car door. 'Well, thanks for your time.' I got in the Alpine and drove off. I could see Moncrieff standing on the school steps watching me all the way down the drive to the coastal road.

I had shown the dog the rabbit. Given the world a push. It was now only a matter of time.

I was almost disappointed by their predictability. It was early evening by the time I got home to my apartment; it had been thoroughly but discreetly gone over. They had done their best to cover their tracks, but I had left little traps: a hair stretched across a door jamb, a book set at a perfectly memorized angle, a puff of talc on the kitchen floor, that kind of thing. They would have been able to take their time: I had 'phoned in advance to make my appointment with Moncrieff, so they would have known for sure when they could turn my place over and I wouldn't be there.

They weren't that good, though. I had always thought that the hidden drawer beneath the hall mirror's shelf was really the result of bad design, rather than deliberate concealment. Whatever the original intention, you wouldn't know it was there unless you looked for it. And my secret visitors *had* been looking but hadn't found the drawer. Maybe McNaught and his people weren't the same, highly professional official snoopers who had turned over Nancy Ross's.

Even if they had found the drawer, they would have found nothing in it. Expecting their visit, I had transferred the gun and knife to the leather satchel briefcase, which had lain stuffed beneath the passenger seat of the Alpine while I'd travelled down to St Andrew's School. My new-found morality notwithstanding, I had thought it best not to leave them in the apartment – and given the fact I was doing all I could to force their hand, there was always the chance that they might have tried to put an end to my snooping on the lonely ribbon of coastal road as I drove home.

I looked at the gun in my hand for a long time before I put it and the commando knife back in the drawer, along with my remaining blue-tabbed key: the one for Tommy's apartment.

I hadn't been to the apartment yet. I would get round to it, but I knew that Tommy wouldn't have left anything of any significance lying around – a lesson that my anonymous guests had just learned in turning over mine. In any case, I had the key by accident, rather than Tommy's design.

After I freshened up and made myself a sandwich and a coffee, I rang Cohen's house and asked to speak to Jennifer. We talked for half an hour, neither of us making reference to the situation we were in, other than when she asked if the journey to and from Ayrshire had been okay. Otherwise, we talked the same way we had in the tearoom: about everything and nothing and I pretended I was something like a normal guy and lived something like a normal life. Talking to Jennifer cheered me up, but when I put down the receiver I felt hollow and dark, like a room where window shutters had suddenly been closed on a sunlit day.

Archie 'phoned about nine. Not much sunlight there – but it was odd how his voice always sounded a little younger and less lugubrious when you couldn't see the doleful eyes and undertaker face. One thing I did notice in his voice was a chord of concern. He was 'phoning, he explained, to find out how I had gotten on at the school, but I could tell he just wanted to check I was back and in one piece.

I gave him a breakdown of everything Moncrieff had said, and hadn't said. Then I told him that they'd been through my flat when I was away.

'Do you want me to come over?' he asked, the chord of concern pulled that little bit tighter.

'No, I'm fine. What you can do for me tomorrow is to get down to the registry of companies and see what you can find about the trust that runs St Andrew's School. Who's involved in it.'

He said he would, told me to take care, and hung up.

I turned in early. I had a big day ahead of me. I switched the light off and lay in the darkened bedroom smoking a cigarette, but I felt restless, itchy. I abruptly stubbed the cigarette out, switched on the light and went through to the hall mirror.

I lay back down and switched off the light again and fell swiftly asleep, aided by my comforter of a Walther P38 next to me on the nightstand.

# 4

It was a different type of operation to the Wishart brothers' set-up. There were no cars for sale, no phoney glitz, just an oily dark cavern of brick garage with a single inspection pit and stacks of car parts and tyres. I had followed Tony the Pole's lead – aided by some additional information supplied by Jonny Cohen – and found my way to the garage in Partick. Tony the Pole had suggested in eloquent Slavic-Celtic that I 'ca' canny' – meaning I should take care. Not that I was to expect Davey Wilson to be dangerous either personally or in criminal connections: he was as straight and honest as his brother was quite the other thing. Tony's advice for caution was because Davey Wilson was very protective of his brother – and Jimmy Wilson was very skilled at keeping himself hidden. If I handled it wrong, Jimmy might just dig himself deeper into his burrow and never be found.

I parked across the street and watched for a while: I could see in through the double-width doorway that there were two men working in the garage, both dressed in mechanics' overalls. One was young, maybe eighteen, and I guessed he was the apprentice. The older man was about forty and moved slowly but purposefully with quiet method from car to bench to parts shelves. As he worked, Davey Wilson had the quiet ease of someone content with his lot, who had found his place in the world.

Watching him was like looking through a window into a different universe, a world of quiet acceptance and contentment that misfits and outsiders the likes of me or Tommy Quaid would never understand.

I waited for the rhythm of a regulated life to take its course: at five-thirty the younger man changed out of his overalls, emerged from the garage and left for the evening. The older man came out a few minutes later, dressed in a battered tweed jacket and corduroy trousers bagged at the knees.

I got out of the car and crossed the road. Wilson had his back to me and was pulling down the garage's shutter-style slatted metal door.

'Hi,' I said. 'Davey Wilson?'

He turned, the door half-closed. Up close I could see he was nearly the same height as me, maybe a couple of inches shorter. He was lean and wiry with hair that might have been blond in childhood but had dulled as he had grown up, as if losing interest. His eyes were a grey-blue colour.

'I'm just closing.' He stated the obvious. 'Did you want to book your car in?' He looked me up and down, then across the road at my gleaming, one-year-old Sunbeam Alpine, doing a quick calculation. His sum clearly totalled *gangster*. I could almost hear the rattling of chains as a mental drawbridge was pulled up.

'My name is Lennox.' I smiled as ungangsterly a smile as I could summon. 'I'm looking for your brother Jimmy. It's very important that I speak to him.'

'I've no idea where he is.' The greyish eyes frosted. 'You're obviously no' the polis, so what's it to you? Why do you want to know? What do you want to talk to Jimmy about?'

I cast an eye up and down the street, checking no one who might have been following me was watching. I regretted it right away, realizing it must have made me looked shady – *shadier* – to Wilson.

'Listen, believe it or not I'm here to help. I know Jimmy's in a bit of a spot.' I nodded to the garage beyond the half-closed roll-down door. 'Could we talk in private? I'm here to help . . .'

Davey Wilson took a moment to think about it, still apprais-ing me. He still looked suspicious, rather than aggressive or tense. He shrugged and ducked under the half-shut door, back into the garage.

The couple of inches or so of difference in height caused me to duck more to get under the door, something he had been counting on. I felt a boot pressed against my shoulder and sud-denly I was on my side on the oily garage floor. It had been a shove, rather than a kick, and when I looked up Wilson had a heavy wrench clutched in his right fist, raised as if ready to bring it down on my head. Except he didn't and he wasn't going to. He'd clearly caught up on the whole aggressive and tense thing, but this was as far as it was going to go.

I'd been in scrapes with a lot of men and you can tell the ones with the killer instinct – with my kind of fury or Baines's kind of professional cool. There were the others who were scared, the ones who cowered and took it. Strangely they could be danger-ous too: if by chance they suddenly found themselves with the upper hand, they were terrified of losing it, beating their oppon-ents until they were incapable of re-turning tables and hurting them. Fear can be more deadly than anger.

And then there were the types like Davey Wilson: the think-ers. In a fight, you can't afford to think; or at least think about anything beyond the fight itself. You have to be committed to win; your head has to be totally in the moment. I could see that Wilson's head was dealing with cause and effect, action and consequence. He stood with a lump of metal in his hand that could send me to the hospital or the graveyard and he knew it. Wilson was of the type that really didn't want to hurt their opponents and would fight only if pushed.

I started to get up and he tensed the arm with the wrench in it. 'Stay where you are,' he said. 'Move and I'll batter you.'

I held one hand up appeasingly as I eased myself into a sitting position. Examining the elbow of my suit, which had taken most of the force of my fall, I sighed: it had a thick black streak of motor oil on it. Another suit ruined. I decided I was going to start a new trend in enquiry agent workwear: dungaree overalls and a fedora.

'Take it easy,' I said wearily.

'I'll take it easy when you bastards leave my brother alone. I've told you I don't know where Jimmy is, and even if I did, I wouldn't tell you. Now get in your fancy car and fuck off back to whoever you work for. Tell them to leave Jimmy alone. He's no threat to anybody.'

'Who is it you think I work for?'

'I don't know who you work for. I don't know why you've got Jimmy so scared. But I'm telling you to leave him alone.'

'Has there been anyone else here, looking for him?'

'It's time you got on your bike.' He braced the arm with the wrench again.

'Okay, okay – I'm going. Take it easy.' I stood up and tried to brush down my suit. I pondered on why everybody seemed to feel the need to hit me, kick me, strangle me or otherwise do me bodily harm: I maybe just had that kind of face.

'Just get out and don't come back.' Davey Wilson kept the wrench raised as if ready to strike.

'I'm going,' I said, again holding up my hands appeasingly.

Wilson did his best to look resolved and not relieved. I made my move. As I passed him, I crossed one of my appeasingly held-up hands and snap-punched him in the face twice in fast succession, with my other hand grabbing and twisting the wrench free from his grasp. I followed up with a jab into his midriff that robbed him of his breath and any fight that was in him. It hadn't taken much and I was sorry that I'd had to lay hands on him at all: the poor guy wasn't a fighter and had just been looking out for his brother. Unlike when I'd been jumped in the street, I'd given this small workmanlike beating without heat; probably with the same amount of passion with which Wilson would have carried out an oil change. As he doubled over I grabbed him by the shoulders and eased him over to the work-bench, leaning him against it.

'Listen, Davey,' I said calmly but firmly. 'I don't want to hurt you and I wouldn't have if you hadn't been waving big chunks of ironmongery at me. And I sure as hell don't want to hurt your brother. I'm here to help him if I can. I have a pretty good idea about the kind of mess he's in and the people he's up against. Now – can we talk this through quietly without you waving tools or car parts at me?'

He glowered at me. 'And if I don't tell you where he is, you're going to try to beat it out of me, is that it?'

I picked up the wrench and handed it back to him. 'Would you feel better if you had your comforter back? I guess I couldn't make you tell me anything that would endanger your brother and, in any case, I have no intention of trying. I understand why you don't trust me. Believe me, I've had people come to me claiming to be one thing and they turn out to be the other.' I took out my silver pocket case, took out a cigarette then offered the case to Wilson. He glowered some more but then took one. I lit us both up.

'Listen, Davey, I was a good friend of Quiet Tommy Quaid and all I'm interested in is getting to the people who killed him. I think I know why they killed him and I think it's the same reason they've maybe been looking for Jimmy. But they got what they wanted. The evidence. So my guess is that they're not going to make a big effort to find Jimmy, but it's still best that he doesn't make it too easy for them to find him.'

'So why do you want to talk to him?'

'I need to know who and where the evidence came from. I have a pretty good idea, but I'm guessing Jimmy can tell me for sure. I also need him to tell me as much as he can about anything else that could help me.'

'And you expect me just to tell you where to find Jimmy?' There was more suspicion forced into the question than was in his expression.

'Not at all. What I want you to do is to tell Jimmy who I am – Lennox – and that I was a friend of Tommy's, and everything else I've told you. Tell him that I'm looking for an officer type with a lopsided face who may or may not call himself McNaught. And tell him that I know that the whole malarkey about Tommy Quaid and Nazi loot is being used as a smokescreen – that I know what Jimmy and Tommy found and the names they found involved in it. Then – and only then – if Jimmy's okay with it, we can meet. I'll meet him anywhere and at any time he chooses. Does that sound fair?'

'How do I get in touch with you?'

I handed him a business card. 'I've written my home 'phone number on the back.'

'You're a private detective?' He frowned as he read the card; I heard drawbridge chains rattling again.

'My interest in this is personal, not professional. Although

I am looking into it for Tommy's sister as well as for myself. Trust me, I have a lot of personal interest in getting to the bottom of why Tommy was killed.'

'I told you I don't know where Jimmy is.' He held the card back out to me. It was a gesture as unconvincing as his spanner waving and I made no effort to take the card back.

'Maybe you don't,' I said. 'But keep that just in case he gets in touch. Jimmy needs all the friends he can get and, believe me, I *am* a friend.'

I had meant every word of what I had said to Davey Wilson. But I was, it has to be said, a less than trusting soul and while I hoped Davey would arrange the meeting, I decided to take a belt-and-braces approach.

After I got back into the car I made a big show of driving all the way down Crow Road to Dumbarton Road, then turning towards the city. I swung the next left and, putting my foot down, hooked back round until I was parked at a junction where I had a clear view of the garage across the street.

The shutter door was still only half-closed and there was no sign of Davey. On the sign above the garage was a business telephone number and I had seen a wall 'phone when I'd been inside talking to him. My guess had been that he would have 'phoned his brother as soon as I had left and there was always the remote chance that he would head off to see him face-to-face, leading me straight to Jimmy and saving me a lot of time and running around.

Davey Wilson reappeared and drew down the door, locking the padlock. Wherever he was headed, I was going to stick to his tail. Hopefully I could be discreet enough: Davey had commented on my 'flash' Alpine and he would be watching out for someone following him.

He was making his way over to his car when a Jag saloon and a Rover P4 pulled up fast into the forecourt. Davey turned, surprised. Two pairs of oversized shoulders got out of the Rover and moved purposefully across to Davey and flanked him. I could see right away that they were helpful types: they grabbed Davey by the elbows and guided him back over to the garage with such helpfulness that his shoes didn't touch the ground.

The driver of the Jag got out and leisurely crossed the forecourt, saying something to Davey and indicating the closed door of the garage. He was shorter than the other two but very solidly built and carried the air of authority. He had a hat on and from a distance you couldn't see the lopsidedness of his face. But I recognized him.

It was McNaught, all right.

## 5

I reversed the Alpine a few yards, hiding it behind the shoulder of a tenement. Cursing the nobility of my motives in leaving the gun and knife back at home in the drawer, I got out, went round to the trunk and took out the Alpine's tyre lever.

By the time I was back around the corner, everyone except one heavy had disappeared back inside the garage and the door had been closed. Avoiding the guard goon's eyeline, I headed down the street in the opposite direction from the garage before crossing the road. Two doors down from the garage was a cheerless-looking pub, its doors closed till opening time, and I slipped up the alley beside it and into a high-walled backyard. A stack of metal beer kegs against the yard's back wall served as steps and I climbed over, dropping down on the other side.

The lane I landed in, as I had guessed it would, ran along the back of the pub, its two neighbouring tenements and the garage beyond them. I ran along it until I reached the back of the garage building, which had no doors directly onto the lane. The garage's back joined seamlessly to a six-feet-high perimeter brick wall that ran around the yard and forecourt; I used the full width of the lane to take a running jump and managed to hook my elbows over the top without dropping the tyre lever and haul myself up and over the soot-grimed wall. The logic of having a tailor run me up some dungarees was gaining appeal as my day progressed.

I was now at the side of the garage and was able to work my way around without McNaught's burly lookout spotting me. I tried to stay close to the wall, but had to weave in and out of piles of tyres and exhaust pipes leaning against it. Coming to a metal-framed window, I had to duck down. Hazarding a quick look through the grimy glass, I could see that McNaught and his other heavy had Davey Wilson hemmed into a corner. He didn't look like he'd been worked over, but he didn't look like they'd dropped round for high tea either. Coercion and threat, of one form or another, hung over the snapshot scene. McNaught said something to the heavy, then turned and headed out of my sight. I heard the door roll up, McNaught say something to the man he'd posted on guard, then the door closing again.

There was the sound of a car starting and driving away. I guessed my opposition had just been reduced by a third.

I edged to the corner of the garage, took a breath and swung around it.

'Hello,' I said cheerily. 'I'm from the better business bureau . . .'

The heavy at the door was built like a weightlifter, was taller than me with a busted nose and red hair cropped short. He looked surprised for a split second, then took a step towards me, recovering his air of authority.

I swung the tyre lever hard and it made a crunching contact. Feeling Quiet Tommy Quaid's ghostly hand on my shoulder, I had deliberately avoided the goon's skull, where I could have done potentially lethal damage. Instead I hit the side of his face, simultaneously depriving him of his air of authority, along with his consciousness and several teeth on the right side.

At least he would now have more in common with his boss, McNaught.

The big guy went down like a felled redwood and I took true Canadian pride in my lumberjacking skill. I crouched down over him and rifled through his pockets, hoping that no one passing along Crow Road, from where the front of the garage was clearly visible, would notice. He was carrying nothing in his pockets in the way of an official ID or that otherwise suggested he was police or from any other official bureau. And anyway, he looked wrong to me for a copper, secret or otherwise: he had more of the dodgy hired muscle look about him. I did, however, feel a bulge under his jacket, tucked beneath his left armpit.

'Naughty, naughty,' I said as I slipped the revolver out of its holster. The heft of it in my hand, I had to admit, felt good. He had started to gurgle on blood and teeth, so I dragged him to one side and propped him up against the garage in a sitting position. I could have done more for him, but he and his pal indoors had the type of beefy arms that had sent me bye-byes in Tommy's lock-up and I was running low on the milk of human kindness.

I checked the forecourt: the Rover P4 was still there but the Jag, presumably with McNaught in it, had gone. I rattled the metal door by knocking on it lightly a couple of times, reckoning goon number two would think I was goon number one. I switched the gun to my left hand and readied the tyre lever in my right.

As I had hoped, the other heavy opened the shuttered door, sending it rushing upwards with a hefty push. His arms were still raised and would have blocked the same kind of round-house swing I'd executed on his pal. I also noted he was even bigger and tougher-looking than his pal, so I brought the lever down hard onto his forehead, deciding to shelve my newly found consideration for my fellow man. There was a gout of blood and he clutched his head with both hands. Dazed, he obligingly leaned forward and I hit him again, this time on the back of the skull, not hard enough to risk killing him, but hard enough. He wished Vienna goodnight and dropped. I threw down the tyre lever and switched the revolver to my right hand. Davey Wilson looked stunned, his mouth open.

'You okay?' I asked.

'I'm fine. But I'm glad you got here when you did. He was about to start work on me. Christ – have you killed him?'

'Where did McNaught go?'

'Who?'

'Their boss.'

'Oh . . . he told that one,' he indicated the muscleman on the floor, 'to get me to tell them what they wanted, then cleared off. He didn't say where. No . . . wait a minute . . . he did say something about seeing them "back at the warehouse".'

'Did he say if he would be coming back here?'

Davey was staring at the unconscious goon, shock beginning to take hold. I snapped my fingers in front of his face to bring him back.

'Davey, stay with me. Did McNaught say if he was coming back here?'

'No. But it didn't sound like he was.'

'What did they want from you? To find out where Jimmy is?'

'Aye. I wasn't going to tell them anything. I think they would have killed me.'

'If you'd told them what they wanted to know they would have killed you anyway, then Jimmy. What I want to know is why they're being less cautious. They went to a great deal of trouble to stage Tommy's death as an accident. Now they're getting plain sloppy.'

'They seemed to think that Jimmy's got something that they'll do anything to get hold of. Something Quiet Tommy Quaid gave him.'

'And does he?'

'Not that I know of. But whatever they think it is Jimmy's got, they're desperate to get their hands on it.'

'Did they say what it was?'

'No. All they wanted to know was where to find Jimmy. That one' – he indicated the unconscious man – 'asked their boss if he wanted them to search the garage, but he said "it wouldn't be here". Whatever "it" is.'

I thought about what Davey had said. What I had seen briefly in Quiet Tommy's lock-up was the kind of dynamite that those involved would go to any lengths to retrieve. But they *had* retrieved it – and had probably by now destroyed it. Everything that had happened, everything Davey was telling me, suggested that it hadn't been the whole picture.

They were desperate because they hadn't got everything back.

'We need to get tidied up,' I said. 'The other monkey is outside . . . let's get him into the garage and shut the door – ideally without half of Partick seeing.'

Once we'd got the other guy inside, I went over to the wall telephone and dialled.

'Who are you calling?' asked Davey.

'Housekeeping . . .' I said.

By the time Twinkletoes McBride arrived, the first of McNaught's men was fully conscious, but had no fight in him. And unless he had always possessed the ability to talk round corners, I'd badly dislocated his jaw with the tyre lever. He sat leaning forward, allowing the blood to flow from his mouth where his teeth had shattered. I could see he was in a lot of pain.

I had done that to him: despite my good intentions and promises of a new start, I was back in the dark. Maybe I really was one of that type who Quiet Tommy had described that night.

The other heavy worried me even more. He too was propped up against a bench, his head also sagging forward, but he was still out for the count and breathed with a loud, harsh stridor like heavy snoring. I could see that Davey Wilson, already shaken up, was really disturbed by the man's condition. I wasn't too happy about it myself, but at the moment, I was more concerned about getting information out of whichever of the goons was capable of talking. Davey was also a little taken aback by Twinkletoes, whose recent presence seemed to fill the space inside the garage. I could see Davey trying to work out if he should offer him a chair or one of the hydraulic ramps.

'What's to do, Mr L?' asked Twinkletoes, looking at the two men on the floor. 'Looks like you's been busy.'

'Just keep an eye on these two, Twinkle. I'm going to bring my car round front. I need to go somewhere with Davey here, but I'll talk to you before I go.'

At that point I heard another car pull up in front of the garage. I took the revolver from my waistband and went over to the door. There were a couple of rattling knocks then a voice.

'Lennox, open up . . . It's me, Jonny . . .'

I opened the door to reveal Cohen and two of his men.

'Thanks for coming, Jonny. Things have gotten messy . . .' I indicated the two injured goons with a nod over my shoulder. 'Let me just get Davey here into the car. I'll be back in a moment.'

Crossing the street, I went around the corner to where I'd left the Alpine parked. I drove back round to the front of the garage and ushered Davey Wilson into the passenger seat.

'We're going to see Jimmy. Okay?'

He nodded.

'Wait here. I'll be right back.'

I went back into the garage, leaving Davey in the car. I knew he was very uneasy about what had happened and I needed him not to hear what I was about to say to Twinkletoes and Jonny. I didn't want to hear it myself: the thing with the two heavies, no matter how many times I ran it in my head, always only ended one way.

I took Jonny and McBride to one side, leaving Jonny's men to watch the injured goons.

'This is a mess, guys.' I kept my voice low. 'Tweedledum and Tweedledee here are McNaught's men. They were going to beat where his brother was out of Davey. I'm pretty sure that if they'd succeeded both Wilson brothers wouldn't see the sun come up tomorrow. I clobbered that one' – I pointed to the still unconscious goon doing the laboured breathing – 'a bit too hard. He needs serious attention.'

'You don't seriously expect us to take him to hospital?' Jonny asked, although I could see in his expression that he already knew the answer. I didn't say anything, but held Jonny's gaze. 'Okay, Lennox. I'll take care of it. What about your pal out there?'

'He'll be happy for the problem to go away, but I won't tell him how.' I looked down at the unconscious man and felt like crap. Jonny and the other two Kings had shares in a meat processing plant with an industrial rendering machine. Quite a few embarrassments had been dealt with that way and I had become circumspect where I bought my meat pies.

'The other one?' asked Jonny.

I turned to McBride. 'Twinkle, I hate to ask you to do this. I know you've been trying to put your past behind you – and you know I have too – but I really need the guy with the busted jaw to talk. Or at least to write down what I need to know. Do you understand?'

'It does put me in a bit of a moral *dial-emma*, Mr L, but I know you wouldn't ask if it wasn't important.'

'It is, Twinkle. It really is.'

'What do you need him to tell?'

'Where I can find their boss. He said something about a warehouse. I need to know where it is. He called himself McNaught, but I need to know his real name and who he works for. Most important, I need to know where to find McNaught, where this warehouse is.'

Twinkletoes nodded his Easter Island head thoughtfully. 'I'll see what I can do.'

I turned back to Cohen. 'These people are connected to something big. We're playing for high stakes, Jonny. After the other guy tells Twinkle what I need to know . . .'

Cohen nodded. And there it was: it had been a brief, business-like conversation. I hadn't even put a square of black silk on my head as I had condemned two men to death.

I headed out to the car without looking back. As I did, I heard Twinkletoes give instructions to Cohen's men.

'Switch on some machinery. Something loud. Then take his socks and shoes off – I need to find a pair of bolt cutters.'

As Jonny Cohen pulled down the garage door, his handsome face stone-set with resolve, I got into the car where a shaken Davey Wilson sat, started the engine and drove out of the forecourt.

I stopped and switched the engine off before I turned onto Crow Road.

'Fuck it,' I muttered.

'What's the problem?' asked Davey.

'The problem?' I said bitterly. 'The problem is something Quiet Tommy Quaid gave me. A conscience. Wait here – I'll be right back.'

I went back to the garage. After I'd talked again with Twinkle-toes and Jonny Cohen, I headed back to the car.

I turned to Davey Wilson when I got in. 'Where to?' I asked. 'Where do I find Jimmy?'

## 6

I knew Jimmy Wilson was desperate, was in terrible fear for his life and willing to go to any lengths to stay safe. But I hadn't known just how desperate and to what terrible lengths: he had chosen to hide in Paisley.

Davey broke the news after we left the garage. He asked if we could stop at a 'phone box on the way so he could make a call to Jimmy to tell him we were coming and to stay put, and another to his apprentice to let him know to keep clear of the garage for a couple of days.

When he got back to the car he told me that Jimmy was okay and would be waiting for us. Davey explained he had rented a small house on the outskirts of the town, paying a couple of months in advance, in cash. He told me it wasn't a bad place and, most importantly, it had a telephone. The landlord had been amenable to a no-paperwork, cash-on-the-table arrangement – mainly because Davey was paying way over the odds – and had no idea what his new tenant's real name was, and he had never clapped eyes on Jimmy. The landlord would be back at the beginning of the next month, however, to collect more rent.

'So there's no way anyone else knows Jimmy's there?' I asked.

'No. Just me. I go down roughly once a week with groceries.

Different times and I'm always careful to make sure I'm not followed.'

I nodded, deciding it wasn't helpful to point out just how experienced in this kind of thing our opposition was, and just how inexperienced Davey was. It didn't matter, anyway: if McNaught had known where Jimmy was hiding, then he wouldn't have set his boys on his brother to beat it out of him.

The two injured heavies were obviously on Davey's mind as well.

'Those men back in the garage ... What is going to happen to them?' he asked, as if uncertain he wanted to hear the answer. 'You hit that one pretty hard.'

'Harder than I meant to ... but don't worry, my friend has a contact, a dodgy doctor whose lost his licence. He's going to get him to fix them both up on the quiet. They'll be *encouraged* to tell us where their boss is, then they'll be kept on ice until we find McNaught and persuade him to leave your brother alone,' I said.

It was the truth: before leaving, I had gone back into the garage and asked Jonny Cohen to get Doc Banks to look them both over – Banks was a struck-off medic Cohen used occasionally and who would do anything to pay for his next drink. I'd also asked Cohen to keep both men alive and suggested to Twinkletoes McBride that he use threat and persuasion rather than a boltcutter pedicure to get the information we wanted.

McBride had been relieved, but still willing to do whatever was necessary. Cohen was less pleased.

'I don't know if the one you clobbered is going to make it,' he had said. 'If he doesn't, his pal could put a rope around your neck – and it's not just your neck we're talking about: these bastards have seen me, Lennox. And they've seen Twinkletoes.

And you know that if they turn out to be in any way official, I won't let them simply walk away.'

'Just keep them locked up for now, Jonny,' I had said. 'We'll work it all out later. Truth is I don't know what we're dealing with, but my gut tells me that McNaught and his boys are unofficial. The kind of fringe scum for hire called in for dirty tricks and clearing up messes.' As I had been leaving, I turned to Cohen and added: 'My time as a life-taker is over, Jonny. The deeper I sink into this mess, the more determined I am to come out with my hands clean. Put it down to the Quiet Tommy Quaid philosophy of life.'

'And a lot of good it did him,' Cohen had said.

As we drove through Paisley, I exercised the same kind of caution that Davey had taken when making his weekly grocery deliveries, taking lots of unnecessary detours to make sure we hadn't been tailed. The cottage was on the south side of the town.

Paisley was famed as Scotland's biggest 'town', not having had its official status elevated to that of a city. Part of the reason had been its sudden and unexpected growth.

Personally I could never see the appeal of Paisley pattern, although I guessed that in Scotland it had a special utility: a fabric design singularly suited to hiding drink and vomit stains. But when fat little Queen Victoria had decided to start wrapping herself in Paisley pattern, there had been an explosion in worldwide trade in Paisley shawls. Although named after the town, Paisley pattern was basically an Indian design; but one of the boons of having had an empire was that you could steal without consequence anything you had a mind to, including intellectual property.

Traditional cottage weavers couldn't keep up with sudden, unexpected demand for the shawls and new mills had been hurriedly built, workers had flooded in, and the town had swelled. A hundred years or so on, just as suddenly, mass shawl production was out and mass unemployment was in, and the town had gone into steep decline.

Any hopes of revival had been kicked into touch after the war with the arrival of new synthetic materials from abroad: the final death knell for many of Paisley's mills had been rung with a pull on a nylon rope.

Commercial history wasn't something that was usually at the front of my mind, but when we arrived at the cottage, Paisley's rise and fall were writ large right there in front of me.

The small cottage Davey had rented for his brother, set a little back from a B-road, was timeworn dark, but well maintained. Low roofed, small windowed and stone built, it was clearly more than a century old and I guessed it had originally been both home and workplace to a weaver when the industry had been cottage based.

But it was the small house's backdrop that provided the starkest reminder of Paisley's unfulfilled ambition. The lane that led to the cottage from the road continued on past it until sealed off by heavy, galvanized steel gates. Beyond the padlocked gates sat the corpse of a vast mill building: a former thread works, Davey told me. The mock-Italianate grandeur of the high, square tower, the high chimney and the cantilever-roofed halls was fading fast: the walls scabbed where the white paint had flaked from the masonry; the windows shattered to black sockets – probably with stones hurled by locals in bitter spite of a pledge broken.

The mill spoke of the end of a story, a future promised but

unfulfilled – it was exactly the same story I saw coming to an end at the foundry in Possilpark and the shipyards in Govan: factories, steelworks, mills and mines built to supply an empire that wasn't there any more. It had been all so predictable but no one seemed to have been able to predict it. I decided I'd suggest to the tourist board that they use the mill scene for a postcard, along with the slogan: *Welcome to Scotland; the place is fucked.*

To be out of sight of the road, I parked on the small square of garden at the back of the cottage.

Jimmy Wilson didn't look much like his brother. He was small and dark but did have something of the same wiry build, although in Jimmy's case it tended to the slight. His complexion was noticeably pale – which, in Scotland, was saying something – accentuated by unruly dark hair that was in need of a cut and the blueing of his unshaven jaw. He had an infectious nervous energy about him: his movements spasmodic, his eyes continually darting, his thin fingers continually twitching. It made him look like some kind of prey animal constantly watchful for predators.

Which, of course, was exactly what he was.

I knew Davey had 'phoned his brother to tell him we were on our way, but I had expected Jimmy Wilson to be alarmed by my presence; to be mistrustful or suspicious. He was none of these things. If anything, he seemed relieved, almost grateful to see me.

'Tommy Quaid told me about you,' he said smiling and shaking my hand. His handshake was weak, his hand soft and slightly damp. Everything about him seemed a little wraith-like and it disturbed me, as if there was already the touch of death on him.

'He did?'

'He told me that you were the one person I could trust . . . other than Davey here. He said that if anything happened to him, that I was to get in touch with you.'

'Why didn't you?' I asked.

'I was scared. I knew they'd come after me too and I had to get away as quickly as I could. I holed up in a lodging house in Edinburgh for a week while Davey got this place sorted out for me. It isn't the first time I've had to lie low, but I couldn't use any of my usual places. I couldn't get in touch with you without coming back to Glasgow and I knew if I did that I'd be putting myself back out in the open.'

He led us into the small, low-ceilinged kitchen, filled a kettle from an ancient brass tap and placed it on the gas stove. Davey and I sat at a wooden table so scarred by time that, if it had been round, I would have said King Arthur had held his weekly get-togethers around it. The whole cottage was like a speck of eighteenth-century dust missed in the sweep of industry that had brought its larger, now abandoned, neighbour. Jimmy brought the tea over to us, his acts of hospitality carried out with the same twitchy nervousness.

'For you to be so scared,' I said, 'I guess you don't believe what happened to Tommy was an accident?'

'I know it wasn't. I know it has something to do with the job we did together.'

I nodded. 'Tommy didn't fall off that roof. Someone broke his neck and threw him off. Tell me about this job you did with Tommy.'

'It was this big house in Hyndland. Huge place – must've belonged to someone minted. Tommy knew it was going to be empty, but needed someone to watch his back and help with the alarm. I did my time as an electrician in the shipyards, so that's my speciality: alarms.' He said it with the same pride he would if he'd just announced he was an Olympic athlete. 'I wasn't in it for a cut, just a straight fee. That way I got paid whether or not we came up trumps. Tommy was always fair to deal with. If it was a good haul he would give me a bonus, even though we'd already agreed the fee. He was always good to me that way, Tommy was.'

'Whose house was it?'

'Tommy didn't say – he just told me he knew it would be empty and that he had good info that there would be a lot of cash and probably a decent haul of jewellery, which there was. But I don't know who owned it. Sorry.'

'That's all right, Jimmy. I think I know whose house it was. Can you remember the address?'

'No' the number, but it was in Langdyke Avenue. Big Victorian place on the corner. It has a huge garden with one of them weird trees in the corner. You know, what do you call them? . . . Aye, a monkey puzzle tree, that's it. The only one in the street.'

'So you dealt with the alarm and you and Tommy broke in . . . but the cash and the jewellery weren't all he found, were they?'

'No.' Jimmy frowned. 'There was a safe, hidden behind a dummy bookcase. You wouldn't have found it if you didn't know it was there – but Tommy went straight for it.'

'How did he know where it was?'

'Tommy didn't share trade secrets. But however he found out, I don't think anyone told him – or knew they had told him, if you know what I mean. He swore blind to me that only him and me knew we was doing the job. He was an expert at getting information on jobs without anyone knowing. That was one of the reasons he was hardly ever caught.'

'So what was in the safe, other than the cash?'

'There were these documents. Two ledgers and a leather case thing – like a big writing case or wallet. Tommy decided to take them to look at later.'

'*Two* ledgers?' I asked.

'Aye. And the leather document wallet.'

'Did you see what was in the document case?'

'No. We didn't have time. Tommy had a rucksack with him and stuffed everything into it. He was working to a timetable, you see. He told me he knew exactly when the owner was likely to be back.'

'You're sure there were *two* ledgers?'

'Aye – I remember one was fancy. Bound in red leather. All fancy.'

'And you never saw what was inside the document case?'

'No. Like I say, Tommy didn't look in it at the time either. It wasn't until the next day that he got in touch. He told me to meet him on Glasgow Green, which was an odd place for him to pick but he said we shouldn't be seen together or meet in any of the usual places. When I did meet him I could see right away something was wrong – that he was really upset about something. And you knew Tommy – he was never usually up or down.'

'Did he say why he was taking precautions?' I asked.

'He said that there had been something terrible in that case we'd robbed and that we could be in trouble – real danger – because of it. He said there were people would do anything to get it back. But he told me not to panic – no one knew we was involved and if it stayed like that we'd be okay. I could tell he was worried though and really upset, like I said. It was then that he told me that I should lie low for a while – and if anything happened to him, I was to make myself really scarce. Make sure no one could find me.'

'And get in touch with me?'

'And get in touch with you . . . He said you would know what to do.'

I sighed, wishing I shared Tommy's confidence in me.

'He also said I was to give you this . . . I've been hanging on to it since.' Jimmy held out a white dish of a palm; in it was a Yale key with a blue tab exactly like the other one I'd had. This time there was nothing written on the tab.

'Do you know what it's for?' asked Jimmy.

'Yep.' I took the key and looked at it. 'I already had one. It's for Tommy's lock-up where he stashed the stuff. Burned to the ground now. Thanks anyway.' I bounced the key in my hand then put it in my pocket. 'I know you didn't see the contents, but did Tommy tell you – I mean when you met him the next day – did he tell you what was in the document folder?'

'No. I asked him, but he said it would be much better for me if I didn't know. Safer. Whatever it was, I've never seen Tommy so wound up. Even on a job he was always calm – but whatever he'd seen in that wallet had shaken him right up. When I met him he looked like he hadn't slept since the job. But he just wouldn't tell me what was in the wallet. He did say that it had a lot to do with high-ups – you know, people in power. Do you know what was in it?'

I nodded, trying to block the images that flashed across my brain. 'I've seen it. Consider yourself lucky you haven't. But whoever it was stolen from has it back.'

'What was it, Mr Lennox? Government secrets?'

I gave a bitter laugh. 'You could say that – but not in the way you think. Anyway, Tommy was right, you're best not knowing.'

'That's what I don't understand,' he said, pleadingly. 'I don't know nothing about what Tommy pinched from that safe.

I don't have it and I don't know what it was. All I had was that key – and you say they've got back whatever it was in Tommy's lock-up anyway – so why are they still after me?'

'You said there were two ledgers. I found where Tommy had stashed the stuff, but there was only one ledger along with the document folder. That's why they're still after you . . . they think you must have the other ledger. The one you said had a red leather binding.'

'Is that what all this shite's about?' asked Davey, incredulously. 'Everything that happened in the garage? The reason poor Jimmy is having to hide? Because of some fucking book?'

'I'm afraid it is,' I said. 'What I saw that night in Tommy's lock-up was bad. The kind of thing once you've seen you can't unsee. It and whatever is in that missing ledger are worth more than people's lives. And who we're up against hold people's lives pretty cheap.'

We sat at the ancient table and drank our tea, Jimmy's thin fingers dancing on the rough wooden table top. I felt frustrated: I had hoped that Jimmy could have given me more, but at least he had confirmed a few suspicions.

'Jimmy, there's this guy, an ex-officer type with damage to one side of his face, like his cheeks don't match up. Davey's met him. Calls himself McNaught, but that won't be his real name. Is that anyone you've come across or heard tell of?'

'Sorry, Mr Lennox.'

'Did Tommy ever say anything to you about his time in the commandos? Did he ever mention anyone called Jack Tarnish, or Dave Baines?'

He thought for a moment, then shook his head. 'Never heard of either of them. And Tommy never talked about the war or what he did during it. You know what he was like – a closed book.'

While we drank tea, the conversation drifted.

'I think it would be a good idea if you followed Tommy's advice to the letter,' I said. 'Have you thought about where you're going to go? I mean, Paisley is hardly a stretch.'

'You're Canadian, aren't you, Mr Lennox?' asked Jimmy.

'That's right.'

'I always wanted to go to Canada. Emigrate. If I could, that's where I would go: Canada. Away from all this shite. I'd go straight as well.'

'So what's stopping you?' I asked.

'My record. I've got three convictions and the Canadians won't let me in. I thought that everyone there had grandparents who were convicts . . .'

'That's Australia, Jimmy,' I said. 'I'm sure once your convictions are time-barred you'd be allowed into Canada. You just have to keep your nose clean.'

'It'd take too long,' he said gloomily. 'I'd be too old, by then. Anyway, I need to find somewhere now, no' in five or ten years' time. Why do you stay here? Why don't you go back? I would if I was you. Glasgow's fucked. This whole country is fucked.'

'I will probably go back, one day,' I said, putting out of my head that he was stealing my best lines for the tourist board. 'I've got a few of my own sins that I'm waiting to become time-barred.' I drained my cup and stood up to go. 'Jimmy, did you get your fee from Tommy?'

'What? Oh aye – Tommy paid me that night.'

Reaching into my pocket, I took out the envelope I had offered Jennifer Quaid, but which she'd refused. I handed it to Jimmy.

'Jeez . . .' he said when he opened the envelope. He held it open and tilted it for Davey to see.

'There's enough in there to keep you hidden here or anywhere else for long enough. Longer than it'll take for me to get this sorted out, hopefully.' I turned to Davey. 'You married?'

He nodded.

'Any kids?'

'Not yet. We've one on the way.' His face lit up. A life organized; a future planned. 'Due in November.'

'I suggest you take some of that cash, shut up the garage for a couple of weeks, and take your wife on a surprise holiday.'

'I can't—'

'Just do what I say, Davey. McNaught is going to realize he's missing two men and the last time he saw them was at your garage. He's probably already been back there with reinforcements to find out why they didn't come back with the song they were supposed to beat out of you. Given all that happened at the garage, I think it's best if you dropped out of sight too. At least till I get something sorted out.'

'What happened at the garage?' Jimmy asked, frowning.

'Long story,' I said. 'Davey can fill you in later. In fact, I think you should get your stuff together too, Jimmy, and make it a family affair. 'Phone your wife, Davey – tell her to pack some things. I'll drop you off and you can drive back down and pick up Jimmy. I suggest the three of you get south of the border. As far south as you can.' I handed Davey a card with both my business and home numbers. 'Let me know when you're settled, but when you 'phone, say it's "Mr Hastings". I'll let you know when the coast is clear.'

'I don't know how to thank you,' said Jimmy, gazing at the envelope of cash in his hands. 'Tommy said you would help. He had a lot of faith in you.'

'Yep,' I said, sighing. 'I know . . .'

## 7

After Davey Wilson had 'phoned his wife and we'd driven back into Glasgow, I dropped him off at his house. It was a small thirties bungalow in a quiet residential street: a place worked hard for, saved hard for; an ambition fulfilled. Like the garden outside the tearoom where I'd had lunch with Jennifer, Wilson's little house was a badge of an ordinary, planned life. It repelled me and excited my envy at the same time.

Getting out of the car, Davey promised me that he would get his wife and head back down to pick up Jimmy as soon as he could.

'You should think about Canada, too,' I said as he got out. 'You've got skills and it's a great place to bring up kids. If you got accepted, you could maybe sponsor Jimmy – get round his past that way.'

He thought about it for a moment. 'Aye . . . aye, maybe that's no' a bad idea. Thanks for all your help, Mr Lennox.'

In the softening light of evening, I watched him go through the gate and up the short path to the small, immaculately tended garden, and puzzled about what the hell he had to thank me for.

I was pretty sure that I'd convinced Davey of the need to get himself and his wife to safety, but I parked further up the street and waited the length of three cigarettes. It wasn't just a lack of confidence in his resolve: I wanted to make sure no one else was watching the house, ready to follow them back to Jimmy's hiding place.

To ease my impatience and my lungs, after the third cigarette I decided to go back and knock on the door, but I saw Davey and his wife come out of the front door, moving with the stiff urgency of the afraid. Davey was carrying two large suitcases, which he put in the trunk of the Ford parked outside while his wife locked up the house.

Despite both looking anxiously up and down the quiet residential street, neither of them saw me watching. I waited until the Ford had turned the corner and onto the main road, unable to get the thought out of my head that Davey and his wife had had a quiet, ordinary life where the future was planned and saved for. Then I had come along, and now they were on the run like criminals. I comforted myself that Davey's brother had been the real agent of chaos, but the truth was it seemed to follow me around.

I started the engine and headed across the river to Tommy Quaid's place, still unable to work out what Davey Wilson could possibly have to thank me for.

The night and my mood were both fully dark by the time I got to Tommy's apartment building in Pollockshields. As I parked in the lamplit street of blond and bland Victorian sandstone villas and flats, it struck me that the last time I'd been there was the night Tommy had patched me up and re-suited me, after I'd been jumped outside the pub.

I parked opposite and looked across at the door of his dark-windowed ground-floor apartment, half expecting him to emerge from it.

Like I had outside Davey's, I sat and smoked for a while, making sure there was no activity in or around the flat. When I got out of the car, I checked the street in both directions. Something tensed in my chest when I noticed a car with two men sitting in it, parked on the same side of the road as mine, a few spaces back. But I could see they were talking and laughing, making no effort to be inconspicuous, and seemed to pay me no heed. In any case, they drove off before I reached the door of Tommy's flat.

I let myself in with the key Jennifer had given me. Everything was pretty much as it had been when I had last been there. Unlike the feeling I'd had seeing the flat from the street, once I was inside I had no sense of Tommy still being there, either in body or in spirit. The truth was he never really had been, even when he'd been alive, and I remembered the feeling of detachment and temporariness I'd had on that last visit.

As soon as I stepped from the hall into the living room, I knew someone had been there.

I didn't know what it was that triggered the instinct, perhaps the slightest change in order, the kind of detail you remember but don't know you're remembering. It was nothing like the certainty with which I'd known that my own apartment had been gone through; and it wasn't like the subtle invasion by shadowy agents of state that Nancy Ross, Tommy's unlikely left-wing academic lover and unlikelier confidante, had described.

It was simply the feeling of recent occupation: that someone had been in the apartment since Tommy's death.

Simultaneously the thought struck me that, for all I knew, they could still be there. Again I cursed my noble gesture of re-drawering Jonny's Walther and Tommy's commando knife. I didn't have the guns I'd taken from McNaught's goons, either: Twinkletoes had one and Jonny Cohen had taken charge of the other.

I went over to the window and eased back the net curtain, checking the street outside. There were no signs of anything odd and the car with the two men hadn't returned.

I went through every room, checking there was no one around. I felt a jolt when I saw Tommy's shaving kit in the bathroom, still looking like it was there temporarily and its owner would be back to pack it away any time. Except he wouldn't.

I decided that I would tell Jennifer that I would help her clear the place out. Once everything was sorted out. If I were still alive.

I spent an hour searching the place. It was more than enough time to go through Tommy's belongings and I was left with the same feeling of impermanence. As I expected, there was nothing there that would have given much of a clue about the apartment's occupant, far less stolen documents.

I sat on the chesterfield in the living room, as if waiting for something to come to me. I *was* waiting for something to come to me: as I had searched through the flat, I had been nagged by the thought that I already knew something important, but I had forgotten it. Something here, in Tommy's place. Whatever it was, it wouldn't come to my recall, sitting tantalizingly just outside my reach.

I picked up the receiver of Tommy's telephone and was surprised to hear the metallic burr of a connection. No one had yet thought to cancel the line. I made another mental note to mention it to Jennifer. I dialled Archie's number and he told me that he had gotten all of the information I'd asked for on the trust that ran St Andrew's School.

'There's one name that sticks out for me,' said Archie. 'You remember I told you about that priest I was warned off about when I was a beat bobby? Father Sean Sullivan – now Monsignor Sean Sullivan?'

'Shit – he's a trustee of the school?'

'Makes you think, doesn't it?'

After I rang off from Archie, I 'phoned Jonny Cohen. He asked me to hold on while he took the call in his study. Why a gangster who ran protection rackets, bookies, strip clubs and organized the odd armed robbery needed a study was beyond me, but I guessed he didn't want to talk where he could be overheard by his family or Jennifer.

'Those birds you left with us,' he said when he picked up the extension. 'I've had the vet look at them. The one with the broken wing is going to make it after all.'

'I'm relieved to hear it,' I said. And I was.

'Aye,' said Cohen. 'But I wouldn't be too relieved. He's going to make it, but he's probably not going to fly that straight from now on.'

'Oh . . .' I said. 'And the other one?'

'I think he's maybe a canary – he's been doing all the singing you wanted him to do. But best not go into that on the 'phone. Where are you?'

'At our late friend's place. I'll come down right away.'

'Oh the birds aren't here,' said Cohen. 'We didn't have the right . . . *cages* for them. But if you meet me here we can go to see them together.'

'I'll be right there.' I hung up, ending our weirdly cryptic exchange. Cohen was right to be cautious, but anyone listening in would hardly have needed Bletchley Park to decode our meaning.

I sat for another minute in an empty flat that had been

empty even when Tommy had lived there, willing whatever it was that had eluded me to come to me.

It didn't, and I left the flat to its dark and emptiness.

The street outside was quiet and empty of people until two men came around the corner, laughing loudly and joking with each other. I guessed they'd had a few and were returning from a pub. I thought about the times Tommy and I had done the same. They were harmless but I decided to let them pass before crossing to where I'd parked.

It was only when they were directly in front of me that I recognized them as the men I'd seen in the car earlier.

By that time it was too late. I almost felt like expressing my admiration, it was all done so quickly and professionally: dropping the pretence of alcohol-fuelled jollity, one man grabbed my wrist and jabbed the pistol he'd drawn from his pocket into my ribs. The other wheeled round to the other side and grabbed my elbow, tight.

'Now we're not going to play silly buggers, are we?' The one with the gun had a nondescript face and a nondescript English accent. 'Play nice and no one needs to get hurt.'

'You're calling the shots,' I said.

'Now that's a good boy . . .' The Englishman smiled, and between them they steered me back towards Tommy's flat.

Once we were inside, the Englishman kept his gun on me while his pal searched me, turning out everything in my pockets and setting it on the coffee table, including the two blue-tabbed keys: the one I'd let us into the flat with and the unmarked one for the lock-up that Jimmy had given me.

From the brief exchanges between them, I could tell the other man was a Scot, sounding like he came from somewhere on the east coast. It was the Englishman who addressed me, telling me to sit down on the chesterfield 'nice and quiet', with my hands on my lap where he could see them.

I knew I was in trouble: there was something about my two captors that was very cool, very assured, very professional; the casualness and familiarity with which the Englishman handled his gun, the quiet calm of both men. They were clearly in a totally different league from the muscle-bound goons at Davey Wilson's garage, and certainly from the Victor McLaglen lookalike and chum who'd jumped me in the street. Maybe it had been one of these two, and not one of the goons Cohen now had on ice, who had killed Baines and put me to sleep in the lock-up.

I sized my opposition up: the Englishman had pale grey eyes filled with cold calm, and his hair was receding at the temples; the Scot was thinner and a little taller, with reddish blond hair. Neither was in any way remarkable in appearance and neither was too tall and, although both had an athletic look, neither was heavily built – but there was something about them that told you they could handle themselves.

Satisfied that I posed no risk, the Englishman put his gun back into his pocket and went across to the telephone.

'We've got him,' is all he said before hanging up. So there it was: a trap had been set and I'd sprung it by walking blindly into it.

The Englishman sat back down in the club chair opposite me while his taciturn Scottish chum leaned against the wall. Both watched me silently.

I smiled. 'Well, this is cosy . . .' I said.

The Englishman smiled back. 'And it's about to get cosier: the boss is on his way.'

I nodded, leaned back in the sofa and waited for McNaught to arrive.

We waited for twenty minutes. My two silent warders watched me unwaveringly and patiently, but without interest, without any sense of heat. It was all very matter-of-fact: they were doing a job, and they didn't feel stretched by it or tense about it. It didn't matter, because I was tense enough for the three of us.

Just like I had when Baines had made me drive to the lock-ups, I tried to think through what moves I could make; again it was a calculation that came out zero every time, no matter what scenario I ran through in my head.

I had no option but to wait until McNaught arrived. When he did, I guessed the rest of my life would be very painful, but very short. I would probably end up envying the quiet death of Thomas Quaid.

At least it would all be over. My life, I had often thought, had pretty much ended in the war. At least that was when the Kennebecasis Kid – the idealistic, ambitious youth from Saint John – had died. It was as if everything since had been on borrowed time; like I'd been a ghost in sharp tailoring overstaying its welcome.

And McNaught was coming to exorcise me.

I had wanted to sort this one out though. My one regret was those kids I'd seen in those photographs: the terror and the pain in their faces. I had made my own silent covenant with them, that the people who had done that to them would suffer. But now the justice I had promised would never come to pass.

Truth was, it probably never would have, anyway.

There was the sound of a car outside; after a while there was a gentle knock on the outside door. My new English friend took the gun out from his pocket and pointed it at me, almost wearily, and nodded to the Scot, who went to answer the door.

There was no move I could make. The Englishman had his gun pointed across the coffee table at my gut. There was nothing you could do when you were gut-shot.

I turned and watched as the Scot came back in, followed by a tall, lean man. Dressed in a lightweight houndstooth sports jacket, Tattersall shirt, knotted plum silk necktie, cavalry twills, and oxblood brogues, he had that landed, privileged look. His very dark hair was swept back from a widow's peak and his features were sharp and angular, giving him a severe, vaguely devilish look – very oddly like an older version of me. No one else came in. No McNaught.

Things fell into place: I realized that this wasn't the game I thought I was playing and tried to disguise the huge sense of relief I felt. I started to rise, but the Englishman in the chair opposite gave a 'tut-tut' and waved the barrel of his automatic: I made an apologetic gesture and eased back into the red leather.

'Good evening, Captain Tarnish,' I said to the tall man in the country-set outfit.

## 8

The Englishman opposite me again pocketed his gun, got up and vacated the armchair so Tarnish could take his place.

'Good evening, Captain Lennox.' Tarnish returned the military courtesy in a cultured, somewhat louche Scottish accent, but didn't look me in the eye, instead casually plucking at the pressed-to-a-knife-edge crease in his cavalry twills to make sure they didn't bag or wrinkle as he sat. 'I wonder if you'd mind telling me what it is you were looking for here?'

I held my hands up. 'Okay, listen . . . before you start with the wet rags in the mouth or the bamboo under the fingernails, I've got some bad news for you: there is no Nazi loot. No hidden treasure. Whatever you think Tommy Quaid stole during the war, it's all just a tall tale.'

Tarnish spoke over his shoulder to his two associates. 'A wet rag in the mouth . . . we've never tried that one, have we, boys?'

'No, sir,' said the Englishman. 'First time for everything though.'

Oh *goodie*, I thought, this is going to be fun.

'Listen, I'm telling you – it's not even that I don't know where Tommy hid it . . . there was nothing to hide. No loot. You and your chum Baines are chasing something that doesn't exist.' I tried to put some force behind the statement.

'So you've met Dave Baines?' asked Tarnish.

I sighed. 'Yes.'

'And would you know where Sergeant Baines would be now?'

I sat silent for a moment, probably open-mouthed as I played through in my head all the ways of saying 'Actually, Baines is dead – and here's the funny thing, you'll really like this – I was the last one to see him alive, just like I was the last to see Tommy Quaid alive, another one of your wartime compatriots. And I know this is going to sound odd, but the thing is that after Baines was murdered – by somebody else, obviously, not me – I burned his body so no one could recognize it. You know, to some people who didn't know better, that would maybe look a little suspicious and they'd almost think I'd killed them both to get my hands on this phantom Nazi loot. Ha, ha, ha.'

'Where is Dave Baines, Mr Lennox?' Tarnish repeated with elegant impatience.

'Dead,' was all I could think to say.

'And would you have happened to be there when he died, by any chance?'

If it was a guess, it was a good one. I nodded. 'In body if not in spirit. Someone came up behind me and put me to sleep. I didn't see who.'

'And these people you didn't see – they killed Baines and left you alive?'

This was going so well.

'That's right,' I said. 'I was meant to take the blame for his murder. Tommy Quaid had hidden something – the something that he was killed for. But that something had nothing to do with anything taken during the war. I found it when I was with Baines. Whoever was looking to get it back bushwhacked us; they killed Baines, put me out, then they took what I'd found, the only evidence, away with them.'

'And all this happened in the storage sheds down by the Clyde?'

I looked at Tarnish, surprised. 'You know about that?'

'We were keeping an eye on Baines. And on you. You made the job easier by getting together. But we already knew about Quaid's lock-up. Tell me truthfully, did you kill Baines?'

'When I woke up Baines was already dead: someone had cut his throat. Commando style. When I woke up I was covered in Baines's blood and had the knife they'd used to kill him in my hand. It was a frame-up and I had to destroy the evidence so I set light to the storage shed. I know how that all sounds, but no, I didn't kill Dave Baines.'

'No,' repeated Tarnish. 'I don't believe you did.'

'At the risk of sounding like a stuck record,' I said, 'there really is no stolen wartime loot. What I found in that storage shed was something else completely. And definitely no treasure. I don't know what you've heard about Tommy scoring big with stolen Nazi booty, but it's all bull.'

'I know,' said Tarnish.

'You know?'

'Tommy Quaid was with us throughout the war. I know there was no job pulled; no "personal enterprises". Trust me, we had our hands too full with achieving our objectives and simply staying alive – which most of the unit didn't. Baines, on the other hand, was transferred elsewhere and heard all kinds of rumours – or maybe he started one himself. There's a mythology in war, as I'm sure you know yourself. A grain of speculation became an obsession with Baines. An imagined Holy Grail.'

'Okay, now I'm confused. You know I didn't kill Baines, and you know there's no hidden loot . . . so what are you doing here?'

'The same thing you are. We're here for Tommy Quaid.' Tarnish reached into his pocket and took out a slab of hallmarked silver and, snapping it open, offered me a cigarette before taking one himself. He lit us up. 'I got a message from Tommy shortly before he died,' he continued. 'We were a tight unit during the war but we had to endure some terrible things . . . we had to *do* some terrible things. That kind of experience binds men together. But after the war things were different: seeing each other just reminded us of all the stuff we'd been through, of all the others who didn't make it – so we agreed never to meet up. But we also agreed that the exception was if any one of us ever needed help – then the rest of us would be there for him. The letter I got from Tommy said he needed help. It said he was in danger and he needed me to take charge of something for safekeeping.'

'And do you have it?' I asked.

Tarnish shook his head. 'We didn't get here in time. By the time I was in touch with Fraser and Mayhew here, and we got to Glasgow, Tommy was already dead. Anyway, how could I have it? I thought you said whoever put you out in the storage shed and killed Baines took everything . . .'

'Apparently not. There's a red leather ledger that wasn't with the other stuff. Our chums are clearly still very keen to get their hands on it.'

'I see.' Tarnish paused, thinking something through; then he said: 'You know, I have to admit that I did find it rather *troubling* that you just happened to be there when two of my former squad members were killed.'

I shrugged, concealing my worry that he'd read my mind when I'd been running through the explanations. 'Trust me, you're not as troubled about it as I am. I need you to know that Quiet Tommy Quaid was my friend.'

'I know that. That's why you're still alive. When Tommy got in touch he told me you were the one man in Glasgow he trusted.'

I said nothing. Truth was, it had stung me: I believed Tommy had said that about me; about the man who had led him to his death. I snapped out of it and tried to process the information – the pile of information – I'd had dumped on me.

'So you're here to seek revenge for Tommy?' I asked. 'That's stretching the old chums thing a bit, isn't it?'

Tarnish looked at me with an elegant, faint disdain. There really was something about him that reminded me of me. In that moment I realized that when Tommy had said I reminded him of a natural-born killer he'd known during the war, it had been Tarnish, not Baines, he had been talking about. The vague mistrust I'd felt since starting the conversation hardened into something more solid.

'There's me, Mayhew and Fraser here – and there was Tommy,' said Tarnish. 'Four of us – five if you count Baines who was only with us for a short time. Four of us out of a unit of fifteen; that's all that survived the war. Does that explain it?'

It did and I nodded.

'But Tommy was very different from the rest of you. He was one of the most peaceable, amenable men I've ever known. One of the least violent.'

Tarnish looked meaningfully over his shoulder at his comrades, both of whom smiled knowingly.

'Am I missing something?' I asked.

'Tell me, Mr Lennox, was Tommy known as "Quiet Tommy Quaid" here?'

'Yes . . .'

'Do you know why?'

'I don't know for sure, but the story here is that it was because if the coppers ever caught him, he would always "come quiet". And of course Tommy was a master at getting in and out of places silently. That and the fact that he never hurt anyone – never used violence in any of the jobs he pulled.'

'That's not the reason. That's not the reason at all.' Tarnish leaned forward, resting his elbows on his knees. 'He had that nickname before he came back to Glasgow. He picked it up during the war. It's true that his ability to get in and out of secure places without detection did have something to do with it – what we used to call in the war a "penetration specialist".'

'Tommy certainly was that,' I said and grinned. Tarnish looked at me wearily and I felt like a schoolboy admonished by the headmaster.

'That's why I recruited Tommy in the first place,' he said. 'Because he was such a skilled burglar and, if we needed, could be in and out without leaving traces. But that wasn't the main reason he was known as "Quiet Tommy".'

'So why was he?'

'Tommy had other skills,' said Tarnish. 'Skills that in peacetime he probably didn't know he had. You're maybe going to find this difficult to believe but, if ever the squad needed someone taken out quickly and silently, then we'd get Tommy Quaid to do it. He killed with ease, even with grace, and always without a sound. Tommy Quaid's speciality was the quiet death.'

I shook my head. 'You're right: I do find that difficult to believe. Impossible, in fact. I knew Tommy as well as anyone, and he was no killer. More than that, he hated violence.'

'Oh it's true, all right. He may not have been a killer in civilian life, but in the field he was one of my best. I'm not saying he relished it, but I also can't say he was disturbed by it. Tommy was quiet in every way. He kept his thoughts and emotions to himself.'

'That I can imagine,' I said.

'You're maybe right that he hated violence, I'm sure he did. That doesn't mean he wasn't good at it.' Tarnish paused to take a contemplative pull on his cigarette. 'There was this one time in particular. We were well behind enemy lines when a young German soldier stumbled right into us by accident. I say soldier, but this was near the end of the war and this kid was *Volkssturm* – you know, children and old men drafted to defend the fatherland at the last ditch. He was nothing but a mere boy, lucky if he was seventeen, and very frightened. We couldn't take him prisoner because we were so far behind enemy lines, we couldn't tie him up and leave him to be found, and no one had the heart to kill the kid.

'We started debating amongst ourselves, what to do with him. And the more we talked the more clearly terrified the boy became. He had probably already worked out he had to die and that we were arguing about who was going to have to do the job. While we were arguing, Tommy Quaid came up behind the boy without making a sound, reached round and stabbed him through the heart, supporting him, almost cradling him, as he fell to the ground.' Tarnish shook his head. 'It was the quietest and gentlest killing I've ever witnessed. Quaid ended the boy's terror, and his life, with the least possible pain and distress. It was probably the most generous act I witnessed in the whole war. But also the most disturbing. Quiet Tommy Quaid.'

It was difficult to hear – and difficult to imagine Tommy as a killer, even a compassionate one – but it squared with some of the things he'd said, and not said, about his time during the war. Again there had been more meaning in the spaces between words. It made me ashamed of the way I had used the war as an excuse for the violence I had committed since, when Tommy had put it all behind him. But maybe, in the unnatural context of war, Tommy really had had more in common with Baines. I brought the thought into the open:

'So where does Baines fit into this? He told me that he and Tommy were close.'

All three men laughed, loudly.

'Tommy hated Dave Baines,' said Tarnish. 'Hated everything about him. Tommy was everything that Baines wasn't, and vice versa. Baines was a self-centred opportunist. Most of the rumours of stolen loot probably came from him telling his story to anyone who would listen.' Tarnish leaned back in his chair again. 'Now, Captain Lennox, I've levelled with you, why don't you level with me? Why don't you take me through the whole story, from start to finish, including what it was you were looking for here?'

So I did. I told him the whole story, starting with McNaught and the offer he had made in my office, through the events at the foundry, all the way to that evening and my coming back to Tommy's apartment. There were details I left out, like Twinkletoes's and Handsome Jonny Cohen's involvement. I also missed out everything to do with Davey and Jimmy Wilson and the goons at the garage.

Tarnish seemed to be on the level, but I was a long way off trusting him completely. As I talked he sat and listened intently, asking the odd question; the other two stayed in the background, still silent.

But I did tell Tarnish about the contents of the document wallet I'd held briefly in my hands. I told him about the photographs; about whom I'd seen in them and what they had been doing. And to who. I spared no detail and, as I talked, I could see Tarnish's demeanour darken, and I heard Fraser, his subordinate, mutter a curse.

I described a lopsided face, then another that looked like Victor McLaglen.

When I was finished, Tarnish sat silent for a while. Then he asked me what the other blue-tabbed key was for. I explained that it was a spare key for the lock-up that had burned down.

'And you have no idea where this red leather ledger is?' he asked.

I shook my head. 'My guess is that Tommy hid it somewhere. That's why I came back here, but I knew he wouldn't be that obvious.'

'There's always hiding in plain sight . . .'

'No . . . I've been through everything. It's maybe not here. There's a good chance Tommy never had it – it was odd that I found everything else in one place. If he has left it behind thinking I'd work out where it is, then he's overestimated my abilities as a detective.'

'It would have been easier if Tommy had simply made a will,' said Tarnish bitterly.

It was like an electric shock, but I tried not to show it. Tarnish's offhand remark had dropped it back into my head: the *something* that had been itching in my head all the time I'd been searching Tommy's flat.

Tommy had intended for me to find it. Me alone.

And now I knew where to look.

We sat talking for another half an hour. Tarnish told me that he, Fraser and Mayhew would do anything to avenge Tommy's death, especially having heard the nature of what I had found in the lock-up. He seemed genuine, and told me that he was willing to work with me – but made it clear that he and his comrades might go about exacting revenge in their own way. I told him

I didn't have a problem with that, but they should leave the investigating to me. I hadn't told Tarnish that I knew where Tommy had stolen the documents from. I also didn't let on that I was now very late for an appointment with Jonny Cohen.

I gave Tarnish my card with my numbers on it; he told me he already had them; I guessed he had built up quite a dossier on me. We agreed to stay in touch.

All the time I had sat, patiently exchanging intelligence with Tarnish, I had to fight the urge to scratch two itches: the first was that insistent grain of suspicion, like grit in my eye, about Tarnish and his men. There was something about them that didn't gel. It was maybe the way his men never spoke, always remaining subordinate and preserving the deferences and hierarchies of thirteen years past; as if Tarnish was their current, rather than former, commanding officer.

The second itch was, of course, to have them gone and out of the flat. All the time I spoke with Tarnish, I had used all of my willpower not to glance over at the bookcase.

*'It would have been easier if Tommy had simply made a will.'* With that comment, Tarnish had unlocked the memory that had lain just beyond my reach.

I remembered that night, after I'd been jumped by the two amateurs in the street and Tommy had strapped me up, standing by the bookcase with the Albert Camus novel *The Outsider* in my hand.

Tommy had said, *'If ever anything happens to me, I'll leave it to you in my will. Remember that.'*

I had no good reason to offer Tarnish as to why I would want to stay behind in Tommy's apartment. I thought of doing the whole shit-I've-left-my-car-keys-inside thing, but Tarnish and his boys were too long in the fang to fall for that kind of malarkey.

And our new found all-pals-together goodwill was paper thin on both sides: I guessed Tarnish had the same grain of mistrust for me as I had for him.

So we all left together and I locked the front door.

'I've got to talk to some people,' I said. 'Why don't we meet here at eleven tomorrow morning?' If the book was still there, it would still be there tomorrow morning. I could of course simply have driven around the block, parked and waited till I thought it was safe to sneak back into the apartment, but the truth was I hadn't been too sharp when it came to spotting Tarnish's surveillance. He'd said that there were only the three of them, but something made me suspect that Tarnish wasn't the type to paint the whole picture. What I'd do was turn up half an hour early, pocket the book, and wait for Tarnish.

As we left, Tarnish explained they were parked around the corner and he rather pointedly watched as I went back to my car and drove off.

As I did, Quiet Tommy Quaid's words echoed in my head: *'Maybe, one day, this'll be a book that will speak to you too.'*

## 9

'Where the fuck have you been?' The normally affable and polite Handsome Jonny Cohen's greeting wasn't the most welcoming I'd had in my time in Glasgow, but neither was it the least. We stood in the marble-floored hallway of his house. You could almost have fitted Tommy's whole flat into the hall alone and the contrast struck me, jarred with me, for some reason.

'I got held up . . .' I explained about Tarnish and goons with gut-aimed guns and how they'd been so insistent that I hang around that it seemed churlish to refuse. Cohen's annoyance gave way to suspicion.

'Do you believe Tarnish?' he asked. 'That he's just here to find out what happened to Tommy Quaid and to get even for it?'

'What other interest could he have?'

'Maybe Baines was right. Maybe Tarnish and Quaid *did* lift something of value during one of their raids and Tommy stashed it away. These things did happen in the war.'

I shook my head. 'This is all about those photographs I found. Those names. Tommy Quaid was killed because he tripped over this little ring of . . . Christ, I don't know what you'd call them – child molesters – who also happen to be in positions of power.'

'So Tarnish has agreed to help out?' Cohen asked.

'Yeah. Help out as an executioner. Speaking of which, thanks for keeping McNaught's goons breathing. Where are they?'

'One of my warehouses. In Clarkston.'

'You said on the 'phone that Doc Banks fixed them up?'

'Aye . . . as best he could. You really went to town on them.'

'It was a tricky situation, Jonny, and they were both armed. I had to think on my feet.' I looked along the hall, into the body of the house. 'Can I see Jennifer before we go?'

'Sure,' said Cohen. 'But make it quick. We're already an hour behind because of your chat with Tarnish.'

It was a concrete-floored, corrugated-iron-walled warehouse filled with crates stacked four high. I didn't ask Cohen what the crates contained, but I guessed that whatever it was was in a state of fluid ownership. In the corner nearest the doors, there was a flat-roofed, shed-like arrangement which obviously served as some kind of office. It was raised on a stilted platform; one wall was all windows and looked over the stacked merchandise.

A man in his late sixties came out of the office and down the steps to greet us. He was short and squat and leathery, his skin thick and dark under a shock of dense white hair, looking as if he'd spent his whole life outdoors. It was a look that sat oddly with the expensive suit.

'Hiya, Yank,' he said good-naturedly.

'Hiya, Pops,' I replied. Pops Loeb had been a gangster in his own right between the wars, when the slums of Govan rather than the semi-detacheds of Newton Mearns had been the centre of Jewish life in Glasgow. He was a tough old buzzard, but the rumour was that in his golden days his protection racket had been more protection than racket, and he had been a popular figure in his community. When the altogether more ruthless Jonny Cohen had become top dog, he had taken over Loeb's operations more as a business merger than gang war. Cohen was clearly fond of Pops Loeb and had kept him close as an adviser; I got the impression that, these days, Loeb's duties were light but his salary was considerable. Loeb had lost his wife to cancer young and his son had been killed in France on the retreat to Dunkirk, and Jonny Cohen had become the closest thing Pops had to family. Like Cohen, I liked Loeb: I always called him Pops and he always called me Yank, no matter how often I told him I was from Canada, not the US.

'No one's been sniffing around, Jonny,' he said. 'Your chums are through there . . .'

'There' was an area cleared of crates in the middle of the warehouse and McNaught's two heavies sat tied to collapsible metal chairs. Twinkletoes McBride sat on a third chair facing them, smoking. Twinkle had his jacket off and his sleeves rolled up over forearms that looked woven from steel cable. He'd unbuttoned his shirt collar and loosened his tie and had slipped the deep red braces from his shoulders so they now hung from his waist. Seeing him like that sent a cold current through me: Twinkletoes McBride was not the kind of person you wanted to see ready for some hard physical work. Especially if you were sitting facing him, tied to a chair.

McNaught's two men didn't look too scared though. They sat limply, without tension, and I guessed that I'd missed the party: Twinkle had already gotten all he wanted from them.

The red-headed boxer type whose jaw I'd dislocated had had his face straightened and a bandage, looped around his head and face Humpty-Dumpty style, held his mouth tight shut. The side of his face that had taken the force of the blow was badly distended and swollen, and had started to bruise dark, which emphasized the large white wound dressing Doc Banks had applied.

He looked at me dully as I approached but didn't seem to recognize me. I guessed that I'd clobbered him so quickly that he hadn't gotten a good look at me, although he had been fully conscious before I left.

His pal, also with a bandaged head, showed no signs of recognizing me, either. That I could understand because I'd belted him as soon as he'd opened the door and this was the first time I'd seen him since. But as I watched him, I noticed the same lack of recognition when he looked at Twinkletoes, at Cohen, at his friend, at his knees, at the crates, at the floor. His egg had been well and truly scrambled. I'd scrambled it. And I felt like shit standing there, looking at him.

'Much trouble?' I asked Twinkletoes.

'Nope. They was very *lock-way-shus*. Or this one was . . .' He pointed to the redhead with the busted jaw. 'I didn't need to do nothing. By the time Doc Banks was finished resetting his jaw, he would have sold his granny down the Clyde. Doc gave them something after I'd finished with them. An injection to kill the pain and they've been as quiet as church mice since.'

Cohen tapped me on the elbow. 'We need to talk.'

He steered me to the corner of the warehouse and the shed-type office. Pops Loeb and two of Cohen's men sat smoking and arguing loudly but heatlessly about something. The air was blue-thick with tobacco smoke, mainly from the stump of stogie that Pops was chewing on. The walls were covered with various pinned-up bills of lading, delivery schedules, freight notes, and a calendar with a brunette spilling out of her bikini. There was a battered old sofa in one corner, on which the two younger men were sitting.

'Could you give us a minute, boys, please? Maybe you could keep an eye on our guests and ask Mr McBride to join us? Thanks. Pops, you hang around.' It was something that I'd noticed about Cohen before: he was invariably polite and courteous, even to his hired thugs. I'd often wondered if, during his time as a bank robber, the demand notes he'd handed bank tellers had had an apologetic addendum: *PS Sorry about the interruption to your routine. Thank you so much for the cash and your kind cooperation.*

'The guy whose jaw you busted told Twinkletoes everything you need to know,' he said when the two heavies had left. 'He told us everything through gritted teeth, though. After Doc Banks stitched up his face and reset his jaw, he bound him up tight and told him to keep his teeth together until he gets to a hospital and has his jaw wired. Or whatever teeth you left him with.'

'The other guy?' I asked hopefully: maybe he had passed the time playing Grandmaster chess with Pops and his vacant look was simply the otherworldliness of the genius.

'You could see for yourself. According to Doc Banks, he could peg out at any time. There could be bleeding in his skull. In any case, his brain's mush. All it'll take is for his ginger chum to point to you across a courtroom and you're looking at attempted murder.'

'I wasn't trying to kill him. The opposite, in fact.'

'Tell that to the judge, as they say.'

'What do we know about them?' I asked.

'They're a couple of heavies for hire from Edinburgh,' said Pops Loeb. 'According to your chum Twinkletoes, they're ex-army and thick as shit – or at least judging from the one you didn't lobotomize. They're not police, government, or anything official.'

'That doesn't mean to say McNaught isn't—' Cohen broke off when Twinkletoes came in.

'Close the door behind you, please,' said Cohen. Twinkle did as he was asked and his bulk seemed to fill the small office shed. 'Could you tell Mr Lennox what you got out of them?'

'Aye – no problem,' said Twinkle. Even the baritone of his voice seemed to fill the shed, reverberating in the wooden walls. 'Both done time inside army and civilian prison. They've done a bit of bare-knuckle and occasional work as bouncers in an Edin-burgh nightclub run by the Ferguson brothers. But they've also done their fair bit of putting people in hospital – aye, and may-bes worse – for cash. Thon feller you talked about – the one with the fucked-up face – hired them directly. McNaught was the name he used with them as well. They'd never knew or heard of McNaught before, but he paid them silly fucking money. He admitted it was made clear from the start that murdering folk was part of the job, and that was why they was being paid so much. If they talked to anyone about it, they'd end up dead too. By the way, I got everything from the ginger-heid with the busted jaw. The other one isn't *cum-puss-menttis*, if you know what I mean.'

'I think I do, Twinkle. Which one of them killed Tommy?'

'They didn't. Ginger swears blind him and his pal had noth-ing to do with it. He thinks McNaught must have other people, but he's never seen them. It could be a load of pish, but if it isn't, then it must've been one of the other teams what killed Tommy.'

'You believe him?'

'Oh aye, I gave his jaw a good wee shoogle and he was

screaming his heid aff an' that, then he passed out for a while. When he came round again he swore blind he didn't know nothing about the foundry or Tommy being chucked off the roof.'

I nodded. I had hoped it had been them. Then I might have felt a little less guilty about leaving one of them with permanent brain damage.

'Where do we find McNaught?'

McBride dipped thick fingers into his shirt pocket; he handed me a slip of paper with an address on it.

'A warehouse. Ginger thinks it's between tenants and McNaught's just making use of it as a headquarters while it's empty. He admitted that McNaught told them to get the information out of Davey Wilson, then do him. They was supposed to make sure the body would never be found.'

'So I wouldn't feel too guilty about your pal,' said Cohen. 'I'm guessing he wouldn't have made *The Brains Trust* even before you malkied him. And the pair of them are life-takers. Live by the sword and all that shite.' He paused, glancing over at Pops Loeb. 'That still leaves the question of what we do with them . . .'

'They're not going anywhere for the meantime,' I said, hoping that it was clear that my definition of 'anywhere' included an industrial mincer or the bottom of the Clyde. I turned back to Twinkletoes, holding up the slip of paper. 'When will McNaught be here?' I was beginning to wonder if any warehouses in Glasgow were actually used to house wares, as opposed to being hubs of criminal activity.

'He was supposed to be going there tonight. Pinky and Perky were to meet him there after they'd got what they wanted out of Davey Wilson and got rid of him.'

I looked at my watch. It was nearly eleven p.m. 'I doubt he's still there, but we should maybe go and take a look. Jonny?'

'I'll get some of the boys together,' he said.

'I'll come too, Mr L,' said McBride.

'And me,' said Loeb.

'No, Pops,' said Cohen. 'I'll be leaving you on your own here to watch our two chums. Do you think you can handle that?'

'Do I think I can handle it?' Loeb looked insulted. 'One of them can hardly move his head and the other's going to be in nappies for the rest of his life and you ask can I handle it?'

'It's no picnic,' said Cohen. 'Their pals could come for them. Are you heavy?'

'No . . . of course I'm not heavy. What for should I be heavy?'

Cohen took an automatic from his waistband and handed it to Pops. 'You should be heavy.'

Pops snorted a scornful laugh, but took the gun anyway.

Leaving Pops Loeb to keep an eye on the two bound men, Cohen rounded up another three goons and they piled, along with McBride, into the back of a Bedford van. Cohen drove and I sat up front next to him. He'd tooled everyone up; Twinkletoes McBride still had the gun we'd taken from McNaught's man.

'You still got the Walther?' Cohen asked before starting the engine.

'It's at home.'

He sighed. 'A lot of fucking good it's doing there.' He handed me a snub-nosed Webley. I looked at it in my hand for a moment, unsure as to what to do, then slipped it into my jacket pocket. In the back two of Jonny's men sat with sawn-off shotguns on their knees.

'I just hope we're not stopped by the police,' I said as we bumped across town.

'I'll tell them we're pest controllers,' said Cohen.

The rest of the journey was in silence.

It was a warehouse that sat pretty much on its own, down by the river. McNaught had chosen well: from the warehouse you would be able to see anyone approaching from either direction along the riverside road. Like us.

The summer night sky still had streaks of paler blue in it, like the lingering ghosts of the day, but even with that it was a gloomy spot. There were streetlamps dotted along the riverfront, small diamond sparkles on dark velvet, but otherwise everything was a cluster of dark shapes. The warehouse itself was a lightless black shadow tight against the dark Clyde; obviously designed originally to be serviced from the river, rather than the road, it had its own small pier.

'What do you think?' Cohen asked.

I jutted my chin towards some open space further along the riverfront. 'Let's park down there and walk it back. If we stick to the shadows as much as possible, they might not see us coming. There's always the chance that there's nobody there.'

Cohen did what I suggested and we drove into the patch of waste ground and parked.

It was a stumbling walk over uneven ground down to the riverfront and along towards the warehouse: it was much darker than I thought it would have been, as if the Clyde, oozing blackly beside us, had gathered the night around itself.

As we grew closer to the warehouse, I saw a goods winch jutting out from the pier-side flank of the building: a geometry of black spars and beams, it looked for all the world like a hangman's scaffold against the paler sky.

I didn't take it as a good omen.

*

The last piece of cover was a long, low boathouse-type building. From there it was a hundred yards in the open to the wall of the warehouse, broken by a fence of steel pillars and wire mesh. It was difficult to tell from this distance, but the fence looked in a pretty bad state of repair and I hoped it wouldn't hold us up too long.

'You ready?' I asked Cohen. He nodded. 'You take the back with your guys . . . Twinkle, you and I will go round the front. And everybody keep low.'

I took the snub-nose revolver from my pocket and waved it in a 'follow me' gesture. I felt sick: the whole set-up took me back to the kind of skulking I'd had to do during the war; the kind of skulking that always ended up with men dead. This whole thing had gotten out of hand.

But the whole thing had been out of hand long before I'd been involved; before Tommy Quaid had become involved. There was nothing more out of hand than a bunch of rich and power-ful perverts torturing kids.

I may have had a gun in my hand, but this time I knew I *was* on the side of the angels.

Despite his nickname – which he'd earned for a completely different skill anyway – Twinkletoes was anything but light on his feet. I had to keep stopping to wait until he got up again, rising as an inhumanly large shadow, every time he stumbled and fell. I took the chance to check on the progress of Cohen's group, but they were obviously keeping low and I couldn't see them.

Twinkle and I reached the fence, found a gap and I slipped through, with Twinkle lumbering behind me. Eventually we were pressed against the bricks of the side of the warehouse.

I took a look around the front. There were no cars parked

there, or anywhere else I could see. I guessed that McNaught had given up waiting for his two hired heavies to return from their task.

'You sure this is the warehouse he said?' I whispered to McBride.

'Aye . . . definitely.' He pronounced it *deh-finn-ately*.

We made our way to the main doors at the front: wooden double doors, fifteen feet high and the same wide, with a smaller, normal-sized door for easier access set into one of them. It was unlocked.

I went first and slipped in, telling Twinkle to wait until I called.

I switched on the flashlight and scanned the warehouse. It was empty, of people, of goods, of anything. I heard the sound of a door at the back yielding to a crowbar.

'It's all clear . . .' I called to Cohen and his men as they spilled in at the opposite side. It was a vast hangar of a place: wide and deep and high. I guessed it had been built to deal with large bales of materials imported from an empire that was now shrinking into insignificance.

And it was dark. Completely dark except for a single point of light.

There was an electric hand lantern, an inspection lamp like the kind mechanics use in garages, hanging from a nail hammered in the wall. Like a lighthouse deliberately set to guide the way, it was the only illumination in the empty dark cavern of the warehouse; its sole function seemed to be to highlight the words daubed in white paint on the grimy red-brick wall beside it.

I held up a hand to stop everybody's advance and straightened up from my half-crouched position. I knew that neither

McNaught nor any of his men were in the warehouse. The painted message had been left for me. For us.

I walked over to it, Jonny Cohen at my side. The white paint hadn't had time to dry and was still tacky; the message was short and simple:

RIGHT IDEA.
WRONG WAREHOUSE.

'Oh fuck . . .' said Cohen. 'Pops . . .'

# Part Five

Part Five

## 1

Handsome Jonny Cohen drove like a maniac, his gaze unblinking and his face set hard the way it had been at Davey Wilson's garage, when he had been prepared to end lives. The gears of the Bedford ground and screeched as he tried to wrest a speed from the van that it was incapable of giving; even at that, we made our way through the city at speeds of around sixty, and I started to worry that the lives he was going to end were our own. When he barrelled through his second red light, just missing a tram, I'd had enough.

'Stop, Jonny.'

He ignored me. Or probably didn't hear me as his mind played through all the possible scenarios that could face us back at the Clarkston warehouse.

'STOP!' I yelled and he looked at me as if I were mad.

He had to slow a little as we approached a junction and I yanked on the handbrake. Jonny pumped the footbrake and steered into the skid as the Bedford slid sideways, tyres screeching. A mountainside fell on me: when Twinkletoes straightened up and I could breathe again, the van was stopped, angled across the road and the guys in the back, who had been thrown about by the sudden swerve and stop, cursed loudly. The sudden halt had killed the van's engine.

Jonny Cohen swung round on the bench seat of the van and glared at me. And there it was, that which Tommy Quaid had talked about: murder in a man's eyes.

'What the *fuck* do you think you're doing?'

'Listen, Jonny, we have a van load of ne'er-do-wells, all armed to the teeth, and you're breaking every road traffic law that there is. I know this is difficult to hear, but whatever has happened back at the warehouse, whatever has happened to Pops, has already happened. We need to get there quickly, all right, but we need to *get there*. If you run us off the road, or if the police pull us over, we won't get there at all. And there's always the chance that McNaught's people could be waiting for us. That message they left for us was intended to make us do what you're doing. I don't want us to go steaming blindly into a trap.'

Cohen still glared at me. He said nothing but started the engine and drove on, although less recklessly than before.

But the truth was, if my guess was right, we really did need to get there quickly.


The large double doors of the warehouse were open to the night, as if expecting a lorry to deliver more crates. All the lights were on but there were no strange vehicles parked outside. Cohen followed my advice and stopped the Bedford some distance from the warehouse, leaving the headlights on.

'Okay, boys,' I said into the back of the van. 'Let's go. But be ready for anything. If these cowboys are still here, don't hesitate to shoot the bastards, because they won't hesitate to shoot you.'

Cohen rested a hand on my arm. 'They're my team, Lennox. I give the orders.' His composure restored, he spoke without anger or heat.

'Sorry, Jonny,' I said. 'I thought your mind would be elsewhere.'

'You're not the only one who fought in the war,' he said. 'I know how to get my head into the game and deal with shite like this.'

Out of the van, I became aware of the almost total quiet around us, broken only by the sound of a distant dog barking somewhere in Clarkston. The sky was cloud-clean and sparkled with stars; even that unnerved me, reminding me of another clear-sky night, when I'd driven a quiet man to his death. The silence and still pressed down on me.

'Okay . . .' Jonny nodded and led the way. We advanced slowly and silently on the warehouse. There was no sign of life. I was pretty sure there would be no one left inside – or at least no one alive – but I knew from bitter experience that McNaught had a penchant for surprises.

When we went in, we all fanned out and searched the place, working from the perimeter inwards; Twinkletoes and I made our way up the wooden steps to the office. If they were still up there, the office windows would afford our opposition a clear view – and shooting – across the whole warehouse.

Every light was on, but the office was empty.

Looking out through the windows, I could see no sign of McNaught or anyone other than our own people. Except for the cleared area where McNaught's two men had been tied to the chairs.

'Oh fuck . . .' said McBride, who was at my side, looking at the same thing I was.

I rushed out of the office and shouted to Cohen and the others that we were alone. With McBride at my back, I ran to the clearing in the heart of the warehouse.

McNaught's two men were still there, as was Pops Loeb. The guy I'd hit too hard was still staring out into the warehouse with a complete lack of recognition. But so was his pal. Neither were capable of recognizing anyone or anything any more because their windpipes had been severed in the same way Baines's had been: from behind with a blade inserted at the back of the windpipe and pushed forward. There was surprisingly little blood, and they would have died quickly and quietly.

I heard Jonny Cohen give a despairing cry when he joined us with his boys.

McNaught may have given his hirelings a quick and quiet death, but not so Pops Loeb. The old Jew sat slumped, tied to the chair Twinkletoes had occupied during his interrogation of the two goons. A hoop of greasy rope from one of the crates bound Pops to the chair, pinioning his arms to his sides. His head was slumped forward, his chin resting on his chest, presenting us with the thick brush of his white hair, flecked crimson. His shirt and suit were sodden dark and a disc of blood bloomed from beneath the chair and around his feet, like a glossy red-black mat on the concrete floor. He had been stabbed multiple times, but care had been taken that not one of the stab wounds would on its own be instantly fatal, and Pops had been left to bleed out slowly.

Cohen placed his fingers under Pops's chin and eased his head up carefully, as if afraid of hurting the old man, who was as far from hurting as it was possible to be. The leathery skin of Loeb's face and forehead was covered in puncture wounds. His tormentors had stabbed him in the eyes and the dark skin of his cheeks was streaked with tears of blood.

Like I'd seen so many times in so many places, it was death as a message: a totem of one human being's absolute power over another.

'I'll fucking kill them,' said Cohen, quietly, almost calmly. 'I will kill every last fucking one of them.'

'And you're welcome to,' I said. 'But, right now, I need you to trust me and do exactly what I tell you to do.'

Cohen looked at me, vaguely confused.

'I need you to get the boys to cover the bodies up with a tarpaulin – or better still hide them behind crates – then get the van inside and cover it up with a tarp as well.'

'Why?'

'Because I think McNaught is trying to pull the same stunt as before. We need to get everyone inside, lock the place up tight and make sure no one can be seen from the windows. It has to look like everything is normal and there hasn't been anyone here all night. We don't have much time.'

'I still don't get—' Cohen stopped mid-sentence and nodded. He barked orders at his team and within a couple of minutes everything was inside the warehouse and the doors shut up tight. There were only two windows, one on each side of the building: small squares of wire-mesh-reinforced glass intended to allow some meagre light into the warehouse during the day. We all lent a hand to move some of the crates in tight around where the bodies of Pops and the two heavies sat, obscuring the line of sight from both windows.

I could simply have slung tarpaulins like curtains over the windows, but I needed whoever came to be able to see inside. See normality.

The only other viewpoint from outside was the small glazed panel, again reinforced with steel wire, set into the access door. We had brought the Bedford into the warehouse, parking it close enough to obscure most but not all of the view of the building's interior from the door panel; two tarpaulins draped hurriedly over the van made it impossible for anyone peering in through the panel to identify it as a vehicle.

I killed the main lights. Cohen, McBride and I stayed in the warehouse hall but sent everyone else up to the office, telling them to switch off the lights, and to keep quiet and out of sight.

Cohen and I flattened ourselves against the wall, next to the window but far enough along to be out of the angle of sight of anyone peering in. The geometry needed to hide Twinkletoes anywhere near the same place would have been beyond Euclid; so, with much grunting and groaning, we got him to fold his bulk, knees tucked up as near as possible to his chin, behind a concealing pyramid of stacked crates.

I heard a single car approaching. No police bells, just the quiet continuous crunch of tyre on asphalt.

'How did you know?' whispered Cohen.

'The same trick they tried to pull with me down at Tommy's lock-up. They got you all fired up by leaving that message and knew we'd come rushing back. The police arrive and find the warehouse doors open and the whole place lit up like Christmas – with three dead bodies and us armed to the teeth.' I held up a hand. Crouching low, I went over to the window and peered out into the night. Only one police car. Two bobbies. McNaught's anonymous tip-off hadn't been taken as seriously as he had hoped.

The beams of the coppers' flashlights swept the approach to the warehouse, flashed briefly into the window, causing me to shrink back, then disappeared.

'They've gone round the front,' I hissed at Cohen.

There was the sound of the door handle being rattled in that way that only bored coppers and night watchmen do. I was about to steal another peek outside when I heard the crunch of a policeman's boot on the gravel immediately outside the window, which suddenly lit up again. This time the copper was right up against the glass, the beam from his flashlight probing the interior of the warehouse. When I'd heard his footfall outside, I hadn't dared try to get back to where Cohen was, so I had dropped to the floor, pressing hard against the wall beneath the window and cursing my own impatience and clumsiness.

The light went out but, looking up from my hiding place, I could now see the policeman clearly as he peered into the warehouse, cupping his hands and pressing them against the window to shield his eyes. I could see him, and that meant all he needed to do to see me was switch his flashlight back on and shine it downwards. I held my breath.

After a few seconds that seemed like an age, the copper removed his hands.

'There's fuck all going on here, Bob,' he called to his invisible partner. 'Are you sure it was this one?'

'Aye . . .' I heard the voice call back from the far corner. They had split up to check out the warehouse. 'This was the one all right. Gunshots, my arse – bloody kids making a hoax call. Either that or somebody's been watching too many cowboy films.'

The copper nearest muttered something as he moved away. I scuttled back across to Cohen, holding my finger to my lips.

There was a dull thud from behind the crates where Twinkle-toes McBride was hiding.

It wasn't a loud noise, but in the absolute quiet around us, and to my adrenalin-heightened senses, it seemed to reverberate through the whole building.

The flashlight was back at the window and again probed the dark warehouse; this time the beam was there longer, more insistent, probing the space more thoroughly. The copper at the window shone his light downwards, to exactly where I'd been hiding only seconds before.

'Are you coming or what?' the further away constable called impatiently. 'This is a complete waste of fucking time.'

'I thought I heard something . . .'

A pause. The insistent beam continued to probe, the light pooling on boxes, tarpaulins, the walls, the floor. It came to rest on the crates behind which the three bodies sat. For a moment, like them, I stopped breathing.

The beam swept to another pile of crates, this time to where McBride was hiding and from where the sound had come. The disc of light sat on one of the crates, midway up. Below it, semi-illuminated, I could see Twinkletoes's ankle and foot jutting out beyond the bottom crate.

The copper hadn't seen it yet, but he would. If he lowered his torch beam a few inches he definitely would. There was no getting out of it if he did. This warehouse was registered to Jonny Cohen. All we could do was maybe overpower the coppers and make it all look like Cohen was the victim of a robbery, but I couldn't see how we could make it work.

I wanted to hiss across to McBride to move his foot, but the copper would hear me too. And maybe it was better that the foot didn't move.

'Aye . . . I'm coming,' the voice from behind the window said eventually, wearily.

The flashlight disappeared from the window.

We waited a good ten minutes. I looked out the window and confirmed that the police car was gone; then Jonny sent one of his men out on foot to go to the road end and check it was out of the area. Only when he returned did we switch on the warehouse lights again, first hanging the tarpaulins over the windows.

'We could have done that to start with,' complained Cohen.

I shook my head. 'The coppers needed to see that the warehouse was empty.'

Twinkletoes McBride looked sheepish. 'Sorry, Mr L.'

'What the fuck happened?' asked Cohen. 'You nearly had the polis down on us.'

'I got cramp,' said McBride. 'I couldn't move in there and I had to straighten my leg and I kicked the—'

'It's all right, Twinkle,' I said. 'No harm done.' I turned to Cohen. 'We've got to get this mess cleared up. Can you take care of it? The bodies, I mean . . .'

We moved the crates we'd stacked around where Pops Loeb and the other two sat tied to their chairs. Cohen looked really distressed. I knew, looking at him, that this was no longer just my fight. What worried me was that it was also a fight no longer under my control: Handsome Jonny Cohen had lost someone close to him and I knew that taking revenge for Pops's killing would become his number one priority.

'What will you do with them?'

'I don't give a fuck about those two . . .' He jutted his handsomely cleft chin at McNaught's dead men. 'They're for the fucking mincer. But not Pops. Pops is going to be buried somewhere. He's going in the ground.'

'Jonny,' I said, 'we can't—'

'I know, I know . . . Pops had no real family left, I'm not talking about an official thing. There'll be no shiva or Kaddish for poor old Pops,' said Cohen sadly, 'but I'll make sure he has a kevura.'

'Kevura?'

'Burial . . . Don't worry, it'll be somewhere he'll never be found. But it'll be a decent resting place for him. And I'll know where he is.'

I let it go. I was never sure what happened to the meat-plant-rendered remains of the Three Kings' victims, but I imagined that any chance of even the smallest part of Pops Loeb ending up in a pork pie probably went against something in the Torah.

'I'm sorry I brought you into this, Jonny. If I hadn't . . .' I looked down at Loeb's body.

'Forget it. These bastards have picked a fight with me. Just promise me that you'll let me deal with McNaught when we find him.'

'Sure,' I said. 'It's the least I can do.' I decided not to bring up that I'd made the same promise to Tarnish, or that I had planned to enjoy the privilege of ending McNaught myself. I was now in a lawless world – where everyone suddenly believed in justice.

We didn't talk much after that, for a while, and set about the business of cleaning up the warehouse and preparing three men for a rest without grace.

# 2

I got there fifteen minutes early. For all I knew, Tommy's apartment was being watched by Tarnish and my arrival any earlier would have looked suspicious.

I didn't need any more time, anyway: what I was looking for would be exactly where I last saw it, or it wouldn't be there at all. I tried to let myself in with the key I had, but it wouldn't fit. When I checked, I realized I was using the unnumbered blue-tabbed key that Jimmy Wilson had given me. Pocketing it, I took out the right key and opened the door.

Before I did anything, I did a quick check of all the rooms to make sure there was no one else in the flat. Once I was reassured there wasn't, I went over to the bookcase and took the copy of *The Outsider* from its shelf. Tarnish and his crew could turn up at any time and I still wasn't in a sharing mood, so I slipped the book straight into my jacket pocket without looking at it. All of my suits were reasonably lightweight: I followed the Italian philosophy that only lightweight cloth hung well. But it was another warm day and I had put on an even lighter than usual, dark-sand cotton weave; the book bulked and wrinkled the pocket.

I went over to the window and looked out. There was no sign of Tarnish yet. My Sunbeam Alpine sat at the kerb directly outside, the convertible top down; I'd left it that way not just because the day was so warm, but to emphasize I had come alone.

Except I hadn't. Before coming, I had arranged with Twinkletoes that he follow me there, keeping his Vauxhall Cresta more than a discreet distance from me. Once I was in Tommy's apartment, I had instructed him, he was to take a couple of spins around the block, then park where he had a view of the street. But only if he could do so inconspicuously. I had to admit that to my mind Twinkletoes McBride and inconspicuousness were about as natural a marriage as Marilyn Monroe and Arthur Miller, but I needed someone to watch my back.

The main reason was that McNaught and his cronies could crash the party at any time. But it was more than that: something didn't gel with me about Tarnish. He seemed genuinely vengeful about Tommy's death, and genuinely revolted by what I had told him about the little club of powerful perverts who had ordered Tommy's murder – but the truth was Tarnish had a look about him that was, well, *bad*. I tried not to dwell on the fact that it was a look I had in common with him.

Tarnish turned up exactly on time. He was alone, but I guessed he was alone in the same way I was, and that he had his men somewhere handy. As I let him into the apartment, I caught him looking at the book-shaped bulge in my jacket pocket. I stepped forward, shook hands with him, and we went through to the living room.

'Have there been any developments since we last met?' he asked, offering me a cigarette from his case. 'Anything in particular?'

'None,' I said. Seeing as we had met only the previous day, I found it an odd question. And his manner of asking suggested he already knew there had been 'developments'. For the meantime, I decided to keep the events in Clarkston to myself.

Tarnish told me that he had been asking around – making 'phone calls to army and commando chums – but my description of McNaught had drawn a blank. It had been a big war, had been a big army, he had said, and maybe McNaught had served in some other branch of the services, if at all.

'Remember, Captain Lennox, that we have an agreement that if you find McNaught, I and my boys get the pleasure of dealing with him.'

'I hadn't forgotten,' I said. I wasn't going to tell him why Handsome Jonny Cohen now had prior claim to McNaught's hide. It was a complication I reckoned would sort itself out. One way or another. 'And when the time comes,' I said, 'I'll be asking a lot of you, you understand that, I hope. The law is no use to me with this. We're talking about people who are beyond the reach of the law. Who *are* the law, in some cases. The justice that finds them has to be natural. And uncompromising. I intend to call on you and your men's special skills when the time comes. Are we clear on that?'

'We are.'

I showed Tarnish out into the hall.

'I'll keep in touch,' I said and opened the door. Tarnish checked its opening with his hand.

'I am a fair man,' he said. 'I like to give people the benefit of the doubt. But that's mainly because I'm not a man friendly to betrayal of any sort. Not the type of man you would want to disappoint. Are we clear on that as well, Captain Lennox?'

'We are, Captain Tarnish. But why do I get the feeling there's a doubt you're giving me the benefit of?'

'Let's just say I hope you're being perfectly open with me.'

'And I hope the same of you.'

A heartbeat's pause. Then Tarnish nodded towards my pocket.

'That,' he said wearily, holding my gaze, 'wouldn't happen to be the ledger bound in red morocco you mentioned, would it?'

'That sounds very much like an accusation.' I instinctively took a step backward. It was a gesture worthy of Roy Rogers and I could almost hear a saloon honky-tonk stutter to a mid-tune halt. Tarnish caught my intention and laughed.

'Just show me. Please.'

I shrugged and took the copy of *The Outsider* from my pocket and held it up for him to see. 'I'm improving my mind. Satisfied?'

'Like I said, it would be unfortunate if you were holding anything back from me. Anything. Goodbye, Captain Lennox.'

'Goodbye, Captain Tarnish.'

I left with him. I wouldn't look at the book until later. I got into the Sunbeam and drove off, heading back towards my apartment. After we were back over the river, I could see Twinkletoes McBride's Cresta in my rear-view; he followed me all the way along Great Western Road.

'Coming up for a drink?' I asked when we were both parked in the car park outside my apartment building. McBride frowned as much as the narrow band between his heavy brow ridge and low hairline allowed.

'Mr L,' he said earnestly, 'I watched for them men with Tarnish. You was right: they was waiting around the corner and he got in with them and they drove away. There's something I've got to tell you about them.'

I placed a hand on his shoulder and smiled. 'Let's go in and get a drink, Twinkle—'

'No listen . . . this is important. I've got to tell you . . . it's something about Tarnish and his men.'

'It's okay, Twinkle.' I steered him in the direction of the apartment building entrance. 'I already know . . .'

After Twinkletoes left – after he told me what he had to tell me and I told him how I already knew – I sat alone in the apartment with my whiskey. I set the book down on the coffee table. I poured myself another bourbon and sat looking at the book without touching it, as if it were a locked box, its secrets still fastened tight within. A Pandora's Box.

I took a sip, then a breath. I opened the book.

I flicked through it all. Nothing. I lifted it up, holding the coverboards like wings and shaking it so that anything trapped in the pages would fall out. Still nothing. Finally, I turned every page individually, methodically, scanning each printed face for notes or highlights. Still nothing. Not even a page corner turned over as a bookmark.

I laid it back down and stared at it.

*'Maybe, one day, this'll be a book that will speak to you too.'*

Except it wasn't saying anything. Its simple cover of orange geometric shapes told me nothing, other than the title, the author's name and that it had an introduction by Cyril Connolly.

After all of that, after all of my investment of significance into an offhand remark; after all my manoeuvres and shenanigans and fancy footwork to retrieve it – maybe all Tommy had meant was a literary recommendation: that he really thought it was simply a book I should read, but he hadn't wanted to lend it to me at the time.

I leaned back in the club chair and lifted my glass to the air.

'Thanks, Tommy. Thanks a bunch for the book recommendation.' I gave a bitter laugh then drowned it with a swig of booze.

It was like Tommy had answered me. It was the weirdest experience, but the rest of what he had said to me that night fell suddenly back into my head: *'And most important of all, always remember that you can never judge a book by its cover. This book particularly.'*

I picked up the hardback again and slipped off the paper dust jacket. And there it was, on the inside of the paper cover in faint yellow pencil; written small and so lightly that its impression wouldn't show through the paper; written specifically for me to read: the words of a dead, quiet man.

As I had asked him to, Twinkletoes had arranged with Archie and Tony the Pole that we meet up at Tony's transport caff. A gloomier than usual Archie was waiting for me, squeezed into the corner of one of the café's booths by the Neanderthal bulk of an equally grim-faced Twinkletoes McBride. When I arrived, Tony the Pole was behind the counter helping Senga, who hypnotized me with her ability to balance a fan of multiple plates in one hand, a cluster of white china tea mugs in the other, while simultaneously squinting through the smoke of her lip-clenched cigarette and containing wet rumbles of rheumy coughs. Not a drop was spilled, even during her worst consumptive spasms.

I wondered idly if she'd trained at Maxim's in Paris.

Tony the Pole beamed at me and came around from behind the counter. We weaved our way through the tables populated by a smattering of early-morning lorry drivers sitting gloomily over their fry-ups and coffees or teas, contemplating arduous journeys to Aberdeen or London, Birmingham or Plymouth.

None of them faced a journey as operose as that which lay ahead of me and my cobbled-together club of allies.

Tony and I slipped into the booth, across the table from Archie and McBride. It was the furthest booth from the other customers and I reckoned we were safe from being overheard.

'I know everything now,' I explained. 'Tommy left it all for me – but I had already worked some of it out. There's more that Tommy couldn't have known about, like Tarnish and his men. But before we get down to that, I need to tell you about what happened last night.' I turned to my business partner. 'Archie, this is all stuff you might not be comfortable with, as an ex-copper. If you want to give this particular conversation a miss, I quite understand.'

'I take it we're talking about criminal acts?' he asked lugubriously. There again, he asked everything lugubriously.

'Not committed by our side,' I said. 'No, wait . . . that's not strictly true. We committed a criminal act in *concealing* worse crimes committed by others.'

Archie shrugged. 'I've already done the same by chucking evidence into Mugdock reservoir. I'm in this already, so I may as well be in it up to my neck. Anyway, with what you said was done – *is* being done – to those children, and who you suspect is doing it, I don't know if I believe in the law any more.'

'Okay,' I said and ran through what had happened, telling Tony and Archie about Pops Loeb and the two hirelings.

'A fucking shame, about that old Jew,' said McBride in doleful support of my tale. 'Very *igg-noh-mine-ee-us* for an old gent like that getting chibbed to fuck all over the coupon the way he was. Real shame.'

We all paused, staring at Twinkletoes; I decided if McNaught came out of everything on top and I ended up dead, then I'd get

Twinkle to deliver my *yule-loggy*. If, knowing what I now knew, McNaught really was the boss.

'What did you find out from Tommy?' Archie asked.

I took a folded sheet of paper from my pocket. I had carefully copied out the names that Tommy had written in his hidden epistle. I handed it to Archie.

'These are the names that were listed in the diary I saw briefly, and more,' I said. 'You already know who some of the names are. The others are mostly, but not all, highly placed people: mostly senior army officers, two MPs, three Glasgow Corporation councillors, prominent law officials, even a couple of police. I have to say it's all very ecumenical: you'll find clergymen from both denominations very well represented.'

'Shit . . .' The normally inexpressive Archie looked shocked and shook his head. 'It's like a list from *Who's Who*, instead of a list of perverts. How did these people get together? I mean, did it come up at the golf club that they all like fiddling with kiddies?'

'It's staggering, right enough,' I said. 'If you look down the list, the reason Robert Weston – the young lad who chucked himself in front of a train – didn't get a fatal accident inquiry becomes pretty clear.'

'Jesus . . .' Archie muttered, staring at the page. He looked back at me, his expression still one of disbelief. '*That* Arbuthnot?'

'The one and the same,' I said.

'Ledd me zee . . .' said Tony the Pole; Archie handed him the paper.

'Everything revolves around St Andrew's School. That's where most, maybe all, of the children involved come from.'

'And zees people – zey are all involved?'

'Yes.'

'Zis iz dangerous shide here, Lennox. Very dangerous shide.'

'You want out, Tony?'

He looked insulted. 'Like fugg . . . you zink I let zees bhazd-ardz gedd avay vid shide like ziss? You dell me vatt I godda do . . . I do it.'

'Okay. Handsome Jonny now has a real dog in this fight, so he'll be doing whatever he has to. Tony, I know you're retired, but I need you to break in somewhere. Open a safe.'

'You vant me to steal zomething?'

I shook my head. 'No, not quite . . .'

## 3

I cut quite a dash. I could be accused of being superficial, but to me the world seemed to be divided between those who had to hire or borrow an evening suit, like Jock Ferguson, and those who owned their own made-to-measure tuxedo and patent blacks. Like me. I could have done with looking less conspicuous, though, given the venue, and I'd been the object of a few bleary-eyed off-duty stares since I'd arrived. On the other hand, lanky Jock Ferguson, in his ill-fitting borrowed outfit, looked like he should be taking orders for drinks.

Ferguson had said that he wouldn't be staying the distance and would get a taxi home later. He still expressed great suspicion about my motives in wanting to attend the retiring Chief Inspector MacIntyre's retirement smoker, but didn't push it.

I'd driven us both to the hotel in the city centre. It was reasonably upmarket and not the type of place you'd usually associate with stripper-and-a-comic stag-dos. But, there again, if the party concerned was the City of Glasgow Police, and you wanted no future trouble with your licences, you pretty much had to put up with it. Even with that, the management had done everything it could to seal hermetically the function suite from the rest of the hotel. When Ferguson and I arrived, we entered directly through a side entrance into the function hall.

The air was steel-blue thick with cigarette smoke and fumed with the stink of free-bar whisky and boiled chicken and vegetables. There were two bars, running the length of each side, working to full capacity, and the main floor area was filled with round tables, each with six or seven bow-tied men around it. The whole space was filled with the ringing clamour of drunken male voices as bawdy conversations were shouted in competition with each other. The attendees, as far as I could see, were all City of Glasgow Police CID officers, most of whom I reckoned were above the rank of sergeant. The night was still young, but many were already fully drunk, the rest halfway there. And this, I guessed, was more decorous than the usual soirée for the ordinary police ranks: it was well known that your average pillaging Viking or pirate would find City of Glasgow Police smokers uncouth.

The room was dully lit, except for the spotlight focused on a small raised stage at the far end of the room. A platinum blonde stripper who was on the obese side of voluptuous was going dully and expressionlessly through her routine, while an equally expressionless drummer beat a tattoo on a snare drum and cymbal. It had several of the audience at the closest tables droolingly captivated, but it was one of the most singularly un-erotic things I'd ever seen. And I'd dated a lot of Scottish women.

'Jesus . . .' muttered Ferguson beside me. 'I'm in hell . . .'

'I'll get us a couple of drinks,' I said. 'We'll need them.'

'Thanks,' said Ferguson when I came back and handed him his glass of blended gut-rot. I had an orange juice; when I'd asked the young barman in his tartan waistcoat and bow tie for a bourbon, he looked at me as if I had come from Mars. When I suggested a Canadian Club, he clearly thought I was looking for a membership, not a drink.

'By the way,' said Ferguson, 'we found Jimmy Wilson. You know, you were asking about him. We were looking for him at Quaid's funeral to serve his warrant . . .'

'Oh,' I said, keeping my eyes on the stage and my cool under control.

'Aye . . .' said Ferguson. 'It's a damned shame.'

'What is?'

'He's dead. He was in his brother's car when it went off the road – way down near the border. His brother and sister-in-law too. The three of them burned in the wreck. My guess is they were heading for England and going too fast. The car went up in flames.'

'That's a shame,' I said and sipped my orange juice. Jimmy Wilson, his brother Davey and Davey's pregnant wife fell into my recall in total, perfect, painful detail. The world shifted beneath my feet and for a moment I thought I was going to throw up. Instead I focused on the stripper's dead, heavily made-up face as she went through her act.

'Oh, and I checked out what you asked,' said Ferguson.

'Sorry, what?'

'You asked me the other day to check out any notable break-ins on that date. I did.' He handed me a folded note from his pocket.

At that point, the stripper revealed all that she had to reveal and several tables exploded into catcalls, drowning out any chance of conversation with Ferguson.

After the stripper quit the stage, followed by her accompanist with his snare drum tucked under his arm, a younger CID man came on and acted as master of ceremonies. He fawningly intro-duced the next act, emphasizing what a great privilege it was to have a star of stage and television appear.

Ferguson leaned his head towards mine to be heard above the drunken applause. 'You know the funny thing about that list of break-ins?' he asked.

'That our star attraction here was a victim of a break-in that night?' I said, slipping the note into my pocket without looking at it.

Ferguson gave a start, surprised; then suspicion settled in his expression. 'How the hell did you know about that?'

'It's a long story. And not one you want to hear.'

I said no more and watched as Frantic Frankie Findlay took to the stage. As he did so, I felt a tidal wave of hate and anger surge up from deep within. For the moment, I forced it down. I also ignored Ferguson who I knew was still watching me, and not the stage.

Findlay's act was all lamentably predictable, but nonetheless shocking as it progressed. He started with a few jokes from his stage act, the usual Scottish parochial line in humour; then – as tradition demanded at such functions – he settled into his 'blue' material. He cracked a few CID in-jokes that he'd clearly been briefed on, naming specific officers, joking about specific events.

After a while, he launched into the real meat of his act. And his audience certainly proved hungry for it, laughing almost mani-acally at every gag. All the usual butts of all the usual jokes were there: sex-hungry and stupid young women; sex-starved and stu-pid older women; and, of course, the Irish, Glasgow Catholics. And Jews.

I could feel Ferguson become more uncomfortable with every gag, adding to impatience with me. Everyone else was lap-ping it up.

'I can't take much more of this,' he said. 'Let's go to a pub and you can tell me how you knew Findlay was on that list.'

'I have to stay, Jock.' I turned to him, faced him straight-on. 'You want me to tell you what I know and why I know it? Okay – I know Frankie Findlay was burgled that night because Quiet Tommy Quaid burgled him. Quiet Tommy Quaid burgled him and was murdered because of it. Tommy knew that Frankie Findlay was appearing at the King's Theatre that night and that his wife, who is his manager and takes care of all of the money, would be there with him. Tommy knew there would be proceeds from Findlay's latest stage tour and that he had the time . . .'

On stage, the man I was talking about was cracking jokes about 'the Jews' being upset because Hitler had sent them his gas bill. Men who had fought in a war that was supposed to have been all about ending that kind of hate roared with laughter.

' . . . had the time to break into the safe and get away with the takings and a pile of jewellery. Except that's not all he found. There were two leather-bound books – a diary and a ledger – and a document folder. It was these he was killed for. The document folder was stuffed with pictures of men raping children.'

'Where is this folder?' asked Ferguson. His face was stone. We stood like an island in the middle of the tumult of raucous laughter and yelling, Findlay's nasal voice microphone-amplified.

'It's gone. They got it back. And one of the books – a diary filled with the initials of those who took part in these sick, perverted parties. By the way, all of the kids involved came from St Andrew's School, down on the Ayrshire coast. Findlay organized these little get-togethers and he kept a record of them, maybe for his own safety, maybe because he had ideas of blackmailing those involved. You see, they were – *are* – all very important people in the Scottish Establishment. Politicians, MPs, army . . .'

'Police?'

I nodded. 'Including your chum you're having the party for here.'

'Bob MacIntyre?' Ferguson looked around the room, as if he suddenly had found himself in a strange land, surrounded by people he didn't know.

'It gets worse, Jock,' I said. 'One of the biggest of the bigwigs involved in this is Donald Arbuthnot.'

'You are fucking kidding me . . .'

I shook my head. 'You don't have much of a chance of justice when one of the people who's sexually assaulted you is the Solicitor General of Scotland. And you should know that Jimmy Wilson was there with Tommy Quaid the night he turned over Findlay's place. Jimmy's death was no accident.'

Ferguson cast an eye around the room, grabbed my elbow and steered me through the function suite, the entrance hall and into the street outside. The air, even Glasgow city air, felt clean and cool and quiet after the smoke and noise of the hall. He checked the side street we were in both ways to ensure he wouldn't be overheard.

'Jesus, Lennox, do you know what you're saying?'

'I know exactly what I'm saying. I saw some of those pictures with my own eyes and there is no way I'll ever be able to unsee them. I thought I would never see anything worse than all the shit I saw in the war. Well, I did. If you'd seen those kids' faces, Jock . . .'

'You're talking about hard evidence. You've got to get those pictures to me and I'll—'

'And you'll what? These people run everything. They run *you*. That evidence will never see the light of day and if you get involved there's every chance you'll stop seeing it too.'

'So why tell me?'

'Because you're a good man. Because you're a good man more than you're a copper, just the way Tommy was a good man more than he was a thief. Because you believe in the right thing. I'm telling you that the right thing here has nothing to do with the law. I'm telling you because I need you to turn a blind eye to what is about to happen. I'm asking you to abandon every instinct you have as a copper and let me handle this.'

'Are you telling me blood is going to be spilt?'

'I'm telling you not to ask me questions like that. But let me say, no innocent blood will be spilt.'

'Fuck's sake, Lennox . . . I'm a detective chief inspector in the City of Glasgow Police. You can't seriously expect me to turn a blind eye to the kind of crime you're talking about – or to you going off on some vigilante crusade.'

'If you get involved right now, all you'll be doing is warning them and they'll get away with it. They'll deal with you somehow. Maybe you'll drive off a road and break your neck, or they'll pin something on you that'll ruin you. Everything you believe is turned on its head with this. If you got involved you'd have to forget everything you believe, everything you think you stand for. You'd have to stop being a copper.' I took a long pull on my cigarette. 'Go home, Jock.'

He made to protest.

'Just go home. You got me into the smoker, that's all I needed you to do.'

He started to walk up the side street towards Argyle Street and the cab rank.

'One more thing, Jock,' I called.

'What?'

'Are you much of a reader?'

He frowned at me in the lamplight, then shrugged. 'Not a big reader. Some Nevile Shute, that kind of thing. Why?'

'I have a book in my apartment: *The Outsider* by Albert Camus. If anything happens to me, I want you to have it. You'll find it very informative, especially if you look behind the dust cover. Then you can decide where you stand.'

He stared at me for a moment, then nodded and headed out onto the main road.

I threw what remained of my cigarette onto the cobbles, ground it out with the pointed toe of my patent black, and headed back into the smoker.

# 4

During the war – or at least during my war – time had split into two types: there was the waiting and preparing for action, and there was the action itself. Sometimes the waiting was worse: you had time for fear, for outcomes imagined. When the time for action came, when you were finally thrown into the storm, the moment of commitment could be a moment of calm.

As I went back into the smoker, I had that strange moment of calm.

My war, like everyone else's on our side, had been all about recovering held territory, and it was always easier to hold and defend than it was to retake and advance. I was ready to retake territory.

I went back into the smoke and the noise of the hall and caught the end of Findlay's act. It was more of the same stuff. Anti-women, anti-Semitic, anti-Catholic, anti-Irish, anti-English. The great thing about the good old City of Glasgow Police, guardians of our lives and property, I thought, was that they really knew how to have a good laugh at a few Fascist funnies.

I checked out the location of the toilets. There was a hallway that led from the main function suite to the double doors of the fire exit. The Gents was off to the left of the hall.

I went back into the bar and decided to risk a Scotch, rather than an orange juice: I needed something to stop my gorge rising while Findlay finished his act. There was a CID copper at the bar: a detective constable I'd had dealings with in the past. As I leaned against the bar beside him, he looked me up and down with drunken, slow-motion contempt – which I rather took umbrage at, considering the last time I'd met him I'd handed him an envelope thick with banknotes in exchange for information. He was at the elision stage of drunkenness, where words slid into each other seamlessly and vowels stretched.

'Whaddafuckyoodoinhere, Lennox?'

I told him I'd been invited along by Jock Ferguson. My new drinking buddy twisted his already ugly face into a gurn that suggested he didn't hold Detective Chief Inspector Ferguson in much regard.

'And of course I wanted to pay my respects to the great man: Chief Inspector MacIntyre,' I explained.

The drunk detective again twisted his features in a kind of gurn and it took me a while to work out that this time it was in approval.

'Aye? Thazzgood, thazzgood. BobbyMacIntyrezza goodbloke. Izzafuckin goodbloke. Zzuckingoodpolisman.'

'Yeah. He's really good with kids, or so I've been told . . .'

'Oh aye?' He raised his eyebrows sluggishly. 'Wouldnaysurpriseme. Wouldnaesurprisemeatall,' he said then squeezed his lips tight to suppress a belch. The belch must have been loaded because he suddenly looked surprised and headed off briskly but weavingly in the direction of the toilets.

I moved along the bar to get a better look at MacIntyre, the man of the moment, who sat at a front and centre table. I watched him through the ever-thickening air. He was over both sixty and six foot. He'd probably been well built once but it had turned to flab; the face pale and thick, his nose and lips fleshy, the cheeks and tip of his nose reddened with broken threads of booze-burst capillaries. He had his thinning grey hair trimmed close to a pink scalp that gleamed through. Everything about him spoke of a boozer, a glutton, a man who gave way to every appetite. I'd seen him before. I'd seen him outside Central Station the day Peter Manuel had hanged and seventeen-year-old Robert Weston had thrown himself in front of a train. I took a good long look at Chief Inspector Bob MacIntyre – a pale, pink, fleshy slug – and I wanted to stamp on him. And I would. But later: this wasn't the time, nor the place.

Frantic Frankie Findlay had ended his act with a routine about the Pope and had quit the stage to enthusiastic applause. The heavy-built stripper and her accompanist retook the stage.

Findlay made his smug-faced way through the tables, stopping occasionally to shake hands and trade gags with his appreciative audience, before finding his way to sit next to MacIntyre at his table.

I watched them for about an hour. During that time a couple of coppers I knew came up to me and asked me with the same bluntness what I was doing there. I explained about being Jock Ferguson's guest and that satisfied them for a while, but Ferguson was becoming conspicuous by his absence. I was on borrowed time.

Eventually, there was an explosion of laughter from the table as Findlay obviously cracked a joke and rose before heading off to the men's room, leaving his companions still laughing. It had probably been one of his best gags: from what I could see a lot of Scottish humour revolved around toilets.

I waited thirty seconds or so then followed him in.

It was a large, bright, Victorian washroom, all white porcelain, mirrors and brass. Tonight its lustre was dulled by cigarette smoke and the stink of stale urine; the average drunk Scotsman viewed a urinal as a general guide rather than a specific target.

Findlay was at a urinal at the far end, bantering over his shoulder to a couple of drunk coppers who were on their way out. I paused at the wash-basins, the one area of the toilets that weren't getting much trade that night, until the two coppers passed. When they did I picked up a folded towelling napkin and dried my hands, watching Findlay as he passed by behind me on the way out.

'I really enjoyed your show tonight, Frankie,' I said to his reflection. He stopped and looked at me. I was probably the only person that hadn't addressed him as Mr Findlay that night.

'Oh aye?' he said. 'That's good.' He started off again.

'Yep. It wasn't your best stuff though.'

He stopped again, looking affronted.

'No . . . You didn't tell that one . . . you know, the one about the kiddie-fiddler,' I continued, throwing the towel into the basin and turning to face him. 'I can't remember *exactly* how it goes, but basically this kiddie-fiddler gets together with his child-raping buddies and they have these parties . . .'

All Findlay's smug assurance washed from his expression and was replaced with alarm. I could tell he was about to make a break for the exit and his copper buddy. Two steps took me to him and I fastened my hand around his throat. His eyes bulged with terror as I pushed him backwards, unresisting, and into a cubicle. I heard voices coming into the washroom and I kicked the door shut behind us, snibbing it with my free hand. Forcing Findlay to sit on the toilet, my hand still tight around his throat, I reached into the waistband of my dinner suit and pulled out the Webley Jonny Cohen had given me. I pushed the barrel hard against his forehead and made a 'not a sound' face. The sight of the gun clearly terrified Findlay and he sat wide-eyed on the toilet.

'We're going for a walk,' I said after a while, when I was sure the coppers had left the toilets. 'If you make a single sound, or try to call for help, know that I'm prepared to hang for you. You got it?'

'Listen,' he said, 'it wasn't me. I didn't do anything to those kiddies.'

I hauled him to his feet and slammed him against the side of the cubicle, ramming the barrel tip under his weak jaw. 'I said have you got it?'

He nodded.

I opened the cubicle door, checked all was clear, and steered Findlay out to the washroom door. Checking the hall outside, I saw there was no one there, but it was at that stage in the evening that there was an increasingly steady stream from the function hall to the toilets, so I had to be quick. I marched Findlay along the hall, shoved the fire exit's push-bar and bustled him out into the side street. It had taken only fifteen or twenty seconds and no one had seen us.

I closed the fire door behind us and steered Findlay, keeping the gun in the small of his back, to where I had parked the car. When I opened the trunk and indicated for him to get in, he hesitated just long enough for me to be grateful for the excuse to slash him across the side of the face with the butt of the gun. I shoved him backwards into the trunk, his knees folding. He started to cry like a woman, coiled up in the dark space and I slammed it shut.

I got into the driver's seat. Before I started the engine I looked at the gun in my hand, trying to work out what the hell was going through my head. Things had taken a deadly turn: people were going to die, either us or them. I was in a game now where I needed to be armed, like tonight, where I needed to be guaranteed Findlay's cooperation. So why had I gone in hunting for him in a hall full of coppers with an unloaded pistol?

I found the house in Langdyke Avenue with very little trouble: just as Jimmy had said, it was one of those big, block-like Victorian villas, sitting in a huge plot on the corner on the avenue, with a tall, primeval-looking monkey puzzle tree, the only one in the street, dominating the garden. There were no lights on when I arrived.

With a jab of the gun and a word of caution that, if he called for help, my silencing of him would be permanent, I bundled Findlay out of the trunk and to his front door. He fumbled with his keys and I took them from him and opened the front door.

It was an impressive place all right. The architect and the builders – who had probably built it for the family of some robber-baron shipyard owner – would never have imagined it falling into the ownership of a sleazy music-hall comic. The marble-pillared vestibule opened into a mahogany-panelled hall. Someone had cut down a forest or two to fashion the staircase at the far end of the hall. I had checked that Findlay's wife would be out of town before pulling this stunt, but the baronial style and size of Findlay's house caused me a second's worry that he actually had a butler. But there was no sound; no Jeeves type appeared to see if we wanted tiffin in the drawing room.

'Take me to where you keep the safe.'

He led me through to a wood-panelled study, two of its walls lined with bookcases filled with antiquarian-looking, leather bound books. Findlay didn't strike me as a big reader and I guessed they had come with the house when he'd bought it.

Findlay's personal touches stretched to an oil portrait of himself and photographs of his yacht. No pictures of his wife, or anyone else.

The safe, predictably, was behind his portrait. I made him open it and rifled through its contents, but didn't find what I was looking for. It didn't surprise me: once bitten, twice shy.

'Where are they?'

'What?'

'The photographs.'

'What do you mean? The photographs are gone. That's wha—'

I hit him again across the side of the face with the butt of the gun. His cheek split and started to bleed, spotting the crisp white of his dress shirt. He bent forward and took his pocket square out, holding it to his face with trembling fingers. He looked at me, his eyes wide with fear and glossed with tears.

'Sorry to interrupt you,' I said, 'but I think you were about to embarrass us both by insulting my intelligence.' I sat down in the button-backed leather armchair behind the desk, motioning with the gun for him to sit opposite me. I laughed a little. 'Makes me feel like a bank manager, all this walnut and leather. Now, let's straighten everything out. All this crap – Tommy Quaid dying and everything that has happened since – has all been about this sick little club of yours. These little parties you throw. All of you are pervert scum – but the rest were *important* pervert scum. You? You're just an end-of-the-pier turn who's had a bit of luck. The only thing you really share with the others is your sick sexual tastes. But you're still the odd man out. You're no Solicitor General, Special Branch copper or soon-to-be cardinal.'

There was a block of silver-trimmed walnut sitting on the desk. I flipped open the lid with the barrel of the gun, took out a cigarette and lit it with Findlay's desk lighter. He sat watching me, still holding the white pocket square to his cheek. A dark red stain bloomed on the cotton.

'You organized the get-togethers, but the real bosses of the group were Arbuthnot, MacIntyre and Sullivan. They're untouchable, but you're not. So, even though everything seemed nice and cosy for the meantime, you decided to take out a little insurance policy. You keep records of who, what, where and when and you keep photographs to back your records up. You maybe even have the idea that you could use them as a *lever* at some time in the future. Not blackmail as such, but maybe just a little extra force to put behind it if you asked one of the others for a favour. Am I right so far?'

Findlay nodded. His face was pale, oiled rat's tails of hair hanging over his forehead.

'And then Tommy Quaid comes along to relieve you of the month's takings, but also takes off with the pictures and the diary. Your insurance policy. You've got to get them back, so all of this shit starts.'

'They'll kill me. They'll kill you, too. You don't know the connections they have—'

I held up a hand to stop him. 'So where is it?'

'Where's *what*?' His voice was pleading.

'Tommy stole the pictures. The danger to you was that he would pass them on to someone who could expose you and the others. Mainly you. But the pictures have been retrieved, and I'm guessing by representatives of the others, not your boys. So we don't have them, and you don't have them. But they were prints. You still hold the negatives. The original film. You're a belt-and-braces kind of guy, so I'm guessing that you kept them somewhere else. That's why Tommy didn't find them in the safe.'

Findlay looked at me pleadingly. 'The negatives are all that are keeping me safe. MacIntyre and the others . . . you don't know what they're capable of.'

'I've got a pretty good idea. But let me make this simple for you: you give me the negatives now or I'll kill you.' I pulled back the hammer on the Webley. Findlay held his hands up.

'They're on my boat. It's moored out at Inverkip. I've got them hidden there.'

I nodded and eased the hammer forward.

'Change into your sailing gear,' I said.

'What?'

'Your clothes for sailing – change into them.'

Racialist and misogynistic jokes must have been worth their weight in gold, judging by the dimensions and furnishings of Findlay's place. Leaving the door open so I could keep an eye on him, I stood in the hall while he changed in his huge bedroom. He started to hang up his evening suit and I told him to leave it lying on the bed. He looked at me oddly: I didn't know if he was just confused, or if he had guessed I was leaving a breadcrumb trail; a story to be read.

The walls of the hall were covered with photographs. It was an inflated ego given physical form: all the photographs were of Frankie Findlay at different stages in his career. Some were full-size front-of-house theatre posters and display cards; others were of him posing with bigger-name stars from England and the US. There was a small cluster of photographs from his time in the war. Findlay's theatre of war had been just that: a theatre. As a member of ENSA – the Entertainments National Service Association – he had pranced about doing his routine on improvised stages before hordes of real servicemen.

There was one picture made me pause. It had been taken

somewhere that saw more sun than Scotland. Frankie Findlay and three other men, all in khaki, all with lance corporal stripes, smiled at the camera. The youngest of the men, immediately to Findlay's right, seemed strangely familiar to me, but I couldn't place him. He was broad-shouldered, handsome and tanned, a Douglas Fairbanks-type pencil moustache lining his upper lip. He looked more the leading-man-actor type than a stage comic, and it itched at me that I couldn't pinpoint who it was he reminded me of. I decided that I must have seen him play a part in something; some movie or TV show.

On its mount, the photograph was captioned: *Singapore, 1941*. The names of the men were listed; next to Findlay's name was *J. P. Gresty*. I was still none the wiser.

I had just turned from the photograph when it fell into place who the handsome young man was. When Findlay came out of the bedroom, dressed in his sailing outfit, I grabbed his arm and pushed him close to the photograph.

I told him who I thought Gresty was. He told me I was right.

Before we left Findlay's house, I made a 'phone call.

## 5

Inverkip, just south of Greenock, was an hour's drive from Glasgow along the southern shore of the Clyde. I couldn't stomach the idea of having to listen to Frankie Findlay's pleadings or justifications, so he spent the trip in the trunk again. This time I tied his hands behind his back and used the canvas bag for the tyre jack as a hood. He had whimpered when I tightened the drawstring around his neck.

Like I had asked, he had changed into white slacks, a blue cotton shirt, a darker blue windcheater and canvas deck shoes. I didn't know what his skills as a sailor were like, but at least he looked the part. I'd fixed his face up and the only discordant note in his nautical ensemble was the pad of gauze held on his cheek by surgical tape. Not once did Findlay ask why I had made him change into his sailing clothes, or why I'd made him leave his clothes scattered in his bedroom.

Inverkip marina was a forest of clinking white masts. I found Findlay's boat at the berth he gave me. It was a thirty-footer and looked reasonably new. Parking at the end of the quay, I left Findlay in the trunk while I checked out the boat. I could see there was no one on board, although I was expecting company soon as a result of my telephone call from Findlay's house.

I went below into the living cabin or whatever the hell they called it on a boat. Like Findlay's study, it was all plush leather and polished wood and brass. An inlaid table was folded flat against the wall and a Tantalus-style double decanter sat above it on a railed shelf. Luxurious. But there was something about the room, about the set-up with the table and the decanter that seemed familiar. I felt sick when I realized I had recognized them from the background of the photographs. This had been one of the venues, maybe the only venue, for Findlay's sick parties. For those children, frightened and vulnerable and uncomprehending of what was being done to them, it had been a polished, luxurious version of hell.

When I went back along the quay to where I'd parked the car, I checked that there was no one around before dragging the bound and hooded Findlay out of the Alpine's trunk and onto the boat. Once he was in the cabin, I snatched the hood from his head.

'Where is it?' I demanded.

'In the galley . . . I'll show you.' Still with his hands tied behind his back, he led me to the boat's kitchen and nodded to one of the cupboards. 'There's an envelope taped to the underside.'

Crouching down, I reached beneath the cupboard and felt a packet fixed there. I was suddenly thrust forward, my head hitting the cupboard, as Findlay rammed the sole of his foot into my shoulder. A second kick caught me in the side of the head.

By the time I was on my feet and turned round in the cramped galley, Findlay was gone and heading up to the deck. I ran after him and saw him as he jumped from the boat onto the quay. He stumbled and struggled to keep his balance with his hands tied behind him.

'Help me!' he yelled as he started running along the jetty. 'For God's sake, somebody help me!'

It only took a matter of seconds for me to catch up with him and bring him down with another blow from the gun butt, this time to the back of his head. He was dazed and brought to silence. I held him down, my knee on his spine, pushing him into the wooden jetty. When I was satisfied no one had been around to hear his desperate cries, I hoisted him back to his feet and frogmarched him back to the boat. I rehooded him with the wheel jack bag and locked him in the toilet.

I retrieved the envelope from under the galley cupboard and took it through to the cabin, folded down the table and spilled the envelope's contents onto its elaborately inlaid surface.

'Son of a bitch . . .' I muttered as I looked down on a small ledger type book, bound in red leather. Red morocco leather.

The strips of photographic negatives had each been carefully interspersed between its pages. On the right-hand page next to each strip was a numbered list: full names of who was on each frame of the negatives and the time and date the photographs had been taken. Whether the photographs had been taken secretly, or whether having pictures of their acts was part of their perversions, it provided a full record of who had done what and when.

There was the sound of footsteps on the jetty and I placed the gun on the table in front of me, sitting facing the steps down from the deck. It was who I was expecting.

'Sit down, gentlemen,' I said. 'And we can begin the entertainment.'

Findlay, still hooded, gave a start when I opened the toilet door. I hauled him to his feet and led him through to the cabin, pushing him down into the seat.

'I've some friends over,' I said. 'I'd like you to entertain them, do some of your act.'

'What? Who's there?' asked Findlay from beneath his hood.

'But first,' I said, ignoring him, 'let's talk about this ledger with the negatives. This is the ledger you've had everyone searching for, when you had it all the time. Your insurance policy. A red morocco ledger. The ledger that Tommy Quaid stole from your safe. How come you've got it?'

'I kept it separate from the other stuff, for safety, like you said. It was just the prints and the diary that went missing.'

'But the ledger? Described exactly like this one. Tommy Quaid *did* take it from the safe.'

The canvas hood moved and I guessed Findlay was shaking his head. 'My wife bought me the ledgers when we were on holiday. Two identical notebooks in red morocco. I told Arbuthnot, MacIntyre and the others that Quaid and Wilson had stolen the ledger with the negatives.'

'So what was in the other ledger – the one Tommy took?'

'Accounts. Details of takings from each of the shows to make sure I wasn't short-changed by the theatres. Nothing more. Honest. I swear it. But as long as the others couldn't find it, they didn't know I still had the negatives.'

I sat for a minute, thinking about Jimmy Wilson, Davey Wilson, Davey Wilson's wife; about carefully made plans for a future that would never come. I resisted the urgent impulse I had to beat Findlay senseless. Instead I said, 'Okay. Do your act.'

'What?'

'I said, do your act.'

'What, now? Are you mad?' Beneath the hood, Findlay's voice was both frightened and incredulous.

I picked up the gun and held it to his head, hard enough for him to feel it through the canvas.

'Do your act. Do the routine you did tonight, you know, the stuff about the Jews. Tell us the one about the gas bill.'

He hesitated and I jabbed the gun harder against his head.

In a halting, frightened voice, Frantic Frank Findlay ran through his material, reciting it without emphasis, without performance, as if reading a grocery list. If he missed anything out, I reminded him of it and made him tell it.

When he was finished his anti-Semitic routine, I picked up the ledger and slipped it into my pocket and stood up to leave. As I did so, I snatched the canvas hood from his head. He blinked, adjusting to the light, then he saw Handsome Jonny Cohen sitting opposite him, flanked by two Jewish heavies in mohair suits.

As I made my way up to the deck and the fresh night air, I heard Jonny say to Findlay in a quiet, almost friendly voice: 'It's a nice night for a little moonlight sail.'

# 6

Twinkletoes McBride and Tony the Pole came round to my place early the following day, as we'd arranged. I ran through what had happened the previous night and told them that our list was now one name shorter. The most important name.

I told them about the ledger and the negatives.

'Tony, you have all kinds of contacts. I need someone to print out these pictures, three sets of each. But the contents of these pictures would turn the strongest stomach and it has to be someone who understands that we're trying to stop this filth, not promote it – otherwise even the most hardened crook would turn us over to the police.'

'Jeez, Lennogs – zat's no gonna be easy. Like you zay, vizz vaht iz in zees pictures. I'll need to think aboud it.'

'We don't have a lot of time, Tony.'

'I'll do it.'

We both turned to McBride.

'I'll do it,' he repeated. 'I've got all the equipment, an enlarger and everything. In the spare bedroom.'

Tony and I still looked at him, stunned.

'It's my hobby,' he explained. 'Photography. Wildlife. Birds, mainly. It's very *therry-pew-tick*.'

It still took me a moment to wrap my mind around the

concept of Twinkletoes McBride discussing technique with Ansel Adams. 'You can do this okay?'

'I'll take them now. Give me a couple of hours.'

I needed to hang on to the ledger, so I had taken the negatives out and placed them in a white envelope. I handed it to Twinkletoes then turned to Tony. 'Once we have the extra prints, can you do the break-in I was talking about?'

'Sure . . .' Tony beamed. 'Izznae a problem.'

'Okay, we'll meet back here at noon. That enough time, Twinkle?'

McBride nodded his Easter Island head.

I drove down to Newton Mearns and spent an hour with Jennifer. We talked about everything else other than the business at hand, then, after a while, I told her that the man who had ordered Tommy's death had been dealt with.

'Will it soon be over?' she asked.

'Very soon. Then we can get on with our lives. In fact, when all of this crap is done with, that's something I want to talk to you about.'

'I'd like that,' she said, and smiled.

I met with Jonny Cohen before leaving.

'Everything go okay last night?' I asked.

'No problems. I got one of the boys to drive Findlay's car to Inverkip. We used a dinghy to get back to shore. Your turn now. You ready?'

I nodded. 'Can I use your 'phone?'

I made sure I was there a full half-hour before the agreed time. I sat in Quiet Tommy Quaid's lounge and smoked a cigarette, taking the time to remember some of the times I'd had with him; some of the conversations we'd had, some of the women we'd picked up, some of the benders we'd gone on. I thought about him because of the time I now occupied, not the space. Tommy's flat still gave me no feeling of his presence.

I'd left the door between the living room and the hall open and when there was a knock on the outer door, I called out that it was unlocked and to come in. Tarnish did so. Cautiously. His two men, Fraser and Mayhew, followed him in.

'I asked on the 'phone if you could come alone,' I said, without surprise or annoyance. 'I thought we could talk privately.'

'Do you have it?'

'What?'

'The ledger,' he said. 'On the telephone you said you'd tracked down McNaught and you had the ledger and the negatives.'

'Oh, of course . . .' I smiled and took the ledger out of my pocket. I held it, rubbing the tooled surface of the cover with my thumb. 'Beautiful leatherwork,' I said.

Tarnish didn't sit, instead remained standing, flanked by his men. 'May I see it?'

'Sure . . .' I didn't get up but tossed the red leather notebook onto the surface of the table. Sighing, Tarnish leaned over and picked it up. He turned to the others and smiled. The smile faded as he flicked through the notebook.

'Where are the negatives?'

'Oh those . . . I'm having several sets of prints made up. One set is going to be found scattered over the desk of the Solicitor General, Donald Arbuthnot, when the police break into his study to find he couldn't live with the shame and committed suicide.'

'When did he commit suicide?' Tarnish did his best to hide his shock.

'Oh, he hasn't, yet. He doesn't even know that he's going to do it. But it will happen tonight. I'm going to pay him a visit and put the idea – or something – into his head. A Polish friend of mine who's good with locks is going to make sure I surprise him.'

Tarnish looked relieved. 'Who's got the negatives now?'

'They're safe.'

Tarnish sighed again, reached into his jacket and pulled out a revolver. 'This is getting tiresome. I want all the prints and all the negatives, and you're going to tell me where to find them. Trust me, it's better that you tell me now. Fraser and Mayhew here will get it out of you anyway and it will be very unpleasant.'

'I suppose so,' I said. 'I saw their handiwork on Pops Loeb.'

'Who?'

'The old guy you did a number on in Jonny Cohen's Clarkston warehouse.'

Tarnish smiled, raising an eyebrow in admiration of my deductive skills. 'How did you know?'

'You described the ledger as having a red morocco cover. I didn't know it had a red morocco cover. All I'd been told was that it had a red leather cover. Of course, it could have been an innocent assumption on your part, but it was as if someone else had described what you were looking for. And I had Twinkletoes McBride watch my back. He saw you get into the same blue van with the Home Office plates that had followed us on the bank run. So which department do you work for?'

'This is unofficial,' said Tarnish. 'Or official-unofficial, if you know what I mean. There has to be a certain order to things; a certain sense of who's in charge and who isn't. Sometimes being in charge makes people feel that they can do anything, get away with anything. My job is to clear up after them. Protect the realm by protecting them. In a way, they're right: they can get away with anything. I was brought up specially for this job because I'd been Quaid's commanding officer.'

'Which one of you killed Tommy?'

'I'm afraid I did,' said Tarnish. 'Shame really, I really did like Quiet Tommy Quaid.'

'Everyone did.'

'He was so surprised,' said Tarnish. 'Confused, when he saw me up there on the roof. It made it easier. Now, where do I find the negatives?'

'You don't,' I said and nodded past Tarnish.

All three men turned around to see Jonny Cohen and his two men, who had been waiting in the bathroom and had sneaked along the hall while I'd talked with Tarnish. Each of them was pointing the armed-robber's weapon of choice, a sawn-off shotgun. I stepped forward and snatched the revolver from Tarnish's hand, then frisked and disarmed the other two. Between us, we tied their hands behind their backs.

'You can't seriously think you'll get away with this,' said Tarnish. 'These people *own* you. They own everyone—'

I shut him up with insulating tape across his mouth.

'Bring the van around to the front,' Jonny said to one of his men. 'When the street's clear, we'll get them out.'

I stepped up to Tarnish, almost nose to nose. 'I swore I would kill the man who killed Tommy. That I would get even for him; repay like with like, an eye for an eye. But you gave Tommy a quick, quiet death and I'd feel obliged to do the same for you. An eye for an eye – it's very Old Testament and so is Jonny here. Pops Loeb didn't have a quiet death at all. That's the debt I think you should pay. I promised Jonny that I'd let him settle accounts. I'm afraid you and your men are in for a somewhat *biblical* experience. You see, Pops Loeb really was like a father to Jonny . . .'

After Jonny and the others were gone, I sat for a while and again thought about Tommy. The dust jacket from *The Outsider* was folded up inside my pocket; I took it out and again read Tommy's secret last testament, written in faint yellow pencil, explaining about the night he and Jimmy Wilson had broken into Frankie Findlay's house, and what they had found. He had avoided naming me, in case someone else found the letter, but explained he had written it after I had left that night. I reread the last two paragraphs:

*Again, I'm sorry for bringing you into this. But it has to be a man like you to put at least some of this shite right. It has to be your kind of justice. There is no bad you can do that matches the evil these bastards have done.*

*My old da was right after all. He was right to spend his life deep in the dark and the dust of a mine. It's cleaner and more honest down there. And you are away from the crap people do to each other.*

*From one Outsider to another, I wish you the very best of luck. Do what you have to do.*

*Your friend,*
*Tommy*

## 7

The more skeletons that tumble out of the cupboard, the deeper you have to dig to bury them; and sometimes there's just not enough dirt to do it. So you have to decide which bones to leave out in the open. The thing of it is, if you pile a scandal on a scandal on a scandal, then it's difficult to cover *everything* up. In Solicitor General Donald Arbuthnot's case, the manner of his death couldn't be hidden from the public. Although the press made no mention of the suicide to start with, it became a matter of public record that the law officer had taken his own life.

It turned out that I didn't have to deal with Arbuthnot personally. When Twinkletoes McBride returned with the prints he'd made from the recovered negatives, he looked a broken man. It was odd to see a mountain of a man, someone who had worked as an enforcer and torturer, crumble under the weight of what the pictures contained.

So Tony the Pole had broken in and Twinkle had put the gun to Arbuthnot's head and pulled the trigger. Tony had typed out on Arbuthnot's typewriter the confession I had written down.

The story that was put about was that Arbuthnot had struggled privately with alcoholism for some time and decided to take the gentleman's way out before disgracing his career and family. No mention was ever made, except probably in hushed whispers in police muster rooms, of the images found scattered on his desk next to his slumped body. Nor was his typewritten but unsigned confession-cum-suicide note naming all of the other great and good personages involved in the pederast ring.

There were, however, a number of surprise retirements and resignations – and two by-elections – over the next couple of months. But no arrests, no prosecutions, no scandals. No justice.

And that, to me and my friends, just didn't seem right.

Particularly galling was the way that Monsignor Sullivan, far from being exposed and punished, actually secured his elevation to cardinal. Archie McClelland reckoned it was because the Catholic Church already had the machinery in place for keeping a lid on this kind of scandal.

I met with Jonny Cohen and we chatted about the injustice of Sullivan not only getting off scot-free, but how powerless we were to do anything about it. Jonny Cohen had looked at me meaningfully when he'd said: 'Maybe he'll get his reward in heaven.'

Two weeks later the clergyman was found hanged in his chambers. Suicide was anathema to the church, but it was better than admitting that the freshly minted cardinal had been found naked from the waist down apart from a floral-design garter belt, women's fishnet stockings and feather-fluffed high-heeled slippers. The automatic assumption would have been that Sullivan had died accidentally while committing some kind of auto-erotic act. This suspicion was probably given added weight by the fact that the priest had been stiff in more than one way. Truth was that post-mortem priapism was a common feature every hangman was familiar with, but the combination of the ladies' underthings and a serious stiffy must have made a big impression on those who found him.

Those were the bones that had to be hidden in Sullivan's case; the greater scandal that had to be concealed.

The church hid all the details of Sullivan's death from the press, even from the police who attended, by which time the clergyman's state of dress had been suitably adjusted. They were hidden from everyone. So how did I come to know?

Handsome Jonny Cohen told me.

Another mystery that was unexpectedly solved was that of who had jumped me that night outside the pub. It turned out to have nothing to do with Tommy Quaid.

Jennifer and I started to fulfil our promise of a normal relationship. About a week after everything had been dealt with, I took her out for dinner and a show in the West End. I was parking outside the restaurant when I saw a taxi pull up across the street and Irene Christie got out, all glammed up for a night out. A heavy-built, joyless-looking man, who I knew instantly was her husband, got out of the taxi behind her. The same thought that had struck me that night hit me again: *fuck-me-he's-the-spit-of-Victor-McLaglen*.

It took them three days to find Frankie Findlay's drifting yacht. There was a heavy smudge of blood on the yacht's boom, which suggested that it had swung and struck Findlay on the head, knocking him into the water. His body was never found, and everyone was mystified as to why he had suddenly left the police function he'd been attending, gone home and changed out of his evening suit, which lay scattered on the bedroom floor. His wife confirmed that his sailing clothes were missing. When his car was found abandoned at the quayside and his boat missing, they had started a sea search for him.

It was all very mysterious, but when rumours started to circulate about Findlay's being one of the names on Arbuthnot's list, the whole thing was dropped.

Newly retired Chief Inspector Bob MacIntyre didn't get a chance to enjoy much of his retirement. His wife had expressed concern about his increasingly anxious state of mind, his constantly seeming preoccupied, which caused him to drink even more heavily than usual. He was making his way home from his local Masonic Club, apparently the worse for wear, when he fell victim to a hit-and-run driver while crossing a deserted street. Neither the vehicle that hit him nor its driver were ever traced. Jock Ferguson told me that the boys who attended the scene said that MacIntyre must have been hit by something the size of a van or truck.

The word 'mince' had been used.

What was confusing was that it looked almost as if the vehicle had reversed back over MacIntyre after hitting him, but for some reason this wasn't pursued and it was treated as an accident.

We hadn't gotten around to discussing what should happen to the retired Special Branch man, so I asked Jonny Cohen and the others if they had been responsible for MacIntyre's death, but no one knew anything about it.

It would have appeared that we weren't the only ones doing some housekeeping.

With Findlay, Sullivan, Arbuthnot and MacIntyre dead, and with the other names on the list disappearing from public life, Jonny Cohen, Twinkletoes, Archie and I all got together at Tony the Pole's transport caff. Rather than feeling celebratory, we were all surprisingly subdued: there really weren't any winners in a game like this, just those left still standing.

'We didn't get them all,' said McBride, gloomily.

'We got the ones that matter, Twinkle. The others will be looking over their shoulders for the rest of their lives.'

'We didn't get all the ones that matter,' said Jonny Cohen. 'I still want McNaught.'

'McNaught wasn't the linchpin we thought he was,' I said. 'But leave him to me. I'll get him.'

'I want that pleasure,' said Cohen.

I shook my head. 'I gave you Tarnish. McNaught's the one who set up Quiet Tommy Quaid. I may never find him, but if I do, he's mine.'

## 8

It took me over a month to track down Gresty, the ENSA actor I had seen in the photograph with Findlay. Guessing that he had some kind of record, I asked Jock Ferguson if he had any details on a J.P. Gresty.

John Philip Gresty had been convicted twice of petty theft, once on an assault charge. His record card stated his profession as 'unemployed actor'. Ferguson had asked no questions, nor had he passed any comment when he handed me the file on Gresty, which included a photograph. It confirmed that it was the same face I'd seen with Findlay in the wartime photograph. Or nearly the same face.

I found Gresty in Edinburgh, living in a run-down flat on the third floor of a Craigmillar tenement. I watched him for a full day and night and it was enough to see that there was nothing to the man's life. He was unemployed and his only social activity had been to buy a bottle of cheap sherry from a corner shop. It was a worn-down stub of a life. The life of a nobody, a loser.

He looked shocked to see me standing there when he opened the door. Then flustered. Whatever the truth of his real identity or background, he was still a big guy and had a record of violence. I decided not to take any chances and waved the Webley vaguely in his direction.

'Now let's not get all silly,' I said. 'Do you mind if I come in, Mr McNaught?'

John Philip Gresty had a face that some event had robbed of its symmetry, making it lopsided. Standing there in the doorway of a low-rent apartment, looking worn-down and frightened, he certainly didn't have the military bearing he had had the day he had walked into my office and announced himself as Mr McNaught. And this time he wouldn't have a script to follow.

He backed away from me into the apartment, which I took as an invitation to follow him in. Gun in one hand, I had a brown paper bag tucked under the other arm. I nudged it upwards a little and inside glass clinked on glass. 'I've brought us something to drink.'

It was a depressing place. A single room served as a kitchen, dining room and living room, a sink and gas cooker in one corner, a bedroom and a small bathroom off. The walls were dressed in a dark wallpaper that had been gloomy when it had been put up, probably before the war, and had darkened to a toffee colour with decades of cigarette smoke and fireplace soot. The furniture looked like Noah had refused to have it on the ark and there was only one piece of soft furnishing: an ancient settee of threadbare chintz.

Like Tommy's apartment, there was no real hint of the personality occupying this space; except in this case, I suspected it had more to do with poverty and the lack of personal belongings. There was one, strangely pathetic, personal touch: a framed photograph on the mantelpiece of Gresty as he had been before his face had been messed up. The glass and frame were clean and dust-free, as if the photograph received care that the rest of the flat missed.

The only other personal touch was a couple of immaculately pressed suits, a lovat raincoat and two pairs of shoes – one black, one burgundy brogues – polished till they gleamed.

I waved Gresty over to the settee and told him to sit, keeping the gun on him. Pulling over one of the dining chairs from the table, I sat opposite him. He asked me how I'd found him and I told him.

I took a bottle of Scotch from the paper bag and placed it on the floor in front of him.

'A present,' I said. 'Do you have glasses?'

I kept the gun on him while he fetched the glasses from the sink in the corner, set them on the floor between us and filled them from the bottle. He winced as it went down.

'Sorry,' I said. 'They were all out of single malt.'

He looked at me steadily and quietly, but I sensed a tremor running through him, like a faint electric current. I guessed he knew what was coming.

'I take it it was Findlay who paid you to act the part of McNaught?'

'Aye.' His natural voice was broader Scots than the one he'd used the day he'd visited me in my office and set the whole ball rolling. 'But I didn't know what was going on until later. Honest. All that stuff with kids . . . I wouldn't have had anything to do with it if I had.' His shoulders slumped and he sighed. 'That's not true . . . I'd have done it anyway. I needed the money. I don't get acting jobs because of this . . .' He pointed to his face. 'Not the romantic lead type any more, you could say. Or even comedy.' He looked at me; at the gun in my hand. 'I'm sorry about your friend, by the way.'

'Did you know they were going to kill Tommy Quaid?'

'That was the plan. Frankie got me to hire those two monkeys.

They were supposed to be waiting for him at the foundry, but it was all taken out of our hands.'

'Help yourself . . .' I twitched the barrel of the gun towards the whisky bottle. He didn't need telling twice. I had left my glass untouched. 'Why was it taken out of your hands?'

'Frankie had those pictures and all those names and details as an insurance policy. He had set the whole thing up for them – where they met, getting the kids from that school. A bunch of sick perverts, if you ask me – but they were all powerful, really powerful, men. Frankie felt reasonably safe because he was so much in the public eye, but he was always a bit worried that the members of his little club might start to think he knew too much. I don't think it was a real worry, because he was into all of that sick shite anyway, but that's why he kept the goods on the others locked up in his safe.'

'What's that got to do with what happened at the foundry?'

'You see, to start with Frankie was shitting himself, realizing someone had all of that stuff. That's why he hired me. He knew me from doing troop entertainment shows together in the war. He also knew that I'd been in trouble with the police since, and that I couldn't get any acting work because of my face. He said he had the perfect part for me and my face was an advantage. It was just the three of us – me and the two boys – and we were to try and get the stuff back. But one of Frankie's pervert chums was the shipyard owner, Sir John MacIlwain. We were drawing blanks and Frankie was getting, well, *frantic* like his stage name says. He went to MacIlwain and told him what had happened.'

Gresty paused to top up his drink. He looked over to me, the bottle in his hand, seeking permission. 'Go ahead,' I said. 'In fact I insist.'

He poured himself another. My first still sat untouched.

'Anyway,' he continued, 'the old guy said – I mean old man MacIlwain – that he had an idea about who could have pulled off the job and gave us Thomas Quaid's name. When I checked around, it seemed like Quaid was definitely the most likely suspect.'

I nodded, remembering what Jennifer had told me about how MacIlwain's pre-war insurance claim, and consequently Tommy's prison time, had both been inflated.

'We came up with the plan to lure Quaid somewhere where his death could look like an accident. After that we would turn over his place and get the ledger back. No one would know that it had never contained the negatives. And that's how you got involved. Frankie did his homework – or got someone to do it for him – and found out you and Tommy Quaid were tight, and heard all the rumours of him doing work for you. Frankie knew Quaid would be on the lookout for someone coming after him, but he would trust you.'

Once more, I had to fight down the rage that rose at the idea that I'd been a collaborator, albeit unknowingly, in Tommy's death. 'I thought you said your boys didn't do it . . .' I said.

'They didn't. After Frankie told him about the break-in, MacIlwain went straight to the others and told them that Frankie had been secretly keeping the goods on them. One of the others was a high-up in Special Branch—'

'Chief Inspector Bob MacIntyre?'

'I don't know his name, but he had connections and he knew that Quaid's old commanding officer worked for military intelligence, or counter-intelligence, or some shite like that. He was an expert in dealing with scandals, apparently, brushing evidence of MPs' indiscretions and stuff like that under the carpet.

He came up north with some of his men and they took the whole thing over. But Frankie kept me and the boys on.'

'Why, if it was all out of his hands?'

'He still had the negatives, but had to keep them safe from the others. Everyone had to think the negatives were missing. Frankie told us we had to make sure the military types didn't get to the stuff and find out the negatives weren't there.'

'And that's why you went after Jimmy Wilson?'

'Aye . . .' Gresty's voice was becoming slurred. 'But we weren't up to it. I'm an out-of-work actor and the other two were a couple of thick-as-shite ballroom bouncers. The military types took it out of our hands. Again.'

'Have another drink,' I said.

'No . . .' He smiled wanly and the damaged side of his face didn't join in. 'I've had enough.'

'Have another drink,' I said. With my free hand I took the two unopened bottles of whisky from the bag. With the other I cocked the hammer on the pistol.

'Oh . . .' he said. 'I see. It's like that.'

'It's like that.'

I could see he was trying to shake off his incipient drunkenness. 'Listen, it doesn't have to be. I'm sorry for what happened, but when I first got into it I didn't know what was planned. I got out of my depth.'

'It does have to be like this,' I said. 'Don't bother with the glass, just drink from the bottle.'

Gresty looked around his grubby room, at his meagre possessions, at the smart clothes incongruously hung on the improvised rail. He was saying goodbye.

'There's no other way?'

'There's a queue of people wanting to get to you. Or get to

McNaught, the character you played. Trust me, you're lucky that it's me. The others wouldn't give you as easy a passage. It's the bottle or . . .' I raised the gun.

He lifted the whisky bottle by the neck and drank from it, keeping his eyes on me as he did so. Half the bottle went down like water.

'How?' he asked.

'The bath,' I said. 'When you've drunk so much you won't know what's happening. A quiet death.'

He stared at me for a moment. Then he said, quietly, 'Okay.'

By the time he'd finished the first bottle, he was very drunk. A cold drunk. The drunk of a man desperately clinging on.

'Will you feel bad about this?' he asked.

'Yes. Yes, I'll feel bad, but there's no other way. The way this was played from the start, the losers don't get to walk away.'

'It's okay,' he said, slurring. 'Don't feel bad about it. Wasn't much of a life anyway. Shite, in fact. I'm a bad sort. Worse – I'm a shite actor.' He waved his finger at me, the bottle still in his hand. 'But I was good with you, wasn't I? I had you convinced . . . the whole ex-officer, hard bastard thing. I carried that off. I *was* fucking good at that.'

'You sure were,' I said, dully. 'You had me hook, line and sinker.' The truth was I'd suspected something from the way he had over-played the military thing. But I said nothing: I didn't think now, when I was soon to hold his unconscious head under water until he drowned, was a good time to give him critical notes. I pushed the second bottle across the floor to him. 'Cheers . . .'

'Cheers . . .' He snatched up the bottle, sneering defiantly at me with the half of his face that was capable of sneering defi-antly, and took two long pulls. He wiped his mouth, his lips now slack with booze.

'Wanna know 'bout my face? What happn'd it?'

'Sure,' I said. There was an etiquette to killing a man in cold blood. An executioner's code. Anyway, it wouldn't be long now. He'd get so drunk that he'd start talking nonsense, then he'd fall asleep, then I'd force more booze down him, then he'd pass out; and then I'd kill him, making it look like a drowning accident in the bath.

'Everybody thinks I was wounded. But I wasn't. I never saw action. Fucking entertainment corps. Along with Frankie fucking Findlay – by the way, you kill him?'

'I didn't play lead, but was in the supporting cast,' I said.

'Good. Surprise t'hear me say 'at? Good fuckin' riddance. No loss either. What he did to those kids. Fucking creep.' He shook his head woozily as if annoyed at losing his thread. 'Anyway, Findlay was in Singapore with me, but fucked off before the Japs came. By the way, he started all this shite as far back as then, out there in Singapore. He used to arrange little parties for officers, local whores an' that. Rumour was he also catered for "special tastes". He made a fuckin' fortune out of it and gained powerful friends. Got himself transferred home. Me?' He stabbed his chest with his thumb. 'Muggins here gets captured in forty-two when Singapore fell. Along with eighty-five thousand other poor bastards.' He shook his head and it nearly cost him his balance, even sitting down. 'All because they put that useless, buck-toothed, lanky streak of piss Percival in charge. Anyway, I was in with the real fighting men – Aussies and Indians who'd been captured after Sarimbun Beach – an' others who'd had to give up without a fight.'

'Keep drinking . . .' I said. He actually made an apologetic gesture and took a couple of hefty swigs.

'*Anyway* . . . I ended up with the others in a prisoner of war camp. A labour camp run by the Kempeitai. Men starved, beaten and worked to death. But I got what everyone else thought was a cushy number. The Nips put me to work as a steward in the Kempeitai barracks. In the non-comms' mess, serving drinks and polishing boots for fuckin' Jap'nese NCOs. For a while it *was* a cushy number. Not as hard work as the others an' I was able to steal scraps of food, sleep separately from the others. Less chance of catching typhus or dysentery, y'see.' He frowned, trying to focus on his story through his growing stupor; or maybe it was the memory that was making him frown. 'But then things started to change: there was this particular sergeant – Sergeant Tsukuda. I can still see the little bastard. A short-arsed, squat, dark-skinned wee sadist. I'd taken the odd beating for being too slow or not serving the *sake* right, but this little shite decided to start a new game. This night they were all pretty pissed and I brought in another tray of *tokkuri* and *ochoko* – you know, the pottery jug and cups the Nips use for *sake*. Anyway, instead of being dismissed, Tsukuda makes me stand to attention and wait. Wee bastard starts waving yen about like he was starting a bet on something. Know what they were bettin'on? Me. Tsukuda walks straight up to me and hits me in the face, hard. That side.' McNaught pointed to the right side of his face.

'I go down, everybody starts fucking laughing. I'm hauled to m'feet and the next Nip has a swing, then the next, then the next. I can hear the sound still – the bones cracking in my face. Eventually I pass out. The bet, I worked out, had been to see how many punches it would take to put me out. I woke up in the dirt outside the mess hut. Next day, they treated me as usual and no one laid a finger on me. They didn't for two weeks. Then they obviously reckoned that I'd healed enough for it to be sport again. So they did the same thing. Did it the following week, and the week after, and the week after. Breaking and rebreaking the bones in my face, always just on that side. It went on for months. That's why I look the way I do.'

I nodded. There wasn't much to say. There were a thousand – tens of thousands – of stories like that, brought back from the war in broken containers.

'But I swore I'd get the wee cunt.' More waving of the bottle. 'After they dropped the bomb and Japan surrendered, the Nips handed over the camp to us. Tsukuda knew what was good for him and fucked off sharpish. I searched for him for days. All I thought about was killing the little bastard, cutting chunks out of him. Payin' him back. Thousand per cent interest. Never did find him though. Never did get justice. Never did.'

He shook his head sadly and looked across the table, his eyes struggling to focus on me. He was now too drunk to be any danger, if he ever really had been any danger, so I tucked the gun back in my waistband, came around to his side of the table. Holding his head back, I poured the rest of the bottle into him. A lot of the whisky was spilled as he coughed, spluttered and gargled on it, but enough went in to finish the job.

I let him go and he slumped onto the settee. I slapped his face a couple of times and called his name, but got no response.

Taking out my cufflinks and putting them in my pocket, I slipped off my jacket and rolled up my shirtsleeves. I went through to the bathroom and ran the bath taps. Gresty didn't regain consciousness while I undressed him, leaving his clothes scattered on the floor. When he was naked, I dragged him across the living room and into the bathroom. It took a lot of effort to get him into the bath, which was filling up. Eventually I got him in and waited until the water level was up to his chest.

I looked at him. A fucked-up man with a fucked-up face and a fucked-up life.

I grabbed his ankles and pulled his legs upwards. Gresty's head went under the water. There was a stream of bubbles from his nose and mouth, then a sudden explosion of them burst the surface as, without regaining consciousness, he bucked and wriggled under the water. He started to drown.

A fucked-up man with a fucked-up face and a fucked-up life, which I was now ending for him. Maybe he had been right: maybe he had played the part well, after all. I was killing McNaught, the character he had played, not Gresty, the actor. For some reason I couldn't get the image of that photograph on the mantelpiece out of my head. A pathetic attempt to brighten up a bleak and empty life with memories of a past life. A life that had been shaped by the cruelty of a little Japanese who'd never been held to account. I was doing Gresty a favour.

'Fuck it!'

I reached into the bath and placing my hands under his armpits hauled his head out of the water. He coughed and spluttered, eventually pulling a long, rasping breath. His eyes opened for a moment and held mine, confused, before he lost consciousness again.

I pulled the plug and let the water drain away.

Before I left the flat, I hauled Gresty out of the bath, through to the bedroom and laid him on his side in the bed, his face turned down and out, pillows behind him to stop him rolling onto his back. After my sudden and inexplicable beneficence, I didn't want him to choke on his own vomit.

I drove back to Glasgow to pick up Jennifer and take her out on the town. Maybe we would just have a laugh, or maybe we could have a serious talk. A talk about how maybe the time was right for a new start for me, for us both, back home in Canada.

As I drove, I tried to work out why I hadn't gone through with killing Gresty, but I felt good I hadn't. Maybe I was developing a conscience.

Or maybe I was being haunted by the ghost of a good, quiet man I had once known.

73